About the

Jennie Lucas' parents owned a bookstore, and she grew up surrounded by books, dreaming about faraway lands. At twenty-two, she met her future husband, and after their marriage, she graduated from university with a degree in English. She started writing books a year later. Jennie won the Romance Writers of America's Golden Heart contest in 2005 and hasn't looked back. Visit Jennie's website at jennielucas.com

Sandra Marton is a *USA Today* bestselling author. A four-time finalist for the *RITA*, the coveted award given by Romance Writers of America, she's also won eight Romantic Times Reviewers' Choice Awards, the Holt Medallion, and Romantic Times' Career Achievement Award. Sandra's heroes are powerful, sexy, take-charge men who think they have it all – until that one special woman comes along. Stand back, because together they're bound to set the world on fire.

USA Today bestselling author **Joanne Rock** credits her decision to write romance to a book she picked up during a flight delay that engrossed her so thoroughly, she didn't mind at all when her flight was delayed two more times. Giving her readers the chance to escape into another world has motivated her to write over one hundred books for various Mills & Boon series.

A Christmas Reckoning

JENNIE LUCAS

SANDRA MARTON

JOANNE ROCK

MILLS & BOON

First Published in Great Britain 2025
by Mills & Boon, an imprint of HarperCollins*Publishers* Ltd
1 London Bridge Street, London, SE1 9GF

www.harpercollins.co.uk

HarperCollins*Publishers*
Macken House, 39/40 Mayor Street Upper,
Dublin 1, D01 C9W8, Ireland

ISBN: 978-0-263-41922-1

MIX
Paper | Supporting
responsible forestry
FSC™ C007454
www.fsc.org

This book contains FSC™ certified paper and other controlled sources to ensure responsible forest management.

For more information visit: www.harpercollins.co.uk/green

Printed and Bound in the UK using 100% Renewable Electricity
at CPI Group (UK) Ltd, Croydon, CR0 4YY

THE CHRISTMAS LOVE-CHILD

JENNIE LUCAS

To my wonderful parents, who taught me to love books and dream of faraway lands.

CHAPTER ONE

JUST when Grace Cannon thought her day couldn't get any worse, she came up from the Tube carrying £1,000 worth of lingerie for her boss's fiancée and got splashed in the face by a passing Rolls-Royce.

Mid-December in London was frosty in the violet twilight. The rain had turned to sleet, but the sidewalks in Knightsbridge were still packed with shoppers. The icy spray of gutter water hit Grace's body like a slap. She stumbled and fell down, her hip hitting the pavement as the shopping bag tumbled into the street. She cried out, holding up her hands to protect her face from the endless crush of feet pushing forward.

"Get back. Get back, damn you."

A tall, dark stranger pushed apart the crowds with his broad arms, giving Grace space to breathe. He towered over her on the sidewalk, black-haired and broad-shouldered in an expensive black cashmere coat.

He turned to face her.

Electric gray eyes stood out sharply against his olive-hued skin. Every inch of him whispered money and power, from his Italian shoes to the muscular shape beneath his black coat and gray pin-striped suit. His lush masculine beauty was like none she'd ever seen before. He had chiseled cheekbones, a strong jawline and a Roman profile. Her gaze fell unwillingly to his mouth, to the sensual lips that curved as he looked down at her.

A bright halo of sunlit clouds silhouetted his black hair as he extended his hand.

"Come."

Dazzled, Grace reached up and placed her hand in his far-larger one. As the handsome stranger pulled her to her feet, she felt a current run through her body more startling than the icy water that had splashed her.

"Thank you," she whispered.

Then she recognized him and literally lost her breath.

Prince Maksim Rostov.

Her throat closed.

She looked again. There could be no mistake.

Prince Maksim Rostov was the man who had saved her.

The lavishly wealthy prince was the most famous Russian billionaire in a city that was full of them. He was so ruthless in his business and personal life he made Grace's boss look like a saint in comparison. For the past two months, since the prince had broken up with his famous fiancée, he'd been photographed with a new woman every night.

Prince Maksim Rostov. Her boss's main rival. His worst enemy.

And that had been *before* last month, when Alan had stolen both the man's fiancée and his merger!

"Forgive me." The prince's cool gray eyes looked

down at her gravely, searing through her like a laser. "It was my car that splashed you. My driver should have been more careful."

"That's…all right," Grace managed to say, utterly conscious of his larger hand still closed over her own. A few minutes before, she'd been icy cold. But her body was rapidly thawing.

Warming.

Boiling.

She tried to pull away. She shouldn't let him touch her. She shouldn't even let him *talk* to her. She was two blocks away from the Knightsbridge town house she shared with her boss. If Alan ever found out that his most trusted secretary had been speaking in private with Prince Maksim, he'd never forgive her. And Grace desperately needed Alan in a good mood, tonight of all nights!

But even knowing this, she found herself unable to pull her hand from the prince's grasp. He was like a rugged, brutal, smooth old-style movie star. Like Rudolph Valentino from the 1920s, seducing women ruthlessly in a savage world of blood and sand. Like a dark angel, sent to lure innocent, helpless virgins to their destruction!

His grip tightened over hers, sending little sizzling currents up her arm, warming her beneath her wet coat.

"I will take you home."

Her teeth chattered. "I…" She shook her head. "No. It's really not necessary."

Prince Maksim pulled her close. He stroked the length of her arm, languorously brushing excess water from her coat sleeve. Feeling his hand move over her clothed body, she suddenly felt so hot she might as well have been lying naked on a California beach. Her skin burned where he touched, as if whipped by a fierce Santa Ana wind.

"I insist."

Beads of sweat formed between her breasts. "No, really," she managed. "I live close. It won't take me long to walk."

He looked down at her, a smile tracing his cruel, sensual mouth. "But I want to take you."

And still he held her hand. Her mouth went dry. Even Alan, the boss she'd loved with hopeless yearning for two years, had never sparked a response like this—never caused her nerve endings to jumble with such an intensity of feeling. Even before he'd taken a new fiancée and asked Grace to buy his Christmas gift…

The lingerie!

Grace gasped, twisting her head to the right and left.

With a little cry, she saw the Leighton bag get nailed by a swerving black cab in the road, causing the embossed lavender box inside it to tumble into the bumper-to-bumper traffic. "Oh, no!"

Ripping away from the prince's grasp, Grace pushed through the tourists to the edge of the sidewalk, looking both ways on the street and preparing to duck between the cars, double-decker buses and black cabs.

But Prince Maksim blocked her with one strong arm in front of her chest.

"Are you suicidal?" His English was perfect, with an accent she couldn't quite place. A little bit British, a bit American, with a slight inflection of something more exotic. He glanced out at the busy road. "You'd risk your life for that blue box?"

"That box," she snapped, "is my boss's Christmas gift for his new fiancée. Silk Leighton lingerie. I can't go back without it!"

"Your boss isn't worth dying for."

"My boss is Alan Barrington!"

Glaring at him, Grace waited for a reaction when he realized she worked for his enemy, his rival in the gas and oil industry, who'd not only just stolen his merger with Exemplary Oil PLC but had stolen his fiancée, the beautiful, tempestuous Lady Francesca in the bargain!

Prince Maksim's handsome face was utterly impassive. She had no idea what he was thinking. A marked difference from Alan, Grace thought. Her flirtatious boss's thoughts were always instantly expressed, either by flippant words or the expression on his good-looking face.

But the image of her boss's toothy smile dissipated instantly from her mind as the dark Russian prince reached out his hand to lift her chin, forcing her eyes to meet his. "Your boss is truly not worthy of your sacrifice."

She licked her lips nervously. "Aren't you w-wishing you'd let me run into traffic now, Your Highness?"

Prince Maksim arrogantly smiled down at her.

"As tempting as it is to cause him staffing problems, I'm afraid I cannot allow you to cover the street with your blood." He gently stroked her hair from her face. "Call me old-fashioned."

He knew she worked for his enemy, so why was he still being courteous? Why wasn't he calling her names or wishing her to the devil? Although, he would have an easy time luring any woman anywhere, she thought. Even to the depths of hell itself.

Frightened by all the new sensations running through her at his touch, she pulled back. "I'll take my chances with the traffic."

"You'll get new lingerie."

"New lingerie?" Safely out of his reach, she regained her equilibrium enough to give an incredulous, scornful laugh. "Right! New lingerie. Maybe in your world Leighton clothes are disposable as baby wipes, but—"

"I will pay for it." He gave her a level look from his steel-gray eyes. "Of course."

If it had been any other person on the planet, she would have accepted gratefully. But not this man. She couldn't accept the help of her boss's worst enemy.

Could she?

As if in slow motion, she saw a red double-decker bus crush the lavender-blue box into a big greasy puddle in the middle of the street.

Alan would be furious if she went home tonight with the expensive charge on his credit card but no lingerie. Alan was completely unforgiving of others' mistakes when they caused him problems. For years he'd hated Prince Maksim, the rival who'd beaten him over and over again. With Cali-West Energy Corporation's stock prices falling, the stockholders had begun to call for Alan's replacement as CEO.

That was before Alan met Lady Francesca Danvers at a charity ball six weeks ago. Their whirlwind romance had gained him the support of her father, the Earl of Hainesworth, who was chair of Exemplary's board of trustees. The deal had changed from a merger of British and Russian energy giants to a British-American one. For weeks now Alan had gleefully recounted to Grace how he'd finally beaten his rival.

Grace hadn't particularly enjoyed his gloating, since it inevitably involved details of how Alan was luring the beautiful, feisty, redheaded Lady Francesca into his bed.

What if Alan was so furious about the ruined lingerie, he demanded Grace pay the bill? What if instead of giving her the advance she so desperately needed, he docked her pay?

She swore under her breath.

"Do not refuse my help, Miss Cannon," Prince Maksim said evenly. "That would be stubborn and foolish."

"Well, Stubborn and Foolish are my middle names!" Grace snapped, furious at herself.

She could have stayed in L.A. and made sure her mother's mortgage was paid each month—but no. She'd been too stubbornly and foolishly infatuated with her boss. *Pathetic,* she thought in disgust. There surely had to be some kind of self-help program for women like her, pathetically in love with a boss who believed her to have no feelings—like an animatronic robot!

"Stubborn and Foolish, Miss Cannon?" Maksim's lips curved. "Clearly American baby-name trends have changed over the years."

"My middle name is actually Diana." Narrowing her eyes, she looked up at Prince Maksim. "But you already know that, don't you? How do you already know my last name?"

"You told me you work for Barrington." He lifted a

dark eyebrow. "Don't you think I know the name of his most trusted secretary?"

Prince Maksim Rostov knew her name.

The fact made her feel warm all over. Made her feel…important.

Until a new, chilling suspicion went down her spine.

He knew her name.

He knew she worked for Alan.

And she was supposed to believe they'd just randomly met on the street two blocks from her home?

Grace was distracted and was nearly knocked over by two heavy tourists decked in cameras, Harrods bags and Santa hats, but she steadied herself to glare at him. "So you'll understand why, as his most trusted secretary, I can't accept any favors from you."

Prince Maksim gave her an easy smile.

"Barrington has nothing to do with this. Replacing the lingerie is repaying a personal debt to you." His smile spread into a carelessly wicked grin that she felt down to her toes. "I can hardly remain indebted to my enemy."

She swallowed, hardly able to collect her thoughts beneath the intensity of his gaze. "I wouldn't say I'm exactly your enemy…"

"Then there is no problem."

"But…"

He enfolded her hand back in his own. The warmth of his naked palm against hers was more erotic than she'd ever thought holding a hand could be. After so many years of useless pining over her boss, this was the most physically intimate she'd been with any man since…since…

Since that brief moment after the Halloween party

when Alan had drunkenly taken her in his arms and given her a big wet kiss before he'd collapsed in a drunken stupor on the office couch.

That sad event had been her first—and only—kiss. In school she'd been too focused on her studies to date anyone. After her father had died and she'd dropped out of college, she'd been too grief-stricken. Then she'd been too busy as a temp in downtown L.A., working to take care of her heartbroken mother and younger brothers.

Grace had become a twenty-five-year-old virgin.

A freak of nature.

And a million miles away from Prince Maksim Rostov's league!

But his car had splashed her, she argued with herself. He'd caused her to drop the lingerie. Wouldn't it be fair to allow him to replace it, when the alternative could mean her ruin?

Tempted, she licked her lips nervously. The sensation of his hand against her own caused a swirling in the tender center of her palm that sent awareness prickling up to the flesh of her ear, tightening her nipples and making her breasts feel strangely heavy. She felt his gaze trace her lips. Her cheeks went hot and her mouth went dry. Every breath she took, every rise and fall of her lungs, became more shallow.

"It is cold," he said. "My car is waiting."

"But, but Leighton clothes are expensive," she stammered, floundering. "They're so expensive they make Hermès and Louis Vuitton look like a bargain-basement fire sale."

He lifted his dark eyebrows.

"I think I can handle the expense," he said dryly. Signaling with one hand, he put the other against the small of her back, guiding her gently toward the curb of a side street where she saw a black Rolls-Royce limousine.

She felt his hand on her back and shook all over. It was that touch which finally forced her surrender.

Looking back at him, she whispered, "Alan must never know."

His lips trembled on the brink of a smile. "Agreed."

The shock waves from his hand on her lower back continued to sizzle up her arms and down her legs as she breathed, "Thank you."

"Thank you." His eyes gleamed down at her. "I always enjoy the company of a beautiful woman."

It broke the spell. She started to laugh, snorting through her nose before she covered it with a cough.

Her…beautiful? That was a good joke! She knew she wasn't anything special. And at the moment, wearing no makeup, with a damp old coat over her second-hand skirt suit and her hair tucked back in a soaked blond ponytail, she looked like a half-drowned refugee from an office in a swamp!

So why had a handsome prince dropped out of the sky to help her? Just because his driver had splashed her with water from the street? Did he have that much honor and generosity of Christmas spirit?

Or was it something else?

The dark suspicion returned to her. When she was younger, she'd believed the best of people. But since she'd started working for Alan, she'd seen how devious people could be. Both in business and in love.

Was Prince Maksim hoping to use her against Alan to take back his merger and his marriage?

"I hope you know," she said evenly, "that doing me this favor won't make me discuss Alan or the merger."

He just gave her a darkly assessing smile. "Do you think I need your assistance?"

"Don't you?" she said uncertainly.

They reached the Rolls-Royce limousine purring next to the curb. With a dismissive shake of his head to the driver, the prince opened her door himself.

"Get in."

Standing on the edge of the sidewalk, against the ebb and flow of Christmas shoppers, Grace looked at the open door of the car and hesitated. She wondered suddenly if she was doing a foolish thing, making a deal with the devil.

When she didn't move, he said mockingly, "Surely you're not afraid of me, Miss Cannon?"

Biting her lower lip, she glanced up at his handsome face. She *was* afraid of him. Afraid of his wealth, his power and well-known ruthlessness.

But even more than that, she was afraid of the sensual reaction that overwhelmed her body every time he touched her. Every time he even *looked* at her.

She shook her head uneasily. "No," she lied. "I'm not afraid of you at all."

He held the door wider. "Then get in."

Flurries of sleet swirled around Grace in a sudden gust of wind. Wet tendrils of blond hair whipped against her cheek, sticking to her skin. But she didn't feel the chill. His gray eyes seared through hers, sapping her will.

And she made her choice—which was really no choice at all. She climbed into the back seat of his Rolls-Royce.

He closed the door behind her.

Once released from his basilisk gaze, alone in the back seat, Grace was as suddenly shocked as if she'd just woken up sleepwalking in Buckingham Palace. What was she doing here? It wasn't a dream. She was really in Prince Maksim's limo. She was consorting with the enemy.

But he's not my *enemy,* she thought in confusion as she watched his dark shadow walk around to the other side. *He's Alan's enemy. And what do people say? The enemy of my friend is my enemy? Or is it that the enemy of my enemy is my friend?*

The door opened, and the most handsome, ruthless man in London climbed in beside her with a dark glance that made her feel hot and sweaty all over.

"Why are you being so nice to me?" she asked.

"Am I being nice?"

"If it's to get secrets about my boss—"

"It's Christmas. The season of joy." Festive lights from the nearby shops glinted off his wolflike teeth as he gave her a sharp smile. "And I'm going to give you joy." He turned to his chauffeur. *"Davai."*

The shadowy Rolls-Royce swept away from the curb. And just like that, Prince Maksim Rostov took her away from the drudgery and crowds and cold, and swept Grace up into his lavish world.

CHAPTER TWO

MAKSIM glanced down at the girl's lovely, dazzled blue eyes as his chauffeur drove east through the crowded traffic on Knightsbridge Road towards Mayfair. She'd called him "nice." He repeated the word in his mind as if he were trying to comprehend it.

Nice?

Prince Maksim Ivanovich Rostov had not become powerful by being nice.

His great-grandfather had been nice during his Paris exile, spending money as if he were still Grand Duke with his own fiefdom in St. Petersburg, giving largesse freely to every hard-luck story that walked into his pied-à-terre.

His grandfather had been nice, spending what little remained of the Rostov fortune down to the last penny in London as he waited impatiently for the Russian people to kick out the Soviets and beg him to return.

His father had been nice, hopelessly trying to support his young, sweet American wife by taking increasingly humiliating jobs until he'd finally followed his father's lead of suicide-by-vodka, leaving his gentle wife, eleven-year-old son and baby daughter to fend for themselves in her native Philadelphia.

But Maksim…

He was not nice.

He was selfish. He was ruthless. He took what he wanted. It was how he'd built a billion-dollar fortune out of nothing.

And now…he wanted Grace Cannon.

For the past hour, he'd been waiting for her. His chauffeur had driven back and forth on Brompton Road, waiting to catch the girl as she came up from the Knightsbridge Tube stop on the way home to her basement flat in Barrington's town house.

This young American secretary was the key to everything.

She would help him finally crush Barrington. The man had been a thorn in his side for far too long, and now he'd finally crossed the line by taking both the deal—and the woman—that rightfully belonged to Maksim.

Barrington thought he'd saved himself from ruin by taking Francesca as his fiancée. He'd soon find it was his last mistake. He would get neither the bride nor the merger.

Maksim would destroy him. As he deserved.

And Grace Cannon would help him. Whether she wanted to or not.

Maksim turned to her with a smile. Unfolding a soft cashmere blanket, he draped it over her shivering body.

"Thank you," she said, her teeth still chattering.

"It's my pleasure."

"You're not what I expected," she whispered,

pressing the blanket against her cheek. "You're not like everyone says."

"What do they say?" He carelessly placed his arm on the leather seat behind her. She was still shivering. He moved closer. Even though she was now covered with a blanket, her shivering only increased when he touched her.

"They say...you're a...ruthless playboy," she said haltingly. "That you spend half your time conquering business rivals...and the other half making conquests of women."

He laughed. "They are right." He moved closer, looking down into her face. "That is exactly who I am."

His thigh brushed against hers, and she nearly jumped out of her skin. She scooted away from him as if he'd burned her.

She was skittish. Very skittish.

There were only three possible explanations.

One—she was afraid of him. He dismissed that idea out of hand. She wouldn't have agreed to get in his car if she'd been truly afraid.

Two—she had no experience with men. He dismissed that idea, as well. A twenty-five-year-old virgin? Almost impossible in this day and age. Particularly since she not only worked for Alan Barrington, she lived in his house. He surely had seduced her many times over.

That left only the third possibility. She was ripe for Maksim's conquest.

He slowly looked her over. She wasn't a girl that any man would immediately notice. Compared to fiery bird-of-paradise Francesca, who had bright-red hair, sharp red nails and a vicious red mouth, Grace Cannon was a drab sparrow, pale and frumpy with barely a word to say for herself.

And yet…

Now that Maksim really looked at her, he saw that the girl wasn't nearly as plain as he'd first thought. Her ill-fitting coat and wet ponytail had made her seem so, but now he realized his mistake.

The fact that she wore no makeup only revealed the perfection of her creamy skin. Her eyelashes and eyebrows were so light as to be invisible, but that proved the glorious pale gold of her hair came from nature, not a salon. She wore no lipstick and her teeth hadn't been bleached to blinding movie-star whiteness, and yet her tremulous smile was warmer and lovelier than any he'd seen. She wasn't stick thin as the strange fashion for women dictated, but her ample curves only made her more lushly desirable.

He suddenly realized the dowdy secretary was a beauty.

A *secret* beauty, disguising herself away from the world. Beneath the unattractive clothing and the frumpy, frizzy hairstyle, her loveliness shone bright as the sun.

She hid her beauty. Why?

"What's wrong?" She frowned up at him suddenly, furrowing her brow in alarm.

Had she guessed his plan? "What, *solnishka mayo?*"

"You're staring at me."

"You're beautiful," he said simply. "Like sunshine in winter."

She blushed, biting her tender pink lip as she looked away. Clutching the luxurious cashmere like a security blanket against her wet, threadbare coat, she scooted further away from him on the car's leather seat. With a swallowed sigh, she stared out through the window at the passing Christmas lights beneath the thickly falling sleet. "Don't be ridiculous. I know I'm not pretty."

She didn't know, he realized. She had no idea. She wasn't purposefully hiding her beauty. *She didn't know.*

"You are beautiful, Grace," he said quietly.

At the use of her first name, she gave him a sudden fierce, sharp glance. "Don't waste your flattery on me, Your Highness."

He gave her an easy smile. "Call me Maksim. What makes you think it's flattery?"

"You might be London's most famous playboy, but I'm not that gullible. A few false compliments won't make me blurt out details about the merger with Exemplary Oil. Alan has Lord Hainesworth's support now. You won't be able to win."

So she was intuitive, as well as lovely. He was growing more intrigued by the moment. "I wasn't lying."

"I'm not a total fool. I know I'm not beautiful. There's only one reason you'd say I am."

"And that is?"

"You want me to betray Alan." She lifted her chin. "I won't. I'd die first."

"Loyalty," he said, staring at her with even greater interest. The girl felt something for her boss beyond what he'd expected. Was it possible she was in love with Alan Barrington?

A pity if the little secretary believed herself in love with him, Maksim thought. He'd just been starting to respect her.

Would money be enough to convince Grace to turn on her lover? Or would Maksim have to seduce her away from him?

Seducing a woman who was in love with another man would be an interesting challenge, he thought. And poetic justice.

But Maksim's interest in Grace was no longer just about revenge. It was no longer just about rivalry or honor.

He suddenly wanted to peel away the deceptive layers of the little secretary's plain clothing. To see her true beauty. To see her naked in his bed. To feel her lush curves against his body and see her bright, unadorned face breathless in the soft pink light of dawn.

Beneath his gaze, her pale cheeks went slowly red, like the blood-colored sun burning through the thick morning mist on the wide snowy fields of his Dartmoor estate. He watched as she nervously licked her full, pink, heart-shaped lips. Her white, even teeth nibbled at her lower lip, followed by a small dart of her tongue to moisten each corner of her mouth.

He felt himself go hard watching her.

He prayed she'd refuse his honest offer of money. Then he could just take her. Without conscience. Without remorse.

"The Leighton boutique is on Bond Street," she stammered, caught in his gaze.

He gave a predatory smile. "My driver knows the way."

"Of course he does. You date so many women, I bet you go there a lot." She turned away, blinking fast as she stared out the window. Beneath her breath, she added wistfully, "It must be nice to never worry about money."

A sudden memory went through Maksim of the bone-chilling winter when he'd turned fourteen. There'd been no heat in their tiny apartment; his mother had been laid off from her temp job. Three-year-old Dariya had been shivering and crying, and their desperate mother had taken her to a shelter to get warm. Wanting to help, he'd cut school to sell newspapers on the street in Philadelphia. Freezing rain soaked through everything. It had taken three days afterward for Maksim's coat to dry—three days of winter so cold it left his skin the color of ash. Three days of a wet, icy wind that seeped beneath his clothes and left him shaking till his teeth chattered.

Three days of hiding the wet coat from his mother, knowing that she would insist on giving him her own, that she'd go without a coat herself as she trudged the distance between employment agencies, desperate to find a job, any job.

Those three days had taught him the most valuable lesson of his life.

Money made the difference between a good life and no life at all.

Money fixed anything. Money fixed everything.

And you didn't get it by being nice.

"What a fairy-tale life," the girl whispered, staring out the window at all the well-dressed shoppers on Bond Street, the expensive cars, the festive decorations and lights of Christmas. "A perfect fairy-tale life."

Looking at her wistful beauty, Maksim suddenly had the strong desire to tell this naive girl the truth about his ruthless soul.

But he didn't. She'd learn it soon enough.

She'd learn it the hard way.

Grace Cannon would tell Maksim what he needed to know. He would try to buy the information. If that didn't work, he'd seduce it from her.

Or maybe, he thought suddenly as he looked down at her, he would seduce her anyway.

He would show this little secretary a kind of romance she'd never seen before. Luxury on a grand scale. He would be lavish. He would kiss her senseless. And like every woman before her, she would fall.

He would make her talk.

He would take her body.

Then…he would drop her.

A man didn't get rich—or win—by being nice.

CHAPTER THREE

ELEGANT shops always made Grace uncomfortable, and the Leighton boutique was the snootiest shop on Bond Street.

She could feel herself tensing up the moment she walked through the door, past grim-jawed security guards in suits like FBI agents. They gave her a hard stare, and she had the sudden feeling they were waiting for her to make one false step so they could take her down as a warning to other broke secretaries who might try to venture inside this rarefied, exclusive world.

Grace swallowed, looking around the elegant primrose-colored boutique. Buying the lingerie the first time had just about killed her. Buying it on behalf of the man she loved, as a gift for another woman—in such a teensy, tiny size, to boot—was just another painful reminder of the fact that Alan had chosen Lady Francesca Danvers over her. The moment Alan had met the beautiful, wealthy aristocrat, he'd forgotten all about the drunken kiss he'd given Grace just the previous night.

It had been Grace's very first kiss. But for him it had been instantly forgettable.

"Back again, I see," the snooty salesgirl sniffed. She looked dismissively from Grace's worn, wet coat to her scuffed-up boots. "Here to do more Christmas shopping for your boss?"

"I, um, yes." She swallowed. "I need more lingerie. The same exact one. I lost—"

But as she spoke, the salesgirl's eyes moved over her shoulder as someone new entered the shop.

Grace didn't need to look around to know it was Maksim. She knew from the immediate electricity in the room. She knew from the thousand watts that lit up the salesgirl's face as she nearly knocked Grace over in her haste to cross the marble floor. Reaching toward him. Wanting him like every woman in London.

Every woman except *her,* Grace told herself. He was dangerous and handsome and powerful, and he was her enemy. She didn't want him. She *didn't.*

"Your Highness! Such a pleasure to see you again," the brunette cried. "We have plenty of new stock—I'd love to show it to you!"

It was painfully obvious to Grace what the salesgirl would really love to show Maksim. For no good reason she felt herself get tight and tense all over. She turned away, used to feeling invisible. In her job, on the street, living alone in a foreign country…invisible. Alone.

Then she felt a strong masculine hand on her shoulder.

"You will start by getting my beautiful friend a replacement of the lingerie she bought," Maksim said to the salesgirl. He looked down at Grace. "Then—you will get her anything else she desires in the store."

"Yes, of course, Your Highness," the salesgirl gasped, her mouth a round *O* as she looked at Grace with new respect.

His steel-gray eyes and the touch of his hand caused a flash of heat to spread through her body.

"I splashed you with my car," he said. "It was an unforgivable rudeness. The least I can do is buy you new clothes. A new coat."

Grace stared at him, warmth cascading all over her. A moment before, she'd felt so invisible and cold, but with one touch he made her feel alive. With one word he'd made her feel she had value in the world.

"Anything you want, Grace," he said softly, stroking her cheek. "Anything at all. It will be my deepest honor to provide."

A shudder of longing went through her. Her face turned involuntarily toward his touch, and his hand cupped her cheek. She tried to pull away from him, but her feet weren't working properly. Neither was the rest of her.

Except for her breasts which started to ache, sending sizzles of longing down to her deepest core.

And at that moment Grace started to realize how dangerous the dark prince truly was.

She licked her lips. "Thank you, but I couldn't possibly accept."

His hand traced lightly down her neck to her shoulder, to her coat. "Why do you hide in these clothes, Grace? Why are you afraid to show the world your beauty?"

He really thought she was pretty? It hadn't just been

flattery? Her mind was spinning a million directions at once, and as long as he kept touching her she couldn't think straight. "I—"

"This would look lovely on you."

He touched a lovely pink nightgown displayed on a white headless mannequin. The silk and lace were the blush color of a spring rose, and while the low-cut neckline was covered in lace, the rest of the fabric went elegantly to the floor.

Grace, who normally slept in T-shirts and flannel pants, couldn't imagine sleeping in anything so sybaritic and luxurious.

Against her will, her eyes traced the shape of Maksim's muscular fingers against the delicate silk. She had the sudden image of what it might feel like to be in that nightgown with his hands on her. To be touched and caressed and stroked through the silk by his strong, powerful touch.

Grace fiercely shook the evocative image out of her mind.

What was wrong with her? She was growing as headless as the mannequin! No man had ever seen her in nightwear. Not even in her flannel pajamas. And it was likely to remain so!

"I'm not in the habit of letting strangers buy me nightgowns," she said, pulling her hand away from him and forcibly turning her back on the lovely pink silk.

"No lingerie, then," he said, sounding amused. "In that case, a coat. This one?"

"A coat?" She turned around, tempted. In spite of the cashmere blanket and warmth of his car, she was still shivering from the melted sleet and slush seeping through her old camel-colored coat. Having never owned a proper coat in California, she'd bought this one at a charity shop in London. It had seemed serviceable enough, and the price had been right. But it didn't hold up very well to rain, and was terribly ugly in the bargain, though Grace tried not to care.

"My car splashed your coat. It's ruined," he pointed out. "Surely even your overheightened sense of honor would allow me to replace it as a matter of course."

He touched a truly beautiful ankle-length black shearling coat with a wide collar. It was a dazzling sight, fit for a princess. She'd admired the coat when she'd first come into the shop a few hours ago. But she'd only admired it from a distance—she hadn't been nearly brave enough to actually touch it. Particularly after her eye had fallen on the price tag. Ten thousand pounds. In dollars, that equaled—

A new car.

She closed her eyes, suppressing her desire.

"And you must have this, as well." He pointed at an exquisite silk cocktail dress. "The color matches your eyes."

She looked at it hungrily. The dress was beautiful—something out of the fashion magazines she saw on newsstands. She reached out to touch the silk, then at the last moment hesitated and took the price tag instead. Four thousand pounds.

What was she thinking? She couldn't allow her boss's rival to buy her even a cocktail, let alone a cocktail dress!

Clothes like these were for glamorous, beautiful heiresses like Lady Francesca. Not for broke, plain girls like her. She'd bought her boots at a discount warehouse. Her shirt had cost less than ten dollars at Wal-Mart, and she'd bought her skirt suit used at a consignment shop in Los Angeles. For the past five years, since her father had died, she'd scrimped everywhere she could to help her family.

A lump rose in her throat. But it still hadn't been enough. She never should have left her mother alone....

"Let me do this small thing for you," Maksim said decisively. "You cannot refuse me this pleasure."

And she almost couldn't. She almost didn't want to refuse him *any* pleasure.

But she couldn't accept. She didn't trust him. And as much as she wanted these beautiful luxuries, she knew they weren't for her. Nothing in the Leighton boutique related to real life!

"And just where do you think I would wear that dress?" she retorted, raising her chin so he wouldn't know how tempted her weak soul had been. "To the grocery store? The post office?"

His lips curved into a smile. "I can think of a few places you could wear it. And not wear it."

Immediately a shiver of longing went through her body at his sensual smile. Why was he acting like this, wooing her as if she were a desirable, demanding woman?

There could be only one reason the ruthless billionaire prince would have any interest in her: he wanted to use her to get back the things Alan had stolen.

The merger.

The bride.

Grace resolutely turned away. From him, from the black coat, from the extravagant teal cocktail dress and the lavish, hedonistic life they represented. She wouldn't sell herself, or sell out Alan.

"No," she said, forcing down the hunger in her soul for everything she knew she'd never have. "I'll allow you to replace the lingerie. No more."

He shrugged. "It's just money, Grace."

Just money. The words made her want to laugh. Easy enough to say just money when you had plenty of it. Just money had made Grace drop out of college when her father died five years ago. Just money had made her mother worry about bills ever since, with three teenaged sons who ate out the refrigerator daily. And just money was about to make her family lose the only home they'd ever known.

"What is it?" Maksim's steel-gray eyes were intent on hers, mesmerizing her will with the whispered promise of all her lost dreams. "Tell me what you want. Anything you desire, Grace. Say the word, and it is yours."

"A couple of mortgage payments," she said under her breath.

"What?"

"I…I…it's nothing." She couldn't possibly ask Alan's enemy for a loan. She could only guess what the cost could be. She'd have to stab Alan in the back. She wouldn't do that, not for any price.

Alan will advance me the money, she told herself desperately. *He will!*

With a deep intake of breath, she turned away from

Maksim to speak directly to the salesgirl. "Just the white silk-and-lace babydoll, please. Size extra small."

"I have it here, miss," the brunette said respectfully. Grace watched as the girl folded the lingerie carefully, then wrapped it in tissue paper. She placed it in a glossy primrose-hued box embossed with the Leighton crest, then tied it with a white silk ribbon.

"Only one woman in a hundred would have turned down my offer," the Russian prince said quietly from behind her. "One in a thousand."

She looked back at him with a trembling attempt at a smile. "You are my boss's rival. I feel enough of a traitor allowing you to replace the lingerie. Accepting a gift from you would not be appropriate."

"No one would ever know about it."

"I would know. And so would you."

"Ah." He looked down at her, his dark eyes intent. "A woman of honor."

She felt uncomfortable, unsure of what response to make. The way he looked at her didn't help. It just made her jumpy in her own skin. After feeling invisible for so long, being so suddenly *seen* by a man like Maksim made her dizzy.

It was like spending years in the darkness and then abruptly being hit by a blaze of sun. It sizzled her all over. She felt blinded by the intensity of his heat.

From the corner of her eye, she saw the salesgirl hold out the bag with a bright smile. "Merry Christmas, miss. Please come again soon."

"Allow me." Maksim took the bag, carrying it for her.

A prince *and* a gentleman?

It shocked her. If she'd been shopping with Alan, he would have made her carry everything. He liked to keep his hands free. After all, he always joked, didn't women love to carry shopping bags? But then, Alan was her boss.

Maksim was…her enemy?

He was different from any man she'd ever known before. Dangerous. Because he was so handsome? Ruthless. Because he was a billionaire? And gallant. Because he was a prince?

Whatever it was, he was just like the Leighton clothes. Not for Grace. Nothing to do with real life. And yet she couldn't look away, and a part of her couldn't stop wondering what it would be like to be his woman.

As they climbed into his waiting Rolls-Royce, she felt the strength of his hand beneath her arm as he helped her in. Felt his touch up and down her body. And she trembled in her wet coat for reasons that had nothing to do with cold.

"Is it strange for you to buy lingerie for your ex-girlfriend?" she murmured as the car pulled away from the curb.

He shrugged, looked away. "She may someday be my girlfriend again."

"But she's engaged to Alan."

She saw the twitch in his jaw. "And two months ago she was with me."

"You can't possibly think—"

"I don't wish to speak of her." He took both her hands in his own. "I wish to speak only of you." He looked down at her and the edges of his lips turned up. "You need warming up."

"I…do?" she breathed.

"Join me for dinner tonight."

He was asking her out on a date? She tried not to tremble. Failed. "I couldn't possibly."

His dark eyebrows lowered. "Why?"

"I'm not hungry, for one." As if on cue, her stomach gave an audible growl and she blushed. She'd worked through lunch writing engagement announcements for Alan's friends and family, while her boss met Francesca for a celebratory lunch at her father's estate outside the city. "If Alan found out…"

"He won't."

"Splurging on dinner is not in my budget."

"I will of course be pleased to—"

"No."

He sighed, clearly exasperated. "You make it impossible to pamper you."

"I don't want you to pamper me." Her stomach growled again, and she bit her lip. "But…perhaps a small snack wouldn't hurt. As long as we go Dutch." *And as long as Alan never finds out.* "There's a tea shop by Harrods, close to our house."

He raised his eyebrows. "'Our' house?" he asked innocently. "You have a roommate?"

She felt a blush go across her cheeks. "I share a house with Alan."

He gave her a knowing glance. "I see."

"We're not lovers, if that's what you think!" But she could see he didn't believe her. She felt her cheeks turn redder still. "I have my own three-room flat in his basement. As his executive secretary, he needs me to always be available. With London rents as expensive as they are, I'm happy to have a place to stay."

"How very convenient for you both," he murmured silkily.

"You don't understand," she stammered. "It's all fair and aboveboard. He deducts the cost of the rent from my salary each month!"

He suddenly laughed. "Does he really? So you're available to him around the clock, running his personal errands on your own time…and he still makes you pay money to live in his basement?" He shook his head. "I can see why he inspires such loyalty."

"Oh, forget it," she said in a huff, sitting back against the seat and staring stonily out at passing Hyde Park. "If you're going to insult Alan, you can forget the tea and just take me home."

"I didn't insult him."

"You did!"

"I'm just surprised at your loyalty. You deserve more."

She stared at him. She deserved more? It was an entirely new thought. She'd spent three years in low-paying temp jobs in downtown L.A. before she'd been hired by Cali-West. She'd been instantly smitten by the powerful, blond, handsome CEO who looked like a young Hugh Grant. She'd thought herself very lucky.

But the darkly handsome Russian prince thought she deserved…more?

"Are we close to the tea shop?" Maksim asked. She saw the driver waiting for directions, glancing at her in the rearview mirror.

She pointed grumpily. "Right there. Just past the light."

The white-haired lady who owned the patisserie appeared flustered by Maksim's broad-shouldered form appearing in the doorway of her dainty shop. He seemed massively masculine, out of place against the faded flowery wallpaper. She immediately seated them at the best table, tucked in a corner window overlooking the crowds and festive windows of Harrods across the street. When the Frenchwoman asked for their order, Grace waited for Maksim to order first, as Alan would have done.

Instead, he looked at her questioningly, reaching across the small table to take her hand. "What do you recommend, Grace?"

"I…um." She glanced down at her hand wrapped in his far larger one. She could barely think with him touching her. "The…er…" She pulled her hand away under pretense of picking up the gently tattered menu that she'd long ago learned by heart. "The English breakfast tea is good. The pastries are excellent, and so are the sandwiches." She looked up at Madame Charbon, handing back her menu. "I'll have my usual."

The woman nodded.

Maksim handed her his menu. "I'll have the same."

"Oui, monsieur."

As the Frenchwoman departed, Grace looked at him in surprise. "You don't even know what you just ordered!"

He shrugged. "You know this restaurant. I trust you."

He trusted her. She tried not to feel flattered. "Want to know what you're having?"

"I like surprises."

Normally Grace didn't, but she was starting to. She

took a deep breath. "I'm sorry I was so upset in the car. I guess you really weren't insulting Alan."

"He is lucky to have you."

She stared down at the tiny table. The truth was it was sometimes grating how small her paycheck was. And never more so than now. She'd been his junior secretary for eighteen months before she was promoted to executive assistant six months ago. But in spite of her additional responsibilities, he'd never given her a raise commensurate with her new position. He'd always managed to put her off with an excuse and a smile.

Then he'd decided to pursue a long-shot merger with Exemplary Oil PLC and he'd abruptly moved them to London in early October. In L.A. Grace had had fewer expenses. She'd been able to live at home and help her family. Now that she lived in London and paid Alan rent, she was barely able to send her mother a hundred dollars a month.

This led to one inescapable conclusion: the looming foreclosure of her family's home was entirely Grace's fault.

As Madame Charbon arrived with the steaming mugs of hot chocolate and croissants, Grace tried to push the depressing thoughts away. They just made her feel more powerless and scared and…angry.

Alan will help me. He will, she repeated to herself.

"What are you thinking about, *solnishka mayo?*" Maksim asked, leaning forward as he looked at her keenly.

She gulped down some hot chocolate, scalding her tongue. "Nothing. Um. I was just wondering if you've ever ridden the Trans-Siberian Railroad."

His dark eyebrows rose. "An odd question."

"You're Russian, aren't you?" She smiled wistfully. "I used to dream about that train when I was a little girl, a train that crosses seven time zones and nearly six thousand miles, going all the way from Moscow to the Pacific Ocean."

"Sorry to disappoint you," he said dryly. "I live in Moscow only a few months a year. When I travel or visit the northern oil fields I go by jet."

"Of course you do," she said with a sigh. "So where do you live when you're not in Russia? London?"

"I have many houses around the world. Six or seven. I live in whichever one is convenient."

She stared at him. "Six or seven? You're not even sure how many?"

He shrugged. "I have as many as I need. I sell them when I'm bored." He licked the thick whipped cream off the top of the mug with his wide tongue, causing her to stare in spite of herself. He took a sip of hot chocolate, then a bite of the croissant. "This is delicious."

"I'm glad you like it. Alan hates hot chocolate."

Maksim's eyes suddenly sliced through hers. "You're in love with him, aren't you?"

She felt sucker punched.

"What?" she whispered. "Who?"

"You're his loyal slave. You live in his house. You spend your free hours running his errands. It's plain you're not doing it for the money, since you have none. There's only one explanation. You love him."

Grace opened up her mouth to deny it, but suddenly she was so tired of lying. Tired of holding everything inside, of keeping it together, of having no one to confide in and no one she could rely upon. She took a deep breath.

"Yes. I love him." Sinking her head into her hands, she whispered, "It's hopeless."

"I know." She looked up, saw surprising warmth and sympathy in his handsome face. "I'm usually on the other side of it. Old or young, secretaries imagine themselves in love with me and drop like flies from my office. It's painful. It causes disruption. I hate it."

"Me, too." She gave a little laugh that ended with a sob—or was it a sob that ended with a laugh? She tried her best at a laissez-faire shrug. "And now he's engaged to someone who's beautiful, wealthy and so, well…"

"Vicious?" His eyes met hers. "Cruel and mean?"

With a gulp, she nodded. "I'm surprised to hear you say that. Didn't you love her?"

He changed the subject. "You don't have to endure it, Grace. Come work for me instead."

It was a good thing she'd already finished her hot chocolate or it would have snorted out her nose. Her eyes flew open, and she saw he wasn't joking. He was deadly serious.

Her throat closed.

"Work for you?" she gasped.

"I could use another secretary. Leave Barrington. Work for a man who will pay you well and take you far." He smiled. "The fact that you're in love with someone else is actually in your favor."

She swallowed. "Even though it's the man who stole your girlfriend?"

He took another drink of the hot chocolate.

"Delicious," he murmured, then looked up at her. "I need a secretary I can trust, Grace. A smart woman who knows the meaning of loyalty. You wouldn't regret changing your allegiance. I swear to you."

For an instant she was tempted. What would it be like to work for this handsome prince, instead of Alan?

Maksim was handsome, dangerous and ruthless. But he was also a man she would be free to fight, free to leave, free to speak her mind with, because she did not love him!

"I would pay you double whatever Barrington's paying you."

Double?

She licked her lips. "Would you consider paying me in advance?"

He didn't even hesitate. "Yes."

She took a deep breath, tempted beyond measure. This could save her mother's house. Save everything.

"And the catch?"

"You would help me win the merger."

"And Francesca?"

He shrugged, then held out his hand. "Do we have a deal?"

Grace closed her eyes, remembering all the times Alan had teased her, flirted with her. He'd told her more than once that he never wanted her to leave him. "I just couldn't survive without you, Gracie," he'd said with his charming movie-star grin. And it had made her so happy! She'd hugged his words to her heart, hoping that he might be starting to see her as more than just a secretary!

Then Lady Francesca Danvers had offered him money and power in such a perfectly beautiful package.

But no matter how Alan had treated her, Grace couldn't betray him.

Stubborn and foolish, she thought sourly, but she shook her head. "Thanks for asking, but my answer is no."

Taking back his hand, he nodded. "I understand."

But he didn't seem disappointed. On the contrary, he seemed to savor her refusal like a cat licking a bowl of cream.

Finishing the last crumbs of her croissant, Grace left some coins on the table and rose regretfully from her chair. She held out her hand.

"Thank you for a very pleasant afternoon, Prince Maksim."

He looked at her, and for a moment she was lost in his gaze, swirling in the endless shades of gray.

"No. I thank you, Grace." He took her hand in his own. A sizzling warmth spread through her body from their intertwined fingers. Then, still holding her hand, he kissed each of her fingers, and she shivered.

"Da svedanya, solnishka mayo. I'll never forget the way you looked in the street, with the last rays of winter twilight in your pale-blond hair. Like an angel. Like the sun." He turned her hand over and kissed her palm. An erotic charge arced through her, making her nipples tight and her breasts heavy. Her whole body was suddenly tense, waiting, waiting...

Looking up into her face, he murmured, "Until we meet again."

He released her, and Grace walked out of the tea

shop in a daze. As she slogged through the crowds outside Harrods, gripping her Leighton bag as if her life depended on it, she could still feel that sensual kiss against her palm.

With one brief touch of his lips, he'd branded her. In the dark winter night lit up by Christmas lights and shop windows, she looked down at her right hand, expecting to see the burn of his lips emblazoned on her skin for all the world to see.

But her skin was bare.

She knew she'd never see him again. Probably a good thing.

Definitely a good thing.

And yet…

When Alan yelled at her for not magically foreseeing his wishes in advance…when a check bounced in her bank account…when she was forced to watch the man she loved get married to another woman…when she felt helpless, hopeless, invisible…

She could treasure this one magical afternoon when she'd spent the day with a handsome prince who'd been kind to her. Who'd treated her like a princess.

As she walked home, the sleet softened to snow in the dark stillness of winter, leaving scattered, twisted flurries of flakes.

She'd loved Alan Barrington in hopeless silence for two years. But he'd never affected her like Maksim Rostov had. He'd never made her tremble and shake and feel hot all over. Maksim had changed her in a way she couldn't understand.

But whatever he'd made her feel didn't matter now.

With a sigh that created a puff of white smoke in the frozen air, Grace climbed slowly up the front steps of the three-story town house she shared with her boss.

The fairy tale was over.

CHAPTER FOUR

ALAN was waiting for her at the door with twinkling blue eyes. He was so boyishly handsome, he could almost be called pretty. Beaming with excitement, he dragged her into his reception room.

"You got home just in time, Gracie! I have a present for you!"

He placed a plane ticket into her hands. She stared down at it, and the sparkling white lights of his elegantly decorated Christmas tree seemed to whirl around her in the front room of his Knightsbridge town house.

"Merry Christmas," he purred.

Sucking in her breath, she looked up at him. And to think she'd wondered in her darker moments if he intentionally used her own feelings against her, taking advantage of her crush to avoid having to properly pay her. But with this gift, there could be no doubt that he truly cared for her…otherwise, why would he have done this?

"Thank you," she whispered. "I wanted so much to go home for Christmas. But I didn't have enough to—"

"I know, Gracie," he said with a big smile.

"Thank you, Alan," she said, feeling as if she was going to cry. "This means so much to me."

"On Christmas Eve, as soon as the deal is finished, you'll fly off to enjoy the sun and surf." He sighed. "I don't know how I'll survive while you're gone."

She took a deep breath. "Alan, I have a really big favor to ask you—"

"Oh, no." He groaned. "Not the raise again. Does it always have to be about money? I'm the CEO of Cali-West and you're my righthand woman." He gave her a wink. "Isn't that glory enough for you?"

His righthand woman, but not the woman in his arms. Grace managed a weak smile. "You said we could talk about maybe a raise or bonus at the end of the year, and I'm really desperate, Alan, because—"

"Sorry, kiddo." He held up his hand. "That'll have to wait a bit longer. I'm late for my date with Francesca."

"But Alan—"

"We'll talk about it tomorrow. I really promise this time." He took her hand, and she felt nothing like the painful zing she'd experienced with Maksim. Alan's hand was just warm and soft. "In the meantime, there's something I need you to do for me. A teensy, small favor." He flashed her a big white grin. "Help me get married."

"Wh-what?"

"Francesca's having trouble setting the wedding date. So I thought—why bother with a wedding at all? Why not just elope? That's where you come in." He gave her a bright smile. "Christmas Eve I want to elope. Scotland. Honeymoon in Barbados. I need you to make the arrangements."

Alan didn't realize what he was asking of her. How could he? To him, Halloween night had been just a kiss. To her, it had been the culmination of two years of fantasies. Which was probably why the kiss hadn't felt nearly as intense as she'd imagined it would. Not even as intense as the way Prince Maksim's lips had felt against her palm an hour before.

Trying to push the memory of the dark Russian prince from her mind, she took a deep breath. "Are you sure eloping is a good idea? The bride might prefer to choose when—"

"It's perfect," he said, frowning.

"All right," she sighed. She suddenly realized she was still clutching the Leighton bag in her hands. "Here's your gift."

"Thanks." Taking his coat from the hall closet, he slung the bag over his shoulder. He stopped at the door with a wink. "I'll need this tonight to close the deal. I'll be getting her something better for Christmas. In the meantime, start working on the elopement plans, will you?"

After Grace locked the door behind him, she turned back with a lump in her throat.

She'd thought buying gifts for his fiancée was bad. Planning their quickie wedding would be a thousand times worse.

It hurt more than she'd expected.

Because she'd spent the afternoon with Prince Maksim, she realized. Because for the first time in years she'd felt the full attention of a man's eyes on her, the consideration of his touch and regard, and it had brought something to life inside her. Something that wanted to be seen. Something that wanted to be touched. It had felt so good. She'd felt…

Alive.

Now she just felt numb.

Grace went downstairs to her basement apartment. Closing the door quietly behind her, she changed out of her damp clothes. She put on an old sweatshirt and flannel pajama pants. She heated some leftover takeaway Thai food in her microwave. She sat down heavily on the couch. She turned on the old television. She placed a fork, the food and a diet soda on the coffee table. She got out her laptop to start making elopement arrangements for Christmas Eve, just two weeks away.

But instead of opening her laptop or watching TV, she wrapped herself in the quilt her mother had made her as a child. She sat on the couch and stared blankly at the wall.

He was really going to marry Lady Francesca Danvers. The vicious, skinny, gorgeous heiress who always got away with her bad behavior because she was so beautiful that men put up with it. Men would put up with anything to be with a girl like that.

While Grace was such a pushover she couldn't even make Alan listen to her beg him for an advance. Not even though her family's security depended on it.

Tears fell softly onto the frayed fabric of the quilt. Why hadn't she found out until that morning that her father's life insurance money was gone? Why hadn't she known her mother had been keeping their financial difficulties secret? And why couldn't she stop loving a man who so plainly saw her as nothing but a secretary?

She jumped when she heard a loud knock at her front door.

Fiercely wiping her eyes, she wrapped her mother's quilt over her shoulders and rose from the couch. Alan had likely forgotten his key again and wanted to go up through her apartment. Her nervous heart beat faster. This time she would make him listen. *I need an advance,* she practiced in her mind. *Please, Alan, I need $10,000 right away or my family will lose their home.*

She opened the door into the dark, snowy night. "Alan, I need—"

Her words ended in a gasp.

The tall, dark-haired man who looked down at her with a gleam in his eye was definitely *not* her boss.

Prince Maksim leaned against the edge of the door, looking dangerous and oh, so seductive in a tuxedo beneath a black coat. Her heart pounded in a whole new way.

"What are you doing here?" she breathed.

"I forgot something," he said, looking down at her tear-stained face.

"What?"

She caught a sudden brief blur of icy moonlight above as she felt his hands, his warmth, wrapping around her. Saw the colors of her quilt blur around her as he cupped her face.

"This," he said simply.

And he kissed her.

The touch of Maksim's mouth on hers was gentle at first. He pulled her close. She felt his hands brush through her hair before they moved slowly down her back. Her breasts pressed against his hard chest. He held her more tightly, deepening the embrace. His lips caressed hers, leading her, teaching her, making her sizzle all the way to her toes. He forced her lips wide, penetrating her mouth, teasing and licking her with the tip of his tongue. Her whole body became tight with longing, and her core poured with heat.

It was the kiss she'd always dreamed of. The whole world seemed to whirl and shudder around her like a tornado as she was swept up in his fierce embrace.

Was she dreaming? She had to be dreaming!

Feeling Maksim's strong arms around her, his lips taking his pleasure and demanding she take her own, was like nothing she'd ever felt before. Nothing like Alan's sloppy, drunken kiss six weeks earlier.

Alan!

She was kissing Alan's enemy in his own house!

"Stop," she whimpered against his lips, shuddering as she pulled away. "Please stop."

He pushed blond tendrils from her face. "Because you're in love with Barrington?"

"No...yes." She shook her head with a tearful laugh. "You just have to go!"

"You just have to come with me."

He wanted her to go out with him? "I don't need your pity—"

"Pity?" His eyes darkened until they were almost black in the snowy, cloud-ribboned moonlit night. "I have been accused of having no heart. I am telling you the truth, Grace. Take this as a warning."

And he kissed her again.

This time he was not gentle. It was a hard plundering of her mouth that bruised her lips and left her dizzy, aching with pleasure.

"Come out with me tonight," he whispered against her cheek. "You cannot refuse me."

Though she'd been standing for five minutes in the below-street-level entrance of her basement flat, she was barely aware of the cold.

But how could she be tempted? She loved Alan!

Didn't she?

"I won't turn on him," she gasped, still trembling with the shock of desire. "Not for any price. You won't kiss a betrayal out of me."

"You think that's the only reason I would kiss you?" The rich moonlight moved against scattered dark clouds above them, wistful and haunted, tracing his razor-sharp cheekbones and chiseled jaw. "You are a desirable woman, *solnishka mayo.*"

"*Solnishka mayo?*" she repeated.

"Sunlight," he whispered.

She choked out a laugh, glancing down at her flannel pajama pants, her ratty sweatshirt. She pulled her mother's quilt a little tighter over her shoulders. "You're blind."

"You don't know your own beauty." He stroked her shoulder, running his hand down the quilt as he looked down into her eyes, towering over her. "Let me show you the truth."

"But I can't trust you," she whispered. Prince Maksim was dangerous and ruthless. Though knowing he was forbidden to her just made her want him more….

He leaned down to kiss one cheek softly, then the other, as he spoke against her skin. "I'm not leaving without you."

The touch of his lips against her cheek sent aching tension to her breasts and down deep in her belly. She longed for him to kiss her again. In his arms she couldn't think, she couldn't do anything but feel. She closed her eyes as she felt his hot breath against the tender flesh of her ear. "I…I can't."

"You can and you will," he said. "Let me show you how pleasurable life can be."

With those words he pulled away from her. She nearly protested aloud and her eyelids reluctantly fluttered open. He was at least six inches taller than her, making her feel delicate. "No."

"Stubborn and foolish," he repeated softly, rubbing his thumb lightly against her swollen lower lip. "Why do you resist me?"

"Because…because…" She couldn't think straight with him stroking her lip like that. Grace's whole body ached. "I…don't have anything to wear."

With a sudden grin, he snapped his fingers. A bodyguard—a dark, hulking man who had to weigh three hundred pounds—ambled down the steps to her basement door with two primrose boxes in his arms. He set them near the doorway, then disappeared back up to the street.

An exclamation of shock escaped Grace as she stared at the two recognizably colored boxes embossed with the Leighton coat of arms.

"What have you done?"

"The coat," he said. "The dress."

She licked her lips. "Not the ones from Leighton."

"I knew you wanted them, though you denied it."

Remembering how she'd yearned for the black coat and the teal silk cocktail gown, a shiver swept through her body. She'd been afraid to even touch them in the store. At the thought of wearing them against her skin, her heart pounded.

He's luring me, she warned herself desperately. *Luring me to my own destruction!*

"I guessed your size, but have others in the car if necessary." His eyes met hers. "Women's clothes have always been a mystery to me. I've always been more interested in taking them off."

She gave an involuntary shiver. Then she looked down at the boxes, licking her lips, torn with longing.

He grabbed her wrist.

"Fair warning, Grace," he said quietly. "I will seduce you tonight."

Caught in his gaze, she couldn't breathe. Her heart almost felt about ready to explode from her chest.

"You're welcome to try," she managed over the rapid pounding of her heart. "I will resist you."

He gave her a slow, seductive smile. "I would expect nothing less."

She looked at the Leighton boxes. "And I can't… won't…accept expensive gifts."

"They weren't expensive."

"I saw one of the price tags in the boutique. The coat alone cost ten thousand pounds."

"You are worth far more than that." He stroked her

cheek. "I would pay any price to give you pleasure. Any price to please you."

The reminder of his wealth and power made her tremble. The money that felt like nothing to him was a fortune to her. More than enough to save her family. She closed her eyes. No. She wouldn't think about it. Asking Alan's enemy for help would blacken her soul beyond recognition. She might be weak, but she wasn't a traitor.

"If Alan found out I went out with you, he'd fire me."

"In which case you could come work for me," he said.

"But—"

"Either wear these clothes or go naked." He gave her a slow-rising smile. "Decide. Or I will."

Without asking permission, he pushed past her into her flat, carrying the boxes and pulling Grace behind him. He closed the door. They were alone.

The air seemed to leave the small apartment.

Prince Maksim Rostov—in her flat? She saw him look around at her sagging, plaid, threadbare couch. The day-old Thai takeout in the cardboard container. The blaring television with faded stars sparkling in sequins dancing to ballroom music. The laptop computer set up by her couch. Her cheeks burned.

He turned to her with a sensual smile. "Or we could just stay in."

Stay here—with him?

Ohmygodohmygod. *No.*

"The dress and coat would have to be a loan," she heard herself whisper. "I would give them back to you at the end of the night."

He smiled down at her.

"I'll look forward to it."

A dark force in his eyes pulled her with all the force of gravity. He looked at her as if he'd already undressed her and tossed her naked into his bed.

Bed? Who was thinking about bed?

Going out with him tonight, she was risking everything for a dangerous feeling she couldn't control. But she suddenly hungered to feel something that wasn't grief, loneliness or fear. She wanted to forget. She wanted to disappear into another world.

Her knees shook as she gathered up the boxes. "I'll be right back."

"I'll be waiting."

She hurried to her tiny bedroom, feeling strangely lighthearted. She brushed out her blond hair for two minutes with a hair dryer, then dabbed on some lipstick. She had no bra that would work with the cocktail dress, so she left her breasts bare beneath the dress. As she pulled the aquamarine gown over her hips, the softness of the luxurious silk slid like the whisper of a caress.

She knew she shouldn't do this.

Just one night, she told herself. *One night to forget my problems. I won't let him seduce me.*

She glanced at herself in the mirror and nearly gasped. She looked nothing like the downtrodden, damp, dowdy secretary she'd been just a few moments before. Aside from her old shoes, the scuffed silver pumps which were her only option, she almost didn't recognize herself. Who was the blond, bright-eyed young woman in the mirror?

The teal silk exactly matched the shade of her eyes.

The rose-pink lipstick made her pale skin look creamy. The cut of the gown made her full breasts look exactly right with her small waist, giving her the hourglass shape of a 1950s pinup girl.

Could clothes and makeup really do so much?

It wasn't just the clothes, she realized. It was *him*. His attention was making her blossom like a flower.

One night, she repeated to herself, and her teeth chattered. Just a few hours to feel pretty. She wouldn't let him seduce her. She couldn't. She was in love with someone else, which meant she was perfectly safe. Right?

Coming out of the bedroom, she stopped abruptly when she saw him leaning against the wall of the hallway. Maksim was so dark and handsome and terrifying. His gaze held her own, electrifying her.

"Sorry to make you wait," she said.

He came forward, stalking her like a jungle cat. He looked slowly over her body, from the blue-green silk skimming her curves to the silver drops dangling from her ears, from her long, thick blond hair to her full pink lips. He gave a long, slow whistle.

"You, *solnishka mayo,*" he said in a low voice, "were utterly worth waiting for."

CHAPTER FIVE

As THE chauffeur drove through the London streets, Grace watched feather-edged moonlight from the window move over Maksim's sharp cheekbones, his angular jawline. He was the most beautiful man she'd ever seen.

Beautiful. A strange word to describe such a powerful, dangerous man. But he *was* beautiful—hauntingly so. The moonlight caressed his straight nose, the cleft of his hard jaw, the hinted strength and latent brutality of the muscular body beneath the tuxedo and black coat.

He turned to meet her eyes, and his gaze scorched her, his gray eyes like smoke twisting from a deep hidden fire.

Grace suddenly realized…he hadn't lied. *He did want her.*

Innocent as she was, she could feel it.

He wasn't showing pity—or even kindness.

He wanted her.

The Leighton clothes had somehow transformed her into a beautiful, desirable woman. She'd felt downtrodden and invisible—now she felt like a goddess. Or possibly a sex kitten. An answering fire burned inside her with his every touch, every hot glance.

It wouldn't last. Like Cinderella's, her dress would disappear at the end of the night. She couldn't keep these things. She wouldn't let him buy her. She wouldn't let him seduce her.

But…for this one night, she could be the woman these clothes had created. She would have one night of magic. One night to be *seen*.

She would be the princess in the fairy tale.

The limo pulled smoothly to a stop at the curb. Maksim got out of the car and opened her door himself. Holding her arm in his own, steadying her on the icy sidewalk beneath the softly falling snow, he led her down a popular Covent Garden street filled with pubs and restaurants. Her black shearling coat swished against her ankles as she walked. Between the coat and Maksim's hand on hers, she felt warm in the frozen winter air.

"This way." He led her into a stately Victorian building, through a hidden door beside a chic tavern. She saw an elegant foyer, complete with a crystal chandelier, a front desk concierge and a security guard.

"Where are we going?"

"The top two floors of this building were converted into a penthouse." He gave her a brief smile. "A loft."

She stopped dead on the marble floor. "I'm not going to spend the evening alone with you at your house!"

"I don't live here. My sister does." He gave a careless shrug as he led her into a gilded elevator. "It's a bit colorful for my taste."

"So why did you buy it?"

Pressing on the elevator button, he looked down at her. "The Sheikh of Ramdah thought he could steal a pipeline deal from me. Instead I took his company and his favorite home in the bargain. To teach him a lesson."

The coldness in his voice made her shiver even more. "That's a bit ruthless, isn't it?" she ventured.

He gave a grim smile. "I protect what is mine."

When they arrived at the top floor, he knocked on the door. A ponderous, stiffly formal butler opened it to welcome them. His eyes widened. "Your Highness!"

"Oh!" A beautiful black-haired girl suddenly pushed past the butler to fling herself into Maksim's arms. "You're here! I can't believe you're here!"

He hugged her awkwardly, then drew back. "I wouldn't miss my own sister's birthday party."

"Liar," the girl said with a laugh. "You've missed the last two! And don't think expensive gifts make up for your absence. I don't need another Aston-Martin con-vertible, I need a brother—" She saw Grace and drew back in surprise. "But who's this?"

"A friend," he said.

"Funny, you've never bothered bringing 'friends' around before." She looked at Grace inquisitively, then pulled them both inside. "But I'm being rude. Come in! Come in!"

As the butler took their coats, the girl turned her piercing gray eyes, so much like her brother's, on Grace. "I'm Dariya Rostova."

Of course Grace knew the famous Princess Dariya, the fun-loving party girl who was constantly in the papers with her gorgeous friends. Pale and model slender in her silver sequin minidress, she wore a diamond tiara in her straight black hair.

Beneath her examination, Grace felt shy and out of place. "I'm sorry, I didn't know we were going to a birthday party," she stammered. "I'm afraid I don't have a gift."

Dariya suddenly smiled, and her lovely face lit up with warmth. "It wouldn't have even occurred to Francesca to bring a gift, so I already like you loads better. If you ask me, that woman was a snooty dry stick draped in furs."

"Dariya," her brother warned.

"What's your name?" his sister said, ignoring him.

She cleared her throat. "Grace."

"Well, Grace, you've actually brought the best present of the night." She beamed up at her brother fondly. "Come say hello to everyone!"

Dariya led them into the enormous loft, with soaringly high ceilings and big windows overlooking St. Martin's Lane. In the center of the room, a sharp, metallic chandelier held multicolored orbs for lights. Amid the vast space of the open-walled apartment, the furniture was a cross between 1960s retro and cartoonish avant-garde. Grace looked with dismay at backless chairs that were shaped like ripe strawberries.

"Look everyone," Dariya announced happily. "Look who came! And he even brought a friend. Everyone, say hello to Grace!"

As a cheer of welcome went around the room, Grace felt happy in a way she hadn't felt for months. She suddenly realized how much she'd missed having friends. She hadn't kept up with her old friends since she'd started working for Alan, much less tried to make new ones. She'd given up the idea of friends or hobbies or anything but being Alan's perfect on-call secretary.

But now…

The laughing, friendly group around her reminded Grace of bonfires on the beach when she'd been in school, before her father had died. Before she'd started working for Alan. Back when her life had been simple and easy. She ached remembering the fun she'd had, getting together with friends to eat, drink, talk and laugh.

The only difference being that these people were all impossibly rich and good-looking. And that the party was in an artistic, soaring two-floor loft that had once been the treasured possession of the Sheikh of Ramdah.

"I told you Maksim would come!" Dariya said triumphantly to a young man hovering nearby. "You owe me ten pounds!"

"Best bet I've ever lost. Hello, Maksim. Lovely to meet you, Grace," he said with a grin. "Thanks for putting a smile on my girl's face."

"*Your* girl?" Dariya tossed her dark hair. "In your dreams, Simon!"

Maksim growled something incomprehensible to the aristocratic young man. He was obviously being protective, but it still seemed rude. Grace cleared her throat and turned to Dariya. "So it's your twenty-fifth birthday?"

"Don't remind me," she groaned. She suddenly looked alarmed, putting her hands on her perfect face. "Do I look it?"

Grace laughed, then pointed at the hand-painted banner slung from the high, frescoed ceiling that read, *Happy Twenty-fifth Birthday, Dariya!* It was a charming homemade touch amid all the exorbitantly expensive, bright, sharp modernity.

"Oh. Right." The girl followed her glance with a sigh. "A quarter of a century, and what have I done with my life?"

"I just turned twenty-five on Sunday," Grace said sympathetically, "and I spent the day huddled in my flat in total denial."

"No, really!" Dariya exclaimed. "Not even a party?"

"My boss gave me a gift card for a week's worth of lunches at my favorite Japanese restaurant."

"You had no party," the girl repeated, shaking her head in horror. "You simply can't turn twenty-five without a party! Maksim," she turned to her brother, "tell her it's ridiculous!"

"Ridiculous," he agreed laconically.

"Lulu," Dariya called over her shoulder, "get a party hat, will you? Right. So this party will be for both of us." When Lulu brought the colorfully decorated hat, Dariya took the tiara off her head and stuck the hat in its place. "This will be for me." She placed the diamond tiara on Grace's blond head. "And that will be for you."

"Oh no," Grace gasped, feeling the weight of the diamonds on her head. She'd come without a gift, and now she was going to upstage Maksim's sister, the famous socialite Princess Dariya, during her own birthday party? "That's so generous of you, really, but I couldn't—"

"To be honest, it suits you better." She leaned forward and whispered mischievously in Grace's ear, "It was a gift from my brother, anyway, and not at all my style!"

"Dariya, you promised to dance!" Simon called from the other side of the loft, where a four-person jazz band had started to play.

"In a mo!" She gave Grace one last hug. "Must go dance, I'm afraid. Otherwise he'll pout, but I'm so glad you're here. My brother looks happy. Make yourself at home!"

After she left, Grace touched the top of her head. Was it possible that they were actually real diamonds? The thought shocked her...frightened her. The wealth around her was already far beyond anything she'd ever seen, even working as Alan's secretary. She felt like Alice who'd just stepped through the looking glass to a world where money really did grow on trees. And the tree branches were made of gold. And the berries were all diamonds, rubies and emeralds.

She felt Maksim come up behind her. Wrapping his arms around her, he kissed the crook of her neck. Her nipples instantly went hard, her breath shallow, her mind went dizzy. Then he whirled her around, handing her one of the crystal flutes from his other hand.

She took it with an awkward attempt at a smile. "My first champagne."

"Cristal is not a poor way to start."

She took a sip. The bubbles floated inside her, all soft and lovely and warm going down.

Maksim tilted her head upward with his hand, looking down at her from his towering height. His gaze was dark and intense. She suddenly knew he meant to kiss her again and she couldn't think. Couldn't even breathe.

Everything about him tempted her. Transfixed her. Made her long to really and truly be the woman who could mesmerize him in equal measure.

When would he kiss her?

Kiss her? What was she thinking? Clearly the tiara had constricted the blood flow to her brain!

Nervously she pulled away. She gulped down the rest of the expensive champagne as if chugging a can of soda, then pushed the tiara back crookedly on her head. "This thing isn't real, is it? The tiara's not real diamonds?"

He took a drink of champagne, his dark eyes resting on hers. "Set in platinum."

She swallowed, thinking that she likely could pay off her mother's whole mortgage with the sparkling tiara on her head. And maybe their neighbor's house in the bargain!

"What if I break it?" She gave a weak laugh. "Do you have insurance?"

"Diamonds don't break." Finishing his champagne, he took both flutes and set them on the tray of a passing waiter. He took her in his arms. "The tiara suits you. You should keep it." He slowly lowered his mouth toward hers. "You were born to wear jewels, Grace," he whispered. "Born to be adored and pampered in a life of luxury."

Someone turned out the side lights, leaving the loft lit only by the multicolored globes of the steel chandelier high above. Wide spotlights of red, green and blue shimmered in the semidarkness. In the wide space, she was aware of other people dancing, laughing, swaying to the music. She was in some strange fantastic world of stylish art, youth and limitless wealth.

But it wasn't the luxury that lured her most.

It was Maksim.

"I won't let you seduce me," she whispered, trying to reassure herself. "I won't."

Every inch of her body, down to blood and bone, ached for him to kiss her. Her body arched toward his, taut with longing as her teal silk dress slid like a whisper against his tuxedo.

Pulling her against his hard body, too arrogant to care who might be watching, he lowered his mouth to hers.

He kissed her so deeply that their tongues intertwined, kissed her so hard that with one embrace he bruised and branded her forever as his own.

No! She sagged against his chest, her heart pounding wildly when he released her from the kiss. She couldn't belong to Maksim. She couldn't!

He straightened the diamond tiara, stroking the long hair that brushed her bare shoulders, making her shiver. He took two more flutes of champagne from a passing tray. Then, taking her hand, he led her to the dance floor.

For the next few hours they drank champagne and danced together, their bodies swaying to the music. Time moved strangely, sliding sideways so hours felt like minutes, and minutes felt like eternity. They danced to the soulful jazz music, to the poignant cry of the saxophone, until finally he pulled her gently to the furthest side of the loft.

There, alone in the shadows and away from the others, he pushed her against the wall. He gently bit at her neck, sucking on her ear. She gasped, breathless and desperate for more.

He finally kissed her mouth, his tongue stroking hers deeply, luring her. And suddenly she could barely remember Alan's name, let alone why she should be loyal to him.

"Grace," Maksim murmured between kisses. "It's time to go."

"Go? Already?" she faltered.

"It's past midnight."

"Oh." And like Cinderella, that meant her time was up. The dream was over. She swallowed. "All right. I have a lot of work to do tomorrow, anyway."

"Then you'll be tired." He held her close, so close she could hear the beat of his heart. "I'm taking you to my hotel."

Hotel? A hard shiver racked her body.

"Come with me now," he whispered. "I can wait no longer. I want you in my bed."

She sucked in her breath, staring up into his eyes, caught by his dark, commanding gaze. She'd somehow wandered into a fairy-tale world, a place beyond her comprehension. She'd been drawn from the real world to become a princess in diamonds and teal silk, enslaved by a fantasy prince who compelled her to follow her deepest desires.

He was so handsome, she thought in a daze. Brutally masculine, like a sixteenth-century barbarian warlord. A dark czar from a mist-shrouded medieval age.

"Can you walk," he asked in a low voice, "or should I carry you?"

Walk? Her knees felt weak, whether from champagne or desire she wasn't sure. She glanced down at feet, at the cheaply made silver pumps, scuffed up at the toes, that she'd bought for fifteen dollars at a discount warehouse in Los Angeles. The shoes threatened to break the spell.

He led her from the dance floor. As he said their farewells to Dariya and her friends, Grace could barely speak as she looked up at Maksim.

He intended to take her to his hotel.

Could she resist?

Did she still even want to?

Maksim put her coat over her shoulders, pulling her close to button it up. She felt every brush of his fingertips like an earthquake through her body. He led her back to the elevator. Suddenly they were alone, and she trembled.

"Do you swear," she whispered, "seducing me isn't some backhanded way to hurt Alan?"

He put his hands on her shoulders and looked down at her.

"I swear it to you."

"On your honor?"

He looked away and his jaw clenched. Then he turned to face her.

"Yes," he said tersely.

When she remembered to breathe, she nodded, believing him. He was a prince. He wouldn't look her straight in the eye and lie.

"So why me?" she said. "Why be so nice—"

"Call me nice again and you'll regret it." His dark eyes gleamed as he pulled her from the elevator and out onto the street. "I am selfish. I take what I want. Any man would desire you, Grace. In his arms. In his bed. Any man would want you."

"Alan didn't." As soon as the bitter words escaped her, she wished desperately she'd kept them to herself.

"Barrington is a fool." He stopped on the sidewalk. His mouth curved into a sensual smile. "He lost his chance. Now you will be mine. Only mine."

He slowly stroked up the inside of her bare arm beneath her coat, causing her to give an involuntary shudder of longing.

"Grace," he whispered. "Let me show you how truly selfish I can be."

CHAPTER SIX

DECEIT was part of the art of war.

The truth could be a flexible thing in Maksim's opinion. Stretching it correctly was partly how he'd built a vast empire out of nothing. As a teenager, he'd gotten investors by pretending to already have them. He'd deceived competitors, making them believe deals were finished when they weren't. He'd bought commodities cheap and sold them high because he knew information that others didn't. Information he'd ruthlessly kept to himself.

It was not Maksim's responsibility to do the due diligence of others and reveal any truth against his own best interests. He looked out for himself. He assumed others did the same. Only a fool would blindly trust the word of another.

But that was business. Lying in his personal life—that was something new.

And swearing on his honor…

His neck broke out in a sweat to think of it. He'd never looked into a woman's face and lied against his honor. It made him feel…cheap.

I had no choice, he told himself fiercely. *She gave me no choice.* And this wasn't personal. It was business.

Wasn't it?

If he'd told Grace the truth, it would have ended everything. And he was getting so close. He could feel her weakening by the moment.

Seducing her away from Barrington was the best thing that could happen to her, he told himself. The man was obviously using her own feelings against her, working her like a slave without pay.

And it wasn't as if she were an innocent. No, her kisses were too perfect for that. She'd kissed Maksim slowly, sensually, holding herself back with such restraint. As if she'd been born to enflame a man's senses and make him crazed out of his mind with longing until he would do or say anything to possess her.

Even lie against his honor.

He took Grace's hand in his own. "I gave my driver the night off," he said. "I thought we'd walk."

"All right," she whispered, never taking her eyes from him.

Snow whitened the sidewalk, covering patches of slippery ice beneath. He held her arm tightly as they walked past the pubgoers enjoying last call, making sure she didn't slip and wasn't accosted by some drunken lad seeking a beauty for his bed.

Grace was all his.

Maksim could see their breath joined in swirling white puffs of air, illuminated by the moon in the winter night. He looked at her as they walked down the snowy street toward the southern edge of Trafalgar Square.

She looked so beautiful, he thought, lit up like an angel in front of St. Martin-in-the-Fields. Her light blond hair tumbled down her shoulders, looking like spun silver and gold in the frosted moonlight. The diamond tiara sparkled in her hair, making her a spun-sugar princess. No. There was a layer of grief, of steel, beneath the sweetness. She was no helpless pink princess. No. She was a Valkyrie, from a Gothic northern land.

Her shoulders were set squarely, her hands pushed into the pockets of her long black coat that whipped behind her like a regal cape; and yet there was a softer side to her as she leaned up against him, her tender pink lips pressed together, as if she were trying to hold herself back. As if she were trying not to think.

"Thank you for bringing me to your sister's party," she said softly. "I'd forgotten what it was like to be around friends."

He felt another pang of an unpleasant emotion perilously close to guilt. It had been ruthless of him to take her to the party. But he'd wanted to see Dariya on her birthday. And, he admitted quietly to himself, he'd known it would lower Grace's defenses to meet his family. She would think she could trust him. Another lie.

The only thing that wasn't a lie: *he wanted her*.

"Are you, Maksim?"

He focused on her. "Am I what?"

She looked up at him as he led her by Charing Cross station. "Are you my friend?"

He brought her hand to his lips and kissed the back of it. He felt her shiver beneath the brush of his lips against her skin. "No," he said in a low voice. "I'm not your friend, Grace."

They passed down a slender street full of restaurants and pubs, crowds of young people and a few Chelsea football fans in blue-and-white scarves celebrating loudly over a pint. He took her hand and led her down to the embankment by the river. As they walked, they passed a dark garden.

"I don't want your friendship," he said. "I want you in my bed."

The intimacy of his words, as they passed the quiet darkness of the park drenched in crystalline moonlight, was perfect. She looked up at him, her mouth a round *O*. A mouth made for kissing. A mouth he wanted to feel under his.

Right now.

But as he stopped, leaning down to kiss her, she suddenly turned away, her pale cheeks the color of roses in the moonlight.

"Did you learn to flirt like that in Russia?" she whispered. She gave a sharp, awkward laugh and started walking again. "You have some skills."

So his beauty wished to wait? He would be patient. "I grew up here."

Her eyes went wide. "London?"

"And other places." He shrugged. "We moved around. My father couldn't keep a job. We were poor. Then he died."

"I'm sorry," she said quietly. "My father died five years ago, too. Cancer." She swallowed, looked away. "My mother has yet to recover. She almost never leaves the house. That's why…" She looked away.

"Why what?"

She turned back, blinking hard.

"I'm sorry I misjudged you," she said. "Thinking you'd never known what it was like to struggle or suffer just because you're a prince."

"Yes, a prince," he said acidly. "Distantly in line to a throne that, if you haven't noticed, stopped ruling Russia nearly a hundred years ago."

"But still…"

"Prince of nothing and nowhere," he said harshly. "Money is all that matters. Only money."

"Oh, Maksim." Tears filled her eyes as Grace shook her head. "Money isn't the only thing that matters. It's the way you love people. The way you take care of them."

"And you take care of them with money."

"No. Like your sister said, she didn't need more expensive things, she wanted *you*. Your time and—"

"A lovely sentiment," he said sardonically. "But my sister is too young to remember how we nearly starved and froze to death the winter we lived in Philadelphia. After that, I made sure I could support us. I made sure no one and nothing could ever threaten my mother and sister again."

"You protected your family." Her eyes suddenly glittered, and her hands clenched into fists before she stuck them in the pockets of her designer coat. "I should have stayed in California," she said softly. "I never should have left my mother alone."

A hard lump rose in Maksim's throat. "Being with the people you love doesn't always save them. I made my first million when I was twenty, but it couldn't save my mother from dying."

"Oh, no," she said softly. "What happened?"

"Brain aneurysm. She died without warning. I…I couldn't save her."

He stopped, choking on the words. He had never spoken about his mother's death to anyone—not even Dariya, who'd been barely nine when it had happened.

Maksim waited for Grace to expose the weakness in his argument. To point out that, by his own admission, money was indeed not everything in life.

Instead she reached up to stroke his cheek. The first time she'd deliberately touched him.

"It wasn't your fault," she said softly. "You took care of your family. You protected them. You tried to save your mother. You did everything you could."

A tremble went through him, and he involuntarily turned his face into her caress. He closed his eyes briefly, taking a deep breath.

"You're a special woman, Grace Cannon," he said in a low voice. "I've never met your equal."

She gave a short laugh and looked away. The street-lights shone a plaintive blurry light on the dark, swift river beneath the bare trees of the embankment. "I'm not special. I'm completely ordinary."

"You're special."

"It's the clothes."

"It's the woman inside them." He looked down at her. "Grace. You are just like your name. Grace." His eyes narrowed. "And did you say your middle name is Diana?"

"Don't laugh."

"Your mother believed in fairy tales."

"Yes." She shook her head. "But her two favorite princesses didn't live happily ever after, did they?"

"What about you, *solnishka mayo?*" he whispered. His eyes drifted to her lips. "Do you believe in fairy tales?"

She briefly closed her eyes. "I used to believe in them. I used to believe with all my heart."

"And now?"

Their gazes locked, held in the moonlight. Her pupils dilated as she looked down at his lips, then licked her own.

An invitation no man could resist.

Taking her in his arms, he lowered his mouth to hers. Kissing her was heaven. He was intoxicated by the taste of her. The feel of her. His whole body tightened and he drew back to stroke her face, looking down into her eyes. "Tonight," he said hoarsely. "Tonight you must be mine."

He saw her dreamy expression suddenly change to shock. She shook her head hard, as if clearing the cobwebs from her mind.

She hesitated, licking her lips. Then she pulled away from him. "Please. Don't."

He reached for her. "Grace—"

"I can't," she whispered, backing away from his reach. "Please don't."

As she blindly stepped back, he saw her ankle twist, saw one of her shoes slide on the black ice beneath the snow. He heard the snap of one high heel. Saw her stumble back—

He caught her before she could fall. He cradled her against his chest. She looked up at him with an intake of breath. He could feel the rapid beat of her heart. She was so light she seemed to weigh nothing at all. That damned diamond tiara probably weighed more than she did, he thought. And as he looked down into her eyes, he felt dizzy for a reason he couldn't explain. As if he were the one in danger of falling.

A flash of fire burned through him as he felt her tremble in his arms. And he knew that nothing on earth would prevent him from possessing her tonight.

Grace would be his.

Without a word he carried her toward his hotel. As they were about to turn near Savoy Hill, he paused in a nearby alley to lean her against the rough wall and kiss her, hot and demanding. She was all woman, he thought, warm and pliant and willing...but with an elegant hesitation and restraint that heated his blood. He wanted nothing more than to take her against this wall, to fill her up, to slide inside her and thrust deeply until she screamed his name.

"Don't deny me, Grace," he whispered against her skin after he'd kissed her. "Don't deny us what we both want."

The dreamy look had returned to her eyes. "You're right," she said so softly he almost couldn't hear it. "I can't fight you."

She was looking up at him with desire, yes. But also something else. Faith? Trust? Pushing that disquieting thought away, he carried her around the corner toward his hotel. But when he saw the brightly lit porte-cochère of his luxury hotel, he hesitated again in spite of himself.

He wanted her so badly that his whole body hurt from it. But he also had a sour taste in his mouth. Because of guilt? Because he'd lied? He'd lied to get revenge against

Barrington. To win back the merger. To possibly take back Francesca.

But most of all…he'd lied to get Grace in his bed.

She's no innocent virgin, he told himself again. And she wanted him as he wanted her. Maksim had nothing to feel guilty about. Nothing at all.

The doorman saluted respectfully, pretending he didn't see the captive woman in Maksim's arms. "Good evening, Your Highness."

"Good evening," Maksim replied shortly.

He carried Grace straight to the waiting elevator and upstairs to his penthouse. He would make her moan with pleasure, he told himself fiercely. He was so hard with need he couldn't imagine letting her go now.

He couldn't.

Damn it, he wouldn't!

He unlocked his door with one hand then kicked it wide, carrying her over the threshold like a bride. He walked past the stark black-and-white furniture, the black leather sofa, the large flat-screen television above the fireplace.

The curtains had been left open. Below, he could see the dark Thames beneath moving lights of the barges, and steady traffic across the bridges. He saw the gleaming buildings of the city across the river and, to the far left, the brilliantly illuminated dome of St. Paul's.

A fittingly celestial image for the heavenly things Maksim intended to do to Grace. He couldn't even make it to the bedroom before he started kissing her.

In answer, her lips moved against his with gentle hesitation, a light tease that made him plunder her mouth with greater desire. Her kiss was like nothing he'd ever known before. Women had always kissed him so eagerly and desperately, matching his fire or surpassing it. Her unusual restraint fired his blood, increasing his need until he panted from it.

Still kissing her, he set her down on the big white bed. He paused to look down at her. Her blond hair was mussed and tousled. Her eyes were deep pools of blue green, like clear pools of mountain water from newly melted snow.

He trembled as he reached down to touch her, stroking down her neck to the soft silk of her teal dress, down the valley between her breasts to her flat belly. She was so soft and warm. So beautiful from her rose-pink lips to her unpolished nails. He leaned over her, brushing blond tendrils from her face to kiss her cheeks, her neck, her throat. Finally kissing her mouth, he teased her tongue with his as he cupped his hands over her full breasts. Discovering that she wasn't wearing a bra, that those high, firm breasts were unassisted by fabric or padding and were all her, he nearly gasped. He touched her in wonder and felt her nipples pebble and harden beneath his fingers. It was too much for him.

Lowering his head, he suckled her through the silk.

She gave a small hushed cry, arching involuntarily against his mouth. Wanting more, he roughly pulled down the neckline and tasted her flesh. She fell back against the bed with a shudder, exhaling her breath in a little mewling sound that made him harden to painful intensity. Lying on top of her, wrapping his hands pos-sessively around her naked breasts, he suckled her more forcefully, not letting her go even as she twisted beneath him. His body was hard against hers. Feeling her beneath him, he wanted nothing more than to pull up her cocktail dress, unbutton his pants and push all the way inside her with one hard, deep thrust.

The thought made him groan aloud.

He shoved her dress up to her hips, revealing simple white cotton panties. Even that surprised him, compared to the lacy, tarty panties his lovers typically wore to entice him. The simplicity was just like Grace, and revealed the perfection of her curvy hips, her creamy thighs. She didn't need to even try to seduce, to drive any man mad with need...

"Stop," she suddenly whispered. "Please stop."

He realized he'd already pushed up her dress to her waist and had started to unbutton his pants. Damn it to hell, after promising himself he would take his time and make her explode with pleasure, had he really been planning to fill her with one thrust, to roughly and savagely take her body like an animal?

Yes.

What the hell was this sweet insanity? She caused him to lose control. No woman had ever done that before.

"I'm sorry," Maksim said roughly, pulling away. His hands shook with the difficulty of holding himself back. "I didn't mean to go so fast."

"You're not." She licked her swollen, bruised lips. "I'm just...new to this."

He looked at her with a sudden frown. "How new?"

Propping herself up on her elbows, she admitted, "Completely new."

He sucked in his breath.

"Are you trying to tell me you're a *virgin?*"

Her cheeks went red. "Don't say that word!"

"How else would you describe it?"

Tears filled her eyes. "I'd describe it as being helplessly infatuated with a boss who's barely noticed I'm alive, except for one kiss."

"He kissed you?" he demanded. The ferocity of his sudden jealousy surprised Maksim. He'd never felt jealous before, not even when Francesca had delivered her little ultimatum and taken off with another man as promised. But then, Maksim's claim on Francesca had always been territorial. His possession of Grace felt…personal.

Very personal.

She looked at him, surprised. "Why are you so upset?"

Yes, why? "Because…because it's sexual harassment," he stammered furiously. "He's your boss. It's illegal!"

"Sexual harassment?" Grace laughed, then shook her head with a tearful little hiccup. "One drunken kiss before he passed out on the office couch? Then he met Francesca, who I'm sure is perfect at everything. That's why I wanted you to know," she said in a rush. "In case…in case I'm *not* so perfect. I'm sure I'm very clumsy."

Clumsy?

That explained her restraint. Her hesitation. *She was a virgin.* A shudder of hard desire went through him when he thought about how close he'd been to just ripping off her clothes and brutally taking her.

"Maksim, please. The fact that I'm—that word—doesn't mean anything," she pleaded. "It truly doesn't."

Clenching his jaw, he shook his head.

"You're wrong."

She was a virgin. She was doubly innocent.

He couldn't use her in his vicious power play.

He'd been prepared for anything but this. He could fight anything…but this.

Her naive faith had conquered the would-be conqueror.

"Maksim, nothing has changed between us." As she timidly reached for him, he grabbed her wrist.

"No, Grace. No."

He pulled her up from the bed and straightened her clothes. He wrapped her coat around her shoulders. Within two minutes he'd led her down the elevator, through the hotel lobby and out onto the street.

"Where are you taking me?" Grace whispered.

He hailed a passing black cab. When the cab pulled to the curb, he turned to face her.

"You're going home," he said tersely. "Alone."

He pushed her into the cab, then leaned forward to speak to the driver, giving him Grace's address and a very large tip with the fare.

"Wait!" Blinking out of her trance, Grace protested, "No. Maksim, please—"

He slammed the door. "Just go."

"But—"

"Go!" he ordered the cabbie.

The man pressed on the gas. Maksim watched her go. Grace turned around in the back seat to stare at him through the back window. She looked hurt and bewildered.

Then the cab turned a corner, and she was gone.

And for the first time that night, Maksim felt the chill in the air.

Oh my God, he thought suddenly. What had he done? Why had he let her go?

Why had he shown mercy?

He'd always laughed at the word. *Mercy*. Another name for weakness! And he'd let her go. He'd been weak.

He clawed back his hair. He wanted Grace so badly it hurt. Knowing she was an untouched virgin made him ache, wanting her still more. He wanted to take her in his soft, wide bed, to teach her everything he knew, to fill himself inside her again and again and watch her face slowly shine with the joy of discovery. To take her hard. To take her slow. To take her any way he could get her, *and be her first.*

Growling a curse that made the doorman's eyes nearly pop out of his head, Maksim strode into his hotel to his penthouse. He undid his tuxedo tie and tossed it on his desk before he poured himself a short vodka. Every ounce of his body was howling for him to take Grace…take her now…take her hard and deep.

Why had he let her go?

Mercy. Staring down at the swirling clear liquid in his shot glass, Maksim said the word aloud with derision. He gulped the rest of the vodka, but his body still hurt with need for her. He glanced across the room to his vast, empty bed. He could have had her, but he'd let her go.

Tomorrow, he promised himself grimly. Tomorrow he would regain control. He would show no mercy. He would be ruthless.

Virgin or not, Grace would be his.

* * *

The next morning Grace stared forlornly out the small window beside her desk at work.

The snow that had made London so magical had melted, turning to rain. And the rest of last night's magic had melted right along with it.

From their suite of offices on the thirtieth floor, where the Cali-West Energy Corporation had leased space, Grace looked down at the people on the street, far below the other high-rise office buildings of Canary Wharf. The city seemed foggy and sad.

Or maybe that was just her today. Foggy. Sad. With a deep breath, Grace tried to turn her attention back to her computer screen, but her focus on work kept getting interrupted by her painful memories of last night.

She'd sworn she wouldn't surrender to Maksim.

Then she'd not only surrendered, she'd thrown herself at him—and he'd rejected her!

She rubbed her temples, then tried to straighten her wrinkled beige skirt and oversize brown cardigan. She'd planned to iron them this morning but she hadn't had time. She'd tossed and turned all night, then fallen asleep around dawn and had nearly slept through her alarm. Now she felt exhausted. Every time she thought about last night, she writhed inside. Her cheeks burned hot with shame.

She'd tried to resist him.

She'd really thought she could.

But then when he'd shown such unexpected gentleness, allowing himself to be vulnerable in front of her when he spoke of his family, she'd been helpless to fight him.

But she must have overestimated Maksim's desire for

her. Big surprise there. What did she know about men? He'd wanted her—she was still sure about that. Then he'd changed his mind. One moment he'd been kissing her senseless, peeling her clothes off, his hands roaming all over her as he'd pushed her back against his bed.

The next minute he'd been shoving her into a taxi without so much as a good-night.

She swallowed. The reason for the change was obvious. He'd been turned off by her virginity. What man would want to initiate a twenty-five-year-old virgin?

It was all too horrifying.

Sometime before dawn, she'd gotten up from bed and packed up the Leighton dress and coat and the platinum tiara. She would send them to his penthouse tonight and be done.

Even now she could hardly believe that she'd worn them to a society party, where she'd been lavished with kisses by the most devastating man in the city, probably the *world*.

She was lucky he'd rejected her, she told herself. She stared blankly at the screen.

She'd thought she was invulnerable, but she'd utterly lost herself in the winter moonlight. He'd stolen her soul away, evaporating it from her body like mist under his power.

The intoxicating force of his touch had done such strange things to her, made her weak inside, made her melt in his arms. She wondered if she'd ever truly loved Alan at all. Because if she had, how could she have surrendered to Maksim?

As if on cue, she heard Alan's peevish voice. "Where

were you last night? I came back early and you weren't in your apartment."

She looked up to see him standing over her desk. It was almost ten-thirty and he was just now coming into the office. That was typical. What was unusual was that his pale, handsome features looked irritated as he looked down at her.

"I was out," she replied shortly. There was not a single detail about last night that she felt like sharing with Alan.

"Did you finish the wedding plans?"

Anger—usually such a foreign emotion—suddenly burned through her. Did he think she had no life of her own? Did he really think after doing his shopping, she would rush to spend her whole night planning his wedding and honeymoon?

The answer was clear as he waited with his arms folded. *Yes*.

Clenching her hands under her desk, she took a deep breath. It wasn't enough that she came into work before dawn while he never bothered to arrive before ten. It wasn't enough that she'd spent the past three hours frantically writing his speech for a charity event that afternoon, a speech he'd insisted for weeks that he would write himself—until she'd found the task waiting in her inbox that morning.

"Look at these!" The front desk receptionist appeared with an enormous arrangement of exquisite long-stemmed white calla lilies, which she set on Grace's desk. "Aren't they gorgeous?"

"Oh, thank you," Alan said with a smile and a wink,

immediately reaching for the card. "I can't imagine who—"

"Oh no, Mr. Barrington," the receptionist said with a giggle. "They're for Miss Cannon."

"For me?" Grace exclaimed in shock.

"For you?" Alan said with equal shock. "What…who?"

Drawing the card from the envelope, Grace silently read a single line written in a rough, sharp hand.

"Last night you dazzled me like the sun in winter. Waiting outside now for the bright burn of dawn—M."

Happiness soared through Grace.

She hadn't made a fool of herself after all! Maksim hadn't been disgusted with her for being a virgin! He'd just sent her away in the taxi because…

Because he wanted more than just a one-night stand? Because he was trying to protect her and take things slow?

It was the only possible reason.

And he already wanted to see her again! She suddenly felt like tap-dancing beneath her desk.

She closed her eyes and inhaled the heady scent of lilies. Maksim thought she was worth such extravagant beauty.

And for the first time in forever *so did she*.

"Well?" the receptionist asked slyly. "Who's the prince charming, Grace?"

"Yes," Alan demanded. "Who?"

She looked up at her boss and saw him with utterly new eyes. She'd suddenly had enough. Straightening in her chair, she gave a dismissive laugh.

"For heaven's sake, Alan, I'm your secretary, not your wife. Why do you care who sends me flowers?"

"I don't," he stammered, clearly surprised. "I just want to make sure that you devote the proper time and energy to your work."

"You mean the time I've spent buying gifts for your various girlfriends?" she said coolly. "Or do you mean the time I've worked for you around the clock without pay?"

The receptionist gasped a laugh. At Alan's dirty look, she gulped and scurried away.

He looked back at Grace. "Look here, Gracie…"

She leaned her elbows against her desk. "Or maybe you mean the times I've asked you for a pay raise." She thrummed her pen thoughtfully against her cheek. "All the times you put me off and said we'd talk about it later. When I was promoted to your executive assistant. When I moved to London with you."

He swallowed, licking his lips as he attempted a weak smile. "You know how valuable you are to me—how much I need you!"

"I'm afraid that's not good enough."

He leaned over her desk. "Is this because of Francesca? Because you don't need to feel jealous," he whispered urgently. "Our engagement isn't real."

"You bought her lingerie!" she gasped.

He gave a bitter laugh. "I *thought* it was real. She set me straight last night when I suggested an elopement. That's why I asked if you'd started the wedding plans yet—you don't need to bother. She only agreed to a fake engagement to make some other man jealous. She has no interest in marrying me—or sleeping with me either." He clenched his jaw. "But as long as I play along with her, she'll make sure her father doesn't know, and the merger will still go through."

Francesca was trying to make some other man jealous?

Grace suddenly feared she knew who that man might be. And she didn't like it one bit.

"So don't give up on me." Alan gave her his old charming, Hugh Grant smile. "In a few months, it will all be over. Things can go back to how they were. Just be patient. I'm asking you, Grace. Wait for me."

Looking into his smiling eyes, Grace sucked in her breath.

Oh my God.

He'd known.

All this time she'd thought he was clueless about her feelings. But *he'd known about her crush all along.* He'd used her own feelings against her. Used her for free work. Used her for a nice ego boost or a snog when it suited him.

"Well? What do you say?"

"I'm sorry," she said evenly.

And she was. Sorry that she'd given him all her time and energy. Sorry she'd thrown away better opportunities with both hands, while pretending he was the solution to all her problems!

With a sympathetic smile, he leaned against her desk. "Sorry you have to wait?"

"I'm sorry, but things have to change." She slowly rose from her desk. "I'm dating someone else. And if you want me to remain your secretary, it's going to cost you."

He gaped at her. "Where else would you go?"

"I've had another job offer."

"From whom?"

"That's irrelevant," she said. "Since I had to move from Los Angeles, my mother's had trouble paying her mortgage. I need ten thousand dollars to stay working for you. Call it a retroactive raise."

"Ten thousand?" he gasped. "Dollars? Are you joking?"

"And effective immediately," she continued sweetly, "I expect a raise in pay commensurate with the increased cost-of-living expenses in London."

"Grace!"

"So what do you say?" She paused. "Shall I stay and finish writing your speech for the charity event this afternoon? Or shall I clean out my desk?"

He stared at her.

"Stay," he muttered. "Finish the speech. You'll get your raise with your next paycheck."

"And my bonus?"

"Ten thousand dollars? That will take longer."

"You have until Christmas Eve."

He ground his teeth. "Fine. Would you perhaps like to take the rest of the afternoon off, as well?" he suggested acidly.

"Yes, thank you." She smiled at him. "I'll go as soon as I'm done with your lovely speech."

Alan tightened his jaw, then turned away. "Fine."

She almost felt sorry for him as she watched his hunched shoulders as he returned to his office and slammed the door. Almost.

Getting one afternoon off wasn't even close to all the hours she'd worked for free over the past two years, but…Maksim was outside at this very moment, waiting for her. Grace's feet tapped excitedly as she polished the last few paragraphs of the speech, making sure it was perfect before she e-mailed Alan the finished copy. Her spirits were soaring as she put on her old coat and came triumphantly out of the building.

She found Maksim waiting for her at the curb in an ultra-expensive, black Bugatti Veyron.

"Thank God," he said with a dark gleam in his eye as she climbed into the car. "It was agony waiting for you."

"It was twenty minutes."

He put on dark sunglasses. "I'm not a patient man."

She laughed aloud, happier than she'd been for years. "Thanks for the flowers," she said. "They really lifted employee morale. I just got a raise from my boss."

"You lift *my* morale, *solnishka mayo*," he growled. He reached over to change gears, and his hand accidentally brushed her thigh. "Ready to celebrate?"

"Yes," she breathed.

"So am I," he said, looking down at her steadily in a way that made her feel hot all over. Then he gunned the thousand-horsepower motor, and the Bugatti flew like a black raven through the mist and rain.

CHAPTER SEVEN

GRACE took a deep breath as she stood on the terrace of Maksim's Dartmoor estate, staring out at the snow-dusted fields. They'd left the London rain far behind. Here the moors were wide and haunted beneath the last rays of fading red sun. A thick white mist was blowing in from the sea.

Tears fell unheeded down Grace's cold cheeks. The sound of her mother's happy crying still echoed in her ears as she tucked her cell phone back into her bag.

She'd done it. She'd told her mother that she would save the house from foreclosure. Now Grace would make sure her family never worried about money again. She took another deep breath, grateful beyond words that she'd found her strength. That she'd found herself.

Thanks to Maksim.

Maksim, who'd treated Grace like a princess. She'd never have imagined that any man, let alone someone so handsome and powerful and rich beyond belief, would treat her that way.

Now Grace realized she should accept nothing less. She would never settle again.

She wanted the fairy tale.

She turned from the wide terrace overlooking the carefully tended classical garden and returned through the back door of his eighteenth-century country house. Maksim was waiting.

The inside of the house was every bit as Gothic and misty as the moors outside. Perhaps because the fifty rooms had no furniture—just white translucent curtains that seemed to move against the windows even when they were closed, twisting eerily in an invisible draft that no human skin could feel.

She'd called her mother outside on the terrace, where the cell phone reception was better, and where she could have privacy. She didn't want Maksim to know how desperate she'd been for money. She didn't want him to think of her as someone who needed saving.

She'd been proud to save herself.

She wanted Maksim as her equal. As her friend. As her…lover? She could barely move her lips to form the word, but there it was. Her secret.

She wanted him as her lover.

She wanted him for the fire he sparked inside her. For the way he'd somehow made her become the woman she'd always dreamed she could be. For the dreams suddenly coming true around her, like roses blooming full and red amid the breathless hush of winter.

Grace walked back through the empty salon. Painted cherubs looked down at her from the two-hundred-year-old painting soaring high above the enormous chandelier.

This house was beautiful, large…and lonely.

No one lived here, Maksim had told her. He'd bought

it to use as his weekend escape, but he'd been too busy with work to bother visiting. The caretaker and his elderly wife, who resided in a nearby cottage, were the only ones who'd entered the estate for the last several years.

Until now.

The house seemed happy to finally have company, she thought, then nearly laughed at her own ridiculous thought. The *house* was happy?

What was it about houses that made people so batty?

Grace wiped her eyes as she approached the dining room. She felt like an idiot for crying because she was happy, but as foolish as it sounded, she felt as if her family—as long as they had their home—could survive and be strong.

She entered the dining room, then stopped in shock.

The room was dark, lit by the fire in the marble fireplace—and by dozens of white pillar candles of various sizes and shapes on the floor.

Maksim was lighting the last candle as she entered. He was darkly handsome, wearing a black shirt and black pants. He looked up at her, then straightened as the expression on his handsome face changed to concern.

"You were crying," he demanded.

"Houses," she sniffled, looking with wonder at all the candles. "They don't make a family, except they do, don't they?"

He frowned. "You're not making any sense."

Laughing through her tears, she shook her head. "I'm just happy. I needed money for my house. Thanks to the raise, I'll have it."

"Good," he growled. "About time you moved out of Barrington's basement."

He'd misunderstood her, but she didn't correct him. Moving out of Alan's house *was* a good idea, and as soon as her family's home was secure, that was exactly what she intended to do.

Blowing out the match and tossing it aside, he put his arms around her. "Now leave his office and come work for me."

"Mixing business and pleasure would be a bad idea," she whispered.

He stroked her chin. "I'll buy you a house as your bonus. Any house you want."

She looked around the eighteenth-century country mansion mischievously. "Really? *Any* house?"

He laughed, then he kissed her. His lips were warm and passionate. She felt his rough chin against her skin as his tongue stroked hers, luring her, intoxicating her. She pressed her body against his. When he pulled away, a little sigh escaped her.

"Let me take care of you, Grace," he murmured against her skin.

"I don't want you as my boss," she managed to say. "And I don't want your money. I just want you."

His eyes flickered.

"And I take care of what is mine," he growled.

She was his? The idea of his possession was like a warm blanket wrapped around her. He cared about her. Hadn't he proved that last night when he'd let her go? He could have easily made her a one-night stand, but instead he was wooing her. Courting her in this romantic way.

And she was starting to care about him more than she wanted to admit.

He sat down on a thick white blanket on the floor near the fire. He patted a spot next to him. "Sit down," he said, quirking a seductive eyebrow. When she did, he handed her a flute of champagne.

"Sure, you have champagne," she teased. "But what about furniture?"

Reaching into the hamper, he held out a chocolate-covered strawberry. "I don't need a bed for what I intend to do to you."

She opened her mouth obediently, and he fed it to her. Then she took the next strawberry from the basket and returned the favor. As he suckled the rich chocolate from the lush fruit, he never took his gaze from hers.

She shivered. When she finished the flute of champagne, he took it from her without a word. Gently brushing her hair aside, he kissed her neck. She closed her eyes, shuddering with desire as he nibbled his way down her throat.

"You're so beautiful," he murmured.

And for no good reason, she felt like crying.

"Thank you," she said, opening her eyes to look directly into his. "Thank you, Maksim."

His dark eyes looked surprised. "For what?"

She looked past him, to the translucent white curtains and lead-paned windows overlooking the winter twilight. Shaking with the force of her emotion, she looked into his face.

"It has been a hard few years for my family." She took

a deep breath. "I didn't know what to cling to anymore. Didn't know what to believe in."

Maksim looked at her steadily above the shimmering firelight. His eyes were deep smoke, his strong jawline shadowed with bristle. Surrounded by the flickering white candles on the floor around them, he looked like a dark king from a medieval fantasy.

"Now I do," she said softly, then took a deep breath. "I can believe in you."

He blinked. Hard.

Clenching his jaw, he looked away.

"I'm no saint," he said in a low voice. "I told you from the beginning. I'm selfish. Ruthless."

"You're wonderful." Reaching her hand up to his rough chin, she gently turned his cheek until he looked at her. "I've never met a man like you before. You claim to be selfish and even cruel, but you're not. You're a good man, Maksim. You don't want anyone to know it. You think it's weakness," she said softly. "But I know your secret."

She felt him tremble in her arms. He took a haggard breath, briefly closing his eyes before he looked down at her. His dark gaze shot through her soul. "I've never met anyone like you, Grace. So determined to see the best in people even if they don't deserve it."

"Because of you." She licked her lips with sudden nervousness. "For the first time in my life, I feel brave. Brave enough to…"

Her words dwindled off as the expression in his dark gaze changed, became fired with heat. He stroked her cheek, looking down at her. Their bodies were so close. She could feel every inch of hard muscle, all the strength of his power. Their eyes were interlocked, and in that moment she could hardly say where her soul ended and his began.

"Grace…"

Lowering his mouth to hers, he kissed her. It was a kiss of anguish and longing and such tenderness that a little whimper escaped her.

Then a Russian curse exploded from his lips. He suddenly pushed away from her.

Rising to his feet, he paced in front of her, clawing his hands through his dark hair.

"What is it, Maksim?" she whispered, staring up at him from the blanket. It was the second time he'd pushed away from her. Was something wrong with her? Something about the way she kissed that he didn't like?

Insecurity went through her. She thought of what Alan had told her, that Francesca only agreed to a fake engagement to make some other man jealous.

What if Maksim still loved Francesca?

"It's all right," Grace said miserably. "I understand. I'm not the one you want."

When he spoke, his voice was low. Harsh. "You think I don't want you?"

"It's all right, truly." She shook her head, trying to keep the tears from her eyes. "I'm not remotely your type—"

Falling to his knees, he grabbed her upper arms so tightly that they bruised.

"Not want you? God! Not want you?" he exploded. "All I can think about is taking you, Grace. In the bed, against the wall, on the floor! Not want you? I want to spread your thighs beneath me. I want to caress and suckle and taste you until you explode and shake around me. I want you and every second I physically hold myself back from making love to you is killing me!"

His voice echoed against the soaring ceilings of the empty dining room as it slowly sank in. *He wanted her.*

"Then why do you keep pushing me away?"

He cradled her face in his hands. "Because you are the only sunlight I've known for years," he said in a low voice. "I can't extinguish that warmth in you, Grace. I can't let the world go dark and cold without your light."

"You're afraid to hurt me?"

Clenching his jaw, he nodded.

"Don't be." She took a deep breath. "After my bad experience with Alan, I've decided love is totally overrated." She wouldn't be stupid enough to risk her heart again. No matter how Maksim made her feel. She reached out to stroke his rough cheek, tracing her fingertips down his throat. "I promise you can't hurt me...."

He grabbed her wrist. "Don't," he said harshly.

"Please," she whispered. "Just kiss me."

Their eyes locked.

With a groan, he surrendered.

His lips brushed hers, then bruised her. The rush that spread through her body was unimaginable. He yanked off her coat. He pulled off her oversize brown cardigan. His hands moved urgently over her plain white shirt, undoing the buttons rapidly, pulling the last one until it ripped. He dropped the shirt to the floor and looked at her in the firelight.

"I will try to go slow," he whispered, visibly shaking

as he touched her bare skin. "But the way you affect me, Grace…"

He kissed her again, reaching his strong arms around her, and her white cotton bra fell to the floor. Then suddenly his shirt was off, as well, and pants and skirt all disappeared in a frantic tumble.

And suddenly he was standing before her.

She'd never seen a naked man before. She took a deep breath and looked at him in the firelight. Candles were glowing all around them in the darkness of the empty mansion as she gently reached her hand to stroke him.

He shuddered, jumping beneath her touch.

"You're beautiful," she whispered.

He gasped. Gathering her up in his arms, he laid her gently beneath him on the thick blanket in front of the fire.

She felt the hard muscles of his masculine body, so much bigger and stronger than she would ever be, and as he stroked her naked body in front of the fire she arched beneath his hands. He slowly kissed down her neck, between her breasts, down her belly.

Did he mean to…? He couldn't possibly intend to…?

Moonlight traced the translucent, gauzy curtains. A sudden frozen rain rattled the windows as he pushed her thighs apart.

Lowering himself between her legs, he kissed the inside of her thighs, slowly licking higher and higher. Her cheeks burned and she tried to scoot out of his grasp, but he held her.

Spreading her wide, he tasted her.

Her nipples tightened so painfully that she gasped

aloud. A thousand zinging sensations went up and down her body like lightning shooting out of her fingertips, her toes, her hair. Every nerve was on fire, and she twisted beneath him.

His tongue changed width and pressure, lapping her widely then swirling lightly against her aching nub. She felt dizzy. She was breathless as her body tightened in agony, wanting…wanting…

She cried out as the first burst rolled through her like thunder, starting low and deep inside her and sweeping through her body until she screamed. At that moment he moved his body and pushed himself inside her.

For an instant the pain was wrenching, but pleasure immediately rode behind it, making her shudder in rhythmic contractions around him. As he thrust inside her, she heard his low gasp. With agonizing slowness, he pulled back, then thrust again. She whimpered as increasing pleasure built inside her. Then her hips rose to meet his as he rode her.

He filled her completely. Slowly, steadily, deeper and deeper until he seemed to reach her very heart. The intensity was too much, pleasure so great it was almost pain.

She looked up and saw his hard masculine body over hers, his chest laced with dark hair and his muscles glistening with sweat in the firelight as he thrust inside her. His eyes were closed. She saw the agony on his face as he held himself back, forcing himself to move slowly. His handsome face was taut as he gasped with every slow, deep thrust, filling her to the hilt.

Maksim.

Her prince.

Her lover.

Her…love?

As if he'd heard her thought, he opened his eyes. Their gazes locked, their souls linked. And as he pushed inside her one last time, her world shattered into a million pieces. She shuddered and shook with him so deeply inside her, deeper, deeper, until she felt like she was being ripped in two by his brutally hard body. Her body arched with electricity as she exploded and gasped out his name.

CHAPTER EIGHT

MAKSIM'S intention in bringing her here had been to seduce her. He'd intended to coldheartedly win her loyalty to get information he could use against Barrington. But his conscience had interfered again. He'd tried to resist. To let her go. To push her away.

Until she'd taken him in her soft arms and asked him to kiss her.

In that single instant he'd tossed aside his plans to get information from her. He'd given up his revenge on Barrington. He'd even given up the merger for the sake of possessing her.

He'd given it all up so he could possess her without guilt and be even half the man she believed him to be.

It had taken all his self-control to go slowly. He was determined to make it good for her. But when their eyes met as he slid deeply inside her, when he saw her beautiful face as their bodies joined, he could barely hold himself back from exploding.

He felt her arch and heard her gasp his name; and then he utterly lost control.

Thrusting one last time, he spilled into her with a hoarse, harsh cry that blended with hers. He closed his eyes as his body was racked with waves of pleasure almost too intense to bear.

He collapsed against her. He must have blacked out for a millisecond before he realized he was crushing her with his weight. And he never wanted to hurt her, never, this fragile innocent beauty who'd given him her virginity….

He rolled to one side of her, cradling her softly in his arms, kissing her forehead. She took several deep breaths before she opened her eyes and looked at him. But she did not speak. What had happened between them was too deep for words.

Candlelight and firelight flickered on the lush curves of her naked body. Grace was everything he'd imagined. Just what he'd fantasized about. But she had more than just an innocent beauty—she had an innocent soul.

He was her first.

Maksim gloried in the thought. It filled him with pride and wonder. No other man had ever touched her. No other man had ever thrust inside her—

Then he suddenly stopped breathing.

Distracted by the conflict between his conscience and his overwhelming need for her, he'd forgotten to use a condom. The first and only time he'd ever forgotten.

Turning from her on the blanket, he stared blankly at the high ceiling. Barely visible cherubs smiled down at him from the shadowed depths.

What if there were a child?

"Maksim." Grace rolled her naked body over his. He

felt the soft press of her breasts into his chest as she looked down at him with concern. "Did I do something wrong?"

"No." Wrapping his arms around her, he kissed her on the temple. "Don't think that, *solnishka mayo*. Never think that."

She ducked her head, placing her cheek against his heart. "Do you feel like you've betrayed Francesca?"

Francesca? He was trying not to think about her— something astonishingly easy to do, considering she'd been his mistress for a full year. He set his jaw. "Why ask me about her? Do you feel you've betrayed Barrington?"

She shook her head. "I never loved him. That was infatuation, nothing more."

For reasons he couldn't explain, those words seeped into him, relaxing him like a warm embrace. He stroked her naked back lazily, appreciating the curve of her body and sweet, smooth skin. "I'm glad to hear that. So there's nothing to stop you from coming to work for me."

"But I thought you said I shouldn't endure sexual harassment from my boss?" she teased.

"You'll enjoy it from me," he growled.

"A lovely offer." She sighed, then slowly shook her head. "But I can't desert Alan. I feel sorry for him."

"Why? He's gotten the deal—and the bride."

"But he just found out she never intended to actually marry him. They haven't even slept together. She's just trying to make some other man jealous." She took a deep breath, then lifted her eyes to his. "I think it must be you."

His hand stroking her back stilled.

"It's not a real engagement?"

"The merger is real. Her father doesn't know. But the

engagement will end." She licked her lips. "And you can have Francesca back, if you want her."

For a moment Maksim couldn't even breathe.

He couldn't believe it.

What a joke of fate. The moment he'd decided to surrender to his conscience, the moment he'd decided he wouldn't try to force information out of Grace— she'd tossed the key to destroying Alan Barrington right into his lap.

With this one bit of information, he could destroy the merger.

Part of him had suspected this all along. Francesca had been so furious when Maksim hadn't caved to her ultimatum in October. After a tempestuous year together, a year of screaming breakups and passionate makeups, she'd demanded that he marry her. "Or else," she'd threatened ominously, "you'll lose me." But Maksim never responded very well to threats or ultimatums. In reply he'd kissed her until she sagged in his arms, then he'd whispered, "In that case, I must lose you."

Typical of Francesca to orchestrate her battle by going straight to his enemy. Managing to string Barrington along without even giving him her body— Maksim was impressed. But the fact that she'd never intended to actually go through with her threat to marry him revealed her weakness.

All Maksim had to do was tell the Earl of Hainesworth the truth, and the merger would be his. Along with Francesca, if he wanted her....

"Do you love her, Maksim?" he heard Grace whisper. "Do you?"

He abruptly focused on the sweet, beautiful girl in his arms.

Grace was so different from his former mistress in every way. She was curvaceous, with full cheeks the color of roses, skin that glowed with health, and natural blond hair that looked like blended gold and silver in the candlelight.

Francesca was tiny and thin in ultrachic designer clothes, with fiery red hair that came compliments of an expensive salon. Natural? Francesca was the type of woman who wore red lipstick to bed!

Grace was poor, young and sweet, and so kind-hearted that she let others take advantage of her, while Francesca gleefully bossed the servants and rode all over anyone weaker than herself.

Grace was honest to a fault. Even now, Maksim could see the vulnerability in her eyes as she anxiously looked at him. Francesca savored nothing more than a viciously well-placed lie. She planned her love affairs like a chess match, or possibly like a general leading troops into a war she intended to win.

"She's so beautiful," Grace said, biting her lip. "She's the kind of woman any man would want."

It would be easy to hurt Grace, Maksim thought. And he never wanted to do it.

"I'm with you now." He rose from the blanket and swiftly blew out the candles around them before he nestled back against her, pressing his naked body against hers. He cuddled her in his arms, turning them both on their sides toward the fire.

With a little sigh she relaxed in his arms. In no time

at all he felt the even rise and fall of her breath as she slept peacefully against his chest. Trustingly.

Normally after he'd been with a woman, he couldn't leave her fast enough. But with Grace, he felt different. She made him feel strangely at peace.

He stared at the fire, waving and crackling and dying in the marble fireplace.

He could complete the merger. Get his revenge on Barrington. Get everything he'd dreamed of: he could create and control the largest oil and gas company in the world.

Or…he could do the unimaginable.

He could forget he'd ever heard the information. And keep Grace as his mistress.

He'd planned to spend the winter in Moscow after the merger was done. He could bring Grace to live in his new Rublyovka estate. He rather liked the idea of having her cook for him, bustling about, making him laugh, sharing his bed at night. How better to keep himself warm through the long, cruel Russian winter?

He could open her credit accounts at all the luxury shops in one of the most expensive cities in the world. He could hire a tutor to give her Russian lessons.

And Maksim could give her other kinds of lessons as well. Personally. He suspected the recent virgin would be a quick and eager student….

Her only job would be to be his mistress, enjoy his company and spend his money. She would be happy.

Maksim stared at the hypnotic dwindling of the fire. Could he let Barrington win? Could he let the merger go? Could he give up his dream of world domination—

and let Barrington have it, while he slipped into a distant second place, possibly making his own company ripe for an eventual hostile takeover?

Giving up this merger meant potentially losing everything he'd ever fought for. But the choice before him was plain.

Grace or the merger.

He couldn't fool himself into thinking he could have both. If Grace found out he'd betrayed her, using her careless words in bed against her boss, she would never forgive him.

But if he didn't betray her, would he ever be able to forgive himself?

Maksim held her in his arms as the moonlight flooded through the high windows. The dying firelight flickered in the sleek marble fireplace.

He'd never appreciated this house quite so much before. Never appreciated anything quite so sharply as this moment. He knew it would never come again. She sighed in sleep, her breasts swaying beneath his arms. He felt himself stir. This woman moved him like no other.

Her eyelids fluttered. She looked up at him with dream-drenched eyes.

"I think I love you," she whispered.

His body went absolutely hard. So hard it hurt.

She blinked. "Oh my God, did I say that aloud? I thought I was dreaming."

"You said it out loud," he said tersely.

"I just meant—"

"I know what you meant."

He gripped her.

She'd just experienced sex for the first time, he told himself. That was what she meant. She loved him in the way a man loved a well-cut suit or a perfect steak or watching sports on Sunday; or crushing an opponent to win a big business deal. She loved him in the way a person loves a pleasure they never want to end.

He told himself these things, but he knew they were lies.

"Maksim…" She touched his shoulder.

"Go to sleep," he told her harshly.

The fire had turned to ashes before he heard her finally fall back into slumber. But he couldn't sleep. He lay awake all night, watching as the pink dawn rose over the misty-white moor.

He had to make a choice.

The warm light of dawn sifted through the high windows, revealing the dust motes trembling in the air. He woke her with a kiss. On her shoulder. On her temple. All over her naked body.

She turned over with a sigh, blinking and not quite awake, but she held out her arms for him. Instinctively welcoming him into her soft body. Into her soft heart.

But this time, as he tenderly made love to her in the pink fresh light of dawn, he used a condom.

Horrible. Unbearable.

When could she leave?

Grace glanced at the clock on her computer screen and tapped her toes impatiently on the floor. She didn't want to be at work on Christmas Eve!

Apparently, no one else wanted to be here, either, since she was the only one left in the office. She'd come to tie up a few loose ends before her two-week vacation in Los Angeles. She smiled as she thought of home. She just needed to wait long enough to pick up the check for $10,000 that would save her mother's house.

But Alan was, of course, late.

Grace was trying to focus on compiling the necessary data for Cali-West's fourth-quarter sales reports. But her mind kept wandering to her favorite subject.

Maksim.

The past two weeks had been the most wonderful of Grace's life. Maksim had taken her out nearly every day. He'd taken her dancing. Out to dinner. And it was hilarious how he kept trying to buy her things. Like yesterday, when he'd suddenly pulled her into a car dealership in South Kensington and wanted to buy her a gold Maserati convertible.

"To match your hair," he'd said, then smiled. "Think of it as a hair accessory."

When she'd refused, he'd tried to argue with her. "It's a small Christmas present," he'd said. "A trifle. A token. *A stocking stuffer!*"

He'd really made her laugh with that one.

She'd steadfastly refused, of course. But later that night in his penthouse suite, he'd made her an offer she could not refuse—he'd made love to her all night.

That must be why she felt so tired today. So absolutely exhausted, and even a little bit queasy.

Especially when she thought about leaving Maksim for the next two weeks.

She was falling in love with him.

She'd already fallen like a brick!

So much for her defenses. Thank God he wasn't in love with Francesca as she'd briefly feared, because she'd started to fall in love with him from the moment he'd taken her virginity in that empty house on the snow-swept moor. She'd even stupidly blurted it out.

Fortunately, by some miracle, telling him she loved him just days into their relationship hadn't scared him off!

Perhaps he was starting to care for her, as well.

The thought made her heart leap in her chest. She wanted to buy him a Christmas present before she left, but what did you get a man who truly had everything? Her naked body wrapped in a big red bow?

Grace glanced down at her form-fitting gray cardigan, yellow silk blouse, pearls and gray wool slacks. Her clothes weren't quite so glamorous as the Leighton cocktail dress, but they were fresh and pretty and new. She grinned down at her feet. She even had new shoes, lovely pale-pink pumps of such sturdy quality that they would never break. They squeezed her a little in the toe, but who cared about that? They were beautiful. She'd put her first paycheck since her raise to good use.

She wanted to look nice for Maksim.

A stronger wave of queasiness went over her. Grace glanced at her lukewarm coffee cup, feeling ill. Had she drunk too much wine last night at dinner with Maksim? Impossible, she remembered, she'd had just half a glass. It must have been the chicken tikka, then.

Picturing the spicy dish, usually her favorite, she felt so nauseated that she almost retched over her keyboard. Rising to her feet, she stumbled to the ladies' bathroom just in time.

Afterward, as she came out of the bathroom she still felt a bit sick and in a cold sweat. She was just grateful she was alone in the office.

Then she saw she wasn't. Alan stood by her desk.

Oh, thank heaven! He was here with the check, and that meant she could go! Hang the data for the fourth-quarter reports. No one would compile the information until January, so why kill herself over it? She'd collect her bonus, brush her teeth then go to the penthouse to see about convincing Maksim to come home to California with her for Christmas.

If all else failed, she'd convince him via that big red bow. She giggled. Perfect.

But she still felt a bit dizzy as she walked toward her boss. "I'm glad to see you!"

"Are you, Grace?" Leaning against her desk, Alan's pale eyelashes blinked rapidly as he stared down at her. He looked strangely grim.

Something seemed to be bothering him, but Grace still felt queasy and couldn't dredge up enough energy to wonder what it was. "Alan, if you'll just give me my bonus check, I think I'll head out. You don't mind if the sales figures wait? I'm not feeling very well." When he folded his arms and continued to glower at her, she added weakly, "It *is* Christmas Eve…"

"You can take as much time as you want."

"Oh, thank you—"

"Because you're fired."

She stared at him for a long moment. "What?"

"You heard me. You have exactly three minutes to pack up your desk before I have you thrown out."

"Is this a joke?"

"Yes, a joke. The secretary I trusted most just betrayed my secrets and caused me to lose the deal of my life."

"What?" she gasped. "How?" She frantically tried to remember saying anything to anyone. Had she mentioned any details? The numbers, the price? She shook her head. "I never breathed a word to anyone!"

"Lord Hainesworth just pulled his funding and support," he said furiously. "He found out this morning the engagement was fake. I've lost the deal and now I'll likely lose my position as CEO. The board has been after me for the past year. I've lost everything. My only consolation is...*so have you.*"

Oh my God, what had happened?

"It's got to be some ghastly mistake," she said. "I would never betray you. Please, I need that bonus—"

"Bonus?" He barked a laugh. "You're lucky I don't have you thrown in jail for corporate espionage! You'll never get hired again by anyone if I can help it. No job recommendation. No back pay." His lip curled. "Now get the hell out before I call the police."

"But I didn't tell anyone about the fake engagement," she cried. An icy trickle went down her back. "Except..."

"When you blackmailed me into giving you a raise, you didn't mention that you were already working on your back for Maksim Rostov!"

She sucked in her breath.

"It wasn't like that," she gasped. "How did you find out about—"

"Francesca heard it from her friends." Alan shook his head with a derisive snort. "Apparently he's been flashing you all over town, his cheap little mistress. You've always been so desperate for money, Grace. Tell me. What did you enjoy more—selling him my secrets or selling him your body?"

She felt like he'd just slapped her across the face.

"I didn't sell anything," she whispered. "He wouldn't do that to me."

"No? You think Rostov wanted you for your intelligence?" he sneered. "For your beauty?" He looked her up and down. "You might have gotten new clothes, but you're way out of your league. This was always a game between him and Francesca—always. He dumped her. She wanted him back. And now they're together."

"No!"

"If you really believe he would choose you over her, you're even more stupid than I thought." He turned his back on her. "I'm sending the security guard up here in two minutes."

Numbly Grace gathered up a few items from her desk, putting a half-dead plant and two framed pictures of her family into a box. She left the building, then realized she'd forgotten her old coat. The security guard refused to let her back inside. Her only option would be to call Alan and ask him to bring it down to her.

Instead she left without it.

Outside, there was a biting chill in the gray afternoon sky. Clutching the cardboard box to her chest, she shivered in her thin cardigan and silk blouse.

Alan had to be wrong. Maksim wouldn't have betrayed her!

She pictured his darkly handsome face. The way he'd

teasingly fed her chow mein noodles at his penthouse last week. The way he'd tried to trick her into accepting expensive gifts. He'd made love to her. He'd made her laugh. He'd been her first.

He wouldn't use her careless words in bed against her, the words she'd spoken when she'd been feeling insecure and had been seeking reassurance!

But she hadn't told anyone else about the fake engagement. Who else could it be?

The answer was shockingly clear.

He'd intended all along to seduce and betray her.

No. A sob escaped her. She felt dizzy as she walked toward the nearest Tube entrance. Another wave of nausea went over her and her knees shook as she went down the escalator. As she sat on the half-empty train, she felt the curious and pitying stares of other passengers. She knew what they saw—a woman without a coat, red-eyed and holding a box with a plant and picture frames. Easy to follow that story. Sacked on Christmas Eve.

Just sacked—or also betrayed?

She found all her clothes stuffed in two suitcases sitting outside her basement flat in Knightsbridge. The locks had been changed. Alan had tossed her out.

Pulling her cell phone from her handbag, she dialed Maksim's number.

No answer. After three rings, it clicked over to voice mail, to his terse voice saying, "Rostov. Leave a message."

Another wave of dizziness washed over her. She started to leave a message. "Maksim, I've just heard something that can't possibly be…"

Her phone went dead. She stared down at it in shock. It had been her business phone, paid for by her company. Alan must have had it disconnected.

Grace took a deep breath, trying to control the rising panic.

She placed her family photos in the suitcases, wrapped herself in her warmest, thickest, frumpiest sweater and left the box and plant in a nearby rubbish bin. She managed to get back on the Tube, dragging both suitcases behind her.

Could it be true?

She heard the echo of his voice. Husky. Deep. Slightly foreign. *I have been accused of having no heart. I am telling you the truth, Grace. Take this as a warning.*

Struggling with her luggage, she came out of the Tube stop near his hotel. He was likely not there but busy at his office, as he hadn't answered his phone. She would wait for him in the penthouse and…

Then she saw he wasn't busy in the office.

Maksim was walking arm-in-arm with Francesca.

He looked ruthlessly handsome in a gray suit and coat. The redhead at his side wore an ivory coat and six-inch heels. Grace watched in shock as they passed the smiling doorman and went inside his hotel.

She saw the look Francesca gave him over the shoulder. Flirtatious. Cozy. Affectionate.

And Grace felt her knees go weak beneath her.

Trembling, she stumbled out into the road to flag down a cab. She shoved the suitcases inside and collapsed in the back of the black cab. "Heathrow," she gasped to the cabbie.

She could no longer deny the painful truth. She'd loved him, while he...

He'd taken her virginity to win back another woman.

Grace needed to get home. Her mother would take her in her arms and stroke her hair and tell her everything would be all right. Her mother knew about broken hearts.

Grace nearly cried with gratitude when a desk clerk at the airport managed to switch her seat to an earlier flight.

Crossing the Atlantic that endless day, crammed into a middle seat between two large, snoring men who both hogged the armrests and overlapped her space, Grace kept her eyes tightly closed. If she started crying, she was afraid she wouldn't be able to stop.

She had more to worry about than a broken heart.

How would Grace save the house? How would she support her family? Now that her father's life insurance was gone, her family was nearly destitute. And the economy was tough. How would Grace find employment when she'd just been fired for blurting out a billion-dollar secret in bed?

Grace clutched the thin airplane blanket to her chest. Funny to think she'd been so determined to not accept any gifts from Maksim. She'd returned the tiara and Leighton clothes. She'd refused his offer of the Maserati convertible and a new house and his many other suggestions of jewelry and clothes and luxury trips. She'd been so proud to stand on her own two feet. So proud to show Maksim she wanted *him,* not his money.

But money, it seemed, was all Maksim had ever wanted. Money. Revenge. Another billion or so dollars to pile on top of his fortune. She'd given him her virginity and her heart, but he'd only wanted money.

Money...*and Francesca.*

CHAPTER NINE

"She's not here."

Maksim looked up to see Alan Barrington staring down at him from the doorway of his town house. It was dark and gray, past twilight on Christmas Eve.

He'd been knocking on the door of Grace's basement flat for the past five minutes without answer. He hadn't expected to be so late. He'd promised he would take her to the airport for her late-night flight, but secretly he'd planned to talk her out of going home for Christmas. His private jet was waiting at a small nearby airport to whisk them away to the South of France.

But he was fifteen minutes late. Only fifteen minutes—that was something of a miracle, given all the surprises today! The merger was nearly a done deal. Thanks to Francesca, it had fallen into his lap, and he'd have been a fool to refuse. But he'd left the meeting halfway through. His people could mop up the details.

He wanted Grace.

He'd called her as soon as he got out of the meeting but hadn't been able to reach her. "Where is she?"

Barrington glared at him. "Why would I tell you?"

"Her phone was disconnected. Any idea why?"

The man folded his arms. "The phone went with her job, which she lost this afternoon."

"After all her loyalty, you fired her so quickly?"

"Loyalty? Some loyalty. Isn't it enough you already took one woman from me? Now you want the other one?" Barrington turned his lips into a sneer. "I'm not her pimp."

In three leaping steps Maksim had run up the stairs and grabbed him by the throat. "Are you calling Grace a whore?"

"Let me go!" the slender man croaked.

Maksim released him with a growl. "Apologize."

"Oh, so now you're her protector?" The blond man gasped, rubbing his neck. "You did this. You seduced and betrayed her. Not me."

"I never betrayed her," Maksim said, even as that strange, unpleasant prickle snaked down his spine. Guilt?

"Why bother denying it now?" Barrington snarled. "You've won. You've taken the merger. You've taken Francesca. You've gotten your payback—you've gotten rid of me for good. My shareholders have already issued a statement asking for my resignation."

"Good." But at this moment, Maksim's revenge didn't feel very satisfying.

"What do you care about some secretary?" Barrington looked at him with shrewd, beady eyes. "You have Francesca."

Right. Francesca.

Maksim's capricious ex-lover had shown up at his penthouse that morning, offering him Barrington's head on a silver platter. "I've just told my father the truth," she'd said, weeping artful tears from her lovely green eyes. "I never wanted Alan. It was you, Maksim, always you!"

Maksim's furious retort had been interrupted by the ringing of his cell phone. Francesca's father had moved swiftly. He'd always preferred that his company accept the offer from Rostov Oil; only his daughter's fake engagement had made him consider Cali-West. Within half a day the merger proceedings had been well started, although it would take another several weeks before they would be fully signed, sealed and delivered.

Maksim had accepted the deal. But he'd chosen Grace. He'd never used the information she'd shared. He'd never betrayed her.

But he realized now it'd worked out exactly the same as if he had.

He clenched his fists. "Just tell me where she is."

"Flying to Los Angeles, I expect, with the plane ticket I bought her. I hope it crashes." Barrington slammed the door.

Coming down the steps from the Knightsbridge town house, Maksim dialed his private investigator to get her address. But that wasn't all he discovered about her family's situation.

An hour later he was on his private jet en route to California.

The little yellow cottage gleamed in the predawn darkness, a shining beacon on the cliff above the soft roar of the Pacific Ocean.

Breathing heavily after her uphill walk, Grace crept back into her house, tiptoeing as she walked past the artificial Christmas tree decorated with ornaments from her childhood, gleaming with colored lights.

"Gracie?" Her mother suddenly peeked around the kitchen door. "You're awake early. I expected you to sleep in this morning."

Grace hid the small purchase she'd bought at the twenty-four-hour drugstore half a mile away. "Um. Jet lag. I couldn't sleep, so I went on a walk."

"Oh, poor dear," her mother said sympathetically, then brightened. "I'll make you some coffee. Come chat while I baste the ham."

"I'll be right there, Mom." Grace tried to calm her rapidly beating heart as she went to her childhood bedroom. She changed out of her jeans and back into her soft, comforting flannel pajamas and red chenille robe.

She set the bag down on her nightstand.

Her mother had been so happy to pick her up at L.A. airport last night, so joyful that she'd come home even earlier than expected. The boys had jumped up and down as they got her luggage from the carousel, and even seventeen-year-old Josh had hugged her, saying in a low voice, "I'm so glad you're home."

Her mother had driven them in the minivan back home to the northern beach town of Oxnard, an hour away, then made them all hot chocolate at midnight with marshmallows. Everyone finally went to bed to dream happy Christmas dreams.

Except Grace.

She hadn't been able to tell them that they were about

to lose the house they were sleeping in. She'd lied. No, not lied, she told herself angrily. Lying was for selfish bastards like Maksim. All she had done was put off the truth that would break their hearts. But she'd barely been able to stomach the hot chocolate, which was usually her favorite. A low-grade nausea had been with her for two days. As she went to bed late that night in her old bedroom still decorated with posters of rock bands and old teddy bears, even her breasts hurt.

That's when the dreadful thought first occurred to her. Nausea…dizziness…exhaustion. Painful breasts.

And so she'd sneaked off before dawn to buy a pregnancy test.

It's a waste of money, she told herself firmly. She and Maksim had only had sex a few times—all right, *many* times—but only just that once without protection. Fate wouldn't be so cruel, would it?

She'd been too carried away, too overwhelmed by sensation to even think of using protection that first time. If she'd thought about it, she would have assumed that a playboy like Maksim would naturally make sure he didn't get his many lovers pregnant. Especially lovers he intended to betray.

Her heart still hurt to think about it.

But the pregnancy test would have to wait. She couldn't take it now, knowing her mother was awake and waiting for her.

Grace went slowly into the kitchen. Sitting at the dining table, she could barely tolerate the smell of the creamy, sweet coffee her mother happily served her. But that was nothing compared to being forced to listen to her mother's delighted praise as she tearfully thanked Grace for saving their family.

"I was silly to live in denial and hide from our problems. You've inspired me with your career, Gracie. I've run this home for twenty years," Carol Cannon said as she put homemade biscuits in the oven. "After raising you four children, I can do anything!" She paused thoughtfully. "I might go back to school to become a tax accountant. I was always good at math."

Grace gulped down a single sip of hot coffee, scalding her tongue. The coffee made her feel nauseous, so she put it down immediately. "I know you can do anything you want, Mom."

Her mother's eyes glistened at her. She leaned forward to kiss the top of Grace's head. "I'm so proud of you, Gracie. I want to come with you tomorrow when you take the check to the bank. I'm so grateful to have such a strong daughter to lean on."

Grace rubbed her temples, feeling like a fraud.

They had no savings. No income now that she'd lost her job. In just one week, they would have to leave their beloved seaside cottage and beg their friends and family for a place to stay. And as there were five of them, including three boisterous teenage boys, they would soon wear out their welcome with even their most devoted friends.

I'll tell Mom tomorrow, Grace promised herself over the lump in her throat. *I just want her to enjoy Christmas.*

The rest of the morning was agony for Grace, as she watched her younger brothers open their presents and saw their joy and the grateful hugs they gave their mother. The gifts would all have to be returned to the store tomorrow. They would need every penny to survive. Seventeen-year-old Josh would have to say farewell to his long-desired iPod. Fourteen-year-old Ethan would be forced to give back his new guitar. And twelve-year-old Connor would tearfully have to return his new drums. Even their mother would return the expensive cashmere sweater the boys had bought for her with their own money earned mowing the lawns of neighbors throughout the fall. When Grace opened her own present from her family, she found a large hardcover picture book about the Trans-Siberian Railroad. Looking up at their beaming faces, she felt like crying.

"Thank you," she said over the lump in her throat. "I love you so much."

"It's 'cause you're such a world traveler," her youngest brother said happily. "I helped pick it out."

At brunch Grace watched her mother serve the platter of ham and scalloped potatoes. The boys cheered the food, but all she could think was that the ham alone was worth two weeks of cheap dinners like ramen noodles and frozen bean burritos.

Tomorrow, she repeated to herself, pasting a frozen smile on her face. *I'll tell them tomorrow.*

But after brunch, when her mother and brothers got ready to attend a Christmas-morning service of songs and carols, Grace pleaded jet lag and stayed home.

Now, finally alone, she stared at the pregnancy test, waiting for the results.

Be negative, she willed with every creative visualization technique she'd ever heard about on morning talk shows. *Be negative.*

Her hands shook as she waited for the results. She squinted in the dark bathroom. Would there be one line? Or two? She thought she saw the lines start to form. She couldn't see.

She ran out into the front room with the sunny windows overlooking the sea. The prewar cottage was small and bright and cozy, with old striped couches and cushions they'd had since Grace's childhood.

She looked down at the test. Negative. It would be negative....

Two lines. Oh my God. Two lines. Positive.

She was pregnant!

She heard a sound and turned to look.

Maksim stood in the open doorway. Brilliant sunlight cast him in silhouette, leaving his features dark. His wide, powerful frame filled the door, instantly filling their cliffside cottage with the force of his presence.

For a moment she thought her knees were going to buckle beneath her. In spite of everything, her heart soared to see him. She longed for him to take her in his arms and tell her everything Alan had said was a lie. To tell her he'd never seduced her to get information about the merger and win back a woman a thousand times more desirable than Grace could ever be.

Thrusting the pregnancy test in her robe pocket, she took a deep breath.

"What are you doing here?"

He stepped over the threshold, his eyes focused only on her. "I came for you."

A shiver spread through her body. She could barely

breathe as she faced him. She gripped her old chenille robe more tightly around her body. "You shouldn't have come."

He strode forward, his face tense. "You shouldn't have left London."

She lifted her chin.

"Why?" she said coldly. "Are there other secrets I might have forgotten to blurt out to you in bed?"

His handsome face closed down, looked grim. "I never betrayed you."

"You didn't take the deal with Exemplary Oil?"

He clenched his jaw. "I took it yesterday."

She briefly closed her eyes. So Alan hadn't lied. Everything he'd said was true.

"You must love her very much," Grace said, her voice barely a whisper.

He shook his head. "Grace, listen to me...."

She sucked in her breath, hating him more than she'd ever hated anyone in her whole life. "What are you even doing here? Shouldn't you be celebrating with Francesca?"

"No, damn you!" His steel-gray eyes blazed as he grabbed her by the shoulders. "I don't want her. I want you!"

"On the side?" She gave a harsh, ugly laugh. "You really think you can have anything you want, don't you? You always intended to seduce me for information, from the moment your car splashed me in the street!"

The rage in his eyes faded. His grip on her shoulders loosened.

"You're right," he said in a low voice. "You were nothing more to me then but Barrington's secretary, and

I thought you were his mistress. I intended to use you to take back what was rightfully mine."

"You took my virginity for that." She fought the angry tears rising to her eyes. She would die before she'd let him see her cry! "What is wrong with you? Don't you have a soul?"

His jaw clenched. "When I made love to you, I gave up my plan," he said, looking down at her. "I couldn't use the information you'd told me in bed. I knew I would lose you. So I kept silent. Francesca was the one who told her father. It would have been foolish and useless for me to refuse the deal she brought to me yesterday." He lifted her chin, holding her in his arms. "But I swear to you. On my honor. I never betrayed you."

She wanted to believe him.

Wanted it so badly it hurt.

But she couldn't.

"You mean the same word of honor," she said evenly, "with which you swore you weren't trying to use me against Alan?"

"My only lie," he ground out. He looked at her, and his eyes glittered. "I hated lying to you. But I made the choice, Grace. I chose you."

He stroked her cheek, looking down at her with emotion. She closed her eyes, her heart pounding at his touch.

"Come with me to Moscow," he whispered. "I want you with me. As my secretary, as my mistress, whatever you—"

Her eyes flew open. "Your…secretary?"

She ripped away from him. After everything they'd

been through together—the romance that had consumed her so utterly that she'd fallen in love with him and was about to have his child—that was still how he saw her. As a secretary?

And now that he'd won the merger with Exemplary Oil, he wasn't even trying to hide it. He was no longer even vaguely trying to pretend that he cared for her.

"You mean because I've helped you steal a billion-dollar deal from my last boss," she said scornfully, "you'll kindly allow me to type your letters and make your coffee in Moscow? Except you'll want different fringe benefits than Alan, I suppose. I assume I'm to spend my evenings and weekends earning my wages on my back?"

His dark brows lowered furiously as he grabbed her shoulders. "You know that's not how it is—"

"You want to hide me away in Moscow, so you can enjoy Francesca in London!" The images she'd seen of Francesca with him outside the hotel went through her. "Marrying her is part of your deal, right?"

"Damn you!" he shouted. "I don't want her! I want—"

"I saw you with her yesterday!" she shouted back.

He dropped his hands from her shoulders. "What?"

Tears filled her eyes. She wiped them fiercely. "After I was fired, I went to your hotel. Stupid me, I actually had faith in all the lies you'd told me."

"They weren't lies, not all of them—"

"Oh, yes, I always get things wrong, don't I?" She could barely speak over the lump in her throat. "Because I'm just a silly little secretary. That's all I've ever been to you."

"You little fool," he ground out. "You know that's not true—"

"Stop trying to have it both ways!" she shouted. "You never cared for me, you just took my virginity, you seduced me, you got me—" *Pregnant with your child,* she almost blurted out, but she stopped herself just in time. Humiliation gnawed at her, causing her cheeks to go hot.

She didn't want to tell him about the baby. Ever.

She just wanted him out of their lives for good.

"I did you a favor to get you away from Barrington," he ground out. "You were letting him walk all over you!"

He'd felt sorry for her?

"Oh, thank you. Thank you so much," she said. Waves of acute misery continued to build inside her, making her feel more ill by the minute. "I wish to God I'd never let you touch me!"

Gut-wrenching nausea waved over her. Covering her mouth, she ran to the bathroom, stumbling on the floor to retch over the toilet just in time.

She heard him come in behind her. His voice was suddenly gentle as he said, "But Grace, you're ill."

"It's nothing—the flu—just go!" She wiped her mouth, looking back at him with eyes of fury. "I hate you!"

"Grace—"

"Just go! You liar, you back-stabbing bastard!" She grabbed a bar of soap and threw it at him. He ducked it easily, enraging her still more.

"I'm not leaving you."

"If I'm sick," she bit out, "it's because looking at your face makes me want to puke! My skin crawls when I think of how I let you touch me." She looked at him with eyes of ice. "You're not a prince—you're not even a *man*."

She'd finally pushed him too far.

He stiffened behind her.

"Fine." His lip curled. "Now that I know your true opinion of me, I won't fight to keep you. I see now there is nothing for me here…"

Turning to go, he stopped.

Bending over the carpet, he picked up something that had fallen to the floor and rolled across the carpet.

The pregnancy test had fallen from the hole in her pocket!

She gasped, rising quickly to her feet. "It's not what you think. It's nothing…an old test…a friend's…left here," she stammered helplessly.

"You're pregnant." He looked at her. "You're pregnant?"

She stared at him. She wanted to deny it, but the lie stuck in her throat.

"Am I the father?"

She gasped at the insult.

"You know you are! Although I wish to God you weren't. I wish any other man on earth was the father but you!"

His eyes focused on her coldly. "And I realize now everything I ever thought about you was wrong. I thought you were special. You're not. You're selfish and deceitful. Jealous and controlling."

She gave a harsh laugh. "More than your precious Francesca?"

"Francesca and I broke up because she tried to push

me into marrying her. You did something far worse. You were going to let me walk right out that door, weren't you? You were going to keep my child a secret. You intended to sacrifice our child's need for a father, and live in poverty without even a home, all for the sake of your own selfish pride!"

He knew the house was in foreclosure? She gasped, feeling as if he'd exposed her vulnerable jugular.

"How did you know?" she whispered.

"I told you. I protect what is mine. That means my child. That means his family." His lip curled. "And whether I wish it or not, that means my child's mother." His eyes were cold as he looked down at her. "You will be my wife."

His...wife?

She sucked in her breath.

His duty bride, the ignored spouse he would leave trapped in a lonely Muscovite palace while he continued to pursue the wickedly lovely Francesca in London?

"No," she whispered desperately. She looked around the sunlit cottage. She desperately wanted her family to keep their home. Then she thought of the tiny life in her womb who needed to be protected. Better to remain in poverty in the warm sunshine of California, near family who loved her, than risk either of them anywhere near Maksim's icy Siberia of a heart!

She shook her head hard. "How many times do I have to say it? I don't want your money!"

"But now you will take it." His voice was low, dangerous. His gray eyes glittered at her as he added maliciously, "As you will take my name. Today."

"No! I won't!"

He grabbed her painfully by the shoulders. "Apparently, I haven't made myself clear. You have no choice."

She was suddenly afraid of him, this dangerous man who seemed to control his anger with such icy reserve.

"Your wife in name only?" she whispered.

He gave a hard laugh. "And now you think to trick your way out of my bed? No. You will be my wife in every way. You will sleep naked in my bed and service me at my will."

It was the final stab to her heart. He'd already made it plain he cared nothing for her. He expected her to surrender her body to his possession, without affection, without love?

"You're worse than Alan," she whispered. "A million times worse. Because, you're not asking me to be your wife. You're trying to make me your household slave, chained to your bed."

He stroked her chin.

"I'm not asking you," he said coolly. "I'm telling you. You are pregnant with my child. You will be my wife. Every jewel and home and luxury you could possibly desire will be yours. You are now mine."

He was offering her money, in exchange for giving her body and soul to a man she hated—a man in love with another woman! "A gilded cage. You're offering me the life of a whore!"

He grabbed her wrist, pulling her hard against his muscular body.

"Have it your way, then. You will be my pretty songbird in a golden cage." He kissed her cruelly, punishing her. As she felt her lips bruise beneath his embrace, a whimper escaped her. He drew away with a hard smile, looking down at her with a gaze like frozen steel. "And, my beautiful one, you will sing only for me."

CHAPTER TEN

MOSCOW, ancient stronghold of czars, was white and frozen in the breathless hush of winter. The sprawling modern city of untold wealth was as brutal as Maksim's will, Grace thought. And in the frosty twilight of New Year's Eve, it was as cold as her husband's icy heart.

Grace stared out the window of her large, elegant, lonely bedroom. After nearly a week in this vast city of old poverty and new wealth, her only outings had been to the doctor and to the exclusive shops of Barvikha Village and Tverskaya Street, driven by bodyguards in a Humvee with darkened windows. She'd shopped beside powerful oligarchs and their pouting trophy girlfriends dripping with furs and diamonds.

She'd seen little of the city. She'd seen traffic, traffic and more traffic on the paved, guarded road to Rublyovka. She'd seen huge billboards on Moscow's ring roads, advertising luxury cars and jewels as they drove past old buildings with aging Communist icons chiseled in stone.

For a woman who'd once hated fancy shops, they were now her only excuse to escape her luxury compound. Surrounded by bodyguards and servants, Grace was never alone.

And yet she was always alone.

She was a captive bride in a guarded palace, and she'd been forced to accept she was completely in Maksim's power. He'd made that clear by coldly marrying her in Las Vegas on Christmas Day.

Once her family came back from their Christmas service, Grace had been forced to tell her mother she was pregnant. Then she lied and said she loved her baby's father. She'd endured her family's delighted surprise and her mother's whispered blessing on their hasty elopement. When she learned they had no ring, Carol had wrenched off the precious ring that hadn't left her finger for twenty-seven years.

"Your father would want you to have this," she'd said to Grace, holding out the simple half-carat diamond ring in rose gold as tears streamed down her face. "He would be so happy for you today. I just wish he could be here now."

Grace had blinked back her own tears two hours later, as she gave her vows to Maksim in the small chapel of the Hermitage Resort, a Russian-style casino owned by his friend, Greek tycoon Nikos Stavrakis. And Grace hadn't been blinking back tears of joy, either. Beneath the candlelight and mournful, painted Russian icons, she'd pledged herself to Maksim for life. Barely looking at her, Maksim had tersely done the same.

After their cold wedding, there had been no sunny honeymoon. Maksim had brought her to Moscow on his private jet and abandoned her in his luxurious palace compound in an exclusive neighborhood outside the city. Grace had no idea where he'd spent his days and nights since they'd arrived. She tried to tell herself she didn't care.

Her only consolation was that her family was safe. They would never lose their home or be worried about money again. Maksim had paid off the entire mortgage and had placed a large sum in a bank account to make sure her family would always be financially secure and her brothers could go to college. They were happy because they believed Grace was, too.

She had been well and truly bought.

I'm sorry I did this to you, baby, she thought, rubbing her flat tummy mournfully. She looked around the large, feminine bedroom with the blue canopy bed and the lady's study beside it. Down the hall, the next room was empty. Maksim had ordered her to create the baby's nursery there, but Grace didn't have the heart. She couldn't accept her new life here. Couldn't accept that this was all the home life her child would have.

As purplish twilight fell softly over the skyline of the distant city, Grace finally saw his armored car pull past their front gate.

Where had he been for the past six days? Where was he sleeping at night? Clenching her hands into fists, she rose from her chair at the window and left her bedroom.

From the high second-story landing overlooking the wide marble floors of the downstairs foyer, she saw Maksim enter the house, followed by assistants and bodyguards. His face was dark and tired. He didn't bother to ask the housekeeper about how his new bride was faring. He didn't bother to even glance upstairs. He simply handed Elena his coat, went into his study and closed the door behind him.

For Grace, it was the final straw.

She ran downstairs. Without knocking, she pushed through his study door.

Sitting at his desk, he looked up at her with infuriating calmness. "Yes?"

She hated his coldness. She envied that he had ice water in his veins instead of blood. She wished she, too, could feel nothing, instead of feeling like her heart was continually breaking anew!

"Where have you been?"

He barely glanced at her as he gathered papers on his desk. "You have missed me, my bride?" he said sardonically.

"I'm your wife. I have a right to know if you've been sleeping with someone else!"

"Of course you do," he said with a cold laugh. "I can tell you I've been working day and night to finish details on the Exemplary merger, sleeping two hours a night on a cot in my office. But of course you will immediately know I have been with another woman. You will immediately suspect I've set up Francesca in a suite at the Ritz-Carlton."

Grace's heart fell to the floor.

"Francesca's in Moscow?" she whispered.

His lips twisted into an ironic smile. "And to think I once believed you had such faith in people."

"You destroyed that!"

"Have no fear, my dear wife," he drawled. "I have no interest in Francesca. How could I, when I have such a warm, loving wife waiting in my bed at home?"

His barb went straight to the heart. She clenched her hands into fists. "Just try getting into bed with me sometime, and you'll see how warm and loving I am!"

Maksim rose wearily from his desk. "Enough." Placing a stack of papers in his briefcase beside his laptop, he started walking toward the study door. "If you have nothing else to discuss, I'll wish you good-night."

She stared at him incredulously. "You're leaving? Just like that?"

He stopped and turned back to her. At the intensity of his expression, she trembled from within.

Then he lowered his head and kissed her softly on the cheek. "*Snovem godem,* Grace," he said softly. "Happy New Year."

She turned her face up toward his, her heart aching with the memory of the man she'd loved in London. She searched his gaze for some remnant of the man she'd laughed with, cared for. *Loved.*

Then he turned from her.

"Don't wait up."

Anguish rose in her heart…then anger. She hated his coldness. How could she have ever thought he was a good man?

"You can't keep me locked up here!"

He glanced back curiously. "Do you not think so?"

"I'm not your slave!"

"No." He gave her a brief, cool smile. "You are my wife. You are carrying my child. You will live in comfort and luxury, with nothing to do but enjoy the pleasure of your own company."

"I'm going insane!"

"How surprising."

She ground her teeth in frustration. "It's New Year's Eve. Elena is going to Red Square…"

Her voice trailed off as she saw him shaking his head.

"There will be half a million people in Red Square. The bodyguards couldn't protect you."

"Protect me? From what?"

He shrugged. "I have enemies. Some hate me for my billions, some hate me for my title. You could be kidnapped for ransom. It's rare but it does sometimes happen. Or perhaps—" he glanced at her keenly "—you'd be tempted to run off in the crowd."

"I won't," she said tearfully. "Please. I just want to live a normal life!"

"Just what every princess wants," he said sardonically. "And cannot have."

He turned away.

"Maksim, please don't leave me here," she whispered. "I can't bear to be left like this."

He paused at the door, not bothering to turn around.

"Have a pleasant evening, my bride."

She stood in shock in his office until she heard the front door slam and the silence as his bodyguards and assistants left with him.

She walked slowly up the wide, sweeping stairs to her lonely bedroom.

He'd left her alone on New Year's Eve.

Was it really possible that Lady Francesca Danvers was in Moscow?

Very possible. The fiery, tempestuous redhead was the woman Maksim had really wanted all along. The woman every man wanted.

She tried to tell herself she didn't care. But still, her heart felt perilously close to despair.

"Can I bring you something to eat, princess?" Elena said softly, and Grace looked up to see the older Russian woman standing in the doorway. She liked the capable housekeeper, who supervised a staff of twenty and spoke fluent English.

But between nausea and fury, food was the last thing on Grace's mind. She shook her head.

"You must eat something, Prince Maksim said, for the baby."

"He's not the boss of me!" Grace shouted, then she felt instantly abashed about her childish behavior when she saw the expression on the housekeeper's face. "I'm sorry, Elena." She paced the luxurious room, then rubbed her forehead. "I'm going out of my mind. I've been trapped in this house for days."

"I'm sorry you're not feeling well, princess. I'm sure His Highness was very regretful to have to leave you alone. He's very busy."

Grace closed her eyes as grief and fury built inside her. Yeah. She could just imagine how he was *busy*.

All week she'd been waiting…for what? For him to

return to the man he'd been in London, the man she'd loved? For him to act like a decent, caring husband?

Well, she wasn't going to wait anymore. She wasn't going to remain jailed here for his convenience!

Grace went to her huge closet and grabbed dark skinny jeans and a snug black cashmere sweater she'd bought at the Leighton boutique on Tverskaya Street. "I'm coming to Red Square with you tonight."

Elena looked alarmed. "Have you asked Vladimir and Igor if it's all right?"

There was no way Grace was going to invite her hulking, overprotective bodyguards to join her tonight! "No. I'll just take the Metro with you."

"It's the train. And, princess, I'd get fired for sure."

"Please, Elena!" She closed her eyes. "I just want a nice, normal life. Just a few hours to breathe fresh air and blend in without big bodyguards hovering over me wherever I go!"

"You don't know this city. You don't speak a word of Russian."

"I do know one word. *Nyet*. And that's my answer to Maksim." She pulled her hair into a ponytail. "*This* princess will have a normal life. I might be his wife, but I won't be his slave!"

Grabbing her warmest coat and hat, she opened the second-story window, peering down at the wide wall. She'd have to climb over on the tree branch and down the other side…

"*Kharasho*," Elena said, sounding resigned. "You can come with me. Just stay close and don't wander off!"

Grace nearly wept tears of gratitude. "I promise I won't tell Maksim!"

"He will find out," the woman said with a shake of her head, then grumbled, "For a new bride to be home alone on New Year's Eve? Bah!" And she muttered something under her breath in Russian.

Grace tapped her black boots on the floor. Every muscle in her body ached to get out of this luxurious palace. Away from her captivity and loneliness.

Away from the fact that she was with yet another man who was in love with Lady Francesca Danvers instead of her.

Was it Grace's fate to always lose every man she cared about to the same woman?

The painfully ironic thought chased her all the way to Red Square an hour later. They followed the currents and crush of people past the twin towers of the Resurrection Gate, with its mosaic icons of favored saints, into Red Square.

"Stay close," Elena said.

Grace took one look at the colorful onion domes of St. Basil's Cathedral and gasped. Standing still in the packed crowd, she slowly turned around, looked at the Kremlin, Lenin's tomb and the red buildings around the square. She'd dreamed about this ever since the Soviet breakup when she was a girl.

Red Square was lit with a million lights and filled with half a million cheering people. It was more fantastically beautiful than she'd ever dreamed. For one moment it made her forget her pain.

Then she saw a nearby man take his girlfriend in his

arms and kiss her. Watching them kiss and laugh and share an intimate moment just a few feet away suddenly made Grace ache twice as much with loneliness.

She turned back to Elena, but the Russian woman was gone! Somehow they'd been separated.

Struggling not to feel alarmed, clenching her gloved hands into fists and shoving them into her coat, Grace looked around through the white mist of her breath.

She felt so alone, and the night was so cold. Here in the far north of the world, she wondered if winter would ever end.

Suddenly she felt a hand on her shoulder.

She turned and saw Maksim standing beside her!

In spite of everything, her heart leaped to see him, dark as night in his black clothes.

"You little fool," he ground out. "I expressly told you not to come here."

She took a deep breath. "I'm not your prisoner."

He looked down at her grimly. "If you risk my child without bodyguards again, you will be."

The threat made her furious. How dare he insinuate that she'd placed their unborn child at risk, just by living a normal life?

"I'm sick of you trying to control me." Furious, she tossed her head, "And where's Francesca?" she taunted. "Don't tell me you've finished with her already?"

"Damn your jealousy," he growled.

"I'm not jealous," she fired back. "I don't care if you make love to her every night. I don't love you. I don't want you!"

He yanked her into his arms.

"Who's lying now?" he growled.

Her eyes suddenly widened when she saw his intent. "No—"

Lowering his mouth on hers, he kissed her savagely.

Beneath the colorful fireworks in the dark wintry sky, he punished her in his embrace, plundering her lips, mastering her with his strength. She tried to resist, pushing at his chest with her small hands, but in the end her own desire overpowered her in a way brute force could not. Surrendering, she sagged in his arms with a whimper, holding his body against hers as she returned his brutal kiss with equal passion.

Beneath the brilliantly lit onion domes of St. Basil's Cathedral, they kissed in a fiery embrace of hate and longing amid the roar of half a million people celebrating the birth of the new year.

From the day he'd married Grace, Maksim had intended to punish her.

And he'd done it. He'd brought her to Moscow, a place where she knew no one, and he'd deserted her in the same palace he'd once dreamed of bringing her to live as his mistress. Except all the tenderness he'd once had for her was long gone. In its place was cold, hard anger.

He'd rushed to her in California. He'd told her the truth. He'd practically begged her to forgive the single lie he'd told her. A small request considering that he'd been willing to give up what he wanted most for her sake.

He'd treated her with better care than he'd ever treated any woman. *He'd placed her interests above his own.*

And all he'd gotten from her in return were insults—and lies. Then, to top it off, she'd tried to steal his child!

He'd thought Grace was different. That she was special. But he knew the truth now. She might have been a virgin when he first bedded her, but in other ways she might as well be Francesca—selfish, cruel and controlling.

When Elena had told him Grace had accompanied her to Red Square against his orders, he'd been furious. Then he'd been frightened—purely for the baby's sake, he'd told himself.

But when he dismissed Elena and saw Grace looking so forlorn and alone amid the festive crowds of Red Square, anger and desire and fury had finally boiled over him.

And something more. Desire. The desire he'd suppressed for days, trying to finish the hellish, endless details of the merger. The desire he'd tried not to feel, staying away from the bride he despised as a way to keep himself from wanting her.

He hadn't meant to kiss her. He'd sworn to himself when he brought her to Moscow that he wouldn't even touch her.

Then she'd taunted him.

Anger and lust had seized him. And he'd seized her. Now…

His need to punish her blended with his need to possess her. Taking her by the hand, he dragged her from the crowds of Red Square to his waiting car. Closing the privacy screen to block the eyes of his bodyguard and driver, he threw her into the back seat and kissed her hard. Her hat had been long lost. Pulling off her coat and gloves, he pressed her body beneath his, kissing her with angry force. She returned his kiss with matching fervor, biting at his lips until they bled.

"I hate you," she breathed against his skin.

For answer, he ripped her black sweater off her body. Yanking her bra to the floor of the car, he pressed his mouth on her breasts, biting and suckling until the mix of pain and pleasure made her gasp and arch beneath him.

"Hate me if you want. You are mine to do with as I please," he said, licking her nipples. "You will pleasure me."

"I won't...ah," she sucked in her breath as he moved his hand between her legs, over her tight jeans, rubbing her until she gripped his shoulders wordlessly seeking release.

He wanted to rip off her jeans. He wanted to thrust inside her hard and deep, until she begged for mercy.

Until she begged his forgiveness.

By the time they made it home, her lips were bruised with his kisses, her blond hair tousled and tangled, her eyes dazed and bewildered with her unwilling longing. Giving his driver and bodyguard a terse order in Russian, he collected Grace in his arms and carried her roughly into the house.

The palace was quiet. The bodyguards were outside celebrating in the guardhouse by the gate. The rest of the servants had been given the night off.

Maksim intended to carry her to the master bedroom, but halfway up the stairs she reached up to stroke his neck and he could bear it no longer. He placed her down on the curving, sinuous staircase, beside the art deco railing that looked like swirls of melting wax in white limestone. Pulling off her jeans, he undid his fly. He was hard as a rock and aching for her.

He didn't tease her.

He didn't ask permission.

Without warning, without tenderness, he pulled down his pants and thrust himself inside her, all the way to the hilt.

She gasped, then moved beneath him, her full, heavy breasts swaying as she arched her back, pulling him deeper still.

She wanted him as unwillingly as he wanted her. He knew it. But suddenly he wanted far more than just to take his pleasure. He wanted her to take her own. To force her to hold nothing back. To surrender herself completely.

Rolling over, with his own back against the shallow, wide steps, he lifted her on top of him. She gasped as he lowered her over him, impaling her.

"Move," he ordered.

As he commanded, she slowly moved against him, sliding her wet, hot body against his in circles that got progressively tighter and smaller. He felt her muscles clench around him, deep inside her, as she closed her eyes. She stopped, fighting her desperate desire.

He stroked her breasts, then, taking one of her hands in his own, he sucked gently on a fingertip. Her blue eyes met his, innocent, shocked. Her pupils were dilated, her nipples painfully tight, her body so hot and wet around him. And as if she could not resist his will, she started to move again. Her heavy breasts bounced softly as she rode him, pushing her hips harder and faster until he was barely able to hold on to his self-control. He looked up at her beautiful face, at her soft, curvaceous, feminine body that was getting tighter and tighter around him as she started to shudder. And he heard a low scream rising from her throat.

As she moved herself against him, rocking back and forth in rhythm, her core slick and impossibly soft around him, he felt her start to tense and shake, and finally he could take it no longer. With a Russian curse on his lips, he exploded into her with a shout that echoed against the high walls of the foyer, mingling with her own ecstatic cry.

Exhausted, her limp body fell against his own. For a moment he held her, feeling her soft body against his chest, listening to the sound of her breath.

But when his sense returned, he was furious.

At her.

At himself.

He had no self-control whatsoever where Grace was concerned.

He'd sworn to himself that he wouldn't touch her. But this proved his desire was stronger than his pride. Proved she still had control over him.

Proved that no matter what she thought of him, he still cared for her.

Pushing away roughly, he rose to his feet on the stairs, furious at himself. Without saying a word, he rezipped his pants and coldly left her on the stairs.

The palace suddenly felt too confining, and outside

he would be watched by guards. With a deep breath, he climbed two floors to the roof garden. Where he went to find peace. Where he went to be alone.

The rooftop terrace was covered with snow and dead branches of the dormant garden. He took several deep breaths, stretching his arms, trying to clear his head. He stared at his own breath, looking past the treetops and lights of the city toward the distant fireworks in the cold clear night.

He heard her come out though the garden door. He couldn't believe she'd followed him out here. He looked at her with narrowed eyes. She'd put her clothes back on, tying her tattered blouse together as best she could. She hesitated, then finally came up behind him, wrapping her arms around him.

For a moment he was tempted to lean into her arms. His heart hungered for her.

Then she spoke.

"Just tell me the truth, Maksim," she whispered. "Admit that you betrayed me. Admit that you lied and I'll forgive you."

His jaw clenched as he turned to face her. "You'll forgive me," he said tersely.

She swallowed, then lifted her chin. "I will try."

Anger rushed through him, pulling away all his remembered tenderness like an overflowing river ripping sediment from the banks.

"I do not want your forgiveness," he said in a low voice.

"Maksim." Her face was tear stained, her voice a whisper. "Just tell me if you love her. Tell me."

Love her? *Her?* Who?

Then he knew. Of course. She was talking about Francesca. He'd never given Grace any reason to feel jealous, but she continued to grind away at him with her insecurity's endless need for control.

Did he need further proof she thought him a man without honor, a man she couldn't trust?

He'd tried to change her mind in California. He wouldn't try again. He wouldn't allow himself to be vulnerable with her. Never again.

He looked at her coldly. "In two days I will introduce you to all of Moscow as my bride. You must be ready for the ballroom reception. You and the child need rest. Go sleep. In your peaceful, solitary bed."

"Maksim..." she whispered.

For answer, he turned and left her without a backward glance, leaving her shivering and alone on the snowy rooftop garden, in the chill black night beneath icy white stars.

CHAPTER ELEVEN

"LADY Francesca Danvers is here to see you, princess."

Grace whirled around in her chair. "What does she want?"

"Nothing good, I wager," Elena said sourly.

Grace turned back to face herself in the mirror. She hardly recognized herself. Wearing a long, sparkling, champagne-colored gown that caressed her body, with her blond hair piled high on her head, she looked like a princess.

For the past two hours, Elena had been helping her get ready for the ballroom reception that would introduce her to Moscow society. But she wasn't sure she could face the woman her husband still loved. She licked her lips nervously. "Do you know her?"

The Russian housekeeper shrugged as one of the maids brought in a small enamel-and-silver box. "She was here once before, long ago. But old lovers should disappear when a man gets married," she said with a sniff. "Let me send her away. Your reception starts in ten minutes. You don't have time to speak to each and every guest before…"

"She's a guest?" Grace gasped. "Who would have—"

But she cut herself off. She didn't have to ask who would have invited Francesca.

She closed her eyes, willing herself not to cry. It would ruin the carefully applied makeup, and she had to look lovely when she was introduced as Maksim's bride.

He must really hate her, to do this, she thought. How could he stab her in the heart, forcing her to publicly meet his mistress? It hurt so badly she thought her heart might crack in two.

Maksim had made his feelings plain. After they'd made love on New Year's Eve, she'd begged him to justify his actions. She'd been so desperate for a fresh start, she'd offered him almost more than she thought she could bear—her forgiveness. If only he would just admit what he'd done, and promise never to see Francesca again!

But he had refused. And in the two days since, he'd avoided her more than ever.

And yet she still couldn't believe Francesca was in Moscow.

When Maksim had said he'd installed her in some fancy hotel, Grace had assumed he was just trying to hurt her.

But the woman was here. Had he been telling her the truth? Had he been spending all his nights with his mistress?

Why shouldn't he? She thought miserably. He'd only married Grace because she was pregnant. A forced marriage wouldn't necessarily stop him from loving Francesca....

"Ah, you look perfect. You just need one last thing.

His Highness sent this." Elena pulled an antique gold-and-emerald tiara from the enamel box and reverently placed it around Grace's high chignon.

"It's beautiful," Grace said in a low voice.

"It used to belong to the prince's great-aunt, the Grand Duchess Olga." Elena pulled back to see the effect in the mirror then nodded her approval. "Now I'll send that wretched woman away," she added, "and I'll be right back."

"No," Grace blurted out, her mouth suddenly dry. "Send her up."

The Russian woman looked at her dubiously. "Are you sure, princess?"

No. "Yes."

A moment later Lady Francesca was escorted into the drawing room beside Grace's bedroom.

The pale redhead was as beautiful as Grace remembered. Petite and very thin, she wore a pink tweed Chanel skirt suit and white peep-toe shoes with flashy red soles. In her perfectly manicured hands, she carried a white quilted bag with a gold chain handle.

She glanced around the pretty, elegant, feminine room. "I see you've set yourself up nicely," she said with a sniff.

"Please sit down," Grace said nervously, indicating the blue high-backed chair. "May I order some tea?"

"No, thank you." Francesca's cold, kohl-lined green eyes looked right through her scornfully. "This isn't a friendly visit." She set her handbag on the tea table, all business. "I've come to ask you how much money I have to pay you to divorce your husband."

Grace stared at her in shock, speechless.

"Oh, come on," she said impatiently. "You were clever enough to get pregnant. You are hoping to profit from your child. I don't blame you. I'm sure I would do the same if I had no money, skills or beauty. So just tell me how much you expect."

Grace tried to speak, but still couldn't.

Francesca pulled her checkbook and an expensive-looking pen out of her wallet, then looked up at her. "Well?"

"I'm not trying to profit from my child!"

"Because you're a decent mother?" Francesca's red lips twisted. "Can we please skip your fervent protestations? We both know that Maksim should belong to me. Tell me how much it will cost to be rid of you."

Remembering all that she'd suffered because of this woman, Grace clenched her hands into fists.

"I gave up one man to you without a fight," she said in a low voice. "I won't do it again."

"So you did have a desperate little crush on Alan," Francesca drawled, glancing down at her flawless scarlet nails. "I wondered. My dear, don't you realize that a woman like you cannot possibly compete against a woman like me?"

Every word was like a stab to Grace's heart. "I never loved Alan," she said in a trembling voice. "You can have him. But I'll die before I give Maksim up to you!"

"You poor fool. I understand Maksim in a way you never will." Francesca tilted her head. "He doesn't love you. If you were any sort of decent woman, you would let him go. If you won't, you're not a decent woman.

You're a gold digger who deliberately got pregnant to trick Maksim into marriage."

Grace's insides twisted. "I never tried to get pregnant. I never asked him to marry me," she whispered. "He insisted."

Francesca nodded. "So you didn't want to marry him in the first place. Perfect. Then take my check and leave him. Find some other man to marry." She stared at Grace with false sympathy. "Someone more at your level."

"He's my husband and father of my child. Now we're married, I won't give him up." She narrowed her eyes, looking up at the other woman as her shoulders shook with emotion. "Not to you or anyone."

With a sigh, the beautiful redhead closed her checkbook. "Fine. Have it your way." She leaned forward across the tea table. "You're not a bad person. I can see that. So if you love him, let him go."

Grace looked up at her rival. "You love him?"

Francesca's green eyes were clear and direct. "And I can help him. In life. In business. I thought a fake engagement would prod him into setting a date to marry me. But he plays the game even better than I do. He actually married you." She gave a thin red smile. "I told my father about the fake engagement to save Maksim's merger. I can make him the richest man in the world. What can you ever do for him…except be a burden?"

"Izvenitche, pojhowsta." Elena suddenly appeared in the door, scowling. "It's time for the princess to make her entrance at the reception."

Francesca rose gracefully to her feet. She paused at

the door, her eyes narrowed and her red lips pulled back to reveal her sharp white teeth.

"If you love him, Miss Cannon," she said softly, "you'll leave him."

After her parting shot the beautiful redhead swept away, leaving pain and regret racking through Grace in waves.

Maksim had told her the truth. Francesca was the one who'd told her father about the fake engagement. Maksim had tried to tell her he didn't betray her. He'd seduced her, yes, but he hadn't been able to use her words against her. He'd protected her honor at the expense of his own. He'd given up what he wanted most—for her.

But she hadn't believed him.

Instead she'd insulted him. She still winced to remember the horrible words she'd thrown at him when he'd followed her to California.

She'd done everything she could to push him back into Francesca's arms. Could he ever forgive her lack of faith?

He has to, she thought. *Even if I have to beg him for forgiveness.*

But what difference would begging make—if he was in love with another woman? She closed her eyes as a stabbing pain went through her heart. Why would he ever choose her over Francesca, after the way she'd treated him?

"Are you ready, Grace?"

She turned to see Maksim standing in the doorway. She sucked in her breath. He looked devastatingly handsome in his tuxedo, her dark Rostov prince, strong and powerful and very, very dangerous.

"She's ready," Elena said approvingly. She adjusted

the tiara over Grace's high chignon, adding pins to hold it as she said softly, "And the most beautiful princess the house of Rostov has ever seen."

Maksim slowly looked her over and then nodded. "You are beautiful."

Grace's heart fluttered in her chest. "You are, too. So handsome, I mean."

His dark eyes were inscrutable as he held out his arm. "Come."

He led her out of the room to the top of the elaborate limestone staircase where they'd made love with such intensity two days before. At the bottom of the stairs, she heard the noise and voices of their guests, the clinking of crystal. She couldn't face them as Maksim's wife.

Not without knowing their marriage had a chance.

She stopped in her tracks, pulling on his hand with urgency to pull him back into the hallway.

He looked down at her impatiently. "What is it?"

"I should have believed you all along. I'm so sorry, Maksim." Her eyes filled with tears as the words spilled out, rushing over each other. "You never betrayed me. Francesca said she told her father about the engagement. Oh, Maksim. Can you ever forgive me?"

His eyes narrowed. "You have spoken with Francesca?"

"She was here."

His eyebrows rose. "Here? What was she—"

She placed her hand over his. "I don't want to fight," she pleaded. "I want to start fresh. To go back to how we were in London. I believe you now. I'm sorry I didn't have faith—"

"It's easy to believe me now, isn't it?" he interrupted

coldly. "You believe Francesca's words, when you wouldn't believe mine."

This was all going wrong. She'd apologized, begged him to forgive her, pleaded for a fresh start. What else was left? What hadn't she said?

Only one thing, and it terrified her. She couldn't possibly lay her soul bare before him, not when his face was so cold, his body so tense and unyielding.

"Come." He turned away, drawing her once more toward the wide sweeping stairs and the marble-floored foyer where she knew hundreds of society guests were waiting.

She grabbed his tuxedo sleeve, pulling him to her, forcing him to listen.

"Maksim, I…" Her heart pounded in her throat. She licked her lips. "I…I love you."

His steel-gray eyes widened, became deep pools of some emotion she couldn't identify, but it caused yearning and fear to spread through her veins.

"I love you," she repeated, her mouth utterly dry. "And I have to know. Can you ever love me?"

She waited for his answer, and as the seconds ticked by, they seemed to last for eons.

Then his handsome face slowly turned to ice. He shook his head grimly. "It's too late."

"How can it be too late?" she gasped.

"I'll always take care of the child, Grace." He looked away, tightening his shoulders. "But I'll never love you again."

Again?

He'd loved her?

He'd loved her—and she'd thrown his love away!

"No!" she cried. "It can't be too late! I love you. And if you once loved me…"

He gave her a sardonic smile, all emotion gone from his eyes. "And how well you repaid me."

"I made a horrible mistake." She was humiliated by the whimper in her voice, but she couldn't lose him. Not now. Not when she'd finally realized he was truly the man she'd always wanted. "Please, Maksim…"

"Stop begging," he said harshly. "You are a princess. Begging is beneath you."

"I can't lose you." She felt a sharp pain in her heart. "But I already have, haven't I?" she whispered. "You want to be with her."

"Who?"

"Do I have to say her name?"

His jaw clenched as he exhaled with a flare of his nostrils. "I am sick of having to defend my actions where Francesca is concerned. You are my wife. You are pregnant with my child. There will be no other woman in my life. There can't be. How clear do I have to make it?"

"But if there were no baby?" she said, her heart in her throat. "Would you still have married me?"

"That is a pointless question. There is a baby. The decision has been made. Love doesn't matter."

She closed her eyes to block out the pain. "You're wrong," she whispered. "It's all that matters."

Maksim had married Grace out of honor. The honor she'd bitingly, insultingly accused him of never having. And for the sake of honor, he was determined to stand by her side.

But if Grace hadn't been pregnant, he would have gone to Francesca like a shot. His heart was with her. She was beautiful and wealthy and a perfect match for Maksim in every way.

"I will always protect you both," he said in a low voice. "Don't ask for more than I can give."

He would protect her with money and his name. Nothing more.

Grace's own parents had had such a blissful marriage. She thought of how they'd laughed together, teased each other. The way her father had playfully wrapped his arms around her mother's waist while she cooked in the kitchen. Her parents' love had shone through everything, especially their children. Grace and her brothers had shared such a happy childhood beneath the umbrella of their parents' love.

She suddenly realized it had never been their house that had made them a family. The house hadn't made them secure and warm. It had been her parents' love. Their mutual adoration that had endured long after her father had died.

The lump in her throat sharpened.

What kind of home life would Grace's loveless marriage create for their baby?

How would their son or daughter feel, raised by a father who'd been forced to give up his own happiness because of the child's very existence?

Grace suddenly felt like crying.

Maksim held out his arm stiffly. "Come. Our guests are waiting."

Her heart felt shattered in her chest as he escorted her down the limestone Art Deco stairs.

In the wide marble foyer, beneath the soaring crystal chandelier, she saw a swirl of faces. Hundreds of people applauded for her as she was introduced as Her Highness Princess Grace Rostova. Gorgeous women in diamonds and Maksim's billionaire friends cheered in both English and Russian, holding up their champagne flutes in a toast to the new princess.

Grace got a glimpse of herself in the enormous gilded mirror across the foyer. She truly looked like a princess. The tiara sparkled in her hair. The champagne-colored gown moved against her like a whisper. This time, even her shoes were perfect, the twenty-first-century version of glass slippers. Beautiful, rather uncomfortable and very, very expensive.

But she would have done anything to go back in time to when she was just a plain, poor secretary, happy in Maksim's arms and bed. Back to when they'd actually had a chance at happiness.

Back to when he'd loved her. He'd never said the words then, but he'd made her feel them.

Grace saw Maksim's sister waiting for them at the bottom of the stairs. Dariya glowed as she hugged them both. "I'm so glad you're my sister," she whispered to Grace. "Not just my sister…my friend. And you're going to make me an aunt!"

"Thank you." Blinking back tears, Grace did her best to smile. "Your friendship means so much…"

She froze when she saw Lady Francesca Danvers over Dariya's shoulder.

She felt her husband stiffen beside her. She glanced at him. His face had closed down, his mouth a grim line, as he looked straight at Francesca.

"Excuse me," he said shortly.

Grace watched as he crossed through the crowd, grabbed the redhead's wrist and dragged her toward his study. His expression looked furious as he closed the door behind him.

And staring at the closed door, everything suddenly became clear for Grace.

He wasn't having an affair with Francesca. She now knew that to her core. He'd promised fidelity to Grace and he would keep to that vow. He was a man of honor.

He hadn't invited her here. He was determined to remain faithful to the wife he'd never wanted. Family and honor meant everything to Maksim. He would remain faithful to Grace.

But did she want him to?

After so many years of being Alan's doormat, desperate for any sign of tenderness, did she really want to be tied forever to a man who didn't love her?

And worse: did she want to raise their child that way?

Could she raise her baby to be happy in this palace of ice? Could she risk her child's bright, joyful new spirit in this frozen place, knowing he'd always be bewildered by his parents' cold misery and might eventually blame himself?

Grace may have sacrificed herself for her baby's sake, but she couldn't allow the life and warmth to be sapped out of her newborn's soul. She couldn't allow her precious baby to grow up suffocated in an endless winter of unspoken blame.

"What's *she* doing here?" Dariya said sourly. "Can't the woman take a hint?"

"I…I'm not feeling very well," Grace said, rubbing her forehead. "Will you please make my excuses and thank everyone for coming?"

"Of course, absolutely." Dariya peered at her in worry. "You do look pale. I'll go get my brother—"

"No! Don't tell him anything. I want to be alone." She ran upstairs with a hard lump in her throat.

Slamming her bedroom door behind her, she collapsed on her bed.

Love made a family.

She loved their baby. She loved Maksim.

But Maksim loved Francesca.

Grace's eyes fell on her battered old suitcase in the massive walk-in closet. It had taken her to London, back to California, to Moscow. It could take her back home.

"If you love him, let him go," Francesca had said.

Grace loved Maksim. She loved her baby. She loved them both so much and there was only one way to save them. One way to make sure they were both safe and happy. One way to set them both free.

Rising from the bed, she picked up her suitcase.

"How dare you show up here?" Maksim said furiously as he closed the study door behind them. "I expressly told you in London—we're through. We were done two and a half months ago when you gave me your little ultimatum."

Francesca looked up at him with her perfectly lined

green eyes. "But I made up for that, darling, when I got the merger back for you!"

"You only gave back something that should always have been mine."

A tremulous smile traced her red mouth. "I rectified a strategic misfire. You won this round."

He stared at her coldly. He expected at any moment, tears would appear—her carefully manufactured tears that never smudged her eye makeup. She was a master at manipulation.

Unlike Grace. Grace who'd looked so vulnerable just moments before they came down the stairway. She'd truly looked like a princess.

"I love you," she'd said. "Can you ever love me?"

His reply to her had been harsh.

Maksim clenched his hands, remembering the stricken look on her face. Grace had no defenses. It had been coldhearted and cruel of him. But she'd kept pushing him for what he wouldn't, couldn't give her...

"Come back with me to London," Francesca said. "It's time."

"Perhaps you haven't noticed," he replied acidly, "but I have a wife."

Emotion turned her thin face pale beneath the rouge. "I never should have given you an ultimatum. But how long do you intend to punish me for my mistake? Let the gold digger go."

"What did you call her?" he said dangerously.

She threw him a scornful glance. "Oh, please. A secretary? She's obviously a gold digger. I just offered her a blank check to leave you, but she refused. She knows she can cash in for more after the little brat is born!"

He clenched his fists. "You tried to buy her off?"

She sniffed. "I was trying to do you a favor, darling. You can't actually want to be married to her. She's not remotely your type!"

His type?

Pictures of Grace went through his mind. Her openness. Her purity. Her laughter and her tears. The way her thoughts were always revealed on her face. Her care and concern for the people around her. Her soft heart.

Gold digger? She'd made it clear from the beginning that she didn't want Maksim's money. He'd tried to spoil her in London, but she'd made it impossible. Over and over again, she'd refused his offers of gifts for clothes, jewels, cars, houses.

The only time she'd accepted anything was to give her family a place to live, when Maksim had black-mailed her into marriage. A strange feeling almost like shame went through him at the memory.

I had no choice, he told himself. *I had to protect my child. I had to make her marry me.* But the oft-repeated reason rang hollow today.

"I love you," she'd whispered. "Can you ever love me?"

"You're right," he said heavily, clawing his hand through his dark hair. "Grace is not my usual type of woman."

"She's not." Francesca gave him a sly smile. "I am."

She was right. Francesca was exactly his type. A selfish beauty who enjoyed playing games and liked to fight dirty. She liked to insinuate they were special due to aristocratic birth, but there was one thing and one thing only Francesca thought was truly noble: money.

Creeping closer to him, she licked her sultry red lips. "You and I are perfect for each other. Yes, we fought constantly, but only because we pursue our own desires no matter the cost. We're both selfish to the bone. Face it, Maksim, we're exactly alike!"

He stared at her.

"That's not true," he said hoarsely. "I'm nothing like you. Now get out."

"Maksim, don't be a fool. You're throwing away a fortune if you don't marry me!"

"We're done, Francesca. Through." He clenched his fists, staring at her coldly. "If I ever see you again—if you ever upset my wife again—you will regret it." Walking to the door, he flung it open. "Now leave."

"Fine," she ground out, tossing her head and exiting toward the curious party-goers outside. "Enjoy your common little wife. You'll be tired of her before your kid's even born!"

In the echo of her departing steps, Maksim closed the door heavily and sank into a chair at his desk. In his heart of hearts, he knew that he *was* just like Francesca.

Or at least he had been. Until he'd met someone who'd inspired him. Someone who with her sweet kindness and natural beauty had made him believe there was more to life than money.

He heard someone come in, and looked up, ready to snarl.

His sister stood in the doorway, her arms folded.

"About time you sent that woman away," Dariya said.

"And I hope you did it more thoroughly this time. Heaven knows she won't take a hint. Maybe you should toss a Rolex into the Moskva River—she'd be sure to dive through the ice. That would be one way to finally—"

"Where's Grace?" he interrupted.

"She wasn't feeling well, so she's gone upstairs to her room." Her eyes met his. "You have a houseful of guests with no host or hostess at the moment. I thought you'd want to know."

He took a deep breath. "Did Grace see me come in here with Francesca?"

"Yes. Everyone saw it. You might want to come and do some damage control."

Maksim clenched his jaw. "I'll go to her now." His encounter with Francesca had left him feeling strangely dirty. Had he really been like that? *Like her?*

He needed to see Grace. To see her calm face and hear her sweet voice. To have her take him in her soft arms so that he could take a deep, clear breath…

"Let Grace rest, Maksim," Dariya said sharply. "Let her sleep and talk to her in the morning. You need to end the rumors going through Moscow, or your marriage will be over before it's begun."

He clenched his jaw. He didn't blame Grace for fleeing to her bedroom. How could he? He'd left her alone during their wedding reception, abandoning her with hundreds of strangers while he disappeared behind closed doors with his ex-mistress.

No wonder Grace had been so insecure, considering that he hadn't bothered to reassure her. He'd just left her, his lonely, pregnant, deserted wife.

He clenched his hands into fists.

He had to make this right.

He had to see her.

"We're exactly alike," Francesca had said.

But fighting that was the soft echo of Grace's voice from long ago. "You're a good man, Maksim. You think it's weakness...but I know your secret."

Which woman did he want to believe?

Which man did he want to be?

He took a deep breath. "I'll just check on her. I won't wake her if she's sleeping," he promised. "Act as hostess until I'm back, Daritchka, won't you?"

But friends and acquaintances were swarming the foyer. Bewildered at the sudden abrupt disappearance of both bride and groom, they stopped him in his path, asking for reassurance and explanations that Maksim hardly knew how to give. It took him almost twenty minutes to cross the marble floor of the foyer to the limestone stairs.

He went to Grace's bedroom and knocked softly on the door. When he heard no answer, he pushed the door open.

Her room was dark. Only in the faintest trace of moonlight from the window could he see her shape in the Wedgwood-blue canopy bed beneath the covers.

He wanted to wake her but held himself back. Waking her would be selfish when it was only to seek his own comfort.

He was a husband.

He was going to be a father.

Everything had changed for him, but he'd been slow to realize it.

Turning away, ignoring the ache in his throat, he went downstairs and did his duty as host. He spent the rest of the long night entertaining his guests and reassuring them that his new bride had just taken ill due to her delicate condition. But all through the endless hours, he couldn't stop thinking of his pregnant wife sleeping upstairs. Lonely in the bedroom that he'd given her as a way to punish her for calling his offer of marriage "a gilded cage."

At dawn, after he'd finally shoved the last guest firmly out the door, Maksim crept back to her room, praying she would now be awake. If she wasn't awake, he didn't know how much longer he could wait.

He needed to feel comforted by her presence. To tell her he was sorry he'd been so cruel. To tell her…to tell her…

The warm blush of a gray-and-pink dawn filled her bedroom as he pushed open the door. She was still in bed, just as she'd been before.

I won't wake her, he told himself. He would just watch her sleep. Even that would bring him some small peace.

But as he walked forward in the lightening room, something didn't look right. Her body beneath the blanket looked strange. The comforter stretched all the way up to the headboard. He pulled back the blanket and discovered…pillows.

She was gone!

He snatched up the note attached to the pillow. It read:

Maksim,
There is no baby. I faked the pregnancy—don't

ask how—to try and get your money. But I can't
do it. Please divorce me immediately and don't try
to find me. I don't want any alimony. I wish you
every happiness in your life with Francesca. All I
want is for you to be with the woman you love.
     Grace

No baby? She'd faked the pregnancy?

Pain ripped through him, pain so staggering it almost
dropped him to his knees.

He couldn't breathe. The tie on his tuxedo suddenly
seemed to constrict his air, choking him. He ripped it
to the ground in a tear of fabric. He read the note
again. And again.

No baby.

She'd faked the pregnancy.

He crumpled up the note in his fist.

He'd been shocked by her pregnancy, but until this
moment he hadn't realized how much the baby had
come to mean to him. In spare moments between the
bone-crushing work of completing the oil company
merger, he'd daydreamed about their coming baby.
Would he have the Rostov profile? Would he have
Grace's pale-blond hair and blue eyes?

He threw the note across the room. It floated gently
to the floor. Not enough. Grabbing the lamp, he threw
it across the room, smashing it against the wall.

No baby.

She'd lied to him. She'd faked the pregnancy to
marry him for his…

Money?

His body snapped straight. Grace, after his money?

He recalled all the times he'd tried to help Grace with money. She'd refused. She'd fought everything—jewels, designer clothes, fancy cars, cash, everything. Beyond having food, clothes and a roof over their heads, Grace didn't give a damn about the so-called finer things in life. All the designer clothes and jewels she'd gotten since their marriage were still hanging neatly in her closet. His eyes fell upon the priceless tiara once owned by his great-aunt, the Grand Duchess.

Grace hadn't lied about the baby.

She was lying now.

He looked back at the note.

Please divorce me immediately and don't try to find me. I don't want any alimony. All I want is for you to be with the woman you love.

Francesca must have somehow convinced Grace that Maksim loved her.

And he'd helped her, he acknowledged to himself grimly. He thought of all the times he could have reassured Grace that he wanted both her and the child. The hours he could have spent with Grace, instead of deserting her in his palace. He'd claimed he wanted to protect his unborn son or daughter, and he'd forced Grace to be his wife, but he'd never acted like a decent husband or father.

He'd withheld the security and comfort and affection he could have given his lonely, pregnant wife.

Grace, on the other hand, wanted him to be happy—

even if that meant throwing him into the arms of another woman.

Shame raced through him, and this time he couldn't deny the emotion for what it was.

He didn't deserve Grace's love. He didn't deserve her. But…he *loved* her.

She was like no other woman he'd ever known. Her faith and honesty. Her willingness to sacrifice herself for others. *He loved her.* He loved her and he'd let his anger and hurt pride get in the way of his own happiness…and hers.

How could he have been such a blind, selfish fool?

Maksim had money, power, influence—everything he'd ever wanted when he'd been desperately poor as a child. But all his success had somehow become meaningless without her.

What use was it to be one of the wealthiest men in the world, if he didn't have the woman he loved?

CHAPTER TWELVE

GRACE rubbed the frost off the edges of the train window and looked out at Lake Baikal and the distant mountains. The endless white of the deepest lake in the world was an eerie expanse of snow. Hillocks of razor-sharp ice, ten feet tall, stabbed upward on the edges of the frozen lake.

How many days had she been on the train? Her journey from Moscow blended together in endless dark days and still darker nights. She looked numbly at the tiny village with a few wooden buildings scattered up the hillside. Grace couldn't read the Cyrillic letters on the sign to even know its name.

Siberia.

She'd hoped taking the Trans-Siberian Railway would raise her desolate spirits, as well as make sure that Maksim couldn't find her. He would check at the airport and possibly trains heading west into Europe. He wouldn't look here.

If he bothered to look for her at all.

Her body felt hot in the sweltering train car as she

leaned her forehead against the steamy, half-frosted window. But instead of enjoying her childhood dream, she couldn't stop agonizing about the man she'd left behind.

This train station was just a small platform covered with snow, on which three women wrapped in coats and hats were selling fish, homemade bread and fruit to train passengers. After so many days spent weeping in her packed third-class compartment, hanging out of the window and trying not to smell the stale smoke and sweat, Grace saw oranges and suddenly hungered for the sweet tangy fruit as fiercely and recklessly as Rapunzel's mother had once longed for rampion in the fairy tale.

Putting her thick coat over her old jeans and sweater, she crawled out of her upper berth and got off the train. She traded a few Russian coins to the old woman in furs, then snatched up the fruit. Grace barely managed to peel off half of the rind before she sank her mouth into the juicy fruit. Tears streamed down her face. It was delicious. It was heaven.

But by the next bite, the orange had suddenly lost its flavor. She stared out at the vast white emptiness of the snow-covered lake and craved something far more.

Her husband.

Her heart twisted in her chest every time she thought of how she'd left him. How she'd lied to him!

I was right to lie about the pregnancy, she told herself. *He doesn't really want to be a husband or a father. I can't keep him from the woman he loves. Not when I all I want is his happiness, and our child's…*

But at this moment she wanted Maksim so badly she

could hardly believe she'd had the strength of will to be so unselfish. She yearned for him. For his touch. For his smile. Even for his haughty glare. She would have taken any and all of it.

The night of the reception, she'd snuck out of the house and managed to sell her mother's wedding ring for the equivalent of a hundred dollars in a pawn shop near Yaroslavskiy Station in the center of the city.

Every day of her journey had been full of tears. She couldn't stop thinking about Maksim in love with another woman...thinking of the fact that she'd sold her mother's wedding ring...thinking of her own unborn child who would have no father.

The kindly Russian *provodnika* who was in charge of their train car had grown so concerned she'd started sneaking Grace dried fish and borscht from the first-class dining car. An invisible alliance of women who'd been hurt in love.

Grace wondered suddenly if everyone on earth was secretly hiding a broken heart.

She stared blindly across the white snowy expanse of Lake Baikal. In the distance she saw a black truck driving across the frozen lake toward her. The image blurred as her eyes filled with tears.

She hated what she'd done. How she'd lied to him.

It was the only way to set him free, she tried to tell herself. She wiped her tears with the back of a gloved hand. If Maksim knew their unborn child still lived, flourishing and growing every day inside her, he would have tracked her down to the ends of the earth. And she would not have been able to give him his freedom.

Now her own freedom stretched before her like a death sentence. In a few days, at the end of the tracks, she would reach Vladivostok. From there she'd get cheap passage across the Pacific. She would find some kind of job and raise her child in California's endless sunny days.

And yet the thought of that sunshine was more bleak to her than any rain.

As she took a deep shuddering breath, the black truck whirled to a stop on the other side of the platform in a scatter of snow and ice.

A dark figure come out of it, slamming the door with a hard bang.

He walked toward her, a dark prince coming from the white mist like a Gothic warlord with a long black coat, surrounded by snow and jagged sharp ice like ancient swords left by northern giants.

The orange dropped from her nerveless hands as he reached her.

"Maksim…?" she whispered.

Taking her in his arms, he kissed her fiercely.

"Grace, oh, Grace," he whispered. "Thank God. I was afraid I would never find you."

"But what are you doing here? In Siberia?" Still believing that she was dreaming, she reached up to touch his rough cheek. It was thick with bristle. She'd never seen him so unkempt. "You haven't shaved…"

"This train was my last hope. Oh God. I've barely slept for the last four days. Thank God I've found you." She thought she saw a suspicious glimmer in his eyes as he stroked her cheek. He lifted her chin. "Both of you."

She gasped. He knew she'd been lying!

She tried to open her mouth to lie to his beautiful, powerful face, but she couldn't do it. A sob rose to her lips.

"I'm…sorry," she cried, pressing her face against his chest.

"Sorry?" he said gently, rubbing her back. "Oh, *solnishka mayo*. I am the one who is sorry."

"I tried so hard to let you go," she sobbed. "I wanted you to be happy, and I've failed…."

"Failed?" He laughed softly, shaking his head. "Don't you think I know you by now? You have a heart as big as the world. I knew almost at once that you were trying to sacrifice your own happiness for mine."

"Just as you once sacrificed what you wanted most for my sake." Tears streamed down her face, wet tears that stung as they froze like hoarfrost against her skin. "But, Maksim, I want you to be with the woman you love—"

"I *am* with the woman I love," he said fiercely. He forced her to meet his eyes, and she couldn't look away from the intensity of his gaze, a whirling blend of black and white, of snow and hot steel. "It's you, Grace. Only you. The only woman I have ever loved. The only woman I will ever love."

"Me?" she whispered, hardly daring to believe she'd heard him right.

"My plane is waiting at a private airstrip across the lake." He put his arm over her shoulders. "Let us go home."

"Home." The thought tantalized her. She looked up at him. "Are you sure?"

"I wish to make one thing clear, *solnishka mayo*." Reaching for her hand, he pressed it against his rough cheek. "I didn't marry you just because you were pregnant. Even when I thought I hated you, part of me always knew you were the only one for me. Now I will be yours to the end. You are my princess. My wife." He put his hand on his heart. "I love you with all my heart, and I always will."

And to her incredulous wonder, he kissed her passionately on the train platform on the edge of the misty Siberian forest and endless white lake.

As if from a distance, she heard a burst of applause, then yells in Russian, Chinese and a few other languages she couldn't recognize. Blushing, Grace pulled away from Maksim to see people young and old hanging out of the sliding windows on the train, beaming down at the two lovers, clearly egging them on.

She saw the impish look on Maksim's face as he wrapped them both in his black coat.

"Today is January sixth," he whispered. "Do you know what day that is?"

She licked her lips. "Epiphany?"

"It's also Christmas Eve."

"Christmas Eve was weeks ago!"

"Russians celebrate Christmas on January seventh. One Christmas isn't enough for a winter as long as ours." He glanced back mischievously at the people cheering and hanging out of the train windows. "So let us give our audience one last gift for the season." He stroked her cold cheek, unfreezing her tears with the warmth of his breath. "Let's show them what love really means."

And this time, when he kissed her, it was so long and deep and true that she couldn't hear the applause or the whistle of the train. She couldn't hear anything but the pounding of her own heart roaring in her ears, in perfect rhythm with his.

A year later Grace crept down the holly-decked stairs in their Devonshire house, weighed down with Christmas stockings.

She heard a noise in the room below and froze. She knew her brothers were far too old to believe in Santa, but she had baby Sergey to think about now. Then she giggled at the thought that her four-month-old son might catch her. He was certainly the smartest, cleverest baby on earth, but that was pushing it a little too far, even for a proud mother.

Santa had already brought Grace everything she'd ever wanted.

She only had to look around this house. The country house had seemed so empty and wistful last year when she and Maksim had first conceived Sergey. But not anymore. She'd spent the last few months of her pregnancy consulting designers, buying furniture from all over the world, making it comfortable and bright. She'd done the same for their other homes in Moscow, London, Los Angeles, Cap Ferrat and Antigua, but this house was her favorite.

This house was their home.

She'd gone into labor three weeks early here, while finishing the baby's nursery. Sergey had been born at the hospital in a nearby village at a healthy seven pounds three ounces, and he'd been growing ever since. The baby was happy here and so were his parents. Grace could feel the house glowing with happiness, the wood of the banister warm beneath her touch as she came downstairs to the family room with the old fireplace and their Christmas tree.

She stopped when she saw her husband, still shirt-less as he'd slept and wearing only the bright red reindeer flannel pajama pants she'd bought him as a joke, walking their baby son back and forth in front of the shining lights of their twelve-foot Christmas tree.

"He's finally asleep," Maksim whispered, and kissed their baby son tenderly on top of his downy head. "I'll take him up to bed."

She nodded with a lump in her throat. As she watched her husband carry their slumbering baby up the stair-case, she wondered what she'd ever done to deserve such happiness. All her dreams had come true.

For her Christmas surprise, Maksim had flown her whole family here from California yesterday to share their baby's first Christmas.

"Oh, my dear," her mother had whispered to her last night, her eyes full of joyful tears as they shared their midnight cocoa, "you're really going to live happily ever after."

Now Grace hung the red stockings—stuffed full of candy, oranges and small gifts—on the marble mantel and stood back to see the effect. She nodded with satis-faction, then placed one last gift in her mother's stocking. Her father's wedding ring. Maksim had tracked it down for her in Moscow two weeks ago. Grace had cried with gratitude, kissing him again and again.

She glanced down at her left hand, which now shone

with a ten-carat diamond surrounded by sapphires, set in gold with a matching wedding band. Maksim had given it to her right after she'd kissed him. "To match your hair and eyes." He'd added with a wicked grin, "I know this time it's a gift you can't refuse."

And she hadn't refused. She couldn't. It fit perfectly with the wedding ring that meant everything to her, the one he'd bought her on Russia's Christmas day last year. She was so happy and proud to be his wife.

And she'd finally found the perfect gift to give him in return. The perfect Christmas present for the man who had everything.

Smiling through the tears, Grace gently placed the small gift in Maksim's stocking. It was a small framed picture of baby Sergey she'd taken last night, while Maksim was in the village doing last-minute Christmas shopping. In the photo, the baby was wearing a T-shirt she'd made herself, with words that read, "I'm going to be a big brother."

Looking at the stocking, picturing Maksim's reaction, she smiled, and tears welled up in her eyes. *Such a ninny I am,* she thought, wiping her eyes and laughing at herself. But was it possible to die of happiness?

Upstairs she could hear her younger brothers waking up. In a moment they would be racing downstairs to open their presents beneath the tree. Her mother would bustle around the enormous, refurbished kitchen, insisting on cooking brunch for them as the staff had the day off. Then she'd sit by the fire, knitting booties for the baby while studying books for next semester's classes.

And Grace could sit on her husband's lap and kiss

him when no one was looking. He would kiss her back, and they would wait with breathless anticipation for their private Christmas celebrations to come during the silent, sacred night.

With a grateful breath, Grace glanced outside through the tall windows at the wide expanse of white fields, the peaceful moment before the world woke. Outside, the first rays of pink dawn were streaking through black trees covered with snow.

It was the winter glow of her heart. Even in the stillness of winter they would forever have the warmth and light of home. And as she heard her husband's step on the stairs coming back to her, she knew the sunshine would always last.

THE SICILIAN'S CHRISTMAS BRIDE

SANDRA MARTON

CHAPTER ONE

THE HOTEL BALLROOM was a Christmas fairyland.

Evergreen garlands hung with silver and gold ornaments were draped across the ceiling; elegant white
faux Christmas trees sparkled with tiny gold lights.
Someone said there'd even be a visit from Santa at
midnight, tossing expensive baubles to the well-dressed
and incredibly moneyed crowd.

Nothing could ever compare with New York's first
charity ball of the holiday season.

Dante Russo had seen it all before. The truth was, it
bored the hell out of him. The crowds, the noise, the in-
your-face signs of power and wealth...

But then, for some reason everything bored him lately.

Even—perhaps especially—the high-octane excitement of his current mistress as she clung to his arm.

"Oh, DanteDarling," she kept saying, "oh, oh, oh,
isn't this fabulous?"

That was how she'd taken to addressing him, as if
his name and the supposed-endearment were one
word instead of two. And *fabulous* seemed to be her
favorite adjective tonight. So far, she'd used it to

describe the decorations, the band, their table and the guests.

A month ago, he'd found Charlotte's affectations amusing. Now, he found them almost as irritating as her breathless, little-girl voice.

Dante glanced at his watch. Another hour and he'd make his excuses about an early-morning meeting and leave. She'd protest: it would mean missing Santa's visit. But he'd assure her Santa would bring her something special tomorrow.

A little blue box from Tiffany, delivered to her apartment building not by Saint Nick but by FedEx.

He would see to it the box held something fabulous, Dante thought wryly. Something that would serve not only as a gift to make up for ending the night early but as a goodbye present.

His interest in Charlotte was at an end. He'd sensed it for days. Now, he knew it. He only hoped the breakup would be clean. He always made it clear he wasn't interested in forever, but some women refused to get the message, and—

"DanteDarling?"

He blinked. "Yes, Charlotte?"

"You're not listening!"

"I'm sorry. I, ah, I have a meeting in the morning and—"

"Dennis and Eve were telling everyone about their place in Colorado."

"Yes. Of course. Aspen, isn't it?"

"That's right," Eve said, and sighed wearily. "It's still gorgeous—"

"Fabulous," Charlotte said eagerly.

"But it's not what it used to be. So many people have discovered the town…"

Dante did his best to listen but his attention wandered again. What was the matter with him tonight? He didn't feel like himself at all. Bored or not, he knew better than to let his emotions gain control.

Giving free rein to your feelings was a mistake. It revealed too much, and revealing yourself to others was for fools.

That conviction, bred deep in his Sicilian bones by a childhood of poverty and neglect, had served him well. It had lifted him from the gutters of Palermo to the spires of Manhattan.

At thirty-two, Dante ruled an international empire, owned homes on two continents, owned a Mercedes and a private jet, and had his choice of spectacularly beautiful women.

His money had little to do with that.

He was, as more than one woman had whispered, beautiful. He was tall and leanly muscled, with the hard body of an athlete, the face of Michelangelo's David and the reputation of being as exciting in the bedroom as he was formidable in the boardroom.

In other words, Dante had everything a man could possibly want, including the knowledge that his life could very well have turned out differently. Being aware of that was part of who he was. It helped keep him alert.

Focused.

Everyone said that of him. That he was focused. Tightly so, not just on his business affairs or whatever woman held his interest at the moment but on whatever was happening around him.

Not tonight.

Tonight, he couldn't keep his attention on anything.

He'd already lost interest in the conversation of the others at the table. He took his cue from Charlotte, nodded, smiled, even laughed when it seemed appropriate.

It bothered him that he should be so distracted.

Except, that was the wrong word. What he felt was— What? Restless. As if something was about to happen. Something he wasn't prepared for, which was impossible.

He was always prepared.

Always, he thought… Except for that one time. That one time—

"DanteDarling, you aren't paying attention at all!"

Charlotte was leaning toward him, head tilted at just the right angle to make an offering of her décolletage. She was smiling, but the glint in her eye told him she wasn't happy.

"He's always like this," she said gaily, "when he's planning some devastating business coup." She gave a delicate shudder. "Whatever is it, DanteDarling? Something bloody and awful—and oh, so exciting?"

Everyone laughed politely. So did Dante, but he knew, in that instant, his decision to end things with Charlotte was the right one.

These past couple of weeks, while he'd grown bored she'd grown more demanding. Why hadn't he phoned? Where had he been when she called him? She'd begun using that foolish name for him and now she'd taken to dropping little remarks that made it seem as if she and he were intimate in all the ways he had made clear he never would be.

With any woman. Any woman, even—

"...would love to spend Christmas in Aspen, wouldn't we, DanteDarling?"

Dante forced a smile. "Sorry. I didn't get that."

"Dennis and Eve want us to fly to Aspen," Charlotte purred. "And I accepted."

Dante's eyes met hers. "Did you," he said softly.

"Of course! You know we're going to spend Christmas together. Why on earth would we want to be apart on such a special day?"

"Why, indeed," he said, after a long pause. Then he smiled and rose to his feet. "Would you like to dance, Charlotte?"

Something of what he was thinking must have shown in his face.

"Well—well, not just now. I mean, we should stay here and discuss the party. When to fly out, how long we'll stay—"

Dante took her hand, drew her from her chair and led her from the table. The band was playing a waltz as they stepped onto the dance floor.

"You're angry," she said, her voice affecting that little-girl whisper.

"I'm not angry."

"You are. But it's your own fault. Six weeks, Dante. Six weeks! It's time we took the next step."

"Toward what?" he said, his tone expressionless.

"You know what I mean. A woman expects—"

"You knew what *not* to expect, Charlotte." His mouth thinned; his voice turned cold. "And yet, here you are, making plans without consulting me. Talking as if our arrangement is something it is not." He danced her across the floor and into a corner. "You're right about one thing. It's time we, as you put it, took the next step."

"Are you breaking up with me?" When he didn't answer, two bright spots of color rose in her cheeks. "You bastard!"

"An accurate perception, but it changes nothing. You're a beautiful woman. A charming woman. And a bright one. You knew from the beginning how this would end."

His tone had softened. After all, he had only himself to blame. He should have read the signs, should have realized Charlotte had been making assumptions about the future despite his initial care in making sure she understood they had none. Women seemed to make the same mistake all the time.

Most women, he thought, and a muscle jumped in his cheek.

"I've enjoyed the time we've spent together," he said, forcing his attention back where it belonged.

Charlotte jerked free of his hand. "Don't patronize me!"

"No," he replied, his voice cooling, "certainly not. If you prefer to make a scene, rest assured that I can accommodate you."

Her eyes narrowed. He knew she was weighing her options. An embarrassing public display or a polite goodbye that would make it easy for her to concoct a story to soothe her pride.

"Your choice, *bella*," he said, more softly. "Do we part friends or enemies?"

She hesitated. Then a smile curved her lips. "You can't blame me for trying." Still smiling, she smoothed her palms over the lapels of his dinner jacket. It was a proprietorial gesture and he let her do it; he knew it was for those who might be taking in the entire performance. "But you're cruel, DanteDarling. Otherwise, you wouldn't humiliate me in front of my friends."

"Is that what concerns you?" Dante shrugged. "It's not a problem. We'll go back to our table and finish the evening pleasantly. All right?"

"Yes. That's fine. But Dante?" The tip of her tongue flickered across her lips. "Hear me out, would you?"

"What now?" he said, trying to mask his impatience.

"I know you don't believe in love and forever after, darling. Well, neither do I." She paused. "Still, we could have an interesting life together."

He stared at her in surprise. Was she suggesting marriage? He almost laughed. Still, he supposed he understood. He didn't know Charlotte's exact age but she had to be in her late twenties, old enough to want to find a husband who could support her fondness for expensive living.

As for him, men his age had families. Children to carry forward their names. He had to admit he thought about that from time to time, especially since he'd plucked the name "Russo" from a newspaper article.

Having a child to bear the name was surely a way to legitimatize it.

Charlotte could be the perfect wife. She would demand nothing but his superficial attention and tolerate his occasional affair; she would never interfere in his life. Never fill his head to the exclusion of everything else.

And, just that suddenly, Dante knew what was wrong with him tonight.

A woman had once filled his head to the exclusion of everything else. And, damn her, she was still doing it.

The realization shot through him. He felt his muscles tighten, as if all the adrenaline his body could produce was overwhelming his system.

"Oh, for heaven's sake," Charlotte said, "don't look at me that way! I was only joking."

He knew she hadn't been joking but he decided to go along with it because it gave him something to concentrate on as he walked her back to their table.

Eva greeted them with a coy smile. "Well," she said, "what have you decided? Will we see you in Aspen?"

For a second, he didn't know what she was talking about. His thoughts were sucking him into a place of dark, cold shadows and unwanted memories.

Memories of a woman he thought he'd forgotten.

Then he remembered the gist of the conversation and his promise to Charlotte.

"Sorry," he said politely, "but I'm afraid we can't make it."

Charlotte shot him a grateful look as she took her seat. He squeezed her shoulder.

"I'll be back in a few minutes."

"Going for a cigar?" Dennis said. "Russo? Wait. I'll join you."

But Dante was already making his way through the ballroom, deliberately losing himself in the crowd as he headed for one of the doors. He pushed it open, found himself in a narrow service hallway. A surprised waitress bumped into him, murmured an apology and tried to tell him he'd taken a wrong turn.

He almost told her she was right, except he'd taken that wrong turn three years ago.

He went through another door, then down a short corridor and ended up outside on a docking bay. Once he was sure he was alone, Dante threw back his head and dragged the cold night air deep into his lungs.

Dio, he had to be crazy.

All this time, and she was still there. Taylor Sommers, whom he had not seen in three years, was inside him tonight, probably had been for a very long time. How come he hadn't known it?

You didn't want to know it, a sly voice in his head told him.

A muscle knotted in his jaw.

No, he thought coldly, no. What was inside him was rage. It was one thing not to let your emotions rule you and another to suppress them, which was what he had done since she'd left him.

He'd kept his anger inside, as if doing so would rid him of it. Now, without warning, it had surfaced along with all the memories he'd carefully buried.

Not of Taylor. Not of what it had been like to be with her. Her whispers in bed.

Yes. Dante, yes. When you do that, when you do that…

He groaned at the memory. The need to be inside her had been like a drug. It had brought him close to believing in the ancient superstitions of his people that said a man could be possessed.

He was long past that, had been past it by the time she left him.

It was the rest, what had happened at the end, that

was still with him. Knowing that she believed she'd left him, when it wasn't true.

He had left her.

He'd never had the chance to say, "You made the first move, *cara,* but that's all it was. You ran away before I had a chance to end our affair."

She didn't know that and it drove him crazy. Pathetic, maybe, that it should matter…but it did. Obviously it did, or he wouldn't be standing out here in the cold, glaring at a stack of empty produce cartons and finally admitting that he'd been walking around in a state of smoldering fury since a night like this, precisely like this, late November, cold, snow already in the forecast, when Taylor had left a message on his answering machine.

"Dante," she'd said, "I'm afraid I'll have to cancel our date for tonight. I think I'm coming down with the flu. I'm going to take some aspirin and go to bed. Sorry to inconvenience you."

Sorry to inconvenience you.

For some reason, the oh-so-polite phrase had irritated him. Was *inconvenience* a word for a woman to use to her lover? And what was all that about canceling their date? She was his mistress. They didn't have "dates."

Jaw knotted, he'd reached for the phone to call and tell her that.

But he'd controlled his temper. Actually, there was nothing wrong in what she'd said. *Date* implied that they saw each other when it suited them. When it suited him.

So, why had it pissed him off? Her removed tone. Her impersonal words. And then another possibility had elbowed its way into his brain.

Maybe, he'd thought, *maybe I should call and see if she needs something. A doctor. Some cold tablets.*

Or maybe I should see if she just needs me.

The thought had stunned him. Need? It wasn't a word in his vocabulary. Nor in Taylor's. It was one of the things he admired about her.

So he'd put the phone aside and gone to the party. Not just any party. *This* party. The same charity, the same hotel, the same guests. He'd eaten what might have been the same overdone filet, sipped the same warm champagne, talked some business with the men at his table and danced with the women.

The women had all asked the same question.

"Where's Taylor?"

"She's not feeling well," he'd kept saying, even as it struck him that he was spending an inordinate amount of time explaining the absence of a woman who was not in any way a permanent part of his life. They'd only been together a couple of months.

Six months, he'd suddenly realized. Taylor had been his mistress for six months. How had that happened?

While he'd considered that, one of the women had touched his arm.

"Dante?"

"Yes?"

"If Taylor's ill, she needs to drink lots of liquids."

He'd blinked. Why tell him what his mistress needed to do?

"Water's good, but orange juice is better. Or ginger tea."

"That wonderful chicken soup at the Carnegie Deli,"

another woman said. "And does she have an inhalator? There's that all-night drugstore a few block away…"

Amazing, he'd thought. Everyone assumed that he and Taylor were living together.

They weren't.

"I prefer that you keep your apartment," he'd told her bluntly, at the start of their relationship.

"That's good," she'd said with a little smile, "because I intended to."

Had she told people something else? Had she deliberately made the relationship seem more than it was?

He'd thought back a few weeks to his birthday. He had no idea how she'd known it was his birthday; he'd never mentioned it. Why would he? And yet, when he'd arrived at her apartment to take her to dinner, she'd told him she wanted to stay in.

"I'm going to cook tonight," she'd said with a little smile. "For your birthday."

He made a habit of avoiding these things, a home-made dinner, a quiet evening, but he couldn't see a way to turn her down without seeming rude so he'd accepted her invitation.

To his amazement, he'd enjoyed the evening.

"Pasta Carbonara," she'd said, as she served the meal. "I remember you ordering it at Luigi's and saying how much you liked it." Her cheeks had pinkened. "I just hope my version is half as good."

It was better than good; it was perfect. So was everything else.

The candles. The bottle of his favorite Cabernet. The flowers.

And Taylor.

Taylor, watching him across the table, her green eyes soft with pleasure. Taylor, blushing again when he said the food was delicious. Taylor, bringing out a cake complete with candles. And a familiar blue box. He'd given boxes like that to more women than he could count, but being on the receiving end had been a first.

"I hope you like them," she'd said as he opened the box on a pair of gold cuff links, exactly the kind he'd have chosen for himself.

"Very much," he'd replied, and wondered what she'd say if he told her this was the first birthday cake, the first birthday gift anyone had ever given him in all his life.

He'd blown out the candles. Taken a bite of the cake. Put on the cuff links and felt something he couldn't define...

"Dante?" Taylor had said, her smooth brow furrowing, "what's the matter? If you don't like the cuff links—"

He'd silenced her in midsentence by gathering her in his arms, taking her mouth with his, carrying her to her bed and making love to her.

Sex with her was always incredible. That night...that night, it surpassed anything he'd ever known with her, with any woman. She was tender; she was passionate. She was wild and sweet and, as he threw back his head and emptied himself into her, she cried out his name and wept.

When it was over, she lay beneath him, trembling. Then she'd brought his mouth to hers for a long kiss.

"Don't leave me tonight," she'd whispered. "Dante. Please stay."

He'd never spent the entire night with her. With any woman. But he'd been tempted. Tempted to keep his arms around her warm body. To close her eyes with soft kisses. To fall asleep with her head on his shoulder and wake with her curled against him.

He hadn't, of course.

Spending the night in a woman's bed had shades of meaning beyond what he needed or expected from a relationship.

Two weeks after that, he'd attended this charity ball without her, listened to people urge him to feed his mistress chicken soup…

And everything had clicked into place.

The birthday supper. The fantastic night of sex. The plea that he not leave her afterward.

Taylor was playing him the way a fisherman who's hooked a big one plays a fish. His beautiful, clever mistress was doing her best to settle into his life. She knew it, his acquaintances knew it. The only person who'd been blind to the scheme was him.

"Excuse me," he'd suddenly said to everyone at the table, "but it's getting late."

"Don't forget the chicken soup," a woman called after him.

Dante had instructed his driver to take him to Taylor's apartment. It was time to set things straight. To make sure she still understood their agreement, that the rules hadn't changed simply because their affair had gone on so long.

In fact, perhaps it was time to end the relationship. Not tonight. Not abruptly. He'd simply see her less often. In a few weeks, he'd take her to L'Etoile for dinner, give her a bracelet or a pair of earrings to remember him by and tell her their time together had been fun but—

But Taylor didn't answer the door when he rang—which reminded him that she'd never given him a key. He hadn't given her one to his place, either, but that was different. He never gave his mistresses keys, but they were always eager to give theirs to him.

And it occurred to him again, as it often did, that Taylor wasn't really his mistress. She insisted on paying her own rent, even though most women gladly let him do it.

"I'm not most women," she'd said when he'd tried to insist, and he'd told himself that was good, that he admired her independence.

That night, however, he saw it for what it was. Just another way to heighten his interest, he'd thought coldly, as he rang the bell again.

Still no answer.

His thoughts turned even colder. Was she out with another man?

No. She was sick. He believed that; she'd sounded terrible on the phone when she'd called him earlier, her voice hoarse and raw.

Dante's heart had skittered. Was she lying unconscious behind the locked door? He took the stairs to the super's basement apartment at a gallop when the damned elevator refused to come, awakened the man and bought his cooperation with a fistful of bills.

Together, they'd gone up to Taylor's apartment. Unlocked the door…

And found the place empty.

His mistress was gone.

Her things were gone, too. All that remained was a trace of her scent in the air and a note, a *note,* goddamn her, on the coffee table.

"Thank you for everything," she had written, "it's been fun." Only that, as if their affair had been a game.

And Dante had swallowed the insult. What else could he have done? Hired a detective to find her? That would only have made his humiliation worse.

Three years. Three years, and now, without warning, it had all caught up to him. The embarrassment. The anger...

"Dante?"

He turned around. Charlotte had somehow managed to find him. She stood on the loading dock, wrapped in a velvet cloak he'd bought her, her face pink with anger.

"Here you are," she said sharply.

"Charlotte. My apologies. I, ah, I came out for a breath of air—"

"You said you wouldn't embarrass me."

"Yes. I know. And I won't. I told you, I only stepped outside—"

"You've been gone almost an hour! How dare you make me look foolish to my friends?" Her voice rose. "Who do you think you are?"

Dante's eyes narrowed. He moved toward her, and something dangerous must have shown in his face because she took a quick step back.

"I know exactly who I am," he said softly. "I am Dante Russo, and whoever deals with me should never forget it."

"Dante. I only meant—"

He took her arm, quick-marched her down a set of concrete steps and away from the dock. An alley led to the street where he hailed a cab, handed the driver a hundred-dollar bill and told him Charlotte's address.

He'd left his topcoat inside the hotel but he didn't give a damn. Coats were easy to replace. Pride wasn't.

"Dante," she stammered, "really, I'm sorry—"

So was he, but not for what had just happened. He was sorry he had lived a lie for the past three years.

Taylor Sommers had made a fool of him. Nobody, *nobody* got away with that.

He took his cell phone from his pocket and called his driver. When his Mercedes pulled to the curb, Dante got in the back and pressed another number on the phone. It was late, but his personal attorney answered on the first ring.

He didn't waste time on preliminaries. "I need a private investigator," he said. "No, not first thing Monday. Tomorrow. Have him call me at home."

Three years had gone by. So what? Someone had once said that revenge was a dish best served cold.

A tight smile curved Dante's hard mouth.

He couldn't have agreed more.

It was a long weekend.

Charlotte left endless messages on his voice mail. They ranged from weepy to demanding, and he erased them all.

Saturday morning, he heard from the detective his attorney had contacted. The man asked for everything Dante knew about Taylor.

"Her name," he said, "is Taylor Sommers. She lived in the Stanhope, on Gramercy Park. She's an interior decorator."

There was a silence.

"And?" the man said.

"And what? Isn't that enough?"

"Well, I could use the names of her parents. Her friends. Date of birth. Where she grew up. What schools she attended."

"I've told you everything I know," Dante said coldly.

He hung up the phone, then walked through his bedroom and onto the wraparound terrace that surrounded his Central Park West penthouse. It was cold; the wind had a way of whipping around the building at this height. And it had snowed overnight, not heavily, just enough to turn the park a pristine white.

Dante frowned.

The detective had seemed surprised he knew so little about Taylor, but why would he have known more? She pleased his eye; she was passionate and intelligent.

What more would a man want from a woman?

There had been moments, though. Like the time he'd brought her here for a late supper. It had snowed that night, too. He'd excused himself, gone to make a brief but necessary phone call. When he came back, he'd found the terrace door open and Taylor standing out here, just as he was now.

She'd been wearing a silk dress, a little slip of a thing. He'd taken off his jacket, stepped outside and put it around her shoulders.

"What are you doing, *cara?* It's much too cold for you out here."

"I know," she'd answered, snuggling into his jacket and into the curve of his arm, "but it's so beautiful, Dante." She'd turned her face up to his and smiled. "I love nights like this, don't you?"

Cold nights reminded him of the frigid winters in

Palermo, the way he'd padded his shoes with newspaper in a useless attempt to keep warm.

For some reason he still couldn't comprehend, he'd almost told her that.

Of course, he had not done anything so foolish. Instead, he'd kissed her.

"If you can get over your penchant for cold and snow," he'd said, with a little smile, "we can fly to the Caribbean some weekend and you can help me house-hunt. I've been thinking about buying a place in the islands."

Her smile had been soft. "I'd like that," she'd said. "I'd like it very, very much."

Instantly, he'd realized what a mistake he'd made. He'd asked her to take a step into his life and he'd never meant to do that.

He'd never mentioned the Caribbean again. Not that it mattered, because two weeks later, she'd walked out on him.

Walked out, he thought now, his jaw tightening. Left him to come up with excuses explaining her absence at all those endless Christmas charitable events he was expected to attend.

But he'd solved that problem simply enough.

He'd found replacements for her. He'd gone through that season with an endless array of beautiful women on his arm.

On his arm, but not in his bed. It had been a long time until he'd had sex after Taylor, and even then, it hadn't been the same.

The truth was, it still wasn't. Something was lacking.

Not for his lovers. He knew damned well how to make a woman cry out with pleasure but he felt—what was the word? Removed. That was it. His body went through all the motions, but when it was over, he felt unsatisfied.

Taylor was to blame for that.

What in hell had possessed him, to let her walk away? To let her think she'd ended their affair when she hadn't? A man's ego could take just so much.

By Monday, his anger was at the boiling point. When the private investigator turned up at his office, he greeted him with barely concealed impatience.

"Well? Surely you've located Ms. Sommers. How difficult can it be to find a woman in this city?"

The man scratched his ear, took a notepad from his pocket and thumbed it open.

"See, that was the problem, Mr. Russo. The lady isn't in this city. She's in…" He frowned. "Shelby, Vermont."

Dante stared at him. "Vermont?"

"Yeah. Little town, maybe fifty miles from Burlington."

Taylor, in a New England village? Dante almost laughed trying to picture his sophisticated former lover in such a setting.

"The lady has an interior decorating business." The P.I. turned the page. "And she's done okay. In fact, she just applied for an expansion loan at—"

The P.I. rattled on but Dante was only half listening. He knew where to find Taylor. Everything else was superfluous.

How surprised she'd be, he thought with grim satisfaction, to see him again. To hear him tell her that she hadn't needed to leave him, that he'd been leaving her—

"…just for the two of them. I have the details, if you—"

Dante's head came up. "Just for the two of what?" he said carefully.

"Of them," the P.I. said, raising an eyebrow. "You know, what I was saying about the house she inherited. A couple of realtors suggested she might want something newer and larger but she said no, she wanted a small house in a quiet setting, just big enough for two. For her and, uh… I got the name right here, if you just give me a—"

"A house for two people?" Dante said, in a tone opponents had learned to fear.

"That's right. Her and—here it is. Sam Gardner."

"Taylor." Dante cleared his throat. "And Sam Gardner. They live together?"

"Well, sure."

"And Gardner was with her when she moved in?"

The P.I. chuckled. "Yessir. I mean—"

"I know exactly what you mean," Dante said without inflection. "Thank you. You've been most helpful."

"Yeah, but, Mr. Russo—"

"Most helpful," Dante repeated.

The detective got the message.

Alone, Dante told himself he'd accomplish nothing unless he stayed calm, but a knot of red-hot rage was already blooming in his gut. Taylor hadn't left him because she'd grown bored. She'd left him for another man. She'd been seeing someone, making love with someone, while she'd been with him.

He went to the window and clasped the edge of the sill, hands tightening on the marble the way they wanted to tighten on her throat. Confronting her wouldn't be enough. Beating the crap out of her lover wouldn't be enough, either, although it would damned well help.

He wanted more. Wanted the kind of revenge that her infidelity merited. How dare she make a fool of him? How dare she?

There had to be a way. A plan.

Suddenly, he recalled the P.I.'s words. *She's done well. In fact, she's just applied for an expansion loan at the local bank.*

Dante smiled. There was. And he could hardly wait to put it into motion.

CHAPTER TWO

TAYLOR SOMMERS POURED a cup of coffee, put it on the sink, opened the refrigerator to get the cream and realized she'd already put it on the table, right alongside the cup she'd already filled with coffee only minutes before.

She took a steadying breath.

"Keep it up," she said, her voice loud in the silence, "and Walter Dennison's going to tell you he was only joking when he said he'd change those loan payments."

Dennison was a nice man; he'd been a friend of her grandmother's. He'd shown compassion and small-town courtesy when Tally fell behind on repaying the home equity loan his bank had granted her.

But he wasn't a fool and only a fool would go on doing that for a woman who behaved as if she were coming apart.

Was that why he wanted to see her today? Had he changed his mind? If he had, if he wanted her to pay the amount the loan called for each month…

Tally closed her eyes.

She'd be finished. The town had already shut down

the interior decorating business she'd been running from home. Without the loan, she'd lose the shop she'd rented on the village green even before it opened because, to put it simply, she was broke.

Flat broke.

Okay, if you wanted absolute accuracy, she had two hundred dollars in her bank account, but it was a drop in the bucket compared to what she needed.

She'd long ago used up her savings. Moving to Vermont, paying for repairs to make livable the old house she'd inherited from her grandmother, just day-to-day expenses for Sam and her had taken a huge chunk of her savings.

Start-up costs for INTERIORS BY TAYLOR had swallowed the rest. Beginning a decorating business, even from home, was expensive. You had to have at least a small showroom—in her case, what had once been an enclosed porch on the back of the house—so that potential clients could get a feel for your work. Paint, fabric, wicker furniture to make the porch inviting had cost a bundle.

Then there were the fabric samples, decorative items like vases and lamps, handmade candles and fireplace accessories… Expensive, all of them. Some catalogs alone could be incredibly pricey. Advertising costs were astronomical but if you didn't reach the right people, all your other efforts were pointless.

Little by little, INTERIORS BY TAYLOR had begun to draw clients from the upscale ski communities within miles of tiny Shelby. Taylor's accounts had still been in the red, but things had definitely been looking up.

And then the town clerk phoned. He was apologetic, but that didn't make his message any less harsh.

INTERIORS BY TAYLOR was operating illegally. The town had an ordinance against home-based businesses.

That Shelby, Vermont, population 8500 on a good day, had ordinances at all had been a surprise. But it did, and this one was inviolate. You couldn't operate a business from your house even if you'd been raised under its roof after your mother took off for parts unknown.

Tally's pleading had gained her a two-month reprieve. She'd found a soon-to-be-vacant shop on the village green. Each night, long after Sam was asleep, she'd worked and reworked the costs she'd face. The monthly rent. The three-months up-front deposit. The fees for the carpenter, painter and electrician needed to turn the place from the TV-repair shop it had been into an elegant setting for her designs.

And then there were all the things she'd have to buy to create the right atmosphere. Add in the cost of increased advertising and Tally had arrived at a number that was staggering.

She needed $175,000.00.

The next morning, she'd kissed Sam goodbye, put on a white silk blouse and a black suit she hadn't worn since New York. She'd pulled her blond hair into a knot at the base of her neck and gone to see Walter Dennison, who owned Shelby's one and only bank.

Dennison read through the proposal she'd written, looked up and frowned.

"You're asking for a lot of money."

"I know."

"Asking for it in a home equity loan."

"Yes, sir."

"You understand what would happen if you were unable to pay the loan off, Ms. Sommers? That the bank would have the right to foreclose on your house?"

Taylor had nodded. "Yes, sir," she'd said again. "I do."

Dennison had looked at her for a long moment. Then he'd smiled. "You've got your grandmother's gumption, Tally," he'd said, and held out his hand.

The loan was hers.

She'd made the first payment…but not the second. Or the third. The contractors demanded their money according to the schedules she'd agreed to. Things couldn't get worse, she'd thought…

And the furnace in the house went belly-up.

Pride in tatters, Taylor had gone to Dennison again. If he could see his way clear to lower the monthly payments…

He'd sighed and run his fingers through his thinning hair. In the end he'd done it.

Which brought her back to today's phone call. It had come while she and Sam were having breakfast.

"I need to see you, Ms. Sommers," Dennison had said. "Today."

She'd almost stopped breathing. "Is it about my loan?"

There'd been a little pause. Then Dennison had said yes, it was, and she was to come to his office at four.

"Four," he'd repeated, "promptly, please."

The admonition had surprised her. So had the change from Tally to Ms. Sommers. She'd told herself it wasn't a bad sign. A man who wanted to discuss a six-figure loan was entitled to be a little formal, even if he'd known you since you were a baby.

"Of course," she'd said, all cool New York sophistication. Then she'd hung up the phone and tried to smile at Sam, whose eyes were filled with questions.

"Nothing to worry about, babe," Tally had said airily.

Sam had grinned a Sam-grin, at least until she said she might not be home until suppertime.

"You can visit the Millers," she'd said reassuringly. "You know how much you like them."

She'd smoothed things over by promising they'd have the entire weekend together, doing what Sam liked most: snuggling with her on the sofa, watching videos and eating popcorn.

Dante Russo had probably never watched a video or eaten popcorn in his life…

And what was that man doing in her head again?

Who gave a damn what Dante Russo did or didn't do? He was history. Besides, he'd never meant anything more to her than what she'd meant to him. New York was filled with relationships like theirs. Two consenting adults going out together, being seen together…

Having sex together.

Tally's eyes closed. Memories rushed in. Scents. Tastes. Sensations. Dante's hands, deliciously rough on her skin. His mouth, demanding surrender as he kissed her. His face above her, his silver eyes dark as storm clouds, his sensual lips drawn back with passion…

She swung toward the sink, dumped her coffee and rinsed out the cup.

What stupid thoughts to have today of all days, when she had to be at her best. Still, she understood why she would think of Dante.

Her mouth curved in a bitter smile.

This was an anniversary of sorts. She'd left Dante

Russo a few weeks before Christmas, three years ago. All it took was the scent of pine and the sound of carols to bring the memories rushing back.

She wouldn't let that happen. Dante had no place in the new life she'd built for herself. For herself and Sam.

He was nothing to her anymore.

Or to Sam.

Sam didn't know Dante existed. And Dante certainly didn't know about Sam. He never would, either. She would see to that.

Tally knew her former lover well.

Dante hadn't wanted her and surely wouldn't have understood why she wanted Sam… But that didn't mean he'd simply let her have Sam, if he knew.

Her former lover could be charming but underneath he was cold, determined and ruthless. She refused to think about how he might react if he knew everything.

Tally sighed and turned on the kitchen lights. Night had fallen; it came early to these northern latitudes. The coming storm the weatherman had predicted rattled the old windows.

She'd fled New York on a night like this. Cold, dark, with snow in the forecast.

What a wreck she'd been that night! Pretending to be sick, then packing her clothes and scribbling that final note. All she'd been able to think about was getting away before Dante showed up.

She wasn't stupid. She'd known he hadn't wanted her anymore. He'd been removed and distant for a while and sometimes she'd caught him watching her with a look on his face that made her want to weep.

He was bored with her. And getting ready to end

their affair, but she wouldn't let that happen. She'd end it first. It would be quicker, less humiliating…

And safer, because by then she had a secret she'd never have been foolish enough to share with him.

So she'd made plans to leave him. And she'd done it so he wouldn't be able to find her, even if he looked for her. Not that she thought he would. Why would a man go after a woman when she'd saved him the trouble of getting rid of her?

Even if he had, maybe out of all that macho Sicilian arrogance made all the more potent by his power, his wealth, his gorgeous face and body—even if he had, he'd never have found her. He'd never dream she'd flee to a tiny village in New England. He knew nothing about her. In their six months together, he'd never asked her questions about herself.

Not real ones.

Would you prefer Chez Nicole or L'Etoile for dinner? he'd ask. *Shall I get tickets for the ballet or the symphony?*

Things a man would ask any woman. Never anything more important.

Well, yes. He'd asked her other things. Whispered them, in that husky voice that was a turn-on all by itself.

Do you like it when I touch you this way? And if what he was doing seemed too much, if it made her tremble in his arms, he'd kiss her deeply and say, *Don't stop me, bellissima. Let me. Yes. Let me do this. Yes. Like that. Just like that…*

She was trembling even now, just remembering those moments.

"You're a fool," Tally said, her voice sharp in the silence of the kitchen.

Sex with Dante had been incredible, but sex was all it was, even though lying beneath him, feeling the power of his penetration, his possession, sometimes made her want to weep with joy. But it didn't make up for the fact that he'd never once spent the entire night in her bed or asked her to come to his.

Stay with me, she'd wanted to say, oh, so many times. But she hadn't. Only the once, when the words had slipped out before she could stop them...

Only the once, when she'd forgotten that all her lover wanted was her body, not her heart.

Tally turned her back to the window.

So what?

Why would she have wanted a man to tie her down, give her a baby and then turn his ever-wandering eyes elsewhere as her father had done, as a man like Dante Russo would surely do?

It was the meeting with Walter Dennison that had her feeling so strange, that was all. Once she put that behind her, she'd be fine.

And it was time to get moving. *Be here at four, Ms. Sommers, and please be prompt.*

She smiled as put on her coat and grabbed her car keys. All those years in New York had made her forget how pedantic a true Yankee could be.

AS USUAL, the weatherman had it wrong. Snow was already falling as if someone were shaking a featherbed over the town.

The snow dusting the woods and fields with a blanket of white as Tally drove past would have made a beautiful Christmas card. In the real world, it made for a dangerous drive. The narrow road that led into the heart of town already wore a thin coating of black ice, and the new snow hid stretches of asphalt as slick as glass.

Her old station wagon needed better snow tires. The rear end slewed sickeningly as she turned onto Main Street and her stomach skidded with it, but there were no other vehicles on the road and she came through the turn without harm to anything but her nerves.

Only two cars were parked in the bank's lot, the aged maroon Lincoln she recognized as Dennison's and a big, shiny black SUV that looked as if it could climb Everest in a blizzard and come through laughing.

Dennison would have sent his employees home early because of the storm. The SUV probably belonged to some tourist on his way to ski country who'd stopped to use the ATM.

Tally parked and got out of the station wagon. The double doors to the bank opened as she reached them, revealing Walter Dennison wearing a black topcoat over his usual gray suit.

"You're late, Ms. Sommers."

He whispered the words. And shot a quick look over his shoulder. Tally felt a stab of panic. The black car. The paleness of Dennison's face. His whisper.

Was the bank being held up?

"I'm sorry," she said, trying to peer past him, "but the roads—"

"I understand." He hesitated. "Ms. Sommers. Tally. There's something you need to know."

Oh, God. It was true. She'd walked into a holdup in progress—

"I sold the bank."

She stared at him blankly. "What?"

"I said, I sold the bank."

He might as well have been speaking another language. Sold the bank? How could he have done that? The Dennison family had started the Shelby Bank in the early 1800s.

"I don't understand, Mr. Dennison. Why would you—"

"It's nothing for the town to worry about. The new owner will keep everything just as it is." Dennison cleared his throat. "Almost everything."

His eyes shifted from hers, and Tally's stomach dropped. There could only be one reason he'd wanted to see her.

"What about the new payment arrangements on my loan?"

She saw Dennison's adam's apple move up, then down. He opened his mouth as if he were going to speak. Instead, he shouldered past her, turned up his collar and went out into the storm. Tally stared after him as his lean figure was lost in a swirling maelstrom of white.

"Mr. Dennison! Wait!" Her voice rose. "Will this affect my loan? You said the new owner will keep everything just as it is—"

"Not quite everything," a familiar voice said.

And even as her heart pounded, as she swung toward the open bank doors and told herself it couldn't be true, she knew what she would see.

That voice could belong to only one man.

DANTE SMILED when Taylor turned toward him.

Her face was white with shock.

Excellent. He'd wanted her stunned by the sight of

him. Things were going precisely as he'd intended, despite how quickly he'd had to work. He'd put his plan in motion in less than a week, first convincing the old man to sell and then getting the authorities to approve the sale, but he was Dante Russo.

People always deferred to him.

This morning, he'd phoned Dennison and told him he'd be there at three. Told him, as well, to notify Taylor to be at the bank at four.

Promptly at four.

And, of course, not to mention anything about the bank's new ownership.

Dante's lips curved in a tight smile. He'd figured Taylor would be on edge to start with. A woman who'd put up her home as equity for a loan of $175,000.00 she couldn't pay would not be at ease. Add in Dennison's refusal to explain the reason for the meeting and the warning to be prompt, her nerves would be stretched to the breaking point.

His smile faded. The only thing that would have made this more interesting was if Samuel Gardner was with her, but from the investigator's comments, he'd gathered that his former mistress's new lover didn't stand up to life's tougher moments.

"Why didn't Sam Gardner sign for the loan?" he'd asked Dennison.

The old man had looked at him as if he were insane.

"Buying a bank on a seeming whim, suggesting something anyone in town would know is impossible… You have a strange sense of humor, Mr. Russo," he'd said with a thin-lipped Yankee smile.

Dante stood away from the door.

Dennison was wrong. There was nothing the least bit humorous about this situation. It was payback, pure and simple.

And it was time Taylor knew it.

"Aren't you going to come inside and face me, *cara?*" he said, his tone deliberately soft and coaxing. "Perhaps not. Facing me is not your forte, is it?"

He saw her stiffen. She probably wanted to run, but she didn't. Instead, she raised her chin, squared her shoulders and stepped inside the bank. He had to admire her courage, the way she was girding herself for confrontation.

She had no way of knowing that nothing she could do would be enough. The news he was going to give her was bad, and it delighted him to do it.

"Hello, Dante."

Her voice trembled. Her face had taken on some color, though it was still pale. Three years. Three years since he'd seen her…

And she was still beautiful.

More beautiful than his memory of her, if that were possible. Was it time that had made her mouth seem even softer, her eyes wider and darker?

Still, time had not been completely kind. It had affected her in other ways.

Purple shadows lay beneath her eyes. Her hair was pulled back in an unbecoming knot and he had the indefensible urge to close the distance between them, take out the pins and let all those lustrous cinnamon strands tumble free.

He let his gaze move over her slowly, from her face all the way to her feet and back again. A frown creased his forehead. He'd never seen her in anything but elegantly tailored clothing. Designer suits and gowns, spiked heels that could give a man dangerous fantasies, her face perfectly made up, her hair impeccably cut and styled.

Things were different now. The lapels of her coat were frayed. Her boots were the no-nonsense kind meant for rough weather. Her hair was in that ridiculous knot and her face was bare of everything but lipstick—lipstick and the shadows of exhaustion under her eyes.

He spoke without thinking. "What's happened to you?" he said sharply. "Have you been ill?"

"How nice of you to ask."

She was still pale but her gaze was steady and her words were brittle with sarcasm. He moved quickly; before she could step back he was a breath away, his hand wrapped around her arm.

"I asked you a question. Answer it."

A flush rose in her cheeks. "I'm not ill. I'm simply living in the real world. It's a place where people work hard for what they have. Where you can't just snap your fingers and expect everyone to leap to do your bidding, but then, what would you know of such things?"

What, indeed? It was none of her business, of anyone's business, that he'd started his life scrounging for money, that he'd worked his hands raw in construction jobs when he came to the States, or that he could still remember what it was like to go to sleep hungry.

He'd never snapped his fingers and never would, but he'd be damned if he'd explain that to anyone.

"And your lover? He permits this?"

She looked at him as if he'd lost his mind. "My what?"

"Another question you don't want to answer. That's all right. I have plenty of time."

Tally wrenched free of his grasp. "I'm the one with questions, Dante. What are you doing here?"

"We haven't seen each other in a long time, *cara*." A slow smile that turned her blood to ice eased across his lips. "Surely, we have other things to talk about first."

"We have nothing to talk about."

"But we do. You know that."

She didn't know anything. That was the problem. What did he know? Did he know about Sam? She didn't think so. Surely, he'd have tossed that at her already, if he did.

Then, what did he want? He wasn't here for a visit. He hadn't bought the Shelby bank on a whim…

The loan. Her loan. Oh God, oh God…

"Ah," he said slyly, "your face is an open book. Have you thought of some things we might wish to discuss?"

She couldn't let him see her fear. There had to be some way she could gain the upper hand.

"What I know," Tally said, "is that we never talked in the past. We went to dinner, to parties…" She took a steadying breath. "And we went to bed."

His mouth twisted. Had she struck a nerve?

"I'm glad you remember that."

"Is that why you came here, Dante? To remind me that we used to have sex together? Or to ask why I left you?" Somehow, she managed a chilly smile. "Really, I thought you'd understand. My note—"

"Your note was a bad joke."

Tally shrugged her shoulders. "It was honest. Or did it never occur to you that a woman is no different from a man? I mean, yes, we can pretend in ways a man can't, but sooner or later, things grow, well, old."

Dante's face contorted with anger. "You're a liar!"

"Come on, admit it. We'd been together for months. It was fun for a long time but then—"

She gasped as he caught hold of her and encircled her throat with his hand.

"I remember how you were in bed," he said, his voice a low growl. "Are you telling me it was all a performance?"

He tugged her closer, until her body brushed his and she had to tilt back her head to look into his eyes. It was deliberate, damn him, a way of emphasizing his strength, his size, his domination.

God, how she hated him! Three years, three endless years, and he was still furious because she'd walked out on him, but she'd done what she had to do to survive. To protect her secret from his unpredictable Sicilian ego.

"You were fire in my arms." His eyes, the color of smoke, locked on hers. She tried to look away but his hand was like a collar around her throat. When he urged her chin up, she had no choice but to meet his gaze. "You cried out as I came inside you. Your womb contracted around me. Would you have me believe you faked that, too?"

"Is it impossible for you to be a gentleman?" Tally said, hating herself for the way her voice shook.

His smile was slow and sexy and so dangerous it made her heartbeat quicken.

"But I was a gentleman with you. Was that a mistake? Perhaps you didn't want a gentleman in your bed." She gasped as he forced her head back. "Is that why you ran away in the middle of the night?"

"I left you, period. Don't make it sound so dramatic."

"Left me for what, exactly? The glory of an existence in the middle of nowhere? A bank account with nothing in it?" His tone turned silken. "I think not, *cara*. I think you left me for a new lover who isn't a gentleman at all."

"I don't know what you're talking about!"

He thrust his fingers into her hair. The pins that held it confined clattered sharply against the marble floor as the strands of gold-burnished cinnamon came loose and fell over her shoulders.

"Is that it? Was I too gentle with you?" He wound her hair around his fist and lowered his head until his face was an inch from hers. "Had you hoped I would do things to you, demand things of you, that people only whisper about?"

"Dante. This is— It's crazy. I don't— I didn't…" She swallowed dryly. "Let me go."

She'd meant the words to be a command. Instead, they were a whisper. He smiled with amusement, and she felt an electric jolt in her blood.

"I said, let go… Or did you come here thinking you could bully me back into your arms?"

His eyes grew dark; she saw his mouth twist. The seconds ticked away and then, when her heart seemed ready to leap from her breast, he thrust her from him, stepped back and folded his arms.

"Never that," he said coolly. "And you're right. Things were over between us. I knew it. In fact, that was the reason I went to see you that night. I wanted to tell you we were finished." He gave a quick smile. "As you say, *cara,* things get old."

She'd known the truth but hearing it made it worse.

Still, she showed no reaction. He wanted her to squirm, and she'd be damned if she would.

"Is that what this is about? That the great Dante Russo wants to be sure I understand I made the first move only because your timing was off?"

Dante chuckled. "Bright as always, Taylor—though you surely don't believe I bought this bank and made this trip only so I could tell you it was pure luck you ended our affair before I did."

Tally moistened her lips with the tip of her tongue. She was dying inside, but she'd be damned if she'd let him know it.

"No. I'm not that naive. You bought the bank because—" Desperately, she ran through the terms of the loan in her mind. Could he do that? Could he cancel what Dennison had already approved? "Because you think you can cancel my loan."

"Think?" he said, very softly. "You underestimate me. I can do whatever I wish, but canceling a loan that already exists would take more time and effort than it's worth." He smiled. "So I'm going to do the next best thing. I'm reinstating the original repayment terms."

Her gaze flew to his. "Reinstating them?" she said stupidly. "I don't understand."

"It's simple, *cara*," he said, almost gently. "As of now, you will pay the amount you are supposed to pay each month."

Tally thought of the four-figure number the loan called for. She was paying a quarter of that amount now, and barely managing it.

"That's—it's out of the question. I can't possibly—"

"Additionally, you will pay the amount that's in arrears." He took a slip of paper from his pocket and held it out toward her. His lips curved. "Plus interest, of course."

Tally looked at the number on the paper and laughed. It was either that or weep.

"I don't have that kind of money!"

"Ah." Dante sighed. "I thought not. In that case, you leave me no choice but to start foreclosure proceedings against your home."

She felt the blood drain from her face. "Foreclosure proceedings?"

"This was a home equity loan. You put up your house as collateral." Another quick, icy smile. "If you don't understand what that means, perhaps your lover can explain it to you."

"Are you crazy?" Tally's voice rose. "You can't do this! You can't take my house. You can't!" Her hands came up like a fighter's, fists at the ready as if she would beat him into understanding the horror of his plan. "Damn you, there are rules!"

"You've forgotten what you know about me," Dante said coldly. "I make my own rules."

He proved it by gathering her into his arms and kissing her.

CHAPTER THREE

HE WAS KISSING HER, Dante told himself, because she'd lied to him a few minutes ago.

Why else would he want her in his arms, except to make her confess to the lie?

Taylor had never faked her responses in bed, and he'd be damned if he'd let her pretend she had.

He was over her, but she knew just the right buttons to push. Well, so did he. He'd kiss her until she melted against him the way she used to and then he'd step back and say, *You see, Taylor? That's the price liars pay.*

Which was why he was kissing her.

Or trying to.

The problem was that he had cornered a wildcat. She fought back, twisted her head to the side to avoid his mouth and pummeled his shoulders with her fists.

When none of that worked, she sank her teeth in his ear lobe so hard he hissed with pain.

"Damn you, woman!"

"Let go of me, you—you—"

Her fist flew by his jaw. Grimly, Dante snared both her hands in one of his and pinned them to his chest. Her knee came up but he felt it happening and yanked her hard against him to immobilize her. She was helpless now, pinned between him and the wall beside the double doors.

"Take your hands off me, Russo! If you don't, so help me—"

"So help you, what? What will you do? How will you stop me from proving what a little liar you are?"

"I don't know what you're talking about. I am not a—"

He bent his head and captured her mouth with his. She nipped his lip, her teeth sharp as a cat's. He tasted blood but if she thought that would stop him, she didn't know him very well.

He would win this battle.

He had the right to know why she'd lied about what she'd felt when he made love to her. And to know why she'd left him.

He wanted answers and, damn it, he was going to get them.

He caught her face in his hands. Kissed her again, angling his mouth over hers, penetrating her with his tongue. He remembered how she'd loved it when he kissed her this way. Deep. Wet. Hot. He'd loved kisses like this, too...

He still did.

Dio, the feel of her in his arms. Her breasts, soft against his chest. Her hips, cradling his erection.

He wanted her, and it had nothing to do with anger.

It was the feel of her. The taste. The scent of her skin. He remembered all of it, everything making love to her had done to them both, and his kiss gentled, his touch turned from demand to caress, and a little sigh whispered from her lips to his.

She was trembling, but not with fear.

It was with desire. For this. For him.

Something began to unlock inside him. Something so primitive he couldn't put a name to it. He only knew that the woman in his arms still belonged to him.

He swept his hands into her hair. All that lush, cinnamon-hued silk tumbled over his fingers.

"Tell me you want me," he said, his voice rough and thick.

She shook her head in denial. "No," she whispered.

But her eyes were pools of darkness as she looked up at him, as her hands spread over his chest.

"I don't," she said, "I don't…"

He took her mouth again and suddenly she gave the wild little cry he had heard her make a thousand times in the past. It excited him as much now as it had then, and when she rose on her toes and wound her arms around his neck, whispered "Dante," as if he were the only man in the world who could ever make her feel this way, he went crazy with desire.

It had been so long. Oh, so long since he'd possessed her. He was on fire…and so was she.

Saying her name, blind to everything but passion, Dante fumbled with the buttons of her coat. When they didn't come undone quickly enough, he cursed and tore the coat open.

He had to cup her breasts or he would die. Had to thrust his knee between her thighs and hear her cry out again as she moved against him. Had to shove up her skirt, slip his hand between her thighs and, yes oh yes, feel her heat, yes, feel the wetness of her desire, yes, yes…

Her head fell back like a flower on a wind-bent stalk.

She whispered his name over and over, knotted her fingers in his hair as she lifted herself to him.

Blindly, he lifted her off her feet. Spread her thighs. Reached for his zipper. Now. Right now. He would be inside her. Lost in her silken folds…

"Mr. Dennison? I didn't finish cleanin' but considerin' the storm's turnin' into a blizzard, an'… Whoa!"

The thin, shocked voice had all the power of an explosion.

Dante whirled around, automatically shielding Taylor with his body. A grizzled old man in overalls and work boots stood next to the tellers' cages, his eyes wide and his jaw somewhere down around his ankles.

"Who," Dante said coldly, "are you?"

Tally pulled the lapels of her coat together and peered past Dante's shoulder, heart thumping in her ears.

"It's Esau Staunton. The janitor," she whispered in a shaky voice.

The old man was also Shelby's biggest gossip. By tomorrow, the whole town would know what had happened here this afternoon. She gave a soft moan of despair, and Dante put his arm around her and drew her forward so that she was pressed against his side. She stiffened and would have moved away but he spread his hand over her hip, the pressure of it insistent.

Was he trying to brand her? Or was he telling her this wasn't finished? Either way, she had to let him do it. Her legs had turned to jelly.

"Is that your name?" Dante said pleasantly. "Staunton?"

The old man swallowed audibly. "That's me." His

eyes danced to Taylor, then back to Dante. "Where's Mr. Dennison?"

"Mr. Dennison no longer owns this bank. I do. And you're right, Mr. Staunton. You should leave now, before the storm gets worse."

"You sure?" Again, the rheumy gaze fell on Taylor. "My boy's just pulled up at the curb in that red pickup, but, ah, if you or the lady wants—".

"Go home, Mr. Staunton," Dante said, his tone still pleasant but now backed with steel.

"Oh. Sure. Sure, I'll do that. Mr., ah, Mr.—"

"Russo. And there's one last thing." Dante spoke softly, in that same polite but unyielding voice. "I'm sure you understand that Ms. Sommers wouldn't want anyone to know about her fainting spell."

"Her fainting—"

"Surely, I can trust you to be discreet. People who work for me always are. And you do want to work for me, Esau, don't you?"

Another audible swallow. "Yessir. I do."

"Excellent. In that case, have a pleasant weekend."

The old man nodded and opened the double doors. The wind filled the room with its icy breath as he scrambled into the red pickup, which disappeared into the swirling snow.

"The old man was right," Dante said. "The storm's turned into a blizzard."

Tally stared at him. How could he talk about the weather after what he'd just done? Forcing his kisses on her. His caresses. If the janitor hadn't turned up, who knew what would have happened?

As for his admonitions to the old man—did he really

think they meant anything here? By tomorrow, this sordid little story would be everywhere.

Not that it mattered.

Without a house, without an income, she and Sam wouldn't be living in Shelby much longer.

"Nothing to say, *cara?*"

She wrenched free of his encircling arm. "You've done what you came to do, Dante. More, thanks to…to that performance just now."

His eyebrows rose. "Is that what you call it?"

Amusement tinged the words. Oh, how she wanted to slap that smug, masculine smile from his face.

"You are—you are despicable. Do you understand? You are the most despicable, contemptible—"

The world blurred. She raised her hand and swung it, but his fingers curled around her wrist.

"Such a temper, *bellissima*. And all because I caught you in a lie." His smile vanished. "You wanted me three years ago and you want me now."

"If you ever come near me again—"

"Don't make threats, Taylor. Not unless you're prepared to back them up."

She wanted to scream. To weep. To lunge at him again—but none of that would change anything. Because of him, her life had almost come apart before. Now, it lay in tatters at her feet.

The only thing left was a dignified retreat.

"You're right," she said, forcing herself to sound calm. "No threats. Just a promise. I don't ever want to see you again. If you come after me, I'll go to court and charge you with harassment. Is that clear?"

He laughed. And, before he could stop her a second time, Tally slapped his face.

Fury darkened his eyes. He reached for her, a harsh Sicilian oath spilling from his lips, but she slipped by him, yanked the doors open and ran.

She heard him shout her name but she didn't look back. The parking lot was a sea of white; the wind tore at her with icy talons as she fought her way to her station wagon, pulled the door open, got behind the wheel and slammed down the lock.

Just in time. A second later, Dante grabbed the door handle, then banged his fist against the window.

"Taylor! Open this door."

Her hands were shaking. It took two tries before she could jab the key into the ignition. The engine coughed, coughed again—and died.

A sob burst from her throat. "Come on," she said, turning the key, "come on, damn it. Start!"

"Taylor!" Another blow against the window. "What in hell do you think you're doing?"

Getting away. That was what she was doing. Dante had destroyed everything she'd built over the last years. He'd taken her home with a stroke of the pen, her pride with a kiss she hadn't wanted, her reputation with an X-rated scene she didn't want to think about.

And all he'd proved was what they'd both already known, that he was powerful and brutal, that he had no heart. That he could still make her respond to him, make her forget what he was and drown in his kisses….

"Taylor!"

She turned the key again. Not even a cough this time. *Calm down,* she told herself. Take it easy. The engine needed work, she knew that, but it had gotten her here, hadn't it?

The car wouldn't start because of the cold, that was all. Or maybe she'd flooded it. You could fit what she knew about cars inside a thimble and have room for the rest of the sewing kit, but wasn't there something about not giving a cold engine too much—

The station wagon rocked under the force of Dante's fist.

"Damn you, woman, are you out of your mind? Get out of that car! You can't drive in a blizzard."

She couldn't stay here, either. Not with him. And there was Sam to worry about. Was Sam safe at the Millers'? Yes. Of course. Sheryl and Dan were Sam's friends as well as hers. Still, she'd worry until she reached home.

If there was one thing life had taught her, it was that anything was possible.

One last try. Turn the key. Touch the gas pedal lightly…

Nothing. Nothing! Tally screamed in frustration and pounded the heels of her hands against the steering wheel.

"Listen to me," Dante said, calmly now, as if he were trying to talk sense to a child.

How could she not listen? They were inches apart, separated only by glass.

"Come back inside until the storm is over. I won't touch you. I swear it."

She almost laughed. What could he possibly know of a New England winter? The storm might last for days. Days, alone with him? With a man who'd just promised not to touch her in a way that made it clear he was sure she was helpless against him?

"Taylor. Be reasonable. We'll phone for help. This town has snowplows, doesn't it?"

Of course it did. But would the phones work? The first thing that always failed in bad weather were the telephone lines.

"Damn you, woman," Dante roared. "Can't you be without your lover for a few hours? Would you risk your neck, just to get back to him?"

So much for logic and reason.

Dante cursed, yanked at the door and it flew open. Tally grabbed for the handle but he was already leaning into the car, gathering her into his arms and striding to the bank through the blinding snow, head bent against the shrieking wind.

When they reached the entrance, he put her down.

"Just stand still," he said grimly. "Once we're inside, I'll call the police. For all I give a damn, you can lock yourself in the vault until they arrive."

He reached for the brass handle and pulled.

Nothing happened.

He grunted, wrapped both hands around the handle and pulled harder. But the doors were locked.

He spat out a word in Sicilian. Tally didn't need a translator to know what it meant. Here was one situation he couldn't control. Neither could she. The doors were probably on a timer. They wouldn't open until Monday.

People died in storms like this, and she knew it.

So, evidently, did Dante.

He picked her up again. She didn't fight him this time. The footing was slippery; he stumbled, recovered his balance and she automatically wrapped her arms around his neck. Snow crunched underfoot as he made his way toward the black SUV she knew must be his. Halfway there, he dug his keys from his pocket, pointed the remote at the vehicle and unlocked it.

He put her in the passenger seat, hurried to the driver's side and got in. For a long moment, they sat without looking at each other. Then he took a cell phone from his pocket and flipped it open.

"It won't work," Tally said wearily, leaning back in her seat.

Dante turned toward her. Her face was pale. He sensed that her anger had given way to resignation. It was an emotion neither of them could afford in a situation like this.

"Well, then," he said briskly, "we'll just have to come up with another plan."

He turned the ignition key so that he could read the instrument panel. The gas gauge, in particular, though he knew what he'd find. He'd been in such a damned rush to get to the bank before Taylor arrived…

One look confirmed what he'd suspected.

"We don't have much gas. Just enough to run the engine for maybe twenty, thirty minutes. After that—" *After that, they'd freeze.* "So," he said, again in that brisk tone, "here's what we're going to do. I'll go for help. You stay here and turn on the engine every ten minutes. Let the car warm up, then shut if off. Do that as long as you can and I'll do my best to find help quickly."

"Don't be a fool! You won't get a hundred yards."

"Why, *cara,*" he said, the words laced with sarcasm, "I didn't think you cared."

She didn't. But she did care about Sam. A moment ago, she'd almost let despair overtake her. Now she knew she couldn't let that happen. She had to live. To live for Sam.

There was only one choice. It was a risk in endless ways, but staying here was worse.

She took a deep breath. "Are you a good driver?"

"Of course."

Such macho intensity! Any other time, she'd have laughed.

"And is there enough gas in the tank to go fifteen miles?"

He nodded. "Just about."

"Then start the car. I'll get us to my house. My neighbor has a truck and snowplow. He can lead you to a place near the highway—tow you, if necessary— where there's a gas station and a motel. You'll be fine there until the storm's over."

"And you? Will you be fine, as well?"

Tally looked at Dante. His eyes were cool, making it clear his was a polite question and nothing more.

"I'm not your concern," she said. "I never was."

A muscle knotted in his jaw. Then he nodded, turned the engine on and headed out of the parking lot and into the teeth of the storm.

THE WORLD HAD TURNED into an undulating sea of white. Shifts in the wind's direction revealed only an occasional landmark, but that was enough.

The heavy vehicle, Dante's skill at the wheel and Tally's knowledge of the roads combined to get them safely to her driveway.

They battled their way to the door. Tally dug out her keys; Dante automatically reached for them as he used to when he saw her home in New York, and they waged a silent, brief struggle until he held up his hands in surrender and let her unlock the door herself.

She paused in the doorway.

The danger of the drive here had deprived her of rational thought. Now she was making up for it with frantic desperation. Were any of Sam's things in the kitchen? She didn't think so. Besides, it was too late to worry about it now.

If there were, she'd come up with some kind of explanation. In the last hour, she'd learned to be an accomplished liar.

She stepped into the room, fingers mentally crossed, with Dante close behind her, and reached for the light switch. The room remained dark. The power was out, as she'd figured it would be. The phone, too. All she heard when she picked up the handset was silence.

"It would seem you're stuck with a guest," Dante said coolly.

Tally didn't answer. She felt her way to the cupboard and took out the candles and matches she kept handy for just such occasions. When the candles were lit, she put one on the sink and another on the round wooden table near the window.

A shudder raced through her. The kitchen was the smallest room in the house but an hour or two without the furnace going had turned it into a walk-in refrigerator.

"Are you cold?"

"I'm fine."

Dante frowned, shrugged off his leather jacket and

draped it around her shoulders. "You'll never be a good liar, *cara*."

"I don't need—"

"You damned well do! Keep the jacket until the room warms up." He jerked his chin at the old stone fireplace that took up most of one long wall. "Is that real?"

"Of course it's real," Tally said brusquely, trying not inhale the scents of night and leather and man that enveloped her. "This is New England, not Manhattan. Nobody here has time for pretence."

A smile twisted across his mouth. "What an interesting observation," he said softly, "all things considered."

She felt her face heat. "I didn't mean—"

"No. I'm sure you didn't." He held out his hand. "Give me those matches and I'll make a fire."

"That's not necessary."

"Nothing is necessary," he said curtly. "Not if it involves me, is that correct?"

He'd come so close to the truth that she was afraid to meet his eyes, but that had been their initial agreement, hadn't it? Their relationship had been based on accommodation, not necessity. No strings. No commitment. No leaning on him for anything…

"Look, I know you want me gone," he said impatiently, "and believe me, I'll be happy to comply, but until then I'll be damned if I'm going to freeze just so you can prove a point. Give me the matches."

He was right, even if she hated to admit it. She tossed him the matches and watched as he knelt before her grandmother's old brick hearth and built a fire. Just seeing the orange flames made her feel better and she moved closer to them, hands outstretched so she could catch some of their warmth.

"Better?"

Tally nodded. All she could do now was wait for the storm's power to abate. At least she wasn't worried about Sam anymore. She'd seen the Millers' lights glowing when they drove past their house. She'd forgotten that Dan and Sheryl had a generator. Their place would be snug. Sam would have a hot meal, a warm bed…

"So. You inherited this from your grandmother?"

Her gaze shot to Dante. Arms folded, face unreadable, he was looking around the kitchen as if it were an alien planet. It probably was, to a man accustomed to luxury.

"Yes," she replied coldly. "And now I'm about to lose it to you."

"And where is your lover? Out of town? Or in another room, afraid to face me?"

"I told you, I don't have a lover. And if I did, why would he fear you? My life is my own, Dante. You have no part in it."

"You made that clear the night you ran away."

"For God's sake, are we going to talk about that again?" Tally marched to the stove, filled a kettle with water, took it to the hearth and knelt down, searching for the best place to put it. "I left you. I was absolutely free to do that. I know it's hard to face, but I didn't need your permission."

"Common courtesy demanded more than that note."

"I don't think so."

"Damn it," he growled, clasping her shoulders and

drawing her up beside him, "I'm tired of you dancing away from my questions. I want to know the reason you left."

"I told you. Our affair was over." She looked straight into his eyes. "And we both knew it."

She was right…wasn't she? Hadn't he come to the same conclusion? That it was time to end things? Not that it mattered. He *hadn't* ended the relationship. She had.

Wasn't that the reason he was here? Except, she was doing it again. Taking the upper hand, and he didn't like it.

"I never gave you the right to speak for me," he said sharply.

"No. You didn't. So I'll speak for myself." She took a deep breath and turned away. "I wanted a change."

Dante's mouth thinned. "You mean, you became involved with another man."

"That's ridiculous! I didn't—"

She cried out as he caught her and swung her toward him. "More lies," he growled.

"For the last time, there is no other man!"

"There is. I know his name." His hands dug into her flesh. "Now I want to know if you respond to him as you did to me a little while ago."

"Respond?" She gave a harsh laugh. "Is that what you call it? You—you forced yourself on me!"

It was a foolish thing to say. His nostrils flared like a stallion's at the scent of a mare in heat.

"You don't learn, do you?" he said softly. "You keep making statements and I end up having to prove that they're lies."

Tally looked up into the face of the man who had once been the center of her universe. How could she have forgotten how beautiful he was? And how cruel?

"We're both adults, *cara*. Why not admit we want each other?"

"Didn't you just say you knew I was eager to see you gone? That you'd be happy to go?" Damn it, why did she sound breathless? "Didn't you say that?"

He didn't answer. Instead, he cupped her face and lifted it to his. "Kiss me once," he whispered. "Just once. Then, if you don't want to make love, I promise, I won't touch you again."

"I don't have to kiss you to know the—"

His mouth took hers captive. Tally made a little sound of protest. Then his arms went around her and she let him gather her into his embrace, let his lips part hers and she knew nothing had changed, not when it came to this. To wanting his touch. His mouth. His body, hardening against hers...

The door flew open; the gust of wind that followed slammed it, hard, against the wall as a small woman cradling a grocery bag in one arm all but sailed into the kitchen.

"Sorry not to knock," Sheryl Miller said breathlessly, "but I don't have a free hand. I brought you leftovers from dinner and a loaf of oatmeal bread I baked this morning. Dan's going to get his mom and I said I'd go with—" Her mouth formed a perfect circle as she peered around the bag. "Oh! Oh, I'm sorry, Tally. I didn't know you had company."

Neither Tally or Dante answered. Both of them were staring at the toddler, round as a snowman in a raspberry-pink snowsuit, who clung to Sheryl's free hand.

"Hi, Mama," Samantha Gardner Sommers said happily, and flew to her mother's arms.

CHAPTER FOUR

FOR A MOMENT, no one moved but the child.

Then, as if someone had pushed a button, the room came to life again. The woman in the doorway, her face a polite mask, put the bag she'd been holding on the counter. Taylor scooped the toddler into her arms, and Dante...

Dante forced himself to breathe.

Mama? Was that really what the child had said? Taylor was staring at him over the little girl's head. Her face had gone white. So, he suspected, had his.

"Who is this?" he said hoarsely.

The woman glanced at Taylor. Then she took a step forward. "I'm Sheryl Miller. Tally's neighbor."

His head swung toward the woman. He thought of saying he didn't mean her, that he didn't give a damn who she was, but that would have been stupid. He needed time to get hold of himself and she had given him exactly that.

Oh yes, he needed time because what he was thinking was surely impossible.

"And you are?" Sheryl said, breaking the strained silence.

"Dante Russo." Dante forced a polite smile. "Taylor and I—"

"We knew each other in New York," Tally said quickly. A little color had returned to her face but it only made her look feverish. "He was in the area and—and he thought he'd drop by."

A horn beeped outside. The Miller woman ignored it. "Funny," she said, "but Tally never mentioned you."

He wanted to tell the woman to get out. To leave him alone so he could ask Taylor who this child was, why she'd called her Mama, but he knew better than to push things. The tension in the room was thick. Taylor's neighbor was already looking at him as if he might be a serial killer.

"No," he said politely, smiling through his teeth, "I'm sure she didn't."

The woman ignored him. "Tally? Is everything okay?"

Tally swallowed a wave of hysterical laughter. Nothing was okay. Nothing would ever be okay again unless she could come up with a story to change the way Dante was looking at her and Sam.

"You want me to tell Dan to come in?"

"No! Oh, no, Sheryl. I mean—" What *did* she mean? "It's as I said. Dante is an old—an old—"

"Friend," Dante said, his tone level. "I thought I'd stop by and see how Taylor was adjusting to small-town life."

The Miller woman looked doubtful but Tally said yes, that was it, and smiled, and finally the woman smiled, too.

"Why wouldn't she adjust? Didn't she ever tell you she's a small-town girl at heart? That she comes from Shelby?"

"No. But then, I'm starting to realize there are lots

of things she didn't tell me." Dante looked at Taylor. "Isn't that right, *cara?*"

Taylor didn't answer. That was good because it meant she knew that whatever she said now would only fuel the fury building inside him.

The horn beeped again. "Dan wants to get going," Sheryl said. She peeled off a glove and offered Dante a brisk handshake. "Nice to have met you." She leaned forward, as if to share a confidence. "Tally can use the company. I keep telling her she needs to get out more but what with Sam, well, you know how it is."

"No," Dante said, forcing another smile, "I'm afraid I don't."

Sheryl grinned. "Men never do. Anyway, it's good to see someone from her old life drop by."

"That's definitely what I am. Someone from Taylor's old life."

This time, the horn beeped three times.

"Okay, okay," Sheryl muttered, "I'm coming. Tally? I was going to say, if you want to come with us, I'm sure Dan's mother wouldn't mind."

For a wild moment, Tally imagined running out into the storm with Sam, getting into the truck, telling Dan to drive and drive and drive until she'd put a million miles between Dante and her—

"Tally?"

What was that old saying? You could run, but you couldn't hide.

"Thanks," she said brightly, "but we'll be fine."

The Miller woman looked unconvinced. Dante put his arm around Tally. When she stiffened, he dug his fingers into her flesh in mute warning.

"Taylor's right. We'll be fine." He drew his lips back from his teeth and hoped the result would still approximate a smile. "The snow, a fire, candlelight…it's quite romantic, especially for old friends. Isn't that right, *cara?*"

The child, thumb tucked in her mouth, looked at him. *Liar,* her round green eyes seemed to say. But the woman's big smile assured him she'd bought the story.

"In that case, I'm off. It was nice meeting you, Mr. Russo."

Dante held his smile until the door closed. *Now,* he told himself, and dropped his arm from Taylor's shoulders.

"Whose child is this?"

No preliminaries, she thought dizzily. No safe answers, either.

"Taylor. I asked you a question. Is the child yours?"

Sam chose that moment to give a huge yawn. Tally grabbed at the diversion.

"Somebody's sleepy," she said, ignoring Dante and the pounding of her heart.

"Am not," Sam said, yawning again.

Despite herself, Tally smiled. "Are, too," she said gently. She buried her face in her daughter's sweet-smelling neck as she carried her to the small sofa near the fireplace and sat her down. She tugged off the baby's boots, zipped her out of her snowsuit but left on the warm sweater and tights beneath it.

"How about taking a nap, sweetie? Right here, by the fire. Would you like that?"

"Wan' Teddy."

"Teddy! Of course. I'll get him. You just put your head down and I'll get Teddy and your yellow blankey, okay?"

"'Kay," Sam said, eyelids already drooping.

Tally rose to her feet and forced herself to look at Dante. "Don't," she began to say, but caught herself in time. Don't what? Go near my child? That wasn't the problem. The questions that blazed in his silver eyes was the problem.

So was answering them.

By the time she returned, Samantha was fast asleep. Tally covered her, tucked the teddy bear beside her, smoothed back the baby's hair...

"Stop playing for time."

She swung around. Dante, standing only inches away, might have been carved from granite. Her heart was beating in her throat but the biggest mistake she could make now would be to show her panic.

"Please keep your voice down. I don't want you to wake Sam."

"Sam?" His mouth twisted. "The child's name. Not your lover's. Why did you let me think otherwise?"

She busied herself picking up the boots and snowsuit from the floor.

"I had no idea what you thought. Besides, why would I care? This is my life. I don't owe you explan—"

She gasped as his hand closed, hard, on her wrist. "No games," he said in a soft, dangerous voice. "I warn you, I'm not in the mood."

"And I'm not in the mood for being bullied. Take your hand off me."

Their eyes met and held. Slowly, he released her. Tally took a last look at her sleeping daughter, then walked briskly into the kitchen with Dante on her heels.

"I'm still waiting for an answer. Is the child yours?"

The million-dollar question. It wasn't as if she hadn't envisioned this scene before and all the possible ways to handle it. Dante would demand to know whose baby this was and she'd come up with a creative reply.

She'd say she was raising the child of a sister or a dear friend. Or she'd tell him that she'd adopted Sam. Any of those explanations had seemed plausible, but now, with his cold eyes boring into hers, Tally knew she'd been kidding herself.

A man with Dante's resources would prove she was lying in the blink of an eye.

"It's a simple question, Taylor. Is the child yours?"

In the end, there was only one possible response. She gave it on a forced exhalation of breath.

"Yes. She's mine."

She steadied herself for what would come next. Anger that she hadn't told him he'd made her pregnant? A demand to claim that which was his? Or perhaps, by some miracle, a thawing of his ice-clad heart at the realization he had a daughter.

Later, she'd weep bitter tears at the memory of those possibilities and how reasonable they'd seemed.

"So, that's the reason you left me. Because you were pregnant."

She nodded and searched his face for some hint of what he was thinking.

"Answer the question! Was your pregnancy the reason you ran away?"

"I didn't run away."

His mouth thinned. "No. Of course you didn't."

"I'm sure you think I should have told you, but—"

"You were quite right, keeping the information to yourself," he said coldly. "However you imagined I'd react, the reality would have been worse."

Tears blurred her eyes. "Yes," she said. "I know that now."

Dante caught her by the shoulders, his hands as hard as his eyes.

"I made myself clear from the start."

She couldn't help it. The tears she'd tried to control trembled on her lashes, then fell. She pulled free of his hands, went to the sink and made a pretense of straightening things that didn't need straightening.

"I know. That's why I didn't—"

"You were my mistress."

That dried her tears in a hurry. "I was never that."

"Don't mince words, damn it!" He came up behind her and swung her toward him. "You belonged to me."

"This jacket belongs to you," she said, shrugging it from her shoulders so it dropped to the floor. "And that vehicle in the driveway." Tally thumped her fist against her chest. "*I* am not property. I never belonged to you."

"No." His smile was as thin as a rapier. "As it turns out, you didn't." His grasp on her tightened. "I knew things had changed between us. I just didn't know the reason."

"I left you. Final answer."

"I thought it was that our relationship was growing old."

Amazing, that such cruel words could wound after all this time, but she'd sooner have died than let him know it.

"You're right. It was. It had. That's why—"

"Now I find out it wasn't that at all." He caught her face, lifted it to him so that their eyes met. "It was this," he said, jerking his chin toward the next room, where the baby lay sleeping. "You had a secret and you were so intent on keeping it from me that you kept yourself from me, too."

"Maybe you're not as thick-headed as you seem," Tally countered, trying for sarcasm and failing, if the twist of his lips was any indication.

"I could kill you," he said softly.

As if to prove it, one cool hand circled her throat. His touch was light, but she felt its warning pressure.

"Let go of me, Dante."

"There's not a court in the land that would convict me."

"This is America. Not Sicily." Tally put her hand over his. "Damn you, do you think I planned to get pregnant?"

He stared at her for a long minute. Then he dropped his hand to his side.

"No," he said. "I suppose not."

He strode away from her, his back rigid, and paced her kitchen like a caged lion.

Her heart thudded.

What was going on in his head? Would he turn his back and walk away? Or would his pride, whatever it was that drove him, demand that he stake his claim to her daughter? She'd do anything to avoid that, anything to keep this heartless man from being involved in raising Samantha.

"Dante." Tally hesitated. "I know you're angry but— but you must believe me. I did what I thought was—"

"You told me you were using a diaphragm."

"Yes. I know. But—"

He swung toward her. "But not with him."

Tally blinked. "What?"

"I want to know who he is."

"You want—you want to know—"

"The name of your child's father. The man you took as a lover while you still belonged to me."

She stared at him in disbelief. He wasn't angry because she'd left him without telling him she was carrying his baby. He was angry because he thought she'd cheated on him.

Was that how little he thought of her? That she'd betrayed him while they were lovers? God oh God, she wanted to launch herself at him. Claw his heart out, except he had no heart.

But then, she'd always known that. It was what had made her weep at night toward the end.

She'd never so much as looked at anyone else while they'd been together. She'd never looked at anyone in the years since, either, because she was a fool, a fool, a fool…

"I am assuming," he said, "that you are not going to tell me I sired this child."

Sired Sam? He made it sound like a procedure performed in a veterinarian's office…but that was fine. Every word he said assured her she'd been right to leave him when she did.

"Damn you," he snarled, catching her by the shoulders, "answer me!"

She could do that. She could do whatever it took, to get this man out of her life.

"You can relax, Dante. I promise you, I'm not going to tell you that you are Samantha's father. If you want that in writing, I'll be happy to oblige."

A muscle bunched in his jaw. "You still haven't said who he was, this man who took you to his bed while you were still sleeping in mine."

Tally wrenched free. "You have it wrong. It was you who slept in *my* bed, remember?"

"Answer me, damn it. Who is he?"

"That's none of your business."

"I told you, you belonged to me. That makes it my business."

"And *I* told *you,* I am not property!" She looked up at him, hating him for what he was, for what he thought, for what she'd once felt in his arms. "What's the matter? Have I wounded your pride? Will I wound it even more if I tell you I was only with him once? That's all it took for him to give me his child."

He grabbed her, his face so white, eyes so hot, that she thought she'd finally pushed him too far, but that didn't matter. She'd wanted to hurt him enough to draw blood and she had…

With the truth.

She knew exactly when their child—when *her* child—had been conceived. On the night of his birthday. She'd learned the date by accident, when he left his wallet open on the nightstand with his driver's license in view. She'd made dinner, baked a cake, bought him a present because she'd—because she'd wanted to.

After, Dante had made such tender love to her that she'd looked into her own heart and come as close as she'd dared to admitting what she felt for him.

"Stay with me tonight," she'd whispered, as they lay in each other's arms.

He hadn't.

After he was gone, she'd felt more alone than she'd ever thought possible. Not just alone but abandoned. Used, not by his heart but by his body.

She'd cried softly as night faded to morning. Hours later, when she got up to shower, she'd discovered that her diaphragm had a pinpoint hole in it. She'd told herself it was nothing. It was her so-called safe time of the month and besides, what were the odds on becoming pregnant after just one night of unprotected sex?

Six weeks later, a home pregnancy kit proved that the odds were excellent.

Tally had considered the life she'd planned. A career, not for her ego but for security. Money in the bank that would guarantee she'd never have to depend on a man the way her mother had.

She'd visited her doctor. Asked tough questions, made tough decisions. And reversed herself on the subway ride home when she saw a young woman with a baby in her arms, the mother cooing, the baby laughing with unrestricted joy.

Her future had changed in that single instant.

Now, it was changing again. If she'd had any last, lingering doubts about her feelings for the man she'd once come close to thinking she loved, they were gone.

She looked pointedly at Dante's hand, encircling her wrist, then at his face.

"I want you out of here," she said softly. "Right now."

He looked at her for a long moment. Then, slowly and deliberately, he took his hand from her.

"I thought I knew you," he said in a low voice.

She almost laughed at the absurdity of those words. "You never knew me," she said.

"No. I didn't. I see that now." He plucked his leather jacket from where she'd dropped it and slipped it on. "Get yourself an attorney. A good one, because I'm going to start foreclosure proceedings as soon as I return to New York."

Panic took an oily slide in her belly. "I can make the payments on the loan. I *have* made them! All you have to do is check the bank records."

"The amount you've been paying each month is a joke. It has nothing to do with the loan agreement."

"But Walter Dennison said—"

"You're not dealing with Dennison. You're dealing with me."

She watched, transfixed, as he strolled to the door. At the last second, she went after him.

"Wait! Please, you can't... My daughter, Dante. My little girl. Surely you wouldn't punish an innocent child for my mistakes. That's not possible!"

"Anything is possible," he said coldly. "You proved that when you took a lover."

"Dante. Don't make me beg. Don't—"

"Why not?" He turned and clasped her elbows, lifting her to him until his empty eyes were all she could see. "I'd love to hear you beg, *cara*. It would fill my heart with joy."

The bitter tears she'd fought to suppress streamed down her cheeks.

"I hate you, Dante Russo. Hate you. Hate you. Hate—"

He took her mouth in a hard, deep kiss, one that demanded acquiescence. Tally fought it. Fought him as he cupped her face, held her prisoner to his plundering mouth until she knew she would kill him when he turned her free, kill him...

And then, slowly, his kiss changed. His lips softened

on hers. His tongue teased. His hands slid into her hair and she felt it again, after all these years, all this anguish and pain. The slow, dangerous heat low in her belly. The thickening of her blood. The need for him, only him...

Dante pushed her away.

"You belonged to me," he said roughly. "Only to me. I could have you again if I wished." His mouth twisted. "But why would I want another man's leavings?"

Then he put up his collar, opened the door and strode into the teeth of the storm.

CHAPTER FIVE

HOW MANY TIMES could a man be subjected to the saccharine nonsense of Christmas before he lost what remained of his sanity?

The holiday was still three weeks away and Dante was already tired of the music pouring out of shops and car radios. He'd seen enough artificial evergreens to last a lifetime, and he was damned close to telling the next sidewalk Santa exactly what he could do with his cheery ho-ho-ho.

New York, his city, belonged to tourists from Thanksgiving through the New Year. They descended on the Big Apple like fruit flies, choking the streets with their numbers, unaware or uncaring of one of the basic rules of Manhattan survival.

Pedestrians were not supposed to dawdle. And they were expected to ignore Walk and Don't Walk signs.

New Yorkers moved briskly from point A to point B and when they reached a street corner, they took one quick look and kept going. It was up to the trucks and taxis that hurtled down the streets to avoid them.

Tourists from Nebraska or Indiana and only-God-knew-where stopped and stared at the displays in department store windows in such numbers that they blocked the sidewalk. They formed a snaking queue around Radio City Music Hall, standing in the cold with the patience of dim-witted cattle. They clustered around the railing in Rockefeller Center, sighing over the too big, too gaudy, too everything Christmas tree that was the center's focal point.

As far as Dante was concerned, Scrooge had it right.

Bah, humbug, indeed, he thought as his chauffeur edged the big Mercedes through traffic.

The strange thing was, he'd never really noticed the inconvenience of the holiday until now. Basically, he'd never really noticed the holiday at all.

It was just another day.

As a child, Christmas had meant—if he were lucky—another third-hand winter jacket from the Jesuits that, you hoped, was warmer than the last. By the time he'd talked, connived and generally wheedled his way into a management job at a construction company where he'd spent a couple of years wielding a jackhammer, he was too busy to pay attention to the nonsense of canned carols and phony good cheer. And after he arrived in New York, earning the small fortune he'd needed to start building his own empire had taken all his concentration.

The last dozen years, of course, he'd had to notice Christmas. Not for himself but for others. Those with whom he did business and the ones who worked for him—the doormen, the elevator operators, the porters at the building in which he lived, all expected certain things of the holiday.

So Dante put in the requisite appearance at the annual

office party his P.A. organized. He authorized bonuses for his employees. He wrote checks for the doormen, the elevator operators and the porters. He thanked his P.A. for the bottle of Courvoisier she inevitably gave him and gave her, in return, a gift certificate to Saks.

Somehow, he'd never observed the larger picture.

Had tourists always descended on the city, inconveniencing everything and everyone? They must have.

Then, how could he not have noticed?

He was noticing now, all right. *Dio,* it was infuriating.

The Mercedes crept forward, then stopped. Crept forward, then stopped. Dante checked his watch, muttered a well-chosen bit of gutter Sicilian and decided he was better off walking.

"Carlo? I'm getting out. I'll call when I need you."

He opened the door to a dissonant blast of horns, as if a man leaving an already-stopped automobile might somehow impede the nonexistent flow of traffic. He slipped between a double-parked truck and a van, stepped onto the sidewalk and headed briskly toward the Fifth Avenue hotel where he was lunching with the owner of a private bank Russo International had just absorbed.

He'd be late. He hated that. Lateness was a sign of weakness.

Everything he did lately was a sign of weakness.

He was short-tempered. Impatient. Hell, there were times he was downright rude. And he was never that. Demanding, yes, but he asked as much of himself as he did of those who reported to him, but the past couple of weeks...

No. He'd be damned if he was going to think about that trip to Vermont again.

He thought about it too much already.

And the dreams that awakened him at night… What were they, if not an indication that he was losing his self-control?

Why would he dream about a woman he despised? For the same reason he'd kissed her, damn it. Because the ugly truth was that he still wanted her, despite her lies and her infidelity. Despite the fact that she'd borne another man's child. Nothing kept the dreams at bay. Each night, he imagined her coming to him, imagined stripping her naked, making love to her until she cried out in his arms and said, *Yes, Dante, yes, you make me feel things he never did.*

And awakened hard as stone, angry at himself for an adolescent's longings, for the frustration that he couldn't lose in another woman's bed though, God knew, he'd tried.

What an embarrassment that had been! *I'm sorry,* he'd said, *that's never happened to me before.*

It hadn't, though he doubted if the lady believed him. *He* could hardly believe it!

He was not himself since Vermont, and he didn't like it. One day in a snow-bound village and he'd discovered he was still an old-world *Siciliano* at heart, reacting to things with emotion instead of intellect.

How could a woman he didn't want ruin his sex life from a distance of four hundred miles?

Taylor had—what was the old saying? She'd put horns on his head, sleeping with another man while she was still his. She deserved whatever happened next.

She *had* been his, no matter what she claimed. So what if she hadn't let him pay her bills? If she hadn't lived with him?

She had belonged to him. He'd marked her with his hands. His mouth. His body.

And she'd let another man plant a seed in her womb. She'd given him a child. A child who should rightly have been—should rightly have been—

Dante frowned, gave himself a mental shake and prepared to vent his anger on the half a dozen idiots who'd come to a dead stop in the middle of the sidewalk.

"Excuse me," he said in a voice so frigid it made a mockery of the words.

Then he saw it wasn't only the people ahead of him. Nobody was moving. Well, yes. The crowd was shifting. Sideways, like a brontosaurus spying a fresh stand of leafy trees, heading for a huge, world-famous toy store.

Dante dug in his heels. "Excuse me," he said again. "Pardon me. Coming through."

Useless. Like a paper boat caught in a stream, the crowd herded him toward the doors.

"Wait a minute," he said to a massive woman with her elbow dug into his side. "Madam. I am not—"

But he was. Like it or not, Dante was swept inside.

A giant clock tower boomed out a welcome; a huge stuffed giraffe gave him the once-over. He was pushed past a tiger so big he half expected it to roar.

Somehow, weaving and bobbing, he worked to the edge of the crowd and found refuge behind a family of stuffed bears. He gave his watch one last glance, sighed and took out his cell phone.

"Traffic," he told the man he was to lunch with, in the tones of a put-upon New Yorker. It turned out the other man was still trapped in a taxi. They laughed and made plans for a drink that evening.

Dante put his phone away, folded his arms over his chest and settled in to wait for a break in the flow of parents and children so he could head for the door.

He didn't have to wait long. A trio of pleasantly efficient security guards cleared the way, formed the crowd into an orderly queue outside. Dante started toward the door, then fell back.

What a place this was!

And what would he have given to be turned loose in it when he was a boy. Just to look, to touch, would have been a time spent in paradise.

His toys had been stick swords. Newspaper kites. And, one magical Christmas Eve, an armless tin soldier he found in a dumpster while he scavenged for his supper.

How could he have forgotten that?

Oh, how he'd loved his soldier! He'd kept it safely buried in the pocket of his sagging jeans, bloodied the nose of a bigger boy who'd tried to steal it.

Was that what Taylor's daughter faced? Improvised toys? If she were lucky, a broken, discarded doll to call her own?

Dante scowled.

Talk about giving in to your emotions! The child—Samantha—was not the Poor Little Match Girl. Neither was her mother. Taylor was perfectly capable of earning a living.

Yes, he'd started the legal procedures that would take her house from her, but she'd reneged on the terms of the loan. It was business, plain and simple. She'd understood the risks when she signed those loan papers.

Besides, she wasn't destitute. She had possessions. She could sell them. She had friends in that town, people who'd help her and the child.

Then, why had her coat looked worn? The house, too. Even by candlelight, he could tell it needed work. The walls needed fresh paint. The wood floors needed refinishing. The furnishings were shabby. And where were the shiny, high-tech gadgets women always had in their kitchens?

Had Taylor deliberately simplified her life...or had fate done it for her?

A muscle flexed in his jaw.

Not that he cared. For every action, there was a reaction. That was basic science. She had deceived him, and he had repaid her.

The child was not his problem. Neither was Taylor. He had no regrets or remorse, and if her daughter didn't have a particularly merry Christmas this year...

Something bumped against his leg.

It was a child. A little girl, older than Samantha, clutching a cloth doll almost as big as she was in her arms.

"What did I tell you, Janey?" A harassed-looking woman caught the child's hand. "You can't see around that thing. Tell the man you're sorry."

"That's all right," Dante said quickly. "No harm done."

The child's mother smiled. "I told Janey that Santa's going to bring her some wonderful surprises in just a few weeks but she saw Raggedy Ann and, well, neither she or I could resist. You know?"

He didn't know, that was just the point. He'd never had surprises from Santa, never fallen in love with a goofy bear, like Samantha, or a rag doll like Janey.

Even if he had, who would have understood how important such a simple toy could be?

Dante watched the little girl and her mother fade into the crowd. He stood motionless, long after they'd disappeared from his sight.

Then he made his way out of the store, took out his cell phone to call his chauffeur... And, instead, called his P.A. to tell her he wasn't returning to the office.

He felt—what was the word? Unsettled. Perhaps he was coming down with something. Whatever the reason, walking to his apartment building on such a cold, crisp day might clear his head.

"You're home early, Mr. Russo," said his housekeeper when he stepped from the private elevator into the foyer of his penthouse.

Dante shrugged off his coat and told her he didn't want to be disturbed. Then he went into his study, turned on his computer and did what he could to further prepare for the meeting he'd have over drinks in just a few hours.

For the first time in his life, he couldn't get interested in the complex facts and figures of an imminent deal.

What kind of Christmas morning would Taylor and her child awaken to? There was a time he'd have assumed Taylor viewed the holiday with as much cynicism as he did. After all, he'd spent six months as her lover. He knew her. He knew her likes and dislikes...

Or did he?

She'd shown him a side of her he'd never suspected. Had she really grown up in a small town? If he hadn't seen her in that shabby little house with a child in her arms, even imagining Taylor in that kind of life would have been impossible.

People didn't even call her by that name in Shelby. She was Tally, not Taylor. A softer, more vulnerable name for a softer, more vulnerable woman.

Dante went to the window and looked down at Central Park. Thanks to the influx of out-of-towners, it was alive with people, even on a weekday afternoon. There were probably more people in the park right now than lived in the entire town of Shelby, Vermont.

If Taylor had stayed in New York, if she'd opened her business here, she'd be turning a handsome profit by now. She had contacts in the city, a reputation.

Dante watched the scene below him for long minutes. Children were sledding down a snowy incline; even from up here, he could see the bright flash of their snowsuits.

Would the little girl in the toy store find a sled under the tree Christmas morning?

Would Taylor's daughter?

A muscle knotted in his jaw.

No. The plan running through his head was clearly insane. She'd made a fool of him, wounded him in the worst way a woman can hurt a man.

But the child was innocent.

It was wrong, that children seemed always to pay for the sins of those who'd given them life.

The muscle in his jaw knotted again. Dante went to the breakfront, took out a bottle of brandy and poured an inch into a snifter. He warmed the glass between his palms, stared sightlessly into the rich depths of the swirling liquid.

And put it down, untouched.

Instead, he went to his desk. Picked up the phone. Made calls to his attorney, to his accountant, to the same private investigator who'd found Taylor for him.

If any of them thought his instructions were unusual, they knew better than to say so.

When he'd finished, Dante picked up his snifter of brandy and went up the spiral staircase to his suite.

The view was even better here. Three walls of glass gave him a vantage point a peregrine falcon would have as it swooped over the city.

Lights glimmered, diamonds sparkling against the pall of encroaching darkness, and he recalled the first time he'd stood here, gazing out into the night, the fierce swell of pride he'd felt at knowing all this was his, that his sweat, his struggles, his fight to get to the top had all been worth it.

Taylor had never seen this view. She'd come here for drinks, for dinner, but he'd never carried her up the stairs to this room.

To his bed.

Dante sipped the brandy.

What if he had? If he'd made love to her while the lights of the city challenged the stars in the night sky? If he'd taken her to these windows, naked. Stood with her as she looked out on his world. Stepped behind her. Cupped her breasts. Bent his head and kissed the skin behind her ear.

She'd always trembled when he kissed her there.

Trembled when he entered her.

He closed his eyes. Imagined entering her now, right now, here, as she looked into the night. Imagined holding her hips, pressing against her, the urgency of his erection seeking the heat, the silken dampness that was for him.

Only for him...

His eyes flew open.

The hell it was.

She'd been with another man, even while she'd been his because, damn it, she *had* belonged to him no matter what she said.

He turned from the window, turned from the images that assailed him.

What he'd just done had nothing to do with Taylor. It was simply an act of charity. This was the season for charity, after all. What he'd done was for a child. An innocent little girl, trapped in a game played by adults.

That the plan he'd set in motion would also bring Taylor back into his life was secondary. Whatever had happened between him and his once-upon-a-time lover was over.

Dante tossed back the rest of the brandy. The liquid burned its way down his throat and, as it did, burned him, as well, with the ugly truth.

Forget charity. Forget pretending that what had happened was over.

It wouldn't be. Not until he slept with the woman who'd made a fool of him, one last time.

CHAPTER SIX

WHEN SHE WAS SIX, Tally stopped believing in Santa Claus.

Her grandmother had taken her to the mall the week before. She'd been terrified of the man with the white beard and the booming laugh, but after a lot of coaxing, she'd sat in his lap and whispered that all she wanted for Christmas was a Pretty Patty doll.

Christmas Eve, she crept out of bed and saw her grandmother putting the doll under the tree.

Even then, she'd understood Grandma had to count every penny. That she'd loved Tally enough to buy the doll meant more than if Santa had brought it.

Now, twenty-two years later, she was close to believing in Santa again.

How else to explain the call from a decorator she'd worked with in Manhattan? He'd been in too much of a hurry to offer details but the bottom line was that he knew someone who knew someone who knew someone who was familiar with her work.

That person had recommended her for the commission of a lifetime.

"The guy's richer than Midas," Aston trilled. "Seems

he just bought out some old-line firm and the digs don't suit him, so he's moving the whole kit and caboodle to that new building on 57th and Mad. You know the one? Baby, this is one plum job! A huge budget, free creative rein... Pull this off, your name will blaze in neon!"

A couple of weeks back, Tally would have been flattered but she'd have turned down the offer. She'd have had no choice, not with a shop to open in Vermont. Now it seemed as if Dante's vicious act of revenge might turn out to be a godsend.

"He wants to meet with you first, of course. See if the synergy's right."

For an assignment like this, she'd do whatever it took to make the synergy right.

She splurged on a haircut, had her black suit cleaned and pressed, charged a new coat which she hated to do but appearance was everything in New York. If things went well, she'd be able to pay for it. If not, she was so broke that the credit card company would have to wait the next hundred years for their money.

She even tried to go back to thinking of herself as Taylor Sommers instead of Tally. Her given name had been the one she'd always used in the city. It suited the image she'd needed, that of a cool sophisticate.

The woman Dante had always assumed her to be. The one she knew he'd wanted her to be.

And yet, today, after leaving Samantha with Sheryl, riding the train into Manhattan, now standing across from the glass tower where she was to meet the Mystery Mogul, she felt more like Tally than Taylor.

Taylor wouldn't have butterflies swarming in her stomach.

Tally did.

She was nervous. Hell, she was terrified about meeting the man who held her future in his hands.

He had no name. Not yet.

"You know how these big shots are," Aston said. "Some of them won't make a move unless a camera's pointed at them, but some guard their privacy like lions protecting a kill. This guy's like that. He wants to stay nameless until the deal is struck."

The Mystery Mogul was meeting her in his new offices. Tally looked up, counting the floors even though she'd already done it twice, head tilted back like an out-of-towner.

The butterflies fluttered their wings again.

She wanted this job more than she'd ever wanted anything. Aston's description of it was almost too good to be true.

Her fee would be—well, enormous. More than she'd earn in five years in Shelby. She'd be able to give Sam everything. New toys, clothes, the best possible nanny to care for her while Tally was at work.

Best of all, she could deal with the loan payments she owed the bank—the payments she owed Dante. So much for his plans to destroy her.

She wouldn't even have to tackle the toughest thing about living in New York. The Mystery Mogul, it turned out, owned an apartment building with a two-bedroom, two-bath vacancy.

"Well, of course he does," Aston had said.

The way he said it made her laugh. It was the first time she'd laughed in weeks.

Since Dante's visit.

Since she'd discovered just how ruthless he could be.

Since she'd found out just how much she could hate him.

"The rent's a perk of the job, can you imagine?"

She could. A picture was emerging of a bona fide eccentric with money to burn. The only thing that almost stopped her was that this meant returning to Dante's city. And that was just plain ridiculous. It was her city, too, or had been for five years. Besides, the odds of running into one person in a city of eight million were zero to none.

And even if there was that eight-million-to-one chance, so what? She'd left Dante so he wouldn't know she was having his baby, but it turned out she needn't have worried. She'd told him Sam wasn't his and he'd been only too willing to believe her.

Tally lifted her chin as she strode through the lobby of the glass tower and stepped into a waiting elevator. She should have spat in his face that night in her kitchen. Given the opportunity a second time, she wouldn't pass it by.

"To hell with you, Dante Russo," she said aloud, as the elevator whisked her to the twenty-seventh floor. "You're a cold, contemptible son of a bitch and—"

The doors slid open.

And the cold, contemptible son of a bitch was standing in front of her, arms folded, face expressionless.

"Hello, Taylor," he said, and that was when she knew she'd been had. All this—the wonderful job, the money, the apartment…

It was all a cruel joke.

A joke only one of them could laugh at, she thought,

and then she stopped thinking, called him a word she had never before thought, much less used, and launched herself at the man she would hate for the rest of her life.

DANTE HAD KNOWN this wouldn't be easy.

Taylor despised him. Well, so what? The feeling was mutual.

And she was proud.

He admired that in her; he always had. She'd never shown the weakness so many women—hell, so many men and women—showed, that of needing someone to lean on. Like him, she was independent and strong.

But things had changed.

She did need someone now. Some no-good SOB had gotten her pregnant and walked away, left her with a child to raise, and that made all the difference.

He'd decided to start by telling her that but she didn't give him the chance. The elevator doors opened, she saw who was waiting for her and she came at him like a tiger.

He got his arms up just in time to keep her from clawing his face.

"Taylor," he said, "Taylor, listen—"

"No," she panted, raining blows on his upraised arms, "I'm done listening, you bastard! Wasn't what you did to me enough? Did you need an encore? You no-good, heartless—"

He caught her hands, yanked them behind her back. "Stop it!"

"Let go. You let go of me or—"

She was still fighting him. Dante grunted, tucked his shoulder down and hoisted her over it like a bag of laundry. She shrieked, kicked her feet and yanked at his hair. What in hell would he say if somebody came running to see who was being murdered?

"Put me down!"

"With pleasure," he said grimly.

The former tenants had left behind a couple of chairs, half a dozen file cabinets and a small black leather sofa. Dante strode to it and dumped her on it. Then he stood back, folded his arms again and glared.

What had made him think helping her would be a good idea?

"Don't even think about it," he warned when she scrambled up against the cushions.

"I hate you, Dante. Do you hear me? I hate you!"

"I'd never have known."

She sat up straight, mouth trembling. "How even *you* could do something like this, you—you—"

"Watch what you say, *cara.*"

"Do not call me that!"

"Is it your habit to attack your clients?"

"If you think I'm going to be party to this—this schoolboy prank—"

"You're so sure you know everything, Taylor. Is it possible you don't?"

"I know what you are. That's all that's necessary."

She rose to her feet, tugged down her coat, smoothed her hands over her hair. She was still shaking and suddenly he wanted to go to her, take her in his arms and tell her everything was going to be all right. That he would take care of her.

Except, that wasn't why he'd brought her here. It was for the child.

And for yourself, a voice in his head said slyly. How

come he'd forgotten his vow to sleep with this woman one last time? That would put her out of his thoughts forever. He didn't need to hear her say she wanted him. Or that she was sorry she'd been unfaithful. He didn't need to hear the words she'd whispered that night three years ago when she'd begged him to stay with her, to stay in her arms, in her bed.

"Get out of my way!"

She was looking up at him as if she wanted to kill him. Fine. The game he'd planned was one that was best played by sworn enemies.

"We'll have our meeting first."

"We've already had it. To think you'd resort to such— to such subterfuge, just so you could make a fool of me!"

"Would you have agreed to this appointment if you'd known I was the man involved?"

"You know I wouldn't." Her eyes filled with angry tears. "Why did you do it? You're taking my house. My livelihood. What more do you want?"

He wasn't going to answer. She could tell by the way he was looking at her but it didn't matter. She already knew the answer. What he'd done to her wasn't sufficient. He wanted to give the knife one more twist.

How? she thought bitterly. How could she have made love with a man like this? How could she have even believed she'd fallen in love with him? Because she had believed it, yes. That was why she'd left him, because she knew he didn't love her, wouldn't love the child they'd created together. She'd left rather than see him look at her as he was looking at her now, as if she had no meaning to him at all.

She took a deep breath, drew what remained of her pride around her like a ragged cloak and started past him.

"Taylor."

She shook her head. She had nothing left to say to him.

His hand closed on her wrist. "You asked me questions. Are you going to leave before you hear the answers?"

She looked pointedly from his hand to hers. "Let go."

"I didn't bring you to New York on false pretenses."

She laughed. "You didn't, huh?"

"Isn't that what I just said?"

"Well, let's see. You got someone to offer me a commission decorating these offices. He mentioned a budget big enough to make my head spin. Oh, and he said there'd be an apartment with the rent a perk of the job." Tally tugged her hand free and put her hands on her hips. "If those aren't false pretenses—"

"The offer is real. All of it. The commission, the budget, the place to live."

Everything from shock to distrust to outright utter disbelief showed in her face. He tucked his hands in his trouser pockets and kept his tone as flat as his eyes.

"It's all yours, if you want it."

She stared at him. "Why?"

"There's an old saying about not looking a gift horse in the mouth."

"I know the saying. Maybe it lost something in the translation. What it means is that an unexpected gift is a gift to beware of."

Dante took a deep breath. "The child," he said.

"What child?" Tally felt her heart beat quicken. Did he know? Had he somehow learned the truth of her pregnancy? "You mean—you mean Sam?"

He nodded. "Yes."

"What about her?"

"I've had time to think." A muscle flexed in his jaw. "And I realized that it's wrong to punish her for your behavior."

He didn't know. Tally almost sagged with relief.

"Your daughter is innocent of all that happened. You deceived me. You left me. But none of that is her doing. The world is filled with children who suffer because of the behavior of adults. I see no reason to add to their number."

She stared at him. Dante Russo, showing compassion to a little girl he thought had been fathered by another man? Why would he show compassion at all? All the months they'd been lovers, she'd waited, she'd yearned to see some show of human emotion in this man.

She never had.

Oh, he supported charities. Smiled at things that were amusing. Frowned at things that were annoying.

But he never lost his composure. Not even in bed.

Not that he wasn't an incredible lover. He was. Alert to her every sigh, her every unspoken desire. He'd given her more pleasure than she'd ever imagined possible.

The way he moved inside her.

The way he brought her to climax.

And yet, he'd always been in control. Always, except that one night when he'd been as tender as he was wild, when she'd asked him to stay with her.

When she'd conceived Samantha.

"Well?"

Tally blinked. Dante was looking at her with barely veiled impatience.

"You asked me why I'd offer this assignment to you and I told you the reason. It's your turn now. Will you accept it? Or will you turn it down because I'm the man making the offer?"

Something was wrong. She felt as if she were looking at a jigsaw puzzle with one piece—the key piece—missing.

"Yes or no?"

She almost laughed. The imperious tone of voice. The straight posture. The cold eyes that said, "I'm in command."

Except, he wasn't.

He couldn't order her around. She wouldn't permit it. She had to think. Nothing was happening the way it was supposed to. She'd worried about being in the same city with this man and now it turned out she'd be working for him.

Impossible.

Better to go home…and do what? Lose the house? Move to a furnished room? Take whatever job she could find? Earn barely enough to live on and, oh yes, impose on Sheryl's kindness by asking her to watch Sam?

"Taylor, I want an answer!"

There was only one answer, but she couldn't bring herself to give it. Not without making him wait.

"I'll call you with my decision."

His eyes narrowed. She tried to move past him as quickly as possible, but his hand clamped down on her shoulder.

"Would you put your pride before the welfare of your daughter?"

"Nice, Dante. Really nice." Tally's eyes blazed with anger. "Don't you try and lay this on me! I never ignored Sam's welfare and I sure as hell never tripped over my own oversize ego! You're the one who came to Shelby, who bought a bank just so you could tear my child's life to pieces."

"That wasn't my intention."

"Maybe not, but it's what you did."

"Yes. And now, I intend to undo it. I will not avenge myself by hurting a child."

"My God, listen to you! So high and mighty. So godlike. Anyone would think you have a conscience. Maybe even a heart."

"Damn you, Taylor!" His fingers dug into her flesh as he pulled her to him. "I want to do the right thing. Why make it so difficult?"

And, in that moment, it came to her. The missing piece of the puzzle. What he'd just called doing the right thing. If that was his intention, there was a much easier way to do it. Why wasn't he taking it?

"If you're serious about not wanting my little girl to pay the price of your revenge—"

"Interesting," he said silkily, "how you manage to misquote me, *cara*. I said I would not avenge myself through her. We both know what that means, that your daughter should not pay the price of your unfaithfulness."

"Put whatever twist you like on it. The point is, if you've suddenly turned into the male counterpart of Mother Teresa, why go through all this? Why not simply stop the foreclosure proceedings?"

There it was, the million-dollar question. The question he'd asked himself a dozen times since coming up with this idea. His attorney and his accountant, each of whom knew only small details of the overall situation, had finally asked it, too, but he hadn't given them any explanations.

A man who answered to no one but himself didn't have to.

That didn't mean it wasn't a damned good question. All he had to do was have the loan payments rescheduled. Or tear up the documents altogether.

End of problem.

Nothing else made sense. Not to his attorney, to his accountant, to him and now to Taylor, who was looking at him with her eyebrows arched.

Dante frowned. She could look at him any way she liked. He didn't owe her an explanation, either.

"It's too complicated to explain."

Her smile was thin. "Try."

"There are banking laws. Rules. And I've already set the foreclosure procedure in motion."

"And I'll unset it by repaying the loan with my earnings from this job." Another thin smile. "Try again."

For a second, he looked blank. "You'd see it as charity. You'd never accept it."

It was a good save. The sudden lift of her eyebrows told him so.

"This way, you'll work for the money," he said, feeling his way carefully through the explanation that had suddenly come to him and knowing it was flawed. Give her too much time, she'd realize that. "I'm simply offering you a practical way out of your dilemma."

Yes, Tally thought. That was how it seemed—but then, the fly that had wandered into the spider's parlor had probably thought she was being asked in for a cup of tea.

And yet, what was the alternative? Could she really say no to his offer and condemn Samantha to financial uncertainty? Besides that, he was right. She'd be working for this money. No favors given, no favors asked.

"Well?"

She looked up. Dante was scowling. Obviously, he had none of her reservations about them being in close contact.

"I can't spend the entire day at this, Taylor. I need an answer. Will you take the job or won't you?"

She took a deep, steadying breath. "I'll take it."

Something flashed in his eyes. Triumph, she thought, but then it was gone, he was smiling politely and holding out his hand. She stared at it. Then, carefully, she extended her hand, too, felt his callused palm against hers as they shook hands.

"I want certain assurances," she said quickly.

"We've already sealed the deal. But go ahead. I'll try and accommodate you. What assurances do you want?"

"Our relationship will be strictly business."

He didn't say anything. His expression didn't change. Was that agreement or was he waiting to hear more?

"Our meetings will occur in public places."

"Such logical choices, *cara*. I'm impressed. Is that all?"

"No. It isn't." She folded her arms. "You're not to call me that."

"What? *Cara?*" He laughed. "You're my employee. I'll call you anything I like."

"I'm not your employee. We'll be working together. Either way, calling me *cara* would be improper."

He smiled, and her heart rose into her throat because everything she'd feared about him, everything she'd adored about him, was in that smile.

"Ah. I understand now." He cupped her elbows.

Slowly, inexorably, he drew her closer. "You're afraid our relationship will become personal."

"It won't," she said stiffly. "How could it, when you're the last man on earth I'd want to become personal with?"

"I used to call you *cara* when you were in my arms. When I was making love to you."

Taylor's breath caught. The sound of his voice at those moments. The feel of his hands on her breasts. The darkness of his eyes as he'd slipped his hands beneath her, as he entered her. Slowly, so slowly, until she cried out with pleasure at the feel of him deep, deep inside her...

"No," she said, "I don't remember. Why would I? It meant nothing. It meant—It meant—"

Dante stopped her lies with a kiss.

Fight him, she thought desperately, *don't let him do this to you.*

But the terrible truth was, he was doing what she had dreamed of. What she ached for. She loved the feel of his mouth on hers. The scent of his skin. The way he moved his hands down her spine and lifted her against him so that his erection pressed against her belly.

"Kiss me back," he said, his voice a rough command, and her treacherous body responded, her lips parted and when they did, he thrust his tongue into her mouth and she felt it happening as it always did, her breasts swelling, her bones melting, her body readying for his possession...

Her heart yearning for what he would never give her.

Tally wrenched free of his embrace.

"No." Her voice was hoarse. "I don't want that from you. Not anymore."

He said nothing for a long moment. Then he let go of her.

"As you wish."

"As I insist."

"Please," he said coolly, "no ultimatums. You made your point. And now…"

He glanced at his watch, then plucked his cell phone from his pocket and made a brief call. It was like a slap in the face, a way of telling her that the kiss had meant nothing to him.

"I've arranged for my driver to come for you."

"That's not necessary. My hotel—"

"I've checked you out of your hotel." His hand clasped her elbow; he moved her into the elevator with determined efficiency. "Carlo will take you to your rooms."

"Rooms?" she said, as the elevator plunged toward the lobby. "Aston said an apartment."

"The rooms for you and your daughter are a separate suite within an apartment."

"Whose apartment?" Tally said, heart suddenly racing.

His eyes met hers. "Mine," he answered.

Before she could respond, the doors swept open on the lobby and Dante handed her over to his waiting driver.

CHAPTER SEVEN

Did he really think she'd live in his apartment?

Not even if the alternative was a tent pitched in the Millers' backyard.

Tally let Dante's driver take her to Central Park West but only because she had to go there if she wanted to reclaim her luggage.

She'd get it, write the imperious Mr. Russo a note telling him, in exquisite detail, what he could do with his contract, phone for a taxi and leave. No. This time, she'd face him. She would not forgo that pleasure.

The driver was new but the doorman was the same as in the past. He greeted her by name, as if three long years had not gone by since her last visit. So did the house-keeper, who added that it was good to see her again.

"This way, miss," she said pleasantly, gesturing not to the library or the dining room or the sitting room, all the places—the only places—Tally had seen when she and Dante had been involved, but to the graceful, winding staircase.

"Thank you," Tally said, "but I'll wait for Mr. Russo in the library. If someone would just bring me my suitcase…?"

"Your things are already upstairs, miss. I'll show you to your rooms."

Arguing seemed pointless. Her quarrel was with Dante, not with his staff. She followed the housekeeper to a door that led into a sitting room as large as her entire house back in Vermont.

"Would you like some tea, miss?"

What she'd have liked was some strychnine for her host, but Tally managed a polite smile.

"Nothing, thank you."

"Ellen's unpacked your things. If you're not pleased with how she's arranged your clothes, just ring."

But I'm not staying, Tally started to say, except, by then the housekeeper had disappeared.

Dante wasn't just arrogant, he was presumptuous. She could hardly wait to see him and tell him so, but where was he? And when was the last train to Shelby? Eight? Nine? She intended to be on it. No way could she afford a night in a hotel now that her prospective job had turned out to be a farce.

Tally took out her cell phone and dialed Sheryl to see how Sam was and to tell her that the plans that had seemed so magical had fallen apart, but there was no answer. What a time to be reminded that cell service in Shelby wasn't always what you hoped.

Was nothing going to go right today?

Twenty minutes passed. Thirty. Tally frowned. Paced the sitting room. Checked her watch again. Damn it, she didn't have time for this! She'd wait another half hour, then give up the pleasure of confronting Mr. Russo and his monumental ego.

Getting on that train, getting back to Sam and the real

world, was more important. In fact, why was she wasting time waiting for Dante when she could be packing? She didn't need a maid to toss things into a suitcase.

Chin lifted, Tally marched through the sitting room, though a light-filled bedroom, to a door she assumed led to a closet…

Her breath caught.

The door didn't open on a closet. It opened on a room meant for a very lucky little girl.

For Samantha.

The walls were painted cream and decorated with murals that spoke of fairy tales, princesses and unicorns. The carpet was pale pink. The crib and furniture were cream and gold. A rocker stood near the window, a patchwork afghan draped over it. Tucked away in one corner, a playhouse shaped like a castle rose toward the ceiling, guarded by a family of plush teddy bears.

The room was a little girl's dream.

For a heartbeat, Tally's mood softened. She could imagine her daughter's excitement at such wonders.

Then she came to her senses and saw the room for what it really was.

Did Dante think he could bribe her into staying?

She turned on her heel. There was nothing she'd brought to the city she couldn't do without. To hell with packing. To hell with confronting Dante. All she wanted was to go home.

Quickly she left the suite, went down the stairs and headed straight for the private elevator…

But it was already there.

The doors slid open just as she reached them and she saw Dante standing in the mahogany and silver car.

Dante, with Samantha curled in his arms.

The blood drained from Tally's head.

Of all the things she'd imagined happening this day, she'd never envisioned this. Not this. Not her former lover, with his daughter in his arms.

Sam was so fair. Dante was so dark. And yet—oh, God—and yet they were so right together. The same softly curling hair. The same wide eyes and firm mouths, curving in the same smiles as they looked at each other, Dante with a softness of expression Tally had never seen in his face before, Sam babbling happily about something in a two-year-old's combination of real and made-up words.

Dante and Samantha. A father and his daughter.

The ground tilted under Tally's feet.

Blindly she stuck out a hand in a search for support. She must have made a sound because suddenly Dante looked up and saw her.

His smile faded. *"Cara?"*

I'm fine, she said. Or tried to say. But the words wouldn't come, nothing would come but another soft sound of distress. Dante barked a command. His housekeeper ran into the room, took Sam from him, and then it was Tally who was in Dante's arms, his strong arms, and he was carrying her swiftly through the apartment.

"Cara," he said again, "Tally…"

He had never called her that before. She thought of how soft the name sounded on his lips. Of how the world was spinning, spinning, spinning…

And then everything went black.

WHEN SHE OPENED HER EYES, she was in an enormous, canopied bed in a softly lit room.

Where was she? What had happened? Something

terrible. Something that carried within it the seeds of disaster.

She sat up against a bank of silk-covered pillows—and everything came rushing back. Dante. Samantha. Her baby in her lover's arms. Her baby, here, in this place, where three years' worth of secrets might untangle like a skein of yarn.

Tally started to push the comforter aside. She had to find Sam. Take her home…

"*Cara.* What are you doing?"

Dante's voice was harsh. He stood in the door between the bath and the bedroom, his tall, powerful figure shadowy in the light.

"Where's my baby?"

"Samantha is fine."

He came toward her, a glass of water in one hand, a small tablet in the other. Tally brushed aside his outstretched hand.

"Where is she?"

"She's in the nursery. Asleep."

"I want to see her."

"I told you, she's fine."

Tally swung her feet to the floor. "Don't argue with me, Dante! I want to see her now."

"The tablet first."

She glared up at him. She knew him well; enough to know he wasn't going to let her get past him until she obeyed his command.

"What is that?"

"Just something to calm you."

"I don't need calming, damn it!"

"The doctor disagreed."

"You called a doctor?"

"Of course I did," he said brusquely. "You fainted."

"Only because—because I was stunned to see my daughter. You had no right—"

"Take the tablet." His mouth twitched. "Then you can tell me what a monster I am, for flying Samantha here so she could be with you."

She glared at him one last time. Then she snatched the glass from his hand, dumped the tablet in her mouth and gulped it down with a mouthful of water.

Tell him what a monster he was? No. She wasn't going to waste the time. You couldn't argue with Dante Russo. He was always right, so why bother? She'd take Sam and leave.

But first, she had to get dressed.

The realization that she was *undressed* surged through her. She was wearing a nightgown of pale blue silk, its thin straps scattered with pink silk rosebuds, the kind of gown only a man would buy for a woman.

An ache, sharp as a knife, pierced her heart. Was the woman Dante had bought it for as lovely as the gown? She must have been, for him to have given her something so fragile and exquisitely beautiful. For him to have made love to that woman here, in his home, where he had never made love to her.

Unaccountably, her eyes stung with tears. Angry tears. What else could they be?

Damn Dante Russo to hell! Who had given him permission to have his housekeeper take off her clothes and dress her in this gown that wasn't hers?

"Well?"

She looked up. Dante was watching her, one dark eyebrow raised.

"Aren't you going to tell me I'm a monster?"

"Get away from me," Tally said, her voice trembling.

"After all," he said, a wry smile curving his lips, "you have every reason to despise me. You pass out, I phone for my doctor.... What woman wouldn't hate a man under those circumstances?"

"I want my clothes."

"Why?"

"Dante. You may find this amusing, but I do not. You seem to think you can—you can take control of my life. Well, you can't. I don't want your job. I don't want your guest suite. I don't want you thinking you can decide what's best for my baby, I don't want your housekeeper undressing me, and I certainly do not want your mistress's cast-offs."

"Such a long list of don'ts," he said mildly, tucking his hands into the pockets of what she now realized were soft-looking gray sweatpants. "Unfortunately, not all of them are appropriate."

"Damn you, I'm not playing games!"

"Let's go through them one by one, shall we?"

"Let's not. I told you—"

"I heard you. Now it's your turn to listen. Number one, I'm not trying to control anything. You agreed to the terms of the job."

"If by 'terms,' you mean me living in your home—"

"Two," he said, ignoring her protests, "I cannot imagine that thinking it best for you and Sam to be together as soon as possible was a mistake."

"I was going home to her. Didn't that occur to you?"

"It did, but I have a private plane. Why would you want to spend hours on the train, only to turn around and make the trip here again when I could arrange to bring her to you tonight?"

"Damn it, who gave you the right to think for me? I was not going to turn around, as you put it, and make the trip here again. I told you, I don't want your—"

"And, finally," he said, "finally, *cara,* you're wrong about the nightgown." He took his hands from his pockets, reached out and trailed one finger deliberately across one rose-embroidered strap, hooking the tip under the fabric, lightly tugging at it so that she had no choice but to sit forward. "I bought it for you, along with some other things I thought you might need to help you settle in." His voice turned silken. "And then there's that final accusation. That my housekeeper undressed you. She didn't."

A rush of color shot into Tally's face. Dante saw it and smiled.

"Why would I have her do that," he said softly, "when I've undressed you myself hundreds of times in the past?"

"The past is dead, Dante. You had no right—"

"Damn it," he said sharply, his smile vanishing, "who are you to talk about rights?" His hands cupped her shoulders and he drew her to her feet. "Such self-righteous garbage from a woman who ran like a coward instead of facing a man and telling him she'd cheated on him!"

"I didn't—"

"What? You didn't cheat? What do you call becoming involved with another man, if not cheating? Come on, Tally. I'd love to hear you come up with a better word."

What could she say to that? Nothing, not without admitting the truth. Telling him he'd fathered Sam would
open her to his scorn, his anger and, worst of all, to the
possibility he'd try and take her daughter from her.

"That's a fine speech," she said calmly, even though
her heart was racing. "But you're only making it because I wounded your ego. You were bored. You were
going to leave me. Instead, I made the first move. That's
what really bothers you and you know it."

Was it? She'd just told him exactly what he'd been
telling himself for three years, but now he wasn't sure
it was that simple. Had he planned on breaking things
off because he was bored, or was there some deeper
reason he hadn't wanted to face?

Was that what had driven her into the arms of a
stranger?

Maybe he'd ask himself that question someday, but
not now. Not when all his rage at Tally had turned to fear
an hour ago, when he'd watched her face whiten as she
crumpled to the floor.

Now she stood straight and tall before him, her eyes
fixed on his and glittering with unshed, angry tears. Her
hair was loose; he'd undone the pins himself, let it
tumble to her shoulders in soft, heavy waves. She wore
no makeup; he'd washed it away with a cool cloth and
it occurred to him that he'd never seen her like this
before, that in all the time they'd been lovers, her appearance had always been perfect.

She'd been beautiful then but she was even more
lovely like this, he'd thought, her lips naked of artificial
color, her hair in sweet disarray. She was what they
called her in Vermont.

She was Tally, not Taylor, and something in the softness of the old-fashioned name had made his throat constrict.

Slowly, he'd undressed her, telling himself it was only so he didn't have to ring for Mrs. Tipton or Ellen.

His hands had trembled as he undid the buttons of her suit, as he slid her blouse from her shoulders.

It was so long since he'd seen her breasts. Her belly. The pale curls that hid the sweet folds of flesh where he longed to bury himself. The long legs that had once wrapped around his hips as he lost himself in her welcoming heat.

And yet, despite those images, what he'd felt, undressing Tally, hadn't been sexual desire.

What he'd felt was the desire to protect her. To hold her close. Rock her in his arms. Tell her he was sorry he'd hurt her, sorry he hadn't understood what she'd needed of him, what he'd needed of her all those years ago....

"Even now," Tally said, her voice tinged with bitterness, "even now, you can't tell me the truth."

"You're right," he said quietly. "I was going to leave you." Tally turned away. He cupped her jaw and forced her to meet his eyes. "But I don't know why, *cara*. I thought that I did, but now I'm not so sure." His gaze fell to her lips. "All I'm sure of is this."

"No," she whispered, but even as he lowered his head to hers, Tally didn't pull back. She shut her eyes, felt the whisper of his breath on her mouth, and when he gathered her into his arms and said her name, she moaned and melted against him.

This was the kind of kiss they'd shared on the night that had changed everything. It was a kiss of tenderness and longing so intense she could feel his heart thudding against hers and with a suddenness that stunned her, she knew she wanted more.

"Dante," she said, the word a soft sigh against his lips. "Dante…"

His name, breathed against his mouth. Her breasts, pressed to his chest. Her belly, soft against his. Dante groaned, slid his hands into Tally's spill of cinnamon hair and gathered her closer.

Passion exploded between them.

Tenderness became desire; longing turned to desperate need. Dante's mouth demanded acquiescence and Tally give it, parting her lips so his tongue could seek out her honeyed taste. He groaned, slid down the delicate straps of the nightgown, baring her breasts to his hands and mouth.

"Say it," he demanded, and she did.

Her whispered "Yes, make love to me. Yes, touch me, yes, yes, yes," rose into the silence of the winter night and filled him with ecstasy.

And he knew, in that instant, that taking her to bed once more in a quest for revenge was not what he needed at all.

He needed her wanting him, like this. Crying out as he bent to her and sucked her nipple deep into his mouth. Tossing her head back in frenzied response to the brush of his hand as he dragged up the skirt of her gown, cupped her mons with his palm, felt her hot tears of desire damp on his fingers and sweet heaven, he was going to come, to come, to come…

He scooped Tally into his arms.

"Now," he said fiercely, his mouth at her throat, and she sobbed his name over and over as he carried her through the vast room, heading not to her bed but to his…

A child's voice cried out.

"Sam," Tally whispered.

Dante shut his eyes. Dragged air into his lungs. Turned and carried her to the nursery, where he set her gently on her feet.

He stood back and let her approach the child in the white and gold crib alone.

"Baby," she murmured, "did you have a bad dream?"

"Mama?"

Tally lifted her daughter in her arms. Sam was warm from sleep, sweet from the mingled scents of soap and baby powder. She sighed and laid her head against Tally's shoulder.

"Teddies are sleepin', Mama."

Teddies, indeed. The bedraggled, much-loved bear from home sat in the corner of the crib, side by side with the smallest new teddy from the bear family Dante had bought.

Unaccountably, Tally's heart swelled.

"Yes, baby," she said softly, "I see."

She went to the rocking chair, sat in it and gently rocked Sam back and forth, back and forth.

"'Hush little baby,'" she sang softly, "'don't you cry…'"

Gradually, Samantha's breathing slowed. Tally waited until she was certain she was sound asleep. Then she carried her child to the crib, laid her in it, covered her with a blanket and pressed a kiss to her hair.

When she turned she saw Dante, still in the doorway, watching her, his face unreadable in the soft shadows cast by the nightlight.

Oh, Dante, she thought, *Dante…*

Slowly, she went to him and looked into his eyes. A muscle jumped in his cheek. He lifted his hand and reached toward her and she shook her head and pulled back, knowing that if he touched her—if he touched her…

"What we did—what we almost did—was a mistake."

"Making love is never a mistake, *cara*."

He was wrong. It was a mistake, and Tally knew it. Knew it because she'd finally faced the truth.

She loved Dante Russo with all her heart.

Bad enough she could never tell him she'd borne him a child, but to lie in his arms and pretend it was only sex would be the ultimate travesty.

A heart could only be broken so many times before it shattered into a million pieces.

Tally put her hands lightly on Dante's chest. "Maybe not," she said softly. "But it can't happen anymore."

A smile tilted at the corners of his mouth. "Does this mean I won't have to sue you for breach of contract?"

She smiled, too. "If you mean, will I take the job, the answer is yes. It's a wonderful opportunity, and I thank you for it. And I'll stay here." Her voice grew soft. "This suite is beautiful, and the nursery you created for Sam is a little girl's dream come true." She drew a breath. "But you have to give me your word you won't try to make love to me."

"Is that really what you want?"

No. Oh no, it wasn't. She longed to tell him that, to go into his arms, lift her mouth to his, plead for him to carry her to bed and love her until dawn lit the sky.…

"*Cara?* Is it really what you want?"

She had lied to him already. Now she had no choice but to lie to him again.

"Yes."

Long seconds dragged by. Then Dante took her hand, pressed a kiss to the palm and folded her fingers over it.

It was only hours later, as she lay in bed watching dawn slip over the city, that Tally realized Dante hadn't actually said he'd agree.

CHAPTER EIGHT

TALLY WAS UP at six the next morning.

Sam was still asleep in the next room, sprawled on her belly in her new crib, flanked by both her teddy bears.

Tally smiled, bent down and pressed a light kiss to her daughter's hair. Then she showered, put on a clean blouse but the same black suit and took a critical look at herself in the mirror.

She needed to buy clothes. If you looked success-ful, people assumed that you were. It wasn't the best way to judge anyone but that was how it went, espe-cially in this town.

Her pay would be based partly on salary and expenses, partly on the cost of the completed project. So far, no one had mentioned when she'd get a check. She hated to ask, especially because it was Dante she'd have to go to, but she'd have to work up to it, and soon.

Tally gave her image another glance, then took a deep breath. Maybe she'd be lucky and Dante would already have left for the day.

No such luck.

He was in the sun-filled breakfast room, seated at

a round glass table with a cup of black coffee in his hand and the business section of the *New York Times* in front of him.

He looked up as Tally entered, and half rose from his chair. She motioned him to stay seated and went to the sideboard to pour herself coffee. It was easier to do that than to think about the fact that this was the very first time they'd had breakfast together.

"Good morning," he said. "Did you sleep well?"

She nodded. "Fine, thank you." A lie, of course. She'd tossed half the night, thinking of him in a room just down the stairs. "Thank you, too, for having that baby intercom installed between my room and Sam's."

"No problem. Actually, I had monitors installed throughout the place. I thought it would make you feel more comfortable, knowing you could hear Samantha no matter where you were."

"That was very thoughtful," she said politely, and sipped at her coffee.

"Sit down and join me."

There was no way to turn down the request, especially since he'd risen to his feet and was pulling out the chair opposite his. She thanked him, slipped into the chair and tried to concentrate on the coffee. It wasn't an easy thing to do.

Dante was a major distraction.

He was—there was no other word for it—he was beautiful. Not in a feminine way but beautiful all the same, wearing what she knew was a custom-made dark-blue suit, a pale-blue shirt from the city's most distinguished shirtmaker, and a maroon silk tie. His dark hair was curling and damp from the shower.

Another first.

They'd never breakfasted together, and she'd never seen him fresh from the shower. They'd had long bouts of incredible sex but afterward, he'd always dressed and gone home to shower. He preferred his own things, he'd told her. His soap, his razor, his toiletries, and she'd understood that what he'd really meant was that sex was one thing but showering was another, that he would only take intimacy just so far....

"Tally?"

She blinked. Dante had pushed a vellum envelope and a leather-bound notebook toward her.

"Sorry." She gave a polite little laugh. "I was—I was just trying to plan my day."

"I've already planned some of it for you. I hope you don't mind, but I want you to get up to speed as quickly as possible."

"Oh. Oh, no. I want that, too."

"There's a check in the envelope. Call it a signing bonus. If it isn't enough—"

"I'm sure it'll be fine. Thank you."

"Don't thank me. You're going to work hard to earn your money. You'll find your appointments for today listed in the notebook. For right now—" Dante glanced at his watch, pushed back his chair and rose to his feet "—I have to get going. Carlo will take you to the office."

"Your driver? Won't you need him?"

"I'm flying to Philadelphia. I'll take a cab to the airport."

Philadelphia. How long would he be gone? Would he be back by evening? It was better if he weren't. Then she wouldn't have to imagine returning here, seeing him, saying something banal as she went to the guest suite and he went out because he would go out, wouldn't he? There had to be a woman in his life. He was too virile a man to be without one.

But if there were, would he have kissed *her?* Would he have said he wanted to make love to her? Would he look at her as he had last night, as if he could almost feel her in his arms, hear her moans, because she would moan if he touched her, and—what was wrong with her today? She couldn't live here and imagine these things.

"Tally?"

"Yes?"

"You seem…distracted."

Heat rushed to her face. "No, not at all." Quickly, to cover her embarrassment, she added, "You said you're flying to Philadelphia?"

"And that my P.A., Joan, will show you around. She took care of furnishing your office. If it doesn't please you, tell her to make whatever changes you wish. Joan's also the one who scheduled your appointments, so if you have any questions—"

"Ask Joan."

Dante nodded and walked around the table to where she sat.

"She's organized meetings for you with half a dozen prospective assistants."

He was leaning over her; his scent drifted to her. Soap, water and pure, sexy essence of Dante. That was how she'd always thought of the smell of his skin. She'd never forgotten it or the memories it evoked.

His taste on her tongue. The feel of him, under her hands.

"I'm right," he said softly.

Tally looked up. His face was close to hers, his eyes a deep, cool gray.

"Something's definitely distracting you, *cara*. What could it be?"

"Nothing. I'm just—I'm concentrating on what you said. My office. Appointments with possible assistants. What else?"

"Did Mrs. Tipton tell you that she and Ellen will be happy to look after Sam, until you've hired a nanny?"

He leaned closer. All she had to do was turn her head an inch and her lips would brush his jaw.

"She told me. That's very—" she cleared her throat "—that's very kind of them. I'll contact an agency first thing and—"

"Joan's already taken care of it. A highly recommended agency is sending over half a dozen women for you to interview. They all have impeccable credentials, but again, if you're not satisfied, all you need do is inform Joan."

His shoulder brushed hers. Was it her imagination, or could she feel the heat of him through all the layers of clothing separating them?

"Tally? Is that acceptable?"

His eyes were on hers. The color had gone from gray to silver. Silver that somehow burned like flame.

"It's—it's fine."

"Because," he said, his voice suddenly low and husky, "because, *cara,* we can always alter the arrangement we made."

He wasn't talking about the office or her appointments, and they both knew it.

"No," she said, "we can't. I want things exactly as we agreed."

"Are you certain?"

The only thing she was certain of was that she had to get herself under control because she couldn't do this. Think about him making love to her, want him making love to her…

She took a deep breath. "Yes."

"In that case, there's nothing left to do this morning." His gaze dropped to her lips. "Except this," he said softly, and brushed his mouth over hers.

"No," she said, hating the soft, breathless quality of her voice.

"You're starting a new career and I'm flying to an important meeting. It's just a kiss for luck. Surely, I'm allowed that?"

"Dante. We can't—"

"We aren't."

He put his hand under her chin, lifted her face and claimed her mouth with his. And she—she let it happen. Let him slide the tip of his tongue between her lips, let him thrust his fingers into her hair, let him deepen the kiss until she was dizzy with wanting him.…

Dante let go of her, straightened and took a sleek black leather briefcase from the sideboard.

And then he was gone.

TALLY'S DAY WAS LONG, exhausting—and wonderful.

Her office was a huge, light-filled room, handsomely furnished and perfectly equipped. Selecting an assistant was difficult only because all the candidates Dante's P.A. had chosen were outstanding.

It would have been equally tough to choose one of the nannies but a middle-aged woman with a soft Scottish lilt made things easier when she spotted Sam's photo on Tally's desk and crooned, "Och, the sweet little lamb!"

There was nothing difficult in deciding that Dante's P.A. was the eighth wonder of the world. Joan was fiftyish, elegant, and as warm as she was efficient.

"Just let me know what you need," she said, "and it's as good as yours."

At lunchtime, Tally dashed to Fifth Avenue and did the sort of lightning-fast shopping trip she used to do in the past. Within an hour, she'd bought several trousers, skirts, blazers, cashmere sweaters and a couple of pairs of shoes.

At four, she met with Dante's architect, who showed her the interior changes he was going to make in the new offices. At five, she met with one of her old contacts at the design center. At six, she dismissed Dante's driver and headed for the subway.

Dante would not kiss her anymore, and she would not accept any more favors from him. She was working with him. It was only right that they maintain appropriate behavior.

There was a delay on the subway line. A quarter of an hour passed before the train came and after that, it sat between stations for five endless minutes. When she reached her stop, she went half a block out of her way to buy a chocolate Santa for Sam.

She'd called to talk with her baby half a dozen times and the last time, she'd promised to bring a special treat.

By the time she reached Dante's apartment building,

Tally was feeling wonderful. She was back in the city she loved, involved in a major project, and she'd made peace with the problem of dealing with Dante.

All she had to do was make sure he understood the parameters of their relationship, and—

"Where have you been?"

Dante stood in the entrance to the building, blocking her way. His voice was rough, his face white with unconcealed anger.

"I beg your pardon?"

Mouth set, he clasped her arm and marched her past the doorman to the penthouse elevator.

"I asked you a question. Where the hell were you? You should have been here an hour ago."

She swung toward him, her temper rising to match his as he pushed her, unceremoniously, into the car.

"I should have been here an hour ago?" Tally slapped her hands on her hips. "Are you out of your mind? I don't have to answer to you!"

"You left the office at six. An hour late."

"How nice. You have people spying on me."

"And turned down the use of my car."

"Is your driver a paid informer?"

"And where did you go for lunch? I phoned and you hadn't told Joan or your new assistant where you'd be."

Tally was trembling with anger. "Where I went and why I went there is none of your business. Unless—" The color drained from her face. "Ohmygod, is it Sam? Is my baby ill?"

"No!" Dante stepped in front of her as the car doors opened on his penthouse. "Listen to me. Samantha's fine. This has nothing to do with her."

Sweet relief flooded through her, but it didn't last. She'd accepted a job from this man and moved into his guest suite. If he thought that made her his property, he was wrong.

"Then, get out of my way," she said coldly. "I don't answer to you."

"You damned well will," he said grimly, his hand closing like a steel band around her wrist. "This is New York, not a blip on the map in Vermont. Anything might happen to you on these streets."

"What a short memory you have, Russo!" Tally jerked free of his hand. "I know all about New York. I lived here for five years!"

She had. He knew that. She'd traveled the city's streets, ridden its subways, lived in an apartment alone. Of course he knew that...but things had changed.

He told her so, and she looked at him as if he'd gone crazy.

"Nothing's changed. The city's the same. So am I."

"You're not." His mouth twisted and the ugly suspicions he'd tried to deny while he'd paced the floor and wondered where she was, burst from his lips. "You slept with another man while you belonged to me. How do I know you're not seeing him again?"

Tally's eyes went flat. "You don't," she said coldly, and brushed past him.

Dante let her go. He had to; he was still rational enough to know that if he went after her now, it was a sure bet he'd do something he'd regret.

So he turned his back, strode along the marble floor to the library, flung open the liquor cabinet and poured himself a stiff shot of bourbon. And began pacing again, back and forth on the antique silk carpet before the fireplace, while the hours ticked away.

She'd all but called him crazy.

Hell, maybe she was right.

How come he hadn't thought about this before? All the plans he'd made to bring Tally back to New York and it had never occurred to him that he might be pushing her straight into the arms of her old lover.

The man who'd made her pregnant.

If he wasn't crazy, he was just plain stupid, because the idea hadn't even popped into his head until he'd been at lunch in Philadelphia after a morning of meetings. Somewhere between the salad course and the entrée, he'd suddenly realized he wanted to hear Tally's voice. He'd excused himself, left the table and phoned.

But she wasn't at her office, and Joan had no idea where she'd gone. He'd started to call her on her cell phone, only to realize that he didn't have the number.

He'd gone back to the table. Shoved the grilled shrimps and vegetables back and forth on his plate. Said "yes" and "no" and "how interesting" when it seemed fitting.

And all the while, he'd been thinking, *Where is she? Where did she go?*

That was when he'd first realized that bringing her back to the city might have been a mistake. That even now, while he pretended to pay attention to the details of a billion-dollar deal, Tally might be lying in the arms of the man she'd left him for. She'd slept with the man only once, she'd said, but Tally wasn't like that.

She wouldn't be anybody's one-night stand.

Had she lied about that? Had the bastard been her

lover for weeks? For months? Did she want to go back to him now?

Why would she, when he'd abandoned her when she was pregnant?

He had abandoned her, hadn't he? Because if he hadn't, if something, who the hell knew what, had kept Tally and the SOB apart and that something no longer stood between them—

You are losing your mind, Dante had told himself.

The warning hadn't helped.

Everyone ordered coffee. He lifted his cup, frowned, put it down untouched. He was sorry, he said; he had to leave. And he walked away from three men who stared at him as if they agreed with the silent assessment he'd made of his sanity.

He'd flown back to New York, angry at himself, furious at Tally because it was her fault, all of this, his rage, his distrust, his inability to do anything except think about her. If only she'd never run from him...

Her fault. Entirely.

At home, he'd paced the floor, planning how he'd tell her that if she thought she was going to live with him and take someone else for a lover, she was wrong.

He'd kill the other man before he let that happen.

Then he'd told himself that she wasn't living with him, not in any real sense. Besides, maybe she hadn't gone back to the other man. Maybe she'd told him the truth, that she'd only been with that faceless stranger the one time.

One time had been enough.

The son of a bitch had planted a seed in her womb. He'd given her a child he hadn't helped support, a child who was solely Tally's responsibility. A child who by all rights should have belonged to—should have belonged to—

The clock on the mantel had struck the hour. Seven o'clock. Seven at night, and where the hell was she?

Carlo had no idea. Ms. Sommers had sent his car away. Joan, reached at home, didn't know a thing, either.

And Dante, fueled with a rage he didn't understand, had lost control. He'd paced some more, snarled at his housekeeper when she came in to ask what time he wanted dinner served and, when he was alone again, punched his fist into the wall with such force he was surprised he hadn't put a hole in it.

He went down to the lobby, about to head into the street to find Tally—though he had no idea where in hell he'd start—and saw her come sauntering toward the door, with a smile for the doorman and a blank look for him.

He'd wanted to shake her until her teeth rattled.

He'd wanted to haul her into his arms and kiss her.

In the end, because he knew doing either would be a mistake, he'd launched into a tirade that settled nothing except to prove, once again, he was an idiot where she was concerned.

Dante looked at the clock on the mantel. The hours had raced by. It was two in the morning; the city below was as quiet as it would ever be.

Two in the morning, and he was still ticking like a time bomb while Tally undoubtedly slept peacefully two floors above him.

He tilted the glass to his lips and drained it of bourbon. Did she get a kick out of this? Out of making him behave this way? Surely, she knew she had this effect on him.

She did it deliberately.

That was why he'd decided to end their affair three years ago. He hadn't been bored. Who could be bored by a woman who could discuss the stock market and football statistics without missing a beat?

A muscle knotted in his jaw.

He could afford a little honesty now, couldn't he? Admit to himself that the reason he'd wanted to end things was because he'd sensed his feelings for her were becoming uncontrollable?

That night she'd asked him to stay, and he almost had. Other nights when she hadn't asked, when he'd had to force himself from her bed because the thought of leaving her had been agony.

Oh, yes.

Tally was manipulating him. Toying with him and the self-discipline on which he prided himself. The self-discipline that had made him a success.

And he didn't like it, not one bit.

Dante's eyes narrowed. But he knew what to do about it. How to regain that control. Of himself. Of the situation. Of Tally.

Back to Plan A. He would take her to bed.

He had perfect control there. Holding back, not just physically but emotionally. Exulting in what happened between them, feeling it as a hot rush of pleasure so intense he'd never known it with another woman and yet, keeping a little piece of himself from her.

Emotions were not things to put on exhibit. Control was a man's sole protection against a hostile world.

Control, goddamn it, Dante thought.

His hands knotted into fists. Anger burned like a fire in his belly. Anger, and something far more primitive.

Tally was asleep, satisfied she'd made a fool of him again, and he was here, wide awake, trapped like an insect in a web of rage.

"Enough," he growled.

Dante flung open the library door and headed for the stairs.

CHAPTER NINE

MOONLIGHT SPILLED from a sky bright with stars and lay like fine French lace across the floor of Tally's bedroom.

Some other time, she'd have noticed and admired it.

Not tonight.

Instead, she sat curled in a window seat, her back to the night, focused only on the turmoil inside her, anger and pain warring for control of her heart.

She hated Dante, hated the things he'd accused her of. How could he think her capable of being a cheat and a liar?

Maybe because you told him you slept with another man while he was still your lover, a voice inside her whispered contemptuously.

Yes. All right, but what else could she have done? She'd wanted to protect herself and Sam. Now she knew she'd done the right thing. Dante had shown a side of himself she'd never imagined.

She'd always believed he was a man who suppressed his emotions.

Tonight, he'd been a man out of control, capable of anything.

Tally shivered and drew the silk robe more closely around herself. The night seemed endless, especially without Sam in the next room. The baby had dozed off in her play crib in the little room next to the housekeeper's.

"Let her stay the night, Ms. Sommers," Mrs. Tipton had said. "Why wake her from a sound sleep?"

Now Tally was glad she'd left Sam where she was. Her little girl needed the rest. Tomorrow was going to be a busy day.

She and Sam were going home to Shelby.

She'd scrub floors for a living, move into a furnished flat above a storefront on Main Street if she had to. Better that, better to raise her daughter in poverty, than to raise her here.

Tally rose to her feet and paced the bedroom, the details of her confrontation with Dante as alive as if they'd happened minutes instead of hours ago.

What gave him the right to ask where she'd been? To accuse her of sneaking off to be with Samantha's father? She'd come within a breath of laughing in his face at that, except it really wasn't funny.

Okay. She'd made a mistake, accepting this job. Well, a mistake could be remedied. And maybe some good had come of it. At least now she knew exactly what she felt for Dante Russo.

She despised him.

Tally paused, wrapped her arms around herself and drew a shuddering breath. She had to do something or go crazy. She'd pack. Yes. That was an excellent idea. She'd pack now. That way, come morning, all she'd have to do was take Sam and get the hell out of this snake pit.

Ellen had hung all her clothes in the closet, including the things Saks had delivered this afternoon. Tally dumped her old stuff in her suitcase and ignored the rest. Let Dante give it away. Let him burn it, for all she gave a damn.

She didn't want anything his money had bought.

He was a heartless, manipulative, controlling son of a bitch and it made her sick to think she'd ever imagined that she loved him. Anybody could be guilty of a bit of self-deception, but once you knew it you had to do something about it.

She'd spent years in the city, though maybe she was still a small-town girl at heart, unable or unwilling to think she'd slept with a man, borne his child without loving him.

But no woman could love a man who thought he owned you. Who believed you capable of lies and deceit and—

The bedroom door flew open, the sound of it sharp as a gunshot in the quiet night. Tally whirled around.

Dante stood in the doorway, and her heart leaped into her throat.

This was a Dante she'd never seen before.

His suit jacket was gone, as was his tie. His shirt was open at the neck, the sleeves rolled to the elbows, exposing forearms knotted with muscle.

But it was what she saw in the way he held himself that terrified her. The tall, powerful body poised like a big cat's. The dark intensity of his eyes as they fixed on hers. The cruel little smile that tilted across his mouth.

Tally wanted to run but there was nowhere to go. She had to face the enemy.

"What are you doing here, Dante?"

He answered by stepping inside the room and shutting the door behind him.

"It's late," she said.

"I agree. It's very late. I'm here to remedy that."

"And—and Samantha is sleeping. I don't want to wake her."

"Samantha is with Mrs. Tipton." He took another step forward. "Taylor."

He was back to using her given name. How could he make it seem menacing?

"Dante." Her voice quavered. "Dante, please. You want to talk. So do I. But it can wait until morning."

"I don't want to talk, Taylor."

A sob burst from Tally's throat. To hell with facing the enemy. She turned and ran. Sam's bedroom was empty. If she could get there before he reached her—

Two quick steps, and his powerful hands closed on her shoulders; he spun her toward him and she looked up into eyes that glittered with the desolate cold of a polar night.

"No! Don't. Dante—"

He captured her mouth with his, forced her lips apart and penetrated her with his tongue. He tasted of anger and of whiskey, and of a primitive domination that terrified her.

"No," she cried, and struggled to free herself from his grasp, but he laughed, pushed her back against the wall and yanked her hands high above her head.

"Fight me," he growled. "Go on. Fight! It'll make taking you even more pleasurable."

"Please," she panted. "Dante, please. Don't do this. I beg you—"

"All those months I made love to you and it wasn't enough. Is that why you went to him? Did he do things I didn't?"

"Dante. I never—"

He ripped the robe apart, tore her nightgown from the vee between her breasts straight down to her belly.

"Tell me what you wanted that I didn't give you."

"You're wrong. Wrong! It wasn't the way you make it sound. I didn't—"

She cried out as he captured one breast in his hand and rubbed his thumb across the nipple, his cold eyes locked to hers.

"Was it the way he touched your breasts?"

Tears were streaming down her face. Good, he thought. Let her weep. It wouldn't stop him. He would do this. Pierce her flesh with his and banish her from his life, forever.

"Was it the way he touched you here?"

He thrust his hand between her thighs, searching, even in his madness, for the welcoming heat, the sweet moisture he had never forgotten...

And found, instead, the cold, dry flesh of a woman who was unready and unwilling. A woman who was sobbing as if her heart were breaking...

As she had broken his.

Dante went still. He looked at Tally's face and felt the coldness inside him melting.

"Tally."

His arms went around her; he gathered her to him, his hands stroking her back, her hair. He kissed her forehead, her wet eyes, and as she wept he whispered to her, soft words in his native language, but she stood rigid within his embrace, still quietly crying as if the world were about to end.

"Tally." Dante framed her face between his hands. "*Inamorata*. Forgive me. Please. Don't cry. I won't hurt you. I could never hurt you." He raised her chin, looked into her eyes and saw a darkness and despair that chilled his soul.

He dragged in a deep breath, hating himself, hating what he had almost done, knowing that what was driving him was not hate or anger but something else. Something foreign to his life and to him.

A fear he'd never known gripped him.

He'd fought toughs on the streets of Palermo. Faced down CEOs in hostile boardrooms. Made believers of financial analysts who'd looked him in the eye and assured him he couldn't do any of the things he'd ended up doing.

He was a warrior. Each battle he survived made him stronger.

But he wasn't a warrior now. He was a man, holding in his arms a woman he'd already lost once before. She had run from him and he knew, in his heart of hearts, that she'd run because he had somehow failed her.

She'd turned to another man for the same reason.

If she ran again, if he lost her again…

"Tally."

He held her closer. Rained kisses over her hair. Said her name over and over, and finally, finally when he'd almost given up hope, she lifted her face to his.

"I wasn't with anyone," she whispered. "I never wanted anyone but you, Dante. Never. Never. Nev—"

He kissed her. With all his heart, his soul, with all he had ever been or ever hoped to be, and Tally wound her arms around his neck and kissed him back. They had kissed a thousand times. A million times…but never like this, as if their lives hung in the balance.

Mouths fused, Dante swept Tally into his arms and carried her to the bed.

At first, it was enough. The taste of her mouth. The warmth of his breath. Her sighs. His whispers. The stroke of her hand on his face, of his hand on her throat…

It was enough.

Inevitably, it changed.

Dante could feel the tension growing inside him. The need to take more. To give more. To suck Tally's nipples, put his mouth between her thighs and inhale her exquisite scent.

It was the same for Tally. She needed Dante's mouth on her flesh. His hands on her breasts. Needed to lift her hips to him, impale herself on his rock-hard erection so that she could fly with him to the stars.

"Dante," she whispered.

Everything a man could dream was in the way she spoke his name.

He eased the robe and tattered nightgown from her shoulders, kissing the hollow in her throat, the delicate skin over her collarbone.

She was lovely. As beautiful as he'd remembered.

There was a new fullness to her breasts now. The child, Dante thought, and felt a swift pain at the realization that someone else had given that child to her, but it left him quickly because there was so much more to the woman in his arms than that one moment of infidelity.

He bent his head, kissed the slope of each breast. Brushed a finger lightly over a pale-pink nipple.

Watched her face as he played the nub of flesh delicately between thumb and forefinger, and felt the fierce tightening low in his belly when she sobbed his name as he drew the nub into his mouth.

She tasted like cream and honey; she tasted like the Tally he'd never forgotten, never wanted to forget, and when she tugged impatiently at his shirt he sat up, tried unbuttoning it, cursed and tore it off. Peeled off the rest of his clothing and took her in his arms again.

The hot feel of her breasts against his chest almost undid him. Dante groaned, clenched his teeth, warned himself to hang onto his control.

But she was moving beneath him, rubbing herself against his engorged flesh. She was slick and hot, and the exciting scent of her arousal was more precious to him than all the perfumes in the world.

"Please," she said, kissing his shoulder. "Please, please, please…"

"Soon," he whispered, but she arched against him and he was lost. Nothing mattered but this. This, he thought, and entered her on one long, hard thrust.

Tally screamed. Her hands dug into his hair; she wrapped her legs around his hips and bit his shoulder and he let go. Of himself, of his past, of the restraints that had always defined his life.

Together, they soared over the edge of the earth, two hearts, two souls, two bodies merged as one.

AFTERWARD, they lay in each other's arms and shared soft kisses. They touched and sighed, and then Tally's breathing slowed.

"Go to sleep, *inamorata*," Dante whispered.

"What does that mean? *Inamorata?*"

He kissed her. "It means beloved."

Tally smiled and he kissed her again.

"Go to sleep."

"I'm not sleepy," she murmured.

And slept.

Dante gathered her closer against him. How had he endured three long years without this woman in his life?

Except, he had never really let her into his life. They'd been lovers for six months back then but he'd kept his distance. He always did. Dinners out at the city's best restaurants instead of pasta and vino by the fire. Center row seats at the newest Broadway show instead of an evening of old movies on the DVD. Dancing at the latest club instead of swaying in each other's arms to a Billy Joel CD.

How come?

And how come he didn't even know if she liked old movies? If she liked Billy Joel or maybe newer stuff?

Because he'd never let her into his life. That was how come. It was the same reason he'd called her Taylor, when any fool could see that under all the urban glamour, she was really a girl named Tally.

And he—and he felt something special for her.

His arms tightened around her. He wanted to make love to her again but she was sleeping so soundly...

Okay. He'd kiss her closed eyes. Gently. Like that. Kiss her mouth. Tenderly. Yes, that way. Kiss it again and if she sighed, as she was sighing now, if her lips parted so that he could taste her sweetness, yes, like that... If her lashes fluttered and she looked up at him and smiled and linked her hands behind his neck the way she was doing now, would it be wrong to kiss her again? To run his hand gently down her body? To groan as she lifted herself to him, cradled his body between her thighs?

"Make love to me," Tally whispered.

And he would. He would—but first, he lifted her in his arms and rose from the bed.

"Where are we going?"

"To my room," he said huskily. "To my bed. It's where you belong, *inamorata,* where you always should have been." He kissed her. "Where you will be, from this night on."

HIS ROOM WAS SHADOWED, his bed high and wide.

They made love again, slowly, tenderly, until passion swept them up and Dante brought Tally down on him, impaled her on him, and watched her face as she rode him to fulfillment. They slept in each other's arms and awakened again at dawn, Tally wordlessly drawing Dante to her, sighing his name against his throat as he rocked into her and took her with him to the stars.

When she awoke next, it was to the kiss of the morning sun. Dante lay next to her, head propped on his fist, watching her with a soft smile on his lips.

Tally smiled, too. "Hello," she whispered.

He leaned over and kissed her mouth. "Hello, *bellissima.*"

She stretched with lazy abandon. The sheet dropped to her waist. Dante seized the moment and kissed her breasts.

"Sweet," he murmured.

She smiled again. She might never stop smiling, she thought, clasping his face between her hands and pressing a light kiss to his lips.

"I love it when you kiss me," he said softly.

She loved it, too. She could spend the morning like this, just kissing, touching, locked away from reality....

Oh, God. Locked away from Samantha.

"Tally. What's wrong?"

Everything, Tally thought, and it was all her fault. She moved out of Dante's arms and sat up, suddenly conscious of her nudity.

Dante sat up, too, and caught her in his arms. "Talk to me. What's the matter?"

"Sam's an early riser."

"Is that what's worrying you?" Smiling, he drew her to him. "So is Mrs. Tipton."

"Sam is my daughter. My responsibility. Not your housekeeper's."

"Damn it, Tally, don't look away from me." He clasped her face, forced her eyes to meet his. "Moments ago you were in my arms. Now you're looking at me as if we're strangers. Talk to me. Tell me what you're thinking."

Tell him what? That the long, wonderful night had been a mistake? Because it had been. Yes, he'd brought her to his bed, but nothing had changed. She loved him. Why lie to herself? She loved him, she always would...

And all he felt for her was desire.

It hadn't been enough three years ago. It was why she'd decided to leave him, even before she'd known she was carrying his baby. She'd loved him so much that hearing him say he'd tired of her would have killed her.

Now she'd put herself in the same position. He wanted her because she'd defied him, but the novelty would wear thin. He'd tire of her as he had in the past and they'd be right back where they started, with one enormous difference.

This time, she wouldn't be the only one who'd pay the price for her foolishness.

Samantha would pay, as well.

Her daughter. Dante's daughter. God, oh God, oh God...

"Tally?"

She pulled free of his embrace, plucked his robe from the chair beside the bed and slipped it on.

"Dante." Tally got to her feet. "This was—it was a mistake."

He sat up, the comforter dropping to his waist. "What are you talking about?" he said, his voice sharp.

"I shouldn't have slept with you." She tried not to look at him as he rose from the bed, naked and beautifully masculine. "I—I enjoyed last night." The look on his face made her take a quick step back. "But it shouldn't have happened. I have a daughter. That makes everything different. I can't just live for the moment anymore, I have to think of her. Of how much what I do affects her."

"You're a fine mother, *bellissima*. Anyone can see that."

"I try to be. And that means I can't—I can't sleep with you and then go about my life as if nothing's happened. I can't—" Tally caught her breath as he reached for her. "You're not listening."

"I am," he said softly. Gently, he brushed his lips over hers. "You don't want your little girl to see her mother take a lover."

"That's part of it."

"To live a life with her, and a separate one with him."

Tally nodded. He was more perceptive than she'd given him credit for. "She won't understand. And I can't do something that will confuse her. Do you see?"

"Better than you think, *cara*." He hesitated. "I only wish my own mother had thought the same way."

The words were simple but they caught her by surprise. He had never mentioned anything about his past before.

"She took lover after lover," he said, his mouth twisting, "if that's what you want to call them. Sometimes she brought them home. 'This is Guiseppe,' she'd say. Or Angelo or Giovanni or whoever he was, the man of the hour. Then she'd tell me to be a good boy and go out and play."

"Oh, Dante. That must have been—"

"When I was six, seven—I'm not certain. All I know is that one day, she took me to my *nonna's*—my grandmother's. 'Be a good boy, Dante,' she said. And—"

"And?" Tally said softly.

He shrugged. "And I never saw her again."

Tally wanted to take him in her arms and hold him close, but she didn't. She sensed that the moment was fragile, that it would take little to tear it apart.

"I'm sorry," she said quietly. "That must have been—it must have been hard."

Another shrug, as if it didn't matter, but when he spoke, the tension in his voice told her that it did.

"I survived."

"And grew into a strong, wonderful man."

Dante looked at her. "Not so wonderful," he said, "or you wouldn't have left me three years ago."

This time, she did reach out, even if it was only to touch her hand to his cheek.

"I grew up living with my grandmother, too," she said quietly.

"In that little house in Vermont?"

She nodded. "My mother was—Grandma called her flighty." She managed a quick smile. "What it really means is that she took off when I was little and never came back. My father had already done the same thing, even before I was born."

Dante gathered her into his arms.

"What a pair we make," he said gently.

Tally nodded again. "All the more reason that I can't—why we can't—"

"Yes. I agree," he murmured, tucking a strand of hair behind her ear, "and I have the perfect solution."

"There is no solution. I have to protect Sam." *Sam and me.*

"Of course there is." Dante tilted her face to his. "You'll move out of the guest suite."

One night? Was that all he'd wanted? Tally forced herself to nod in agreement.

"Of course. I'll find an apartment and—"

"And," he said softly, "you'll move in with me. We'll let Sam see that we are—that we are together. That we are part of each other's lives, and that she is, too."

Tally stared at him, her face a mask of confusion. Was she trying to find a way to tell him she wouldn't go along with his plan? It had come to him during the night; he'd been pleased with it until this moment, when he realized that Tally might not want to be with him this way.

"Tally." His hands slid to her shoulders. "Please." His fingers bit into her flesh. "Tell me want to be with me. I don't want to lose you again. Say yes."

Her head whispered of reservations, of questions, of why the arrangement would never work...

But Tally listened to her heart and said, "Yes."

CHAPTER TEN

THROUGHOUT THE AGES, wise men caution that a man who makes decisions in the heat of the moment might very well live to regret them.

Dante had always agreed.

He was not impulsive. He made choices only after he had examined all the facts. If a man did anything less, he might, indeed, live to regret his decisions.

And yet, he'd acted on impulse when he'd asked Tally to live with him.

It should have been a mistake. The worst mistake of his life, considering that he'd never asked a woman to do that before. Living together, spending your days and nights with one woman, was the kind of involvement he'd always avoided. He liked to come and go as he pleased, to spend time in a woman's company only when he was in the mood.

Add a small child to the mix and a man would surely go crazy.

At least, that was what he'd have said of this new arrangement a week ago. A disaster in the making, he'd have called it…

Dante smiled as he stood at his office window and watched the lights wink on over Manhattan.

He'd have been wrong.

Asking Tally to live with him had turned out to be the best decision he'd ever made. Being with her, with Samantha, had already changed his life.

He'd lived in New York for more than a dozen years and most of that time he'd lived very comfortably. As his fortune grew, he'd become accustomed to a certain start and finish to his day.

In the morning, his housekeeper would ask if he'd be home for dinner; in the evening, she'd inquire pleasantly as to how his day had gone. If the doorman made a comment beyond "Good morning" or "Good evening" it was about the weather. His driver might exchange a few polite words with him about European soccer or American football.

Dante's smile became a grin. How that had changed!

Mrs. Tipton regaled him with stories about Sam. Carlo, whose grandson turned out to be Sam's age, was a font of helpful advice. Even the doorman got into the act with details of Sam's latest adventure among the big potted plants in the lobby.

Sam herself, a bundle of energy with big green eyes and a toothy grin, started and ended his days with sloppy kisses.

Amazing, all of it.

But most amazing was his Tally, who fell asleep in his arms each night and awoke in them each morning. She was the most incredible woman he'd ever known, and he wasn't the only one who thought so.

His architect told him she had the best eye for detail

he'd ever seen. His contractor said she made suggestions that were as innovative as they were practical. Even his P.A., a woman who had seen everything and was surprised by nothing, called her remarkable.

His household staff flat-out adored her.

But not as much as he did.

Dante tucked his hands in his trouser pockets and rocked back on his heels. He'd never believed in luck. What you got out of life was in direct proportion to what you put into it, and yet he knew it was luck, good fortune, whatever you wanted to call it, that had given him this second chance with Tally.

He'd lost her through his own callous behavior. He understood that now. He'd treated her like a possession, taking her from the shelf when he wanted to show her off, returning her when he'd finished. It was how he'd always treated his lovers. Kept them at a distance, bought them elaborate gifts, and politely eliminated them from his life when he got bored.

Dante's jaw clenched.

But Tally had never behaved like his other lovers. She'd kept herself at a distance. That was why she'd refused his elaborate gifts and left behind the ones he'd insisted she accept. And she had never bored him. Never. Not for a moment, in bed or out.

At some point, he'd realized it. And it had shaken him to the core. He'd reacted by pushing her away because he hadn't been ready to admit what she had come to mean to him. As recently as a few weeks ago, he'd still been lying to himself about his feelings for her.

That whole thing about wanting to sleep with her to get revenge, get her out of his system…

Sheer, unadulterated idiocy.

It had always been easier to pretend she was just another woman passing through his life than admit his Tally was special. That what he felt for her was special. That what he felt for her was—that it was—

"Dante?"

He swung around, saw her in the doorway and felt his heart swell. And when she smiled, he thought it might burst.

"I knocked," she said, with a little smile, "but you didn't—"

Dante held out his arms. She went into them and he held her close.

"You look beautiful," he said softly.

She leaned back in his embrace. "Not too dressed up?"

He shook his head. "Perfect."

That was the only word to describe her in a softly clinging silk dress and matching jacket in a color he'd have called green but he suspected women gave a more complex name. Her shoes were wispy things, all straps and slender heels, the kind that made a man imagine his woman wearing them with whatever was under the dress and nothing else.

Dante had a pretty good idea of what was under that dress. He'd bought Tally a drawer full of wispy lingerie from The Silk Butterfly, a shop he'd passed on Fifth Avenue.

"Hand-sewn lace," she'd said, her cheeks taking on a light blush. "I'll feel naked under my clothes." And he'd taken her in his arms and shown her just how exciting that would be for them both.

"I know tonight's important to you."

"You're what's important to me."

"Yes, but tonight—the Children's Fund dinner…"

"Tally. We don't have to go. I told you that. We can have a quiet dinner at that little place on the corner and—"

"No. No, I don't want you to change anything because of me. Everyone you know will be there."

"Everyone *we* know. And they'll see how happy we are to be together again."

She nodded, but her eyes were clouded. "There'll be questions."

Dante raised one eyebrow. "No one will dare to ask questions of me." That made her laugh, just as he'd hoped it would. He took her hand, brought it to his mouth and kissed it. "I missed you."

"You saw me an hour ago," she said with another little laugh.

"And that's far too long to be without you." He drew her closer. "It's going to cost you a kiss."

"Dante. Someone will see."

"I don't care."

"But—"

"If I don't get a kiss from you this very minute," he said dramatically, "my death will be on your hands."

She laughed again. He loved the sound of her laugh, the way her lips curved into an eminently kissable bow. He loved everything about her.

The truth was, he loved—he loved—

Dante bent his head and kissed her.

THEY ARRIVED a few minutes late and found five of their dinner companions already at the table. A well-known real estate agent and his third trophy wife. Dennis and Eve. A used-car salesman turned self-help guru, whose latest feel-good book had just gone into its fifth printing.

Tally remembered them all.

And, clearly, they remembered her. She could almost hear their jaws hit the table when they saw her.

Dante had his arm firmly around her waist.

"Good evening," he said pleasantly. "Tally, I think you know everyone here, don't you?"

"Yes," she said brightly, "of course. How are you, Lila? Donald? Eve and Dennis, how good to see you again. And Mark. Your newest book just came out, didn't it? I hope it's doing well?"

Dante pulled out her chair, whispered, "Good girl," as she slipped into it. He sat down beside her, took her hand and held it in his, right on the tabletop where everyone could see. Five pairs of eyes took in the sight. Then someone said, "Well, I see we're going to have chicken for the main course. Surprise, surprise."

Everyone laughed, and that broke the ice.

People began chatting. Wasn't the weather particularly cold for December? Was snow in the forecast again? Wasn't the ballroom handsomely decorated?

I might just get through this, Tally thought...

"DanteDarling," a woman screeched.

And Tally looked up, inhaled a cloud of obscenely expensive perfume, saw Charlotte LeBlanc swoop down to plant a kiss on Dante's mouth even as he jerked back in his chair, saw the woman's hate-filled gaze fix on her before she switched it to a big, artificial smile...

And knew, instinctively, that Charlotte LeBlanc had, probably until very recently, been Dante's mistress.

"Taylor," Charlotte said. "What a surprise!"

"Yes," Tally said, "yes, I—I suppose it is."

"A wonderful surprise," Dante said, squeezing Tally's hand, but he was looking at Charlotte, his eyes cold with warning, and any doubts Tally might have had about her lover's relationship with the LeBlanc woman vanished.

Conversation swirled around her, the polite stuff people discussed when they were casual acquaintances. Eve talked about her new hair stylist. Dennis said he was buying a new yacht. The self-help guru was also buying one. The real estate agent was too busy eating his shrimp cocktail to say anything. His trophy wife was silent, too, perhaps because her face was frozen in Botoxed bliss.

And suddenly, in a lull in the chatter, Charlotte leaned over, her breasts almost spilling from her neckline, and laid a taloned hand on Tally's arm.

"Taylor," she cooed, "you must tell us all where you've been the last few years."

"She's been in New England," Dante said smoothly. "Building a successful business."

"New England. How quaint." Her smile glittered with malice. "And are you here on business?"

"Taylor's working on a project of mine."

"How nice." Her head swiveled toward Dante. "And you, DanteDarling. Are you and I still on for Christmas in Aspen?"

Dante's eyes went black. "No," he said coldly, "we are not. I told you that weeks ago."

"Oh, but everyone knows how you tend to change your mind, DanteDarling. How fickle you are, well, not about business but about, you know, other things."

There was no mistaking what "things" she meant. Heads swiveled from Charlotte to Tally to Dante, who snarled a word no one had to speak Sicilian to comprehend.

Charlotte turned red. Everyone else gasped. And Tally pushed her chair back from the table.

"Tally! Damn it, Tally…"

Luck was with her. The band was playing and the dance floor was crowded with couples. Tally wove through the mob, pulled open the door to the ladies' room and slammed it behind her. A sob burst from her throat.

How could she have been so stupid? He'd been with that woman. With Charlotte. He'd been with God only knew how many women these last three years. She'd dreamed of him, yearned for him, wanted only him despite all the lies she'd told herself, but Dante…

"Tally!"

His fist slammed against the door.

"Tally! Open this door or I'm coming in."

One of the stall doors swung open. A woman stepped out and stared at her.

"Tally, do you hear me? Open this goddamned door!"

Tally went to the sink, splashed cold water on her face. She would have ignored the hammering on the door but the woman who'd come out of the stall was looking at her as if she'd somehow wandered into the sort of situation that ended in bloodshed.

There was nothing for it but to square her shoulders and walk out of the ladies' room, straight into a muscled wall of male fury.

"Dante," she said quietly, "please, step aside."

He answered by clasping her shoulders and hauling her to her toes.

"If I'd known that bitch would be at our table," he demanded, "do you really think I'd have brought you here tonight?"

"It doesn't matter. Step aside, please."

"Of course it matters! Damn it, she means nothing to me!"

"Dante. Get out of my—"

"Are you deaf?" His hands bit hard into her flesh as he lowered his face to hers. "She doesn't matter."

"She matters enough so you were going to take her to Aspen."

"She suggested it. I said no. In fact, I never saw her after that evening. We were finished and she knew it."

Tally looked into his eyes. They were the color of smoke, and without warning, the pain inside her burst free.

"You slept with her," she whispered.

His mouth twisted. "Tally. *Bellissima…*"

"You should have told me. So I—I could have been prepared to see the way she looked at you. To know you'd been with her, made love to her—"

"It was sex," he said roughly. "Only sex. Never anything more."

She stared into his eyes again. *And what is it with me?* she longed to say, but her heart knew better than to ask.

"How many were there?" Her voice trembled and she hated herself for it. She'd known a man virile as Dante wouldn't live like a monk but to see the proof for herself… "How many women after me?"

His grasp on her tightened. "What does it matter? All

the years we were apart, I never stopped thinking of you. I hated you for leaving me, Tally—and hated myself for not being able to get over you."

Tally looked away from him, certain that her heart was going to break. If he couldn't get over her, how could he have betrayed her with other women? In the endless years since leaving him, she had never even thought of anyone else. She had never betrayed him...

But she had.

Running away had been a kind of betrayal. Even the cold, cleverly worded note she'd left had been a betrayal.

And then there was the cruelest betrayal of all. She'd told him she'd cheated on him with another man, that she'd given birth to that man's child.

"Tally." His voice was thick with anguish. "There's never been anyone but you. You must believe me!"

Slowly she lifted her eyes to his. "What I believe," she whispered, "is that we've both been fools."

He nodded. She could see color returning to his face.

"Yes. We have been, but we won't be any longer." He framed her face with his hands and raised it to his. "I'm not going to lose you again, *inamorata*. I won't let it happen."

Tears gathered on Tally's lashes. Gently Dante kissed them away. Then he wrapped his arm around her shoulders.

"Let's go home."

She smiled. "Yes. Let's go home."

He led her past the curious little group that had been watching them, out of the hotel and into his waiting limousine. Part of him wanted to go back to the ballroom, put his hands around Charlotte's throat and make her pay for what she'd done.

But he was every bit as guilty.

Not for having slept with Charlotte. Tally had been out of his life then. Not even for having not told her about Charlotte. He was a man, not a saint. What man would deliberately tell the woman he cared for that he'd slept with someone else, even if he'd been absolutely free to do so at the time?

He pressed a kiss to Tally's hair as she sat curled against him, her head on his shoulder.

His guilt was over what he'd done three years ago.

He'd let Tally slip away. And he should have gone after her. Should have faced what she meant to him because the truth was he didn't just care for her, he—he—

"Dante?"

Dante cleared his throat. "Yes, *cara?*"

"I'm sorry."

"No! It wasn't your fault."

"Not about tonight. I'm… I'm sorry for…for—" She took a deep breath and sat up straight, her eyes locked to his. "We need to talk. But not here. Someplace… someplace where we can be alone."

Suddenly he knew that was what he wanted, too. A quiet place where they could be alone. Where they could talk—and he could finally confront what was in his heart.

"I have an idea," he said slowly. "Christmas is next week. What if we spend it alone? Just the three of us. You and me and Samantha. We'll go somewhere warm, where we can lie in the sun in each other's arms, where Sam can run around to her heart's content. Would you like that?"

"A place where we can talk," Tally said softly.

Talk about what had really made her run away, she thought as Dante drew her against him, because tonight, she'd finally faced the truth.

No matter what happened, she had to tell Dante that she loved him.

That there'd never been another man.

That he was Sam's father.

CHAPTER ELEVEN

WHAT COULD BE more wonderful than lying in the curve of your lover's arm on a white sand beach under the hot Caribbean sun?

Tally turned her head and put her mouth lightly against Dante's bronzed skin, savoring the exciting taste of salt and man.

How she adored him!

Her Dante was everything a man should be. Strong. Tender. Giving. Demanding. Fiercely passionate, incredibly gentle. She loved him, loved him, loved him…

And it killed her that she'd lied to him.

That she was still lying to him, because she'd yet to tell him the truth about Sam.

Soon, she thought, as she closed her eyes and burrowed closer to his warm, hard body. She'd confess everything to him this evening, after dinner, when they were both tucking Sam in for the night. Or tomorrow morning, at breakfast. And if the time didn't seem right then, she'd wait just another few hours. Another few days…

Tally swallowed hard. *Liar,* she thought, *liar, liar, liar!*

She wouldn't tell him tonight, or tomorrow. Or ever,

at the rate she was going. She wanted to. Wanted to say, *Dante, I've done an awful thing. I lied to you about Sam. About being with someone else. Sam is your child. Ever since we met, there's only been you.*

The problem was, she could see beyond that.

She had let him think she'd been unfaithful.

She had denied him knowledge of his own child.

Who could predict how he'd react?

Some days, she was sure he would understand. Others, she was afraid he wouldn't. She'd thought it would be so easy to admit everything once they were here, on this beautiful island in the midst of a sea as clear as fine green glass, tucked away from the world in a magnificent house on its own long, pristine, private beach. Just the three of them: she and Dante and Samantha. No housekeeper. No maid. No nanny or chauffeur. Just she and the man she loved and her little girl.

Their little girl.

Except, Dante didn't know that yet because she was a coward, because she was terrified of what he'd say, what he'd do when he knew she'd deceived him in the worst way possible—

"*Bellissima,* what's wrong?" Tally's eyes flew open as Dante brushed his lips over hers. "You were whimpering in your sleep, *cara*. Were you having a bad dream?"

"I… I… Yes. Something like that."

Smiling, he kissed her again. "You've been in the sun too long. That's the problem."

Now. Tell him now!

"Dante."

"Hmm?" He bent to her and kissed her again, parting

her lips and slowly slipping the tip of his tongue into her mouth. "You taste delicious."

So did he. Oh, so did—

"Dante." Her breath caught. His mouth was at her throat, her breast, nipping lightly at the rapidly beading tip through the thin cotton of her bikini top. "Dante…"

"I'll bet you taste even more delicious here," he whispered as he slid his hands behind her, undid the top, his eyes shining brightest silver as he exposed her breasts. "Let me see if I'm right."

Tally cried out, arching against him as he drew her nipple into the wet heat of his mouth; even as he began easing her bikini bottom down her thighs, she felt it starting to happen, the shimmering heat building inside her, the hot rush of desire as he stroked her dampening curls, put his mouth to her until she was begging him, pleading with him, to take her.

Slowly, so slowly that she thought it might never end, prayed it might never end, he entered her. Filled her, stretched her, moved deep inside her while he whispered to her in Sicilian, words she didn't know but somehow understood, and she thought, *I love you, Dante. I've always loved you. Only you.*

And shattered like crystal in his arms.

AFTER, HE CARRIED HER into the house, past the room where Samantha lay sleeping, to their bedroom and their canopied bed overlooking the sea.

Gently, he lay her in the center of the white sheets, came down beside her and drew her into his arms. Tally put her face in his neck and sighed.

"I love it here," she said softly.

"I'm glad."

"The house is so beautiful. And the sea… I've never seen a sea this clear."

Dante smiled as he stroked his hand gently up and down her spine. "There's a beach on the Mediterranean where you can stand knee-deep in the water and watch tiny fish swim by like flashes of blue and green light."

Tally tilted her head back so she could see his face. "Is that where you lived with your *nonna?* In a town by the sea?"

"Nothing so postcard-perfect, *cara*. I grew up in Palermo, on a street that was already old when Rome ruled the world."

"It sounds wonderful. All that history—"

"Trust me, Tally. There was nothing wonderful about it. Everyone was dirt-poor, except for us." He gave a self-deprecating laugh. "We were poorer than that."

"Then, everything you have today—you built it all, from scratch?" She smiled. "The amazing Mr. Russo."

He grinned, lifted her so that she lay stretched out along his length.

Well," he said, "if you want to call me that—"

Tally rolled her eyes, brought her mouth to his and kissed him. "Don't let it go to your head," she said softly, "but you really are. Amazing."

Dante framed her face with his hands. "What's amazing," he whispered, "is you."

That brought her back to reality. "Dante," she said carefully, "Dante, do you remember what I said the other night? That we have to talk."

"I agree. We do." His eyes grew hooded. "But not right now."

"Dante. Please—"

"Please what?" He cupped her hips, eased her to her knees above him. "Please, this?" he whispered, and she felt the tip of his erection kiss her labia. "Tell me and I'll do it. I'll do whatever you want, *inamorata*. Anything. Everything…"

Then he was inside her, and words had no meaning. All that mattered was this. This…

This.

AN HOUR LATER, Dante eased his arm from beneath Tally's shoulders, touched his mouth lightly to hers, slipped on a pair of denim shorts and went to check on Sam.

The baby woke just as he peeked into her room. When she saw him, she grinned, said "Da-Tay" and held out her chubby arms. Dante grinned back, picked her up and gave her a kiss.

"Hello, *bambina*. Did you have a good nap?"

"Goo'nap," she said happily.

"I'll bet you need a diaper change."

"Di-chain," Sam gurgled, and Dante laughed.

"You're a regular little echo chamber, aren't you?"

"Eck-chame," Sam said.

Dante laughed again, put her on the changing table and replaced her wet diaper with a fresh one. Then he carried her through the house, into the kitchen, put her in the booster chair at the table while he filled a sippy-cup with milk. She liked it warm so he heated it in the microwave oven, tested a drop on his wrist, screwed the top on, plucked her from the booster, went out on the porch and sat down with her in his arms.

She could handle the sippy-cup herself and he knew

it, but he liked holding her, liked the warm weight of the baby, her sweet smell, the little noises of delight she made as she fed.

He liked caring for Samantha in general. Well, maybe not the poopy-diapers part, which he'd done when he heard her babbling softly to herself early this morning. Why wake Tally when he could change the diaper himself, even if it had been a rather interesting learning experience?

The truth was, he'd never imagined himself with a baby in his arms. Oh, he'd figured on having children someday. A man wanted children to carry on his genes, his life's work, but his thoughts had been of faceless miniature adults and a faceless perfect wife. Now, of course, he knew better.

He wanted a little girl exactly like Sam.

A wife exactly like Tally.

Dante caught his breath.

And, just that easily, came face-to-face with the truth.

He loved Tally. He loved her daughter. He had his family already, right here, the baby in his arms, the woman he adored in his bed.

He rose to his feet, ready to rush to the bedroom, wake Tally with a kiss, tell her what was in his heart—

No. He wanted this to be just right. All the romantic touches he'd always scoffed at. Candlelight. Flowers. Champagne.

The travel agent had given him the name of a respected island family that lived nearby. He waited until Sam finished her milk. Then he kept her safely in the curve of his arm while he made some phone calls. When he was done, he'd arranged for a babysitter, reserved a secluded table at a five-star restaurant on the beach, and ordered a ten-carat canary-yellow diamond in a platinum setting from the delighted owner of the island's most exclusive jewelry shop, with instructions to have a messenger bring the ring to the restaurant promptly at nine that night.

He was about to order flowers when Sam giggled and said, "Mama!"

Dante looked up and saw Tally.

"Hey," she said, smiling.

"Hey," he said softly, smiling back at her.

"You should have woken me."

"Your hear that, kid? Your mother doesn't think we can handle the tough stuff on our own." He paused. "Tally?"

"Hmm?"

I love you. I adore you. I want to marry you and adopt Sam, raise her as our very own daughter…

"What on earth are you thinking" she said, with a little laugh. "You have the strangest look on your face!"

"Do I?" He cleared his throat. "Maybe it's because— because what I was thinking was that I want to celebrate Christmas this evening."

Tally laughed. "Christmas is two days away!"

"You don't think I'm going to permit a little detail like that to stop me, do you?" Smiling, he came toward her. Sam held out her arms and he handed her to her mother. "In fact, I've already made plans for us tonight."

"What plans?" Tally said, hugging her daughter, putting her face up for Dante's kiss, thinking how right all this was, being here together, the man she loved, the child they'd created together. "What plans?" she said again and knew that tonight, no matter what happened, she would tell him everything.

His smile tilted. "It's a surprise. A good one," he added softly, "one I hope will make you happy." He put his arms around them both, the woman he loved and the child he would make his.

The child that should have been his, if he hadn't been so stupid and self-involved.

He felt the dull pain of regret settle over him.

If only Sam really were his. He loved her but sometimes—sometimes it hurt to know that Tally had lain with another man. That someone else had joined with her to create this beautiful little life.

"Dante," Tally said softly, "what's wrong?"

"Nothing." He cleared his throat. "I was just thinking about tonight."

"You looked—you looked sad."

"Sad?" He smiled, forced the dark thoughts away. "Nonsense," he said briskly. "I'm just making sure I've thought of everything. Sam's babysitter. Our dinner reservations."

"Are we having dinner out?"

"We are. At that place on the beach."

Tally gave him the look women have always given men who are too dense to understand life's basic rules of survival.

"That place? But I don't have anything to wear! You said we'd only need swimsuits. Shorts. Jeans. I can't go there in jeans, Dante!"

He thought she could go there in what she wore now and still be more beautiful than any woman in the place, but this played right into his hands. He still had things to arrange. The flowers for their meal and for the house when they returned to it later. Candles for the bedroom.

More champagne, to drink on the beach once she had his ring on her finger.

"I agree," he said solemnly. "That's why you're going to take my credit card, taxi into town and buy whatever you need for tonight."

"But—"

He silenced the protest with a kiss.

"Find something long and elegant. Something so sexy it will make every man who sees you want me dead so he can claim you for his own." He kissed her again and she leaned into him, the baby gurgling happily between them, and half an hour later, holding Sam in his arms, both of them waving as the taxi and Tally pulled away, Dante knew he was, without question, the luckiest man alive.

HE MADE THE BALANCE of the phone calls, arranged for the delivery of white orchids, white candles and bottles of Cristal. The last call went to his attorney in New York, where he left a message asking him to research the state's adoption laws and to determine the quickest way to effect an adoption.

"I think that about does it, Sammy," he said, grinning at the way Samantha looked when he called her that. It wasn't elegant, but he liked it.

Then he turned all his attention on the child who would soon be his.

He took her into the pool, rode her on his shoulders in the warm water as she laughed and clutched at his hair with her fists.

He held her hand as they walked along the beach, helping her pick up shells, making a show of putting them into his pocket for later while surreptitiously letting ones that were too small for her safety fall to the sand.

He made himself a cup of coffee, handed Sam a sippy-cup of juice and shared an Oreo cookie with her, chuckling as he imagined what all those who trembled at his presence in a boardroom would think if they could see him eating the chunks she handed him, baby drool and all.

Late afternoon, with the sun high overhead, he sat on the palm-shaded patio, Sam playing at his feet. She gave a huge yawn.

"Nap time," he said.

Sam, who was, of course, brilliant for her age, puckered up her baby face and yowled.

"Okay, okay, forget I mentioned it."

The baby smiled, yawned again, put her head down and her rump up, and promptly fell asleep on the blanket at his feet. Dante yawned, too, picked up the magazine he'd been leafing through, wondered if Tally—his Tally—would be as happy as he wanted her to be when he proposed tonight.

She would—wouldn't she?

She loved him—didn't she?

He hadn't really thought about it until now. Yes. Of course she loved him. The way she sighed in his arms. Smiled into his eyes. The way he caught her watching him sometimes, that little smile curving her lips—

What was that? A dark shape, near his foot.

"Dio mio!"

Sam woke up screaming as a thing with eight legs raced across her outflung hand. Dante scooped the child into his arms, stomped on the ugly black thing and saw the bite marks of its fangs on Sam's tender wrist.

"Sam," he said, "Sam, *mia figlia—*"

Her shriek of pain rose into the air. Even as he scooped her into his arms, Dante saw the flesh around the bite start to swell. He paused only long enough to tie a scarf around her arm above the bite and to pick up the dead spider, place it in his handkerchief and tuck it into his pocket.

Heart racing, he ran for his car.

HE PHONED THE HOSPITAL when he was two blocks away. Two physicians and a nurse were waiting outside the emergency room. The nurse tried to take Sam from his arms but he refused to give her up.

"I'm staying with her," he said, and neither the doctors nor the nurse doubted his determination.

They led him into an examining room. Sam clung to his neck, sobbing. He soothed her with words he barely knew, things he'd heard people say to weeping children, things he'd once wished his *nonna* had said to him when he was small and he'd skinned his knee or bloodied his nose, except this wasn't a bloody knee or nose, he thought, as he dug in his pocket and produced the ugly corpse.

The nurse grimaced; one of the physicians barked out a command, and Dante's heart turned over when the nurse appeared with a tiny needle and reached for Sam's hand.

"Shh, *bambina,*" he whispered, "everything will be all right."

But Sam was past listening. Her little body arched; Dante cursed as a convulsion tore through her.

"Do something," he snarled.

"Wait outside," the doctor snapped.

Dante flashed him a look the man would never forget. "I will not leave my baby," he said.

He didn't. Not until Sam finally opened her eyes and looked at him.

"Da-Tay," she whispered, and for the first time since his mother had left him, Dante wept.

IT TOOK TWO HOURS and a dozen calls to the house by the sea before Tally answered the phone.

She was, as Dante had anticipated, frantic.

"Dante! Dear God, where are you? Where is Samantha? I came home and the place was empty and—"

He interrupted. Told her everything was fine, that they were at the hospital, in the emergency room. Lied and said he'd let his worry over a little bug bite get out of hand. He didn't want her to know the truth until he could take her in his arms and hold her and she could see for herself that the crisis was over.

He was waiting at the big double doors of the emergency room when she came flying through them.

"Where's my baby?"

Dante caught her in his arms. "She's fine, *cara*."

"Tell me the truth. My baby—"

"Tally." He held her by the shoulders, brought his eyes level with hers. "I would never lie to you. Never."

She nodded, though he could feel her tremble in his embrace. Slowly, carefully, he explained what had happened. When she swayed, he gathered her against him, rocked her gently until she pushed her hands against his chest and looked into his eyes.

"Where is she?"

He kept his arm around her, let his strength seep into her as he led her to Sam's room. The room was private; so was the nurse who sat beside the baby in the white crib, peacefully sleeping. The danger was past but the IV was still in her arm.

Tally bent over the crib and put her hand on her daughter's back. Tears fell from her eyes.

"My baby," she whispered, "oh, my sweet little girl! I could have lost you."

"Your husband did all the right things, Mrs. Russo," the nurse said softly. "Without his quick thinking, things would have been much worse."

Tally looked at the woman. "But he isn't—"

Dante slid his arm around her shoulders. "Let's let Sam sleep, *cara*. Come into the hall and we can talk."

Bewildered, Tally followed him from the room. "She thinks you and I are married?"

"I don't know the laws here, *cara*. But I remember reading about a child somewhere who died because a hospital wouldn't provide emergency treatment without the permission of a parent." He clasped her shoulders. "I wasn't going to run that risk. Not with our little girl."

Tally swallowed hard. *Our little girl. Our little girl.*

"Don't look at me that way, *cara*. I had no choice. Our Samantha—"

It was her fault, all of it. She had denied Dante knowledge of his child, denied Sam her father. And now, dear God, and now Sam might have died if Dante hadn't thought quickly—

"Tally."

She looked up at him. His face was drawn. He had gone through so much today for a child he didn't know was his, a child he loved.

"Tally." Dante paused. "I know my timing is bad but—*cara*, I want to marry you. And I want to adopt Sam. I want to be her father."

Tears swam in Tally's eyes. "Oh, Dante…"

"I love you. And I love her, as much as if she were my daughter."

Tally began to weep. There was no hiding her secret, not anymore.

"Dante," she said brokenly, "Sam *is* your daughter!"

There was a long silence, broken only by the sound of Dante's breathing and Tally's sobs. When he finally spoke, his voice was without inflection.

"What do you mean, Sam is my daughter?"

"I should have told you. I wanted to tell you—"

She gasped as his hands bit into her shoulders. "Tell me what?"

"There was no other man. I made it up. Samantha is—she's your child."

Moments, an eternity, slipped by. Tally waited, trying to read Dante's face, to see something of what would come next.

"Let me make sure I understand this. You didn't sleep with someone else."

"No."

"You didn't get pregnant by another man."

"I know I should have told you, but—"

"You knew you were pregnant, and you left me anyway?"

"Dante. Please. Listen to what I'm saying. I knew

you'd grown tired of me. How could I have told you I was having a baby?"

"My baby." His voice was like a whip; he caught her wrists and pushed her back against the wall. "*My* baby!"

"It isn't that simple!"

"On the contrary, Taylor. It's brutally simple. You became pregnant with my child and didn't tell me. You were going to raise her to think she had no father."

Tally wrenched her hands free and slapped them over her ears. "Stop it!"

"You were going to raise Samantha—my daughter— as I was raised. Fatherless. Impoverished."

"It wasn't like that, damn it! I did what I thought was right."

"For who? Surely not for Samantha. And not for me."

"Remember when I said I wanted to talk to you? It was about this. About you and Sam. But I had to wait for the right time."

He gave a hollow laugh. "Another lie. How many more will you tell before I know the entire truth?"

Tally stared up into her lover's enraged eyes. He was right. It was time for the truth. All of it.

"No more lies," she said, her voice trembling. "Here's the truth. Sam is yours. There was never anyone else. And I left you—I left you because I knew I'd fallen in love with you."

"Such a pretty story."

"I swear it's true! I still love you. I always will."

"As soon as my daughter is fully recovered," he said, as if she hadn't spoken, "we'll fly back to New York."

"Damn you, Dante! Listen to me!"

"You will move back into the guest suite. I'll permit

that because I don't want my child to be traumatized by too many changes all at once."

A cold knot of fear gripped Tally's stomach. "What does that mean?"

Dante smiled thinly.

"It means," he said silkily, "that Samantha is mine. That you stole her from me. That you are an unfit mother." He paused. "And that I intend to gain custody—sole custody—of her."

"No!" Tally's voice rose in horror. "You can't take her from me. No court will permit it!"

Dante ignored her, walked to the room where Sam lay sleeping and sat down in a chair beside the crib. So much for love. For putting your heart in someone's hands. For being foolish enough to think life was ever anything but a cruel joke.

He took his cell phone from his pocket, called his attorney, cut through the man's perfunctory greeting and told him he'd just learned he was the father of a two-year-old child.

The lawyer, who dealt with several wealthy clients, cut to the chase.

"How much does the woman want?"

"You misunderstand me," Dante said. "I don't want to deny my paternity of the child, I want to claim her. I want full custody. Will that be a problem?"

He listened, answered a couple of questions, then smiled.

There were times having money, power and the right connections paid off.

CHAPTER TWELVE

MOMENTS LATER, TALLY entered the room.

Dante, still seated beside the crib and the sleeping baby, looked at the nurse.

"Please take your dinner break now."

He spoke politely, but that didn't lessen his tone of command. The woman left without a backward glance. Tally looked at him, but he didn't acknowledge her presence.

Anyone looking at him would assume he was angry.

She knew better. He was furious. And it frightened her. Dante was a powerful adversary in any situation. Now he would be formidable.

But he wouldn't win. She would do whatever it took to keep her child and defeat him, and that meant facing up to him, starting now.

She moved the nurse's abandoned chair to the other side of the crib and sat down. Her face softened as she looked at her little girl, so peacefully asleep.

Samantha was hers.

No court in the land would separate a mother from her child, not even to satisfy Dante Russo. None, she thought…and maybe because she wished she really believed it, she spoke the words aloud.

"You won't win," she said.

He looked at her, his eyes empty. "Of course I will."

Her face paled. Good. He was happy to see it. She deserved what would come next. She had brought it on herself with her lies.

His attorney was already earning his million-dollar-a-year retainer, drawing up motions and citing precedents even though the hour was late and Christmas was only a couple of days away.

Dante had no doubt as to which of them would gain custody. Tally had apple pie and motherhood on her side, but he had the things that really mattered.

What a fool he'd been, imagining himself in love. He almost laughed. He, of all people, knew that the word had no meaning. His mother had claimed to love him, right up to the day she kissed him, told him to be a good boy, and vanished. His *nonna* had claimed to love him, too, and proved it by beating the crap out of him at every opportunity until he finally ran away.

Emotion was weakness. Self-discipline was strength. This woman had made him forget that, but he would not make the same mistake again.

The one thing he couldn't understand was why she had kept her pregnancy from him. He was rich. She could have milked him for a lot of money. He knew men who'd had that happen to them. A woman got pregnant, deliberately pregnant, and dipped her manicured hands into a man's bank account.

Anyone could see that Tally could have used the cash. The old house in Vermont, the business she'd attempted… An infusion of dollars would have changed her life.

All right. She had not been after his money. He had to admit that. And he had to admit that she seemed to be a good mother.

Why, then, had she lied? Why had she left him?

Because she loved him. That was what she'd said.

What a joke!

A woman who loved a man didn't run from him. She didn't give birth to his child and tell him the child was someone else's. *Dio,* the anger and pain that had caused him. The nights he'd lain awake, held Tally in his arms, tried not to wonder if she were dreaming of him or of her other lover.

His mouth thinned.

It was some consolation, at least, knowing she had not belonged to anyone else. That she had been his. Only his. That no one else had made love to her, held her close, felt the whisper of her breath against his throat while she slept in his arms.

He'd blanked his mind to the rest. To what she'd looked like when she was pregnant. Now, knowing Sam was his, that was impossible to do.

Her breasts would have been full, the skin translucent over the delicate tracery of her veins. Her belly would have been round, lush with the life they'd created. She had denied him the wonder of those months. The feel of his child, kicking in her mother's womb. The moment of his child's entry into the world.

All those signs, the proof of their love…

Except, it had never been love.

Never. Love was just a polite four-letter word men

and women used in mixed company. Taylor's lies were the issue here, not love.

He'd had the right to know the truth. She should have told him.

He looked up. Tally sat with her head bowed. "You should have told me," he said coldly.

She raised her eyes to his.

"You're right. I should have."

"But you didn't."

"No. I didn't. I've tried to explain, to say I'm sorry—"

"I'm not interested in apologies or explanations."

She gave a sad little laugh. "No. You're only interested in you. That's one of the reasons I didn't tell you I was pregnant. I was afraid you'd react exactly this way, as if our baby's existence concerned only you."

"You're good at making excuses."

"Not as good as you are at feeling nothing for anyone but yourself." Her voice trembled. "I think you do care for Samantha, though. And that surprises me."

"A compliment, *cara*. I can hardly bear it."

"Dante. Don't take her from me. I know you want to hurt me, but you'll hurt her, too."

"Hurt her?" His lips drew back from his teeth. "You have nothing. I have everything. I'll give my daughter a life you can only imagine."

"She's my daughter, too. And what she needs is love. It's what everyone needs. How can you not understand that?"

"*Love,*" he said, his mouth twisting, "is a word without meaning. *Honesty. Responsibility.* Those are words that matter. How can you not understand that?"

Then he folded his arms, fixed his eyes on the sleeping baby and ignored Tally completely.

DAWN HAD JUST TOUCHED the sky with a delicate pink blush when Samantha stirred.

"Mama?"

Tally, who'd fallen into a fitful sleep, sprang to her feet, but she was too late. Dante had already leaned into the crib and lifted the baby into his arms.

"Bella figlia," he said huskily, *"buon giorno."*

Sam grinned. "Da-Tay," she babbled, and wrapped her arms around his neck.

Tally felt her throat tighten. All the time she'd been pregnant, the months and years after, she'd never pictured this. Dante and Samantha as father and daughter. She'd never dreamed of this softness, this sweetness in her lover.

The door opened. The physician who'd treated Sam stepped into the room.

"Well, look at this! It doesn't take a trained eye to see that our patient's made a full recovery."

"Thank you, Doctor. For everything."

"My pleasure, Mr. Russo. Just let me give your little girl the once-over and you can take her home."

"To New York?"

"I'd wait a couple of days, just to be on the safe side." He grinned. "Quite a hardship, having to spend Christmas in the Caribbean, huh, folks?"

Tally made a choked sound. Dante forced a smile.

"We'll manage," he said.

Tally hoped he was right.

COEXISTING in a three-level penthouse, as they'd initially done, was simple.

Coexisting in a one-level house built to take full advantage of the sun was not.

Rooms opened into rooms; doors were almost non-existent. Tally moved her things into the third bedroom, but it was impossible to walk to the kitchen or Sam's room without running into Dante.

"Excuse me," she said, at the beginning.

After a while, she stopped saying it. What was there to apologize for? He was as much in her way as she was in his.

And how did he manage to get to Sam's side so quickly? All the baby had to do was whimper and Dante, damn him, was there.

Tally told herself she'd at least have the pleasure of watching him suffer through the horrors of a full diaper but apparently he'd mastered Diaper 101 on his own. All right, she thought with petty satisfaction, at least he wouldn't know how to mash a banana just the way Sam liked it—and she was right. He didn't.

It didn't matter.

Her sweet little traitor liked Dante's method just fine. She liked everything he did, including taking her for hand-in-hand walks along the beach, the warm water lapping at her ankles.

When Tally attempted the same thing, Sam shrieked with horror.

Dante could charm any woman he set his eyes on, including two-year-old females.

But he couldn't charm Tally. Not that he tried. He looked right through her. That was fine. She'd gone back to hating him. She'd never let her little girl be raised by such a cold-hearted tyrant, never mind the performance he was putting on with Sam, never mind the way his face lit each time the baby toddled toward him…

Never mind the numbing sense of sorrow in her own heart at glimpses of what might have been.

As midnight approached, with Sam sound asleep and the house silent, Tally was close to tears, but it wasn't over Dante.

Never over him.

"Never," Tally whispered, and wept as if her heart might break in half.

TALLY'S SOFT SOBS carried through the walls.

Lying on his bed, arms folded beneath his head, Dante stared up at the dark ceiling. Let her cry, he thought coldly. For all he gave a damn, she could cry enough salt tears to fill the sea.

After a long time, the sound of her weeping grew softer, then stopped. A muscle in his jaw flexed. Good. Now, at least, he might get some sleep.

Half an hour later, he sat up.

To hell with sleep. He was going crazy, trapped in a house that was rapidly becoming a prison. He pulled on a pair of shorts, opened the patio doors and strode over the beach until he reached the surf.

The moon, full and round, was bright enough to carve shadows into the sand. Dante's mouth thinned. It was the kind of night you saw on picture postcards. The endless stretch of sand. The white ruffle of the surf. The dark sea stretching to the horizon under the elegantly cool eye of the moon.

Once, he'd considered buying a house in these islands. He'd even mentioned it to Taylor. The idea had come from out of nowhere…or maybe not. Maybe he'd thought of the beauty of this place because Taylor was so beautiful. Because, fool that he was, he'd imagined he was feeling something for her he'd never felt for another woman.

He'd stepped back from that precipice.

And here he was, three years later, with her in the very setting he'd imagined, except all he wanted was to get away from her and return to New York.

Dio, the irony of it!

Dante kicked at the sand as he walked slowly along the beach.

A beautiful island. A beautiful woman, but what good was her beauty if she had no heart? Not when it came to him.

And why should that mean a damn anyway, when he'd never thought the human heart was responsible for anything more than pumping blood through the body?

Wrong, he thought, tilting back his head and staring blindly at the moon. Dead wrong, and it had taken a two-year-old imp to teach him the lesson.

A painful lesson.

For the first time in his life, he'd begun to think about a different existence from any he'd ever known. A house in the country. A dog, a couple of cats, a station wagon. A little girl to run to the door when she heard his key in the lock and maybe a little boy, too…

And a wife, to step into his embrace.

Not just a wife. Tally. His Tally. Because that was how he thought of her, how he'd always thought of her, even three years ago…

What was that?

Dante cocked his head. Music? Chimes. No. Not chimes. Bells. Church bells. Of course. It must be midnight, and this was Christmas Eve.

He swallowed hard. So what? Christmas was for fools. A holiday that celebrated a miracle, except miracles were in painfully short supply in today's world.

When was the last time he'd seen anything remotely like a miracle?

When was the last time he'd held Tally in his arms?

The sound of the bells came to him again, filled with poignancy and hope that floated on the soft sea breeze. Dante swallowed again but he couldn't ease the constriction in his throat.

"Tally," he whispered, and the name was sweeter than the music of the bells.

Tally was his miracle. She always had been.

And he'd turned his back on that miracle, ruined his one chance at love, at happiness, out of pride, arrogance, all the things she'd accused him of, rather than admit the truth.

He loved Tally. Now, three years ago, forever. He adored her.

And he knew exactly why she'd left him.

He *had* been about to end their affair, just as she'd said, and it hadn't had a damned thing to do with boredom. The truth was the great Dante Russo had been terrified of putting his heart in a woman's hands, of saying, *Here I am, cara. A man, nothing more. A man who loves you and can only hope you love him in return because without you, I am nothing. My life is nothing....*

Dante took a shuddering breath.

"Tally," he whispered, and turned toward the house.

TALLY LAY HUDDLED in her bed, eyes hot and gritty with tears.

Ridiculous, wasn't it? To weep over Dante? He wasn't worth it. Not anymore.

He had shown his true colors today. He was the cold, brutal, arrogant tyrant she'd always called him...

Tally rolled onto her back and stared up at the dark ceiling. No. That wasn't true. Dante had been wonderful today, quick and courageous and tender with Sam, and with her...

Until she'd told him what she should have told him a very long time ago.

She could be honest about this, at least. Dante wasn't a tyrant, he was a man in pain. She had told him a lie that had cut to the bone. Now he was hurting. And a man like Dante Russo knew only one way to deal with pain.

He struck at its cause.

And she—she was the cause.

A sob caught in Tally's throat and she rolled over and buried her face in the already-damp pillow.

If only she'd told him the truth that day in Vermont, when he'd first seen Sam. If only she'd said, "Dante, this is your child. I kept her from you and I kept myself from you, too, because—because I loved you. Because I knew I'd die if you turned away from me."

Would he have laughed? Or would he have opened his arms to her? She'd never know. It was too late. She'd finally told him the truth, that Sam was his and that she loved him, but it didn't matter.

He wanted Sam, not her. And she couldn't blame him for that. Her lies had destroyed everything.

Too late, the beat of her heart said, too late, too late, too—

What was that?

Tally sat up, head cocked. Bells? Yes. Bells, chiming sweetly through the night. Why would bells be...

Of course.

It was Christmas. Christmas! The bells were heralding the start of the holiday, singing of joy, of wonder...

Of miracles.

Tears streamed down Tally's face. She'd had her own miracle. A man. Proud. Strong. Protective and, yes, loving. And she'd let that miracle slip through her fingers out of cowardice. She'd been afraid to tell him about Sam.

And terrified to tell him about herself, that she loved him, that she'd always love him, until it was too late.

Almost too late, she thought, and drew a ragged breath.

Tally threw back the covers and rose from the bed. Her footsteps were hesitant at first but they quickened as she ran from room to room.

"Dante," she said brokenly, "my beloved, where are you?"

The bells rang out again, just as she hurried into the sitting room. A beam of ivory moonlight illuminated the French doors that led to the beach. Tally flung them open—

And saw Dante, just as he turned toward the house.

"Dante," she said, and she began to run across the sand, "Dante..."

Moonlight touched his face. She saw love, understanding, the same hope that burned in her heart, and she flew into his embrace and clung to him.

"I heard the bells," she said, crying and laughing at the same time, kissing his mouth as she rose to him, luxuriating in the racing beat of his heart. "I heard them calling and I thought, I can't lose him again, I can't, I can't, I can't—"

"I love you," Dante said fiercely, cupping her face in

his hands. "I've always loved you, *inamorata,* but I was too proud—and too afraid of needing you—to admit it."

"And I love you," Tally said, "I always have. It's why I left you three years ago. The thought of having you end things between us was more than I could bear."

"I was a fool, *cara,*" he said, tightening his arms around her. "How could a man end what is destined to last through eternity?"

Tally laughed through her tears. "Is that all?"

He smiled, too. And then his mouth was on hers, the taste of her tears was on his lips, and as he lifted her into his arms and carried her to the house, the bells rang out, telling the world that miracles are always possible.

All you have to do is believe.

SOMETIMES, HAVING WEALTH and power and all the right connections really did pay off.

They flew back to New York early in the morning the next day, Tally wearing the diamond solitaire Dante had bought for her in the Caribbean.

"It's beautiful," she whispered, when he slipped the ring on her finger.

"Not as beautiful as you," he said, and kissed her.

All the municipal offices were closed, but such details weren't enough to put a crimp in the plans of Dante Russo.

"I know someone who knows someone who knows someone," he said, laughing when Tally rolled her eyes.

"Such arrogance," she said, but her smile, her voice, her eyes shone with love.

By noon, they had a wedding license and a judge who said he'd be happy to marry them in Dante's penthouse.

By one, the penthouse was filled with Christmas

garlands. Mistletoe hung from every doorway. Dante loved catching Tally under the mistletoe, whirling her in a circle and kissing her.

The enormous sitting room was filled with baskets of crimson and white poinsettias. Holly leaves, bright with berries, lay draped over the top of the fireplace mantel. But the room's centerpiece was a blue spruce so tall its branches reached the ceiling.

The tree was beautiful.

It filled the air with its fragrance; it glowed with what Tally was sure were a thousand white fairy lights. The flames on the hearth in the wall-long fireplace danced on the gleaming surfaces of the gold and silver balls that hung from the tree. Gaily wrapped packages spilled from under the branches, though Sam, squealing with delight, had already opened most of hers.

Champagne was chilling in silver buckets; caviar sat in a silver dish. Everything was perfect…and a little before two, the doorman brought up an enormous white box. Inside was a magnificent gown of lace and seed pearls, straight from the atelier of a world-famous designer.

It was the sort of gown princesses wear in the fairy tales little girls read.

Except, Tally thought when she finally stood beside her gorgeous groom and looked up into his eyes, except, this was no fairy tale.

This was real. It was true love, and it would last forever.

"Do you take this woman," the judge intoned, and Dante short-circuited things by saying "Yes."

The perfect P.A., who was one of the guests, laughed. So did Mrs. Tipton and so did Samantha, who she held against her bosom.

Dante brought his bride's hand to his lips. They smiled into each other's eyes. Then they gave the judge all their attention. Slowly, and with deep meaning, they took the vows that would forever unite them.

Moments later, they were husband and wife. Dante gathered his bride to him and kissed her again.

"I will love you forever, *inamorata,*" he said softly.

Tally smiled through tears of happiness. "As I will love you," she whispered.

"Me, too," Sam said.

Everyone laughed as the baby made her pronouncement.

"Down," she told Mrs. Tipton, with all the imperiousness of a two-year-old. She toddled to her parents and held up her arms. "Up," she commanded.

Dante, a man who never took orders from anyone, happily took this one and settled his daughter into the curve of his arm.

"Mama," Sam said, touching a chubby hand to Tally's cheek.

She looked at Dante, who smiled and waited for her to call him Da-Tay.

But she didn't.

Instead, she put a little hand on each side of his face and said, "Dada."

Dante's eyes filled. He looked at his wife, and Tally smiled.

"Merry Christmas, beloved," she whispered.

"Buon natale, inamorata," he said softly.

Their daughter laughed, and flung her arms around them both.

THE RIVAL

JOANNE ROCK

To the new bride Susan Newkirk Heath,
who shares my romantic streak.

One

As she worked in the tack room at Mesa Falls Ranch, Regina Flores caught sight of her reflection in a shiny halter plate bearing one of the horse's names. Even six months after her makeover, it still surprised her sometimes to see another woman's face staring back at her.

Bypassing the fancy dress tack, Regina chose an everyday bridle and rushed back to the stable to finish saddling a second mount. She'd wheedled her way onto the ranch staff as a trail guide the week before and still hadn't found an opportunity to get close to Devon Salazar, whose company was overseeing the social media marketing and launch event for the ranch's rebranding as a private corporate retreat. Getting close to Devon was the only reason she'd taken the job. And she never could have accomplished that if she'd borne any resemblance to her old self—Georgiana Fuentes.

Tightening the saddle girth on the second horse, Regina finished tacking up quickly before unhooking the crossties. She brought both horses through the paddock area before mounting her own and leading the second. She'd heard Devon had a meeting coming up at the main lodge and there was a chance she could talk him into riding there with her. But only if she hurried.

She nudged the bay mustang faster until the main buildings were out of sight. The ranch owners had given Devon a two-bedroom cabin right on the Bitter-root River, a more remote property with beautiful views and a multilevel deck to take in the sights. She'd made careful notes about all the ranch's buildings in order to land the trail guide job. Regina had sacrificed every-thing to be here now—for this chance to learn the truth about the Salazar heirs.

How much did Devon Salazar know about the book his dead father had penned under a pseudonym eight years ago? A tell-all that had caused life as she'd known it to implode? She'd overheard him deny all knowledge of it to his brother in a conversation last week, but she'd also learned the siblings didn't trust each other, so she didn't put much stock in what he'd told Marcus.

Her private investigator had only recently discovered the identity of the author—two months *after* Alonzo Salazar's death—so she'd had to transfer her need for revenge from the father to the sons. Because she didn't believe for a second that they hadn't benefited from their father's decision to unmask her family's secrets for financial gain.

A light snow began to fall as she guided the horses off the trail to a shortcut that would bring her to Dev-on's cabin faster.

She should be thankful she bore no resemblance to the woman she used to be. If she'd still looked anything like sweet, innocent Georgiana Fuentes, Devon might have recognized her as one of the thinly disguised real-life characters in his dad's supposed work of "fiction." Or, more accurately, from the endless images of her in the press after a Hollywood gossip columnist had linked the novel's characters to their real-life counterparts.

But stress had stolen thirty pounds from her frame. Relentless workouts in an effort to excise her anger had sculpted a much different body from the soft curves of her teenage self. Even worse, being hounded by the tabloids for her story had caused a car accident three years ago that required enough facial reconstruction to alter her features. Finally, to complete the transformation, six months ago, she'd hacked off her long blond waves to just above her shoulders and dyed the remaining hair a deep chocolate brown. Regina had effectively scrubbed away every last remnant of the woman she used to be.

Devon would never guess she'd once been the spoiled heiress of a powerful A-list actor who'd disowned her and her mother when he learned that Georgiana wasn't his biological daughter, thanks to the tell-all book. She'd done therapy for her anger issues with her family long ago. But she'd then realized she couldn't really start building a new life until she understood why her old one had been taken from her.

And whether or not Devon and Marcus Salazar had profited from the book that had cost her everything.

Leaning back in the saddle, she slowed the lead horse just before Devon's cabin came into view. She needed to brace herself mentally for seeing the man who had almost assuredly built his business empire thanks to her misfortune. He was her enemy.

So it threw her that he was absurdly handsome. His green eyes had sparked an unwelcome heat inside her the only time she'd spoken to him two days ago, when she'd invited him on a trail ride.

Being around him rattled her, but she had to hide it. Had to stay focused. Because she would do whatever was necessary to uncover the truth.

"You're leaving?" Standing in the living area of his two-bedroom cabin on the Mesa Falls Ranch property, Devon Salazar glared at his half brother, Marcus, knowing he shouldn't be surprised by the news.

When had they ever seen eye to eye on anything?

They'd only come to the ranch to honor a deathbed promise to their father before his passing. Because even though they ran a company together, they did so from offices on opposite coasts—Devon in New York and Marcus in Los Angeles. Devon had assumed their father wanted them to spend time in the same place so they would work out their differences and settle the future of Salazar Media. Little did he know Alonzo Salazar had only called them there to drop a bombshell on them, which they discovered in the paperwork he'd left with the ranch owners before his death.

"I know the timing is unfortunate," Marcus conceded, prowling around the living area in a dark blue suit, his sunglasses still perched on his head from when he'd shown up at Devon's cabin twenty minutes ago. His only nod to the fast-dropping Montana temperatures was the wool scarf slung around his neck. "But Lily and I have left you a thorough plan for the launch event. All you need to do is execute it."

Barely hanging onto his patience, Devon stared out at the densely forested mountainside just beyond his luxury cabin's tiered deck.

"All I need to do is execute?" he repeated, glaring

at the sea of ponderosa pines just beyond the big windows. He hadn't been brought up to speed on the client yet, and most of the ranch owners—it was jointly held by six friends—were still aggravated with Devon for showing up more than a week late at the ranch and delaying the work on the relaunch. "While you and Lily gallivant around Europe for a few weeks?"

Marcus had fallen in love with the COO of Salazar Media, Lily Carrington. While Devon had delayed his trip to Montana to hire a private investigator to look more deeply into their father's mysterious past, Marcus had been at the ranch wooing the woman Devon had sent in his absence. Losing both of them during the launch event for a new, prestigious client was a hard hit.

"We did the setup. Now it's your turn," Marcus explained, his usual antagonism noticeably absent. Maybe romance agreed with him. "Besides, I'm hoping this trip turns into an elopement," he confided, the announcement a total surprise.

Knowing what a difficult—and long—engagement Lily had to her previous fiancé, Devon could see the wisdom of that move. Some of his anger leaked away. He and his half brother might not get along, but Devon wanted Lily to be happy. Hell, he didn't begrudge Marcus being happy, either.

"You haven't asked her yet?"

Marcus shook his head. "No. I was thinking of surprising her in Paris. Pulling out all the stops."

"That's a good idea, actually." Funny to think their shared business—and a shared father—had never brought them together, but if Marcus married Lily, they might finally have an effective tie. "I only want what's best for her, you know."

"I know." His sibling's dark eyes met his for a moment before he glanced away. "And so do I. She hasn't taken a vacation in years. She deserves for someone to put her first."

Devon didn't need to be reminded of the particulars. Lily had been raised to feel like an intruder in her grandparents' wealthy world and she'd worked tirelessly to feel deserving of all they'd done for her. Their backgrounds weren't all that different, since Devon's single mother had moved back in with her old-money family after Alonzo Salazar had abandoned her shortly after Devon's birth.

"Agreed." He would find a way to make the launch event work on his own. He would bring in more staff, for starters. "But you realize the bigger issue right now is not the launch, but trying to contain the fallout from whatever new scandal Dad's book could cause."

Hammering out an agreement for the future of Salazar Media—and who would take the helm of the business—would have to wait.

"But for now, no one knows about that. If the secret comes out somehow, we'll deal with it when it happens," Marcus assured him, checking his watch. "In the meantime, I've got to pick up Lily so we can head to the airstrip. We're flying out this afternoon."

Devon resisted the urge to argue. The ramifications of the secret leaking out were bigger than they knew. But Marcus had been the one to nail down the ranch as a client, and he'd kept the situation under control with the owners until Devon had arrived, so he'd done his part. Now Devon would have to find a way to keep any revelations about their father's book from ruining everything they'd both worked so hard for.

"Good luck," he told him simply, extending a hand. Marcus stared down at it for a beat too long, but he squeezed Devon's palm in the end. "Thank you. And you'd better get moving if you want to make that meeting with Weston Rivera. It's almost noon."

Devon swore as he shoved his phone in his pocket and headed toward the coatrack to retrieve a fitted black parka. "I won't bother you unless all hell breaks loose."

"I can give you a ride over there—"

"No need." The main lodge was in the opposite direction from Marcus's cabin. "You added the ranch to our client list. I'll make the rest of it work."

His brother gave a clipped nod before stepping out into the December chill, a burst of cold air lingering in his wake when he closed the door.

Devon shut his laptop and hunted down a hat and a pair of gloves, already mulling over how he was going to juggle orchestrating the kickoff party with digging deeper into their father's secrets. He hadn't wanted to share with Marcus his own reasons for needing to keep the Salazar dirty laundry out of the headlines for at least two more weeks. Devon's socialite mother was set to wed an international banker on Christmas Eve in a highly publicized ceremony. She had found happiness at last, and Devon refused to let a scandal about his father overshadow her well-deserved spotlight.

Maybe Devon's paranoia about his father's secrets leaking now were misplaced, considering Alonzo had kept his double life as an author on lockdown for eight years. But Devon's gut told him that his dad's death was going to bring everything to light.

The papers Alonzo had left for his sons here at the ranch revealed all the details. Under the pseudonym A. J. Sorensen, Alonzo had released an international bestselling novel about Hollywood power brokers and scandals. The book had caused an uproar a year after its release, when a Beverly Hills gossip columnist cracked the code on the identities of the people who inspired the characters.

Real people had been hurt by the book. A Hollywood marriage had been torn apart. A daughter disowned.

Devon pulled a gray knit cap over his ears and tugged open the cabin door just as a light snow began to fall. He spotted a woman on horseback heading toward him. She had a dark Stetson pulled low on her forehead, and it was difficult to see her features through the swirl of snowflakes, but Devon recognized her as the trail guide employed by Mesa Falls Ranch. She'd approached him two days ago about taking a tour of the property to familiarize him with the ranch, an idea he might have jumped on another time, but he'd been reeling from the news about his father's secrets.

Regina Flores had made an impression, though.

With her silver-gray eyes and dark hair, she'd captured his attention right away. She had a thoughtful, brooding air about her; she seemed to be a woman of deep, mysterious thoughts. Until she smiled. She had a mischievous, quick grin that made him think wholly inappropriate things. Today she wore a black duster that flared over her horse's saddle and a purple scarf tied around her neck. She held the reins to a second mount, a sturdy chestnut quarter horse.

"Hello, Mr. Salazar." She flashed a smile his way, two deep dimples framing her lips as she drew to a stop in front of the cabin.

He wasn't a man easily distracted by physical attraction, but something about this woman's ease in her own skin called to him in spite of his looming worries. It made him very aware of how long it had been since he'd shared his bed. He'd been so focused on growing the company he hadn't made time for anything but the most fleeting encounters over the past two years.

"Good morning." He stepped down the deck steps to ground level as the snowfall began picking up speed. "And call me Devon."

Her mustang whinnied a greeting, shaking its mane. Devon stopped near the horse's head to stroke the muzzle, noting the flurries melting on its nose. Safer to look the animal in the eye than its appealing rider.

"I heard from Mr. Rivera that the two of you have a meeting, so I thought I'd offer you a lift." She jutted her chin in the direction of the chestnut mare behind her. "Nutmeg is saddled and ready to go if you are."

"You came all the way out here on the off chance I'd need a ride?" His gaze skimmed up her denim-clad thigh, over her feminine curves, to study her expression. Was there a chance Regina Flores felt the same pull he did when they were near one another?

The idea revved him up.

"I didn't have any trail rides scheduled for today and both these animals were due for some exercise, so my offer isn't quite as generous as you make it sound." Her smile was self-deprecating this time. "I had to get Nutmeg out either way."

She might well be telling the truth.

But the alternative—that she harbored a personal interest in him—was far more intriguing. Especially during a tense week, with his business hanging in the balance. He could see the potential benefit of a distraction.

"To tell you the truth, I'd be grateful for the company," he said at last, reaching up to take Nutmeg's reins from Regina.

He briefly caught her hand in his, leather on leather, before sliding the horse's lead free.

Regina's quicksilver eyes tracked him, her smile fleeing as awareness flickered between them. At least, he'd like to think that she'd felt it, too.

"Do you need a hand up?" she asked even as he slung a leg over Nutmeg's back.

"I'll be fine." He urged the chestnut forward two steps so he was beside Regina.

Close enough to touch.

"Suit yourself." Her gaze darted around, as if unsure where to land. "Just keep in mind some of our horses are more spirited than others. It's a good idea to get acquainted with their quirks first."

"In that case, anything I need to know about Nutmeg?" He was far more interested in getting to know the trail guide than the gentle mare.

"She's a follower." Regina shifted in the saddle and her horse eased back a step from his. "She'll be more comfortable letting me take the lead."

"Fair enough." He opened his hand with the reins still balanced on his palm, giving the horse her lead. "But since I'm most definitely not a follower, next time feel free to give me something feistier." He allowed his words to sink in before leaning fractionally closer. "I like a challenge."

Her swift intake of breath, a soft and sexy gasp, was the most pleasant sound he'd heard in days.

And just like that, he had something to look forward to during an otherwise hellish week. Regina Flores was a welcome feminine distraction when all the rest of his world was falling apart.

Pull it together.

Regina cursed herself for finding anything remotely attractive about a man she knew to be her enemy.

Tall and leanly muscled, Devon carried himself with athletic grace in dark jeans and a fitted black parka. A gray ski cap covered his light brown hair, the knit fabric framing thick eyebrows and pale green eyes. With sculpted features, he was handsome in a way that should have been boringly traditional. Except there was something undeniably compelling about the way his eyes followed her. He didn't seem like the kind of man who paid attention to every random woman in his field of vision. She'd had time to observe him unnoticed, and he was normally all business. Yet, around her, she felt the heated spark of masculine interest.

She put the bay in motion. The hoofbeats were softened by the layer of snow sticking on the trail back to the main lodge at Mesa Falls Ranch. The wind picked up, swirling flakes that tickled her cheeks. She appreciated the icy kiss on her skin, needing something to cool her frustration.

Her keen awareness.

She'd worked too hard to get close to him to lose focus now. Her whole point in bringing Devon a mount had been to talk to him. Earn his confidence. Instead, the moment he'd gotten close to her, she'd felt the most bizarrely unexpected reaction to him.

Blatant physical attraction.

It would have been unsettling enough if it had been one-sided. But Devon's comment about liking a challenge hadn't only been about the horses.

Breathing out slowly, she told herself to let go of the moment and focus on salvaging this time with Devon. His younger brother and business partner, Marcus, was leaving the ranch today with the COO of Salazar Media, Lily Carrington. The pair had fallen in love and spent so

much time together during their stay at Mesa Falls Ranch
that Regina had had no opportunity to get near Marcus.

Devon was her last chance to find out how much the
Salazar family knew about their father's book. She'd
risked her cover to eavesdrop on a conversation between the brothers the week before, enough to learn
that Marcus and Devon didn't trust each other at all
even though they were business partners. And that fact
alone called into question everything that had trans-
pired between them.

They'd spoken like they didn't know about their father's book. But could one—or both—of them have
been lying?

One thing was certain: she wasn't going to learn
any more if she didn't try to get to know Devon better.

Slowing her horse's step, she waited until he was
close to her again. She noticed he allowed her to keep
the lead, however.

"You ride very well," she observed lightly, daring a
glance toward him as they followed the Bitterroot River
toward the lodge. "Did you grow up around horses?"

He stared out through the snow-covered field where
a few deer picked their way back into a thicket.

"Not really. I went to school with a guy who lived on
a Kentucky Thoroughbred farm and I spent a couple of
summers with his family." He pointed toward the woods
where the deer had disappeared. "Look. The fawn wants
to come back and play."

Sure enough, the smallest of the deer hopped out
into the field again, running in a circle before it darted
back into the trees in a flash of white tail. She felt herself smiling along with Devon until she remembered
she had to keep up her guard.

"Now that I know what a strong rider you are, I'm all

the more determined to take you out on one of the trails while you're here." She figured a little flattery couldn't hurt her cause. "You must want to see the full spread of the ranch while you're preparing for the launch party?"

"I do." He turned those pale green eyes her way, his expression serious. "As long as you're my guide."

Her heart pounded harder.

Only because she was circling the enemy, damn it.

She ground her teeth together. *Focus*.

"Deal." She forced a smile as they rounded the last bend before the main lodge came into view. "Name a time. I actually need to put in more trail ride hours myself, familiarize myself with the place, before Mesa Falls Ranch opens to the corporate retreats at the end of the month."

"How's tomorrow morning?" His breath huffed a cloud in the cold air as he spoke. "I can clear my calendar and spend the day taking in the sights."

"Excellent." She'd have Devon all to herself. Surely she'd find out something about his father and what kind of relationship Devon had with the man who'd used Regina's family secrets to make a fortune. "Should I meet you at your cabin?"

"I'll come to the stables." He nudged Nutmeg in the flank, turning her toward the lodge. "You can help me choose the right mount."

"Of course." She wondered if his knowledge of horses was better than hers. She'd had to exaggerate her skills a bit to land the trail guide job. "We can have the kitchen pack us a meal if you think we'll stay out through the lunch hour."

"Absolutely." Devon nodded. "I had a lot on my plate when you first mentioned the idea of a trail ride, but I'll be ready to give you my full attention tomorrow." Slowing his horse to a halt, he let his gaze linger on Regina. "In fact, I look forward to it."

She stared back at him for a moment too long, trying to read the undercurrent between them. Trying to ignore the pull of attraction.

"Sounds good," she said finally, needing to stay polite. Professional. Friendly.

No matter that her feelings for him veered between suspicion and simmering awareness.

Dismounting, he turned to stride into the lodge for his meeting, leaving Regina to bring Nutmeg back to the stables. She watched him walk away, his dark boots leaving an imprint as he charged through the coating of powdery snow.

Tomorrow, he'd promised her his undivided attention. That had potential for her investigation into what the Salazar heirs knew about their father's activities. But he'd also made it clear he was interested in her, and that complicated things considerably. For some reason she was okay deceiving him about her identity, but not okay using the attraction between them as some sort of bargaining chip.

She'd have to find a way to get the answers she needed without succumbing to the draw of the man.

And even after spending only ten minutes with Devon Salazar, she knew that wasn't going to be easy. But failure wasn't an option. One way or another, Regina would find out where the profits from Alonzo Salazar's book were going. If it turned out Devon Salazar had benefited financially from the wreckage of her world?

She would use everything in her power to make sure he paid.

Two

Regina stayed up late and awoke early, wanting to ensure she was well prepared for the outing with Devon. She had studied everything she might possibly need to know for the trail ride—weather conditions, interesting sights along the way, a refresher on the native plants and animals. She'd also spent some time rehearsing a few basic details of her cover story since she couldn't reveal anything personal for fear of giving away her past as Georgiana.

Now she was huddled inside the barn, checking the map on her phone so she didn't get lost during the ride, when Devon arrived.

"Morning." The deep masculine voice warmed her insides even before she turned to see him standing under the arch of the doorway.

Snow stirred behind him in a misty white cloud as he pulled on a pair of leather gloves. From his jeans and boots to his dark sheepskin jacket, he looked ready for the outing and not at all like her idea of a Manhattan executive. Straightening, she tucked her phone in the pocket of her jacket.

"Good morning, Devon." She forced a smile in spite of the weird mixture of nervousness and tamped-down attraction. "Are you ready to ride?"

"I've been eagerly anticipating this." His green eyes lingered on her as he stepped deeper into the barn. "And I hope you don't mind, but I took the liberty of making a few adjustments to the lunch you ordered from the kitchen."

He held up a sleekly packaged parcel that she hadn't noticed he was carrying.

"Perfect." She'd been planning to stop by the kitchen on their way out. She opened one of the saddlebags. "You can slide it in here."

He was by her side in a few steps, the heat and warmth of him blocking the cold air blowing in through the open doors.

He smelled like pine trees and soap. A fact she wished she hadn't noticed. He stepped back from the Appaloosa.

"I see you saddled a different mount for me today." He patted the mare's flank while she closed the flap on the saddlebag.

"I know you hoped for something more spirited. Your brother was partial to Evangeline," she told him smoothly, pretending not to know anything about their enmity. "I thought maybe you'd enjoy her, too."

Leading his horse out of the barn, he gave a humorless laugh. "Marcus and I have rarely agreed on anything, but I won't hold that against Evangeline."

A few moments later, they were mounted and trotting away from the barns at a good clip. Regina tipped her face up into the falling snow, enjoying the fresh air and the beauty of Big Sky Country despite the rider beside her. She found it difficult to relax around him, given her overwhelming need to learn more about his connection to his father and the book that had destroyed her life. But at least his remark about Marcus had given her a toehold into that conversation.

Her cheeks tingled with the chill of the icy snow as she began her most basic introduction to Mesa Falls Ranch, outlining the size and rough parameters of the place, skimming over the ownership, since she assumed Devon knew all about the unique group who managed the property.

"Have you met all of the owners?" Devon asked as they began the steep trek out of Bitterroot Valley.

"I haven't." She hadn't really understood the point of the shared ranch venture. Most ranches were either family owned or held by a major corporation. Yet Mesa Falls was owned equally by six friends who had never made the bottom line a primary concern. "I've only met Weston Rivera, who spends the most time on site over-seeing things." She pointed to a break in the trees ahead. "We'll be able to see his house from just up there."

"I've been to his home. I got to meet a few of the owners at a welcome party they threw at Rivera's place last week." Devon appeared more relaxed than he had the day before, even though his mount was definitely more energetic.

For her part, Regina felt on edge, wanting to remain alert to any clues he might give her about his family, his business and his sources of income.

Swaying with the mustang's movements, she debated the best way to broach those topics.

"I remember hearing about that. Your brother went, too, I think." She knew a lot about Marcus's movements even though she hadn't spoken to him directly. Last week, she'd still been feeling her way around the ranch after landing the job. She'd spied on Marcus more than once.

"He did." Devon's answer was clipped.

"The two of you have a business together, and yet you mentioned you don't see eye to eye on many things." She glanced his way to gauge his expression. "Doesn't that make working together difficult?"

"Absolutely," he said without hesitation. "Thankfully, we have offices on opposite coasts, and that helps."

She wanted to ask a follow-up question but didn't want to sound like she was interrogating him. So she waited.

"Do you have siblings, Regina?" he asked as they cleared a rise. The terrain leveled off slightly as the horses picked their way along the narrow trail under the shelter of the pines.

"No." That wasn't strictly true since she had two half siblings, her father's kids she'd never been allowed to meet. Her birth father's wife was highly protective of her family, resenting Regina's late appearance in their lives. "I've always envied people with bigger families."

Families that didn't disown their children.

Birds squawked in the trees overhead, their movements causing more snow to rain down on them as they disturbed the branches.

"Marcus and I didn't spend any time together growing up," Devon explained as they left the trees behind and arrived on a plateau above the river. "Our mothers viewed one another as rivals, so Marcus and I did, too."

"Yet you started a very successful business together."

He looked sharply at her. "You've done your homework."

Her cheeks heated; yes, she had dug through everything she could find about Salazar Media. Especially since Devon's father had been a part owner. "You and Marcus are the first guests since I've been a trail guide. I figured it doesn't hurt to know who I'm talking to."

"I'm flattered," he admitted. "I'm usually the one doing all the studying about new clients. I can't remember the last time anyone tried to impress me."

His gaze collided with hers and she felt the prickle of awareness all over her skin, even with the cold wind blowing off the mountains. Her mouth dried up as she debated how to respond. Thankfully, he had questions about their direction and the next two hours passed uneventfully enough.

She kept up a running patter about the sights, the history of the Bitterroot River, and the best spots for fly-fishing according to the locals she'd asked. They were far from the main ranch house when she spotted a creek side lean-to that one of the ranch hands had told her about. Built by one of the owners for a winter retreat, the lean-to was open on one side, with a picnic table tucked under the shelter.

"Are you ready for lunch?" she asked, shifting in the saddle to see Devon better. "There's a good spot to make a fire by the water if you want one."

She could see the fire ring between the lean-to and the creek, the spot sheltered from the wind.

"Sounds good." He followed her down the snowy hill to the open hut with its bark and branch roof.

She settled the horses close to the water while Devon unpacked the food. She found a few promising sticks to build a fire, kicked away the excess snow, then got to work starting a blaze. By the time she turned around, Devon had flannel blankets on both benches, a clean linen over the table and two glasses of wine poured into stemless glasses. A centerpiece of bread, meats and cheeses was surrounded by fruit, nuts and even a small jar of honey.

With the fire snapping behind her, the flames giving the winter picnic a burnished glow, things had taken a turn for the romantic.

"Wow." She darted her gaze to his, not sure what to say. "That definitely looks better than the turkey sandwiches I asked the staff chef to make us."

He waved her closer. "I hope you don't mind. But I like to combine work with pleasure whenever I can, and Montana is too beautiful not to savor."

Her heartbeat jumped nervously as she neared him to slide onto one of the bench seats. She needed to be wary of this man's idea of pleasure. She had too much at stake to lose focus now.

"Of course," she tried to say in a normal tone, but her voice cracked like a twelve-year-old boy's. She cleared her throat and tried again. "It's a treat for me, too."

"I'm glad." He took the seat opposite her and waited while she removed her gloves and filled a plate for herself. "So how long have you worked here?"

She took a sip of her wine to steel herself for the inevitable questions and hoped she could change the topic fast.

"I just started last week. I'm having a hard time deciding on a career path since I finished college, so I've been testing out different jobs, trying to figure out what I want to do and where I'd like to live." It was close enough to the truth.

She didn't mention that she couldn't properly get

her life underway until she had the answers she needed about A. J. Sorensen's book and where all the profits from it had gone.

"Really?" Devon stretched his long legs under the table, one knee bumping hers. "Where did you attend college?"

"Online." That wasn't true. She'd taken most of her classes on the UCLA campus—right up until her accident. "It was easier that way, since I enjoy moving around."

"And where's home?" he asked, dipping a corner of the fresh bread into the honey.

"My mother lives in Tahoe." That was true. "I guess home is there." Technically, Regina had only ever visited for a couple of days at a time.

Her mother had left Hollywood as soon as she could after the scandal broke, but Regina had remained in Los Angeles with her grandmother to finish high school. At the time, she couldn't imagine living without her friends, but one by one her friends had all fallen away after the scandal. Even Terri, her best friend, had eventually disappeared from her life when Terri's parents realized how dangerous it was for two teenage girls trying to flee tabloid reporters on their own.

Regina understood—especially after the late-night car wreck while trying to shake the paparazzi had almost killed her during her undergraduate years. But understanding why her friends had vanished didn't make those years any less painful. She nibbled a square of smoked gouda and hoped she could change the subject soon.

"Well, I'm glad our paths crossed," Devon said, lifting his glass. "Here's to finding new friends in unexpected places."

She felt her chest constrict, hating the lies but knowing she had no choice if she wanted to discover the truth about his father's finances.

"To new friends." Raising her glass, she clinked it gently against his.

Their eyes met as they drank. She glanced away fast, but not before she felt an undeniable spark between them. The thought he'd put into the meal, the curiosity he'd shown about her personally, the way he looked at her—all of it added up to frank male interest that would have been flattering if it hadn't been so dangerous to her mission.

"What about you?" She reached for another topic of conversation to steer things away from herself. Away from the slow simmer of awareness in her veins. "Where's home for you?"

"New York. I bought a place on Central Park West when I heard about a potential vacancy and jumped on it before the apartment went on the market." Crunching into an apple slice, he pointed to a low-flying hawk circling nearby. "My family is in Connecticut. Except, of course, for Marcus out in Los Angeles."

She tracked the bird while she thought about how to steer the conversation to find out more about his father. The hawk flew for long moments without flapping its wings, angling through the air in a graceful, soaring flight.

"Do you travel to a lot of different places for work?" She needed to be subtler than she'd been earlier. She might have admitted she'd read up on his family, but she didn't want him to know how much.

"I was in India last week, meeting with an international client, but that's rare." He removed a sheaf of paperwork from his jacket and laid it on the table. She recognized a map of Mesa Falls Ranch with a few of the buildings marked on it. "Montana is new for me, too, and I appreciate the tour today." He spun the map around so she could see it better, then pointed to a few pen markings. "I want to make sure we hit these places."

She recognized two of the owners' homes as well as a peak with renowned views of the valley. But her eye was drawn to the papers that had been behind the map—the ones now partially covered by his forearm. The top sheet appeared to be contact information for someone—part of a phone number and an email address that looked like it ended "...tigations.com."

Mitigations? Litigations? Investigations?

"Of course." Her brain worked double time to come up with other words even as she forced herself to make eye contact with him. "No problem."

Crazy though it might seem, she couldn't shake the feeling the information was related to his father's estate. Or the book. Or something that might shed light on her quest. But how to steal a peek at it?

"Excellent." He started to slide the map back into his stack, then paused. "Did you need this for reference?"

Her gaze flicked back to the sheaf on the table, where she caught the word "April." Or was it a name?

"Sure." She reached for the map, trying not to stare at the place where his elbow hid whatever came after "April."

"That would be great."

He hesitated before passing it to her. "Are you okay?"

She forced her attention back to his green eyes. "Of course. Why?"

Tucking the map into her jacket pocket, she watched him fold his documents and return them to his coat.

"You just seem a little distracted." He studied her,

and for a moment she feared he could see right through her. But then he clinked his glass to hers again. "Drink up, Regina. We should probably pack our things so we have time to see the rest of the ranch."

Nodding, she finished her meal and wondered how to see those papers before they disappeared for good. One way or another, she needed a plan to separate Devon from his jacket as soon as possible.

Something seemed off about the lovely Mesa Falls Ranch trail guide.

Devon couldn't quite put his finger on what it was, though. After they returned their mounts to the stables shortly before sunset, Regina had invited him to brush down the horses with her, one of many little things that struck him as odd. He didn't mind taking care of an animal he'd ridden all day—that was far from the point. Mesa Falls Ranch was positioning itself as a high-end corporate retreat, secondary to its main ranching mission. They had plenty of ranch hands to oversee the stables. If anything, they had too much help in the weeks before the launch party. So certainly, Regina didn't need his help.

As much as he'd like to think the sexy trail guide was unwilling to part with his company, he didn't think attraction factored into her request. There'd been plenty of opportunities to act on the awareness between them today—during lunch especially. But Regina had seemed distracted, her thoughts elsewhere.

He ran the brush over Evangeline's flank, working in tandem with Regina in the quiet barn. The riding arena close to the lodge was more of a showplace than part of the working ranch—here, inexperienced riders could receive pointers about horsemanship, or try their hand at simple rodeo events in a well-monitored setting. Only a handful of horses were housed here tonight. The sweet smell of hay circulated in the cool air from a high, open window.

Evangeline whinnied as he moved the brush down her back, and he caught sight of Regina working silently at the crossties, next to him. Her dark hair caught the overhead lights, revealing a healthy shine. She'd shrugged off her jacket when they'd started working and now he did the same, draping it over the hook near hers. Even with the window open, the big animals warmed the space.

Regina caught him staring then, and for a moment the temperature spiked hotter. Her eyes darted over him before she shifted her attention back to her work. What was it about her silvery gaze that made him so damned curious about her? Maybe the odd signals he'd gotten today came down to attraction after all.

Perhaps she was simply shy. Or maybe she felt an abundance of caution since she was employed by the ranch and didn't wish to risk a new job by fraternizing with a client. While he considered his next move, his phone rang. He'd had it turned off during their ride, so he checked the screen now just in case it was important.

The caller ID showed his mother's photo.

"Regina, I just need five minutes, but I really should grab this."

"Of course." She waved him along, her smile transforming her face from pretty to breathtaking. "Take as long as you need."

Nodding his thanks, he set down the brush and hit the button to connect the call.

"Mom?" He moved toward the barn doors, sliding one open to step outside.

"Hello, Devon." Her voice was lowered, and he could hear what sounded like a dinner party in the background—indistinct music, soft chatter and laughter. "I just saw your note about extending your stay in Montana for the launch party. I wanted to be sure you'll be here for the wedding."

"Of course I will." He thought he'd made that clear in the text he'd sent earlier, but he knew his mother was nervous about her upcoming nuptials. "Mom, I wouldn't miss it for the world. You know that."

"Okay." Her small laugh sounded relieved more than anything. "I thought so, but I wanted to be sure. There's so much booked for the week before that the sooner you can be here the better."

Devon breathed in the deep stillness of the Montana mountains, wishing he could trade places with his mother for a few days so she could enjoy the peace of this kind of setting. Then again, she wouldn't want to travel anywhere that his father had frequented. She'd never forgiven him for not sticking around after Devon was born, and although Devon understood why, he wished—for her sake—she'd been able to put Alonzo firmly in her past a long time ago.

"I'll be at the rehearsal dinner." He glanced behind him at the barn door, which he'd left open a few inches. "Is there anything else going on that I should know about?"

He tried his damnedest to be an attentive son. His mother had never held it against him that he was a Salazar, the way Granddad did, even though Devon had worked hard to make sure he didn't overtly share any of his dad's qualities.

"Most of Bradley's family will be in town, so Granddad wants to roll out the red carpet," his mother explained. Bradley Stewart's family was a force to be reckoned with in banking, a well-connected clan Devon's grandfather would leverage at first opportunity. "There will be a welcome party, a few media interviews, that sort of thing. You're always so good with the press, Devon. I'd love it if you could be here."

He closed his eyes, resenting his grandfather for making this wedding about business. And he hated knowing that news of Alonzo Salazar's salacious book could steal the spotlight from what should be the happiest day of his mother's life.

"The launch party is only two days before the wedding." He couldn't leave before then. Still, guilt gnawed at him that he couldn't be there for her when she'd given up so much for him. "But I'll get a flight as soon as it ends."

"Of course. I understand." The music in the background of the call grew louder. "I'd better go now, darling. Good luck, and I'll see you soon."

He disconnected the call, not happy to disappoint her, but knowing that it was more important for her to have him here—though she'd never understand why.

Devon needed to speak to all the owners of Mesa Falls Ranch to see what they knew about his father's past—about the book, about the proceeds, about their relationship with him. But he needed to keep a lid on scandal at all costs. Keep his family's private business just that—private.

And yet, as he peered through the opening of the barn door, Devon spotted Regina Flores hunched over his discarded jacket, his personal papers spilled over her lap while she helped herself to the confidential contents.

Anger flared—fast and hot.

Shoving open the door the rest of the way, he charged

toward her. Her guilty scramble to stash the papers would have been damning even if he hadn't already seen her reading them.

He stopped a foot away from her, quietly seething. "May I ask what in the hell you think you're doing?"

Three

Regina froze.

She'd thought she'd been keeping an ear out for Devon's return, but she'd gotten engrossed in reading the files she had only meant to photograph. Had he seen her with the papers? Or had he only noticed her rifling through his jacket?

Her heart pounded harder as she relinquished her hold on his coat, letting it fall back on the chair as she straightened.

"I'm so embarrassed." She only had so many ways to play this without alienating him. For that matter, if she didn't find a way to smooth this over, he could have her fired from her job and then she'd *really* have no options left to track down the profits from the book that had ruined her family.

"With good reason." Devon glared at her, his shoulders tight and his jaw clenched. He stalked closer, his dark brows furrowed.

Behind her, Evangeline tossed her head and exhaled on a long, shuddering snort. Regina moved away from the mare, not wanting the animals to feel the nervous energy pinging through her. Stepping from the straw-covered grooming area onto the cement walkway down the center of the barn, she kept her gaze trained on Devon.

"I only wanted to touch your jacket." She knew her cheeks were bright red, and in this case that was surely to her advantage. "I'm sure it's obvious to you that I'm…" She forced herself to pause, wishing there was another way out of this mess. She took a deep breath. "Attracted to you."

It wasn't a lie. She let him see the truth of it in her expression. Her pulse galloped faster while his green eyes narrowed.

"And what did you think you might find out by snooping around in my personal papers?"

Did he know that for certain? Or was he guessing?

"Call me crazy." Shrugging, she folded her arms around herself to ward off the chill of his doubt. "But I just wanted to breathe in the scent of you." That part was—sadly—true, as well. The first thing she'd done when she picked up his coat was to bury her nose in the lining. "And the papers fell out."

Her face must be on fire by now. She swore she could feel where every single capillary pulsed with heat just below the skin.

She was worried about his reaction, yes. And she'd stretched the truth. But maybe the biggest reason for her blush was that she was baring a secret she hadn't wanted to admit—even to herself.

"I find that difficult to believe when you seemed careful to keep me at arm's length today." He spoke softly, studying her carefully as he stood just inches away. "Our picnic certainly offered an opportunity for that."

"Fraternizing with a guest will surely be frowned upon by my new employer." Her breath came fast. Out of the corner of her eye, she could see a stray hair flutter in her exhale. "I didn't think acting on the attraction would be wise." She saw some subtle shift in his expression. His pupils widened, maybe. Or his nostrils flared. "I still don't," she rushed to add.

"Nevertheless." He shifted closer, his right hand grazing her jaw to lift her chin. "I'd like to test the truth of that claim."

The green of his eyes was just the slimmest of rings around the dark centers as he peered down at her. Her thoughts scrambled.

"That I don't think we should act on it?" Her breathless voice sounded nothing like her.

"That you're attracted to me." His thumb skimmed along her lower lip and pleasure trembled through her even though she tried to hold herself very still.

Electrified, she sucked in a breath. And then his lips were brushing hers. Once. Twice. Just feather-soft touches that made her knees weak, right before he kissed her.

For real.

Desire streaked through her and stole her reservations. Her arms fell to her sides for only a moment before she wrapped them around him, drawing him closer. The woodsy bergamot scent of his skin filled her senses while his hands slid around her back, pressing her closer. His fingers flexed against the hem of her sweater, stirring an awareness of how much more pleasure awaited her. The hard wall of his chest called to her palms to explore all the intriguing ridges and planes of muscle...

He broke away suddenly. For a moment, she was utterly disoriented, blinking back at him in the glow of the barn light overhead. Her breath came hard, and she noticed his did, too. His hands lingered on her back, while hers still clutched the shoulders of his gray flannel shirt. With an effort, she unclenched her fingers, letting go of him.

"The chemistry is real enough." He didn't seem in any hurry to release her, his fingers skimming around to her waist. Stroking up her arms. "But is your story?"

His icy words jerked her back to reality.

He let go of her then, pacing away from her. For a moment she didn't even remember what he was talking about. She'd been that caught up in the kiss.

Panic lodged in her throat.

"What do you mean?" She stalled for time, not sure how to fix this.

How could she have let him catch her snooping? And why hadn't she used the time when they'd been kissing to work out a plan B? Absurdly, her lips still tingled from that damned kiss, and it was all she could do not to brush her fingers over her mouth to still the quivery feeling.

"I mean I'm not convinced about your motives." He turned to study her, and she wondered how he could flip the switch from passion to interrogation so fast. "You could be using the attraction as a smoke screen. A very hot, very effective smoke screen, from whatever it is you're up to."

Her throat dried up.

She was on the verge of blurting the truth—that she didn't trust him, either, and she wanted to know what his father had done with all the profits from her misery. But then, Devon took a step closer to her again, his head tilting to one side as if he was considering a new idea.

"Maybe the best solution is for me to keep you close so I can have my eyes on you all the time." His wolfish smile shouldn't have been a turn-on, but she'd be lying if she denied a flare of heat inside her.

"I don't understand," she told him flatly, folding her arms across her chest to quiet all the ridiculous reactions of her body.

"We'll act on the attraction, Regina," he announced, like it was already decided. "Explore this chemistry for as long as we have together." He lowered his voice, the silky tone stroking over her senses like a caress. "Starting now."

Checkmate.

He'd effectively cornered her, and he wondered if she'd give up the game. No more pretense.

Because while there was attraction at work here—without question—he felt like she'd been searching his jacket with a purpose. His every instinct screamed at him that she was looking for something specific. Was she with the press? Had someone in the media gotten wind of his father's secret identity?

Or had she been tasked by her employer to find out more about him before the launch party? Devon suspected the Mesa Falls Ranch owners would have preferred to work with Marcus on the launch since Devon had arrived late and had asked a private investigator to look into his father's doings before he'd arrived. Weston Rivera hadn't been pleased to be contacted by the PI.

Devon had hoped that was water under the bridge

after the welcome reception the owners had thrown last week. But now he wasn't so sure.

"You're suggesting we...date?" When she raised one eyebrow and pursed her lips, there was something familiar about her features.

For a moment, he could almost swear he'd seen her before. But that made no sense. He shoved aside the thought to lock things down with her.

"Date. And wherever that might lead." He wandered closer to her again, taking pleasure in the way her gaze dipped to his lips for a moment.

"I have to admit, now I'm the one confused about your motives." She turned to release her horse from the crossties so she could lead the bay back to a stall.

It forced Devon to back up a step. The scent of hay and horses stirred while the mustang swished her tail, settling into the space before dipping her muzzle into the feed bucket.

"I thought I made myself very clear. I'm attracted to you. The feeling is reciprocated." He shrugged as he moved toward Evangeline so he could put her in for the night, too. "What's confusing about that?"

"You don't seem to trust me." She eyed him warily, opening another stall door and showing him where to lead Evangeline. "That kiss felt like some kind of test. You walked away from it easily enough. And now you toss around the idea of dating like it's a dare."

"In a way, it is." He led Evangeline to the stall, then passed the bridle to Regina. "Do you dare?"

She slanted a sideways glance at him while she waited for Evangeline to get comfortable. Then she pulled off the bridle and latched the stall door.

"That's beside the point. I can't risk my job by dating one of the patrons." She brushed past him with two bridles in hand.

He followed her into the tack room, where the scent of leather cleaner and polish hung heavily in the air. The walls were lined with saddles, blankets and all kinds of riding accessories. There were a few highly decorative pieces, but most were well-used plain leather.

"I'm not a guest of the ranch, though," he reminded her as he watched her wipe down the bridles. "I'm a freelance contractor providing a service. That's something very different. No one will object to you seeing me for the next ten days until the launch party."

He needed to keep her close to him to find out what she was doing. If she was trying to dig up information about his family, he'd find out soon enough. He watched as she hung the clean bridles on an iron peg over her head. She arched up on her toes, fitting the pieces over the hook.

"How do I know that?" She lifted her hands in exasperation.

"I'll inform Rivera personally." He rested his hands on her shoulders, feeling the tension threaded through her muscles under the fabric of her soft chambray shirt. "That way, he'll know I'm the one who initiated this relationship. So tell me, what would you like to do tomorrow to celebrate our first date?"

He caught a hint of her fragrance, something green and fresh like spring. Jasmine, maybe. He could feel some of the knots sliding away as he worked over the muscles. Not all. She was far from relaxed. Because she was nervous? Or was it more of that attraction at work? The kiss had rocked him, too, even if he'd managed to hide his reaction better than she had.

"You're serious about going through with this?" Those silver eyes were so wary.

"I want you," he told her simply. "I'm sure you could tell how much when I kissed you."

He saw a shiver pass over her and it filled him with satisfaction. No matter what other dynamic was at work between them, he couldn't wait to touch her again. Taste her thoroughly.

She gave a quick, fast nod.

"Okay."

It wasn't the most enthusiastic of receptions, but the shiver—and the kiss—had been enough.

"Okay." He confirmed it, gesturing her to lead the way out of the tack room.

She sidled past him, careful not to touch.

He retrieved her discarded jacket and helped her on with it. "Would you prefer I make the plans?"

He took his time easing the heavy duster over her shoulders, then lifted her hair out from under the collar. It brushed in a silky waterfall along the top of her back.

"Maybe that would be best." She turned to face him while he shrugged into his own jacket. "The picnic was nice today," she admitted, a smile animating her features for the briefest moment.

"I'm glad you had fun." He looked forward to getting to know Regina Flores much, much better. "I'll find a way to top it tomorrow."

She tugged her gloves from her pockets and pulled them on, flexing her fingers into the leather. He wondered what she was thinking. Feeling.

There were mysteries in her eyes he couldn't wait to unravel.

"I'll pick you up at six?" He pulled open the barn

door so he could walk her back to her cabin or wherever it was she stayed on the ranch.

Snowflakes still fell in slow whorls. She glanced up at the sky and then back at him as she stepped outside.

He couldn't miss the steely gleam in her eyes when she nodded.

"I'll be ready." Bracing her shoulders, she headed into the wind.

Devon followed and escorted her toward the main lodge. He'd have time to do his homework on Regina tonight, even if that meant asking his private investigator to do some digging on her. And when it was time for his date with the mysterious trail guide?

He'd be ready, too.

She was dating the enemy.

An hour after she'd made the deal with Devon, Regina couldn't decide if she was grateful for her quick thinking that had made her tell him she was attracted to him. Because she sure had put herself between a rock and a…very hard place. Memories of that kiss still scorched her insides if she let her thoughts linger on it too long.

Back in the comfort of her own quarters that night, she tried to focus on what she'd learned from her gamble instead of the dicey situation she'd put herself in. With a pillow propped behind her back as she worked in bed, she recorded everything she remembered from her quick glance through Devon's papers, entering the information on her laptop.

The women's bunkhouse accommodations were snug but comfortable, especially since half of the beds were still vacant. But then, the guest ranch portion of Mesa Falls was all new, with the service positions still being filled. She'd chosen a top bunk in the corner, and between the location and the curtains she could draw closed across the open side of the bed, her work on the laptop was private enough.

One of the other women she roomed with had come in briefly to shower before heading out for the night, and another had gone to sleep early. In the common room where there were a few couches and a television, a couple of older ladies who worked in the kitchens were reading. Someone had flipped on Christmas country tunes in that room, the occasional twang of a fiddle or a steel guitar filtering back to the bunk area. Regina didn't think anyone would disturb her for the rest of the evening with her curtain closed. She had her phone charging next to a bottle of water in a canvas cupholder that dangled from the top rail against the wall.

Regina searched online for the name she recalled from Devon's papers: April Stephens. She was a private investigator. She hadn't recalled the contact information other than that the woman was based in Denver. Regina found her easily and read her bio on a website for an agency specializing in forensic accounting and tracking down hidden assets.

Why did Devon have her card? And whose assets did he need to trace? Delving further into the website, she found links to articles about tracking missing persons. Apparently the two investigative specialties often went hand in hand since tracing missing money often led to missing people.

For the first time, Regina felt a twinge of guilt about invading Devon's privacy. She'd been so convinced he was profiting from the story about her family, but what if he wasn't? What if she was being as careless sifting through his personal business as his father had been with her family's secrets?

The scent of popcorn from the common room pulled her out of her thoughts, making her remember she hadn't eaten since the picnic she'd shared with Devon. Her stomach rumbled.

The other papers she'd glimpsed in Devon's coat were return plane tickets and a printed schedule for an East Coast wedding. A quick scan online confirmed the woman getting married was Devon's mother, Katherine "Kate" Radcliffe. Regina had read about Kate briefly in her earlier investigation into the Salazar family, but since the woman had never been a Salazar and didn't stay with Alonzo for long, Regina hadn't devoted much time to learning about the Radcliffes.

She dug deeper now, clicking through article after article online to discover all she could about Philip Radcliffe, the aging patriarch who oversaw a global pharmaceutical company. It was possible his wealth had helped Devon fund Salazar Media, and not Alonzo Salazar's ill-gotten gains. But an interview with the billionaire in a business publication suggested otherwise. In it, Philip talked about the need for "the Radcliffe fortune to remain in Radcliffe hands" for future generations.

That sounded like a deliberate slight to his grandson with a different last name, and the author of the article had speculated as much.

Fingers hovering over her keyboard, Regina found herself empathizing—at least a small amount—with Devon. She recalled how it felt to be dismissed based on lack of birthright.

While she mulled over the new twists, the sound of footsteps in the bunkhouse made her click off her screen right before a shadow loomed on the drawn curtain around her bed.

"Hon, you still awake?" It was a woman's voice, warm and kind.

Regina pushed aside the lined cotton fabric to see Millie, one of the new line cooks, holding a bowl of popcorn. Millie seemed close to retirement age, but she had an energetic vibe and fully embraced ranch life. Her long blond braid rested on the shoulder of a red thermal shirt that read Santa, I Tried.

"Just doing some research before bed," Regina replied, pointing to the closed laptop.

"We made a second batch of popcorn, so I thought I'd see if you wanted a bowl." Millie winked as she extended a red plastic dish decorated with green horseshoes and Christmas trees, with a paper napkin underneath. "It's got extra butter."

Touched by the gesture, Regina smiled, her mouth watering. "That's so kind of you to think of me. Thank you."

"It's no trouble." Millie was already backing away, her voice quiet as she passed another bunk where one of the room attendants was sacked out cold.

Millie disappeared into the common room, leaving Regina with the popcorn and a surprise dose of holiday spirit she hadn't been expecting. It was strange that she felt sort of at home at Mesa Falls Ranch, given that she'd only come here to learn more about the Salazar heirs. But it had been a long time since she'd been able to work with horses; the man she'd thought was her father had confiscated her beloved Arabian when the book scandal broke. She'd missed that equine companionship almost as much as she'd missed her father figure. More, perhaps, since the horse hadn't discarded her the way her dad had.

Mesa Falls Ranch gave her the gift of horses. And, it seemed, the gift of friendly faces in the form of people like Millie. As Regina munched the popcorn, she reminded herself not to get too attached. Because she was only in Montana for one reason.

To find out where Alonzo Salazar's profits went on the book that stole Regina's life out from under her. And to do that, she was going to get closer to Alonzo's oldest son than she'd ever imagined.

Starting tomorrow, on whatever date Devon dreamed up for them.

She wished she could concentrate on how that would benefit her cause. Yet long after she'd finished the popcorn and tried to fall asleep, Regina's thoughts returned again and again to the spark of awareness she'd felt when Devon had kissed her. And the knowledge that she was getting in too deep with a man who compelled her like no other.

Four

April Stephens tipped her face into the wind off the Bitterroot Mountains, breathing in the freedom of Big Sky Country just before sunset on her first day in Montana.

Gripping the smooth trunk of a sapling close to the campsite she'd just finished securing, April took in the beauty of Gem Lake, a frozen patch of opalescent blue in the gully between sharp gray peaks. Her work as a private investigator for Devon Salazar may have paid for her plane ticket, but that didn't mean her new client owned all of her time. As soon as she'd settled her things in her room at the Great Lodge at Mesa Falls Ranch, April had stuffed her camping gear into a backpack and requested a ranch utility vehicle to take her to one of the trailheads for Trapper's Peak.

She had no need to summit, and there wouldn't have been enough time if she'd wanted to. She just needed this moment in the outdoors with space and air around her, so different from the crammed suffocation of her mother's house, full of things from years of hoarding, every precarious pile providing tangible evidence that April could never save her.

Her trip there this morning, before her flight to Montana, had been a typical exercise in futility. She'd wanted to bring her mom some basic groceries, encourage her to get in the shower and alert her that April was going out of town. Instead, Mom had spent the whole time fretting over where to put a recent purchase of fabric remains from a local shop going out of business. By the time April had left for the airport, her mother— once a beloved schoolteacher and warm-hearted homemaker—had been in tears trying to cram bolts of fabric around the refrigerator in a way that would still allow the fridge to open.

Shoving aside the memory, April breathed deep, savoring the clean air before turning back to her camp and the small fire she'd started. She took a seat in front of the blaze to enjoy the warmth for another hour until she crawled inside her small tent for the night. She needed to be ready to break camp at dawn and get back to the lodge. For now, however, the cold wind tore through her clothes, whipping them against her in a way that felt like Mother Nature shaking out the cobwebs. Snow swirled in white eddies, the damp iciness scrubbing away the detritus of the messy life she kept hidden from everyone.

Was it any wonder she enjoyed tracking down secrets? She spent so much time concealing her own it was a weird sort of therapy to rip away the subterfuge from other people's. Sometimes it felt cruel. But it was cathartic, too.

Like with her work for Devon Salazar, who now wanted answers about Regina Flores on top of his original request. Tomorrow, she would meet with him about his more difficult project—tracking the proceeds from his father's book. But tonight, before his date with the mysterious Regina, she'd had to message him a warning that the woman's identity was an obvious fake.

That facet of the job had been easy—she'd been able to do the search on the flight. Without further information, she couldn't pinpoint the woman's real name. But as for the lady she claimed to be?

Regina Flores simply didn't exist.

The bunkhouse bustled with activity late the next afternoon while Regina dressed for her date. The second-shift workers had already left, and several of the women who held first-shift jobs were also getting ready to go out to local pubs, enjoying the start of the weekend.

Christmas pop music played over someone's speaker while women traded news about the workday. Most of the chatter was about the influx of reservations for the launch party week. Apparently, the lodge was already booked to capacity for the four days leading up to the event, and even now they were near 80 percent.

After pulling a heavy fisherman's sweater over her T-shirt, Regina double-checked an earlier text she'd received from Devon asking her to dress warmly since their date would have them outdoors for an hour. She was curious what he had in mind since the sun went down early this time of year. It was dark outside already.

She grabbed a pair of mittens and her jacket and was heading for the door when a snippet of conversation from the common room caught her ear.

"…I think his name is Devon. And he's smoking

hot," a feminine voice spoke in a breathless rush, bringing Regina to an abrupt halt. "He came into the lodge today to make a reservation and I was so tongue-tied I don't even remember what he said to me."

Regina couldn't help but listen. But the response of the woman's friend was lost to Regina's ears when someone flipped on a hair dryer nearby. Of course, she shouldn't be eavesdropping anyhow, but it seemed reassuring to know she wasn't the only one who found the marketing executive from New York to be ridiculously appealing. Clearly, he affected total strangers that way, too.

Charging into the common room, she gave a wave to the three younger women decorating a small Christmas tree someone had put up in a corner. There were popcorn strands all around it. Regina guessed that was what Millie and her friends had been working on the night before. Now the younger group—all from guest services, she thought—were hanging pine cones and small, glittery stars on the tree.

"Have a good night," one of them called to her as she left for her date.

She hadn't even pulled the door closed behind her when she spotted the sleigh.

The huge wooden contraption rested across the walkway in front of the bunkhouse. It was outlined in white lights and decorated with pine branches and a few red bows. A driver in a parka and Stetson held the reins to matching Friesian horses stamping and snorting in the chilly evening.

Devon stood beside the sleigh in a dark overcoat, jeans and boots, with a bouquet of white poinsettias in one hand.

Behind her, Regina felt her fellow bunkmates jostle

for position to see. One woman let out a dreamy sigh while another squealed. Reactions Regina could completely understand.

But she knew this romantic display wasn't so much for her as a way for Devon to keep close to her. He was as suspicious of her as she was of him, and she couldn't allow herself to forget it.

"Are you ready for a sleigh ride?" he asked, striding toward her.

She met him halfway, bearing in mind the charade was temporary and strictly for the convenience of keeping an eye on her, so there was no reason to feel flattered he'd gone to this much trouble for their evening together.

"Very ready." As her boots crunched in the snow, her gaze fixed on her companion for the evening.

His green eyes held hers, his shadowed jaw calling to her fingertips to test the feel of his skin there.

"For you." His breath huffed in the air between them as he handed her the poinsettia bouquet tied with a red bow. The scent of his aftershave, something woodsy with a hint of spice, made her want to lean closer.

"Thank you." She clutched the cloth bow and inhaled the bouquet made fragrant by the balsam greenery around it. "They're beautiful."

"Good." He nodded his satisfaction, his breath puffing in the space between them. "I hope it's one of many things you enjoy about the evening." His hand landed on her back as he guided her toward the sleigh. "I've heard this tour is fun at night even though you aren't able to see the sights, as well."

Stepping up into the vehicle, she said hello to the driver before taking a seat on the bench padded with blankets in back. She'd worn a short wool jacket over her sweater, but there was a stack of extra quilts neatly folded in an open shelf under the front seat.

Regina set the flowers on one side of her while Devon settled into the spot on her other side. She could see her bunkmates still crowded in the front door, peering out at them. Their relationship had gone public in a hurry. No doubt it all looked wildly romantic to an outsider. Who would ever guess at the strange way she'd fallen into this evening with Devon?

"Did you speak to Mr. Rivera about…us?" She didn't want to give her boss any reason to fire her.

"I did." He nodded as he leaned back in the seat, draping one arm across the back of the bench behind her before giving the driver the cue they were ready. "And it's a nonissue as far as the ranch is concerned. He said they welcome a lot of couples who take temporary jobs together to experience ranch life."

The sleigh ride began while Regina digested the news, realizing there would be no getting out of the date for that reason. For better or worse, she was committed to this fake relationship if she wanted to learn more about Devon. But she planned to proceed with caution since she had the feeling Devon Salazar was a man who wouldn't take kindly to being deceived.

"I appreciate you checking with him," she told him sincerely, figuring if she spoke the truth as often as possible, it would go a long way to putting them both more at ease.

She glanced out over the moonlit snow as the horses trotted away from the ranch buildings on the trail connecting grazing pastures. The lane was well packed here because trucks and ranch utility vehicles used it frequently. The sleigh moved faster, the runners making a gentle swishing sound.

The evening was clear and starlit, but now and then she felt the kiss of snow against her cheeks from drifts blowing along either side of the trail.

"I'm glad I could put your mind at ease," Devon assured her, tipping his head back to stare up at the tree branches when they entered a heavily forested area next to a pasture. "Now that there's no reason to fear repercussions for you at work, we can relax and get to know each other better."

He turned toward her, his presence suddenly very near. Close enough for her to feel the warmth of his chest near hers, the brush of his arm against the back of her shoulders. His leg grazed hers. Her throat dried up at the physical proximity, at the appeal of hard male muscle just underneath a layer of clothes.

She hid a shiver that was more pleasure than worry.

Frowning, he leaned forward to retrieve one of the linens folded beneath the vacant seat in front of them.

"Are you cold?" he asked, already unfurling the red plaid wool and laying it over their laps. "There are plenty of blankets if you want another."

His fingers tugged the fabric around her, tucking it behind her hip, igniting a slow burn of awareness in her belly. And lower.

"I'm fine," she protested, mostly because his hands were a major distraction.

Her breath came faster as they emerged from the trees back out onto an open field, where it was brighter.

"Are you sure?" He studied her in the moonlight. "Just say the word if you want to turn back at any time." His concern sounded genuine.

"I'm warm enough." She fought the urge to lick her dry lips—and battled an even stronger urge to taste her way along his shadowed jaw. She dragged her gaze from him to gesture toward the scenery. "And this is really pretty."

The Montana countryside unfolded in shades of gray and white around them as they skirted the western bank of the Bitterroot River. In the river valley, the waterway was a frozen layer of ice under snow, the area around it devoid of trees.

A few deer lifted their heads as the sleigh neared, keeping watch over Regina and Devon while other members of the herd nosed through the snow for a drink.

"We lucked out with the moon almost full." Devon shifted on the bench seat beside her as the sleigh took a hard turn away from the water. "I'd heard that the sleigh rides are worth it even when it's fully dark because of the sensory experience, but we're getting to see quite a bit, too."

"Sensory experience?" She wasn't quite sure what he meant. She pulled back to look at him.

"You know how your senses are heightened when your eyes are closed? You're more attuned to what you hear or feel? I heard this trip in the dark is fun like that—you can really enjoy the experience of the sleigh ride." A wolfish smile flashed as he lowered his voice. "Sort of like closing your eyes when you kiss so you can appreciate everything else that's going on."

Her belly flipped, feeling almost airborne for a moment.

Her brain refused to think of a single response that didn't sound like flirting. Because suddenly, all she could think about was pressing her lips to his.

Maybe it was unwise to kiss a woman who was hiding something from him.

Everything about Regina Flores—from her fake

name to the way she'd rifled through his jacket the night before—had warned Devon she was trouble. At the very least, she was being dishonest with him.

Yet something about her called to him anyway.

Because he wasn't thinking about kissing the woman who was doing her best to deceive him. No, he was mesmerized by the one who could handle a horse in icy trail conditions and build her own fire. Captivated by the woman who knew about Montana wildlife and whose breath caught when he got close to her.

Like now.

"Should we try it?" he asked her now, skimming away a few dark strands of her hair where they blew across her cheek.

Her ivory-colored knit hat framed her face but didn't constrain her hair.

"Try what?" Her voice was a barely-there whisper of sound that was almost lost in the swish of the runners through the snow, the clop of hooves and the jangle of sleigh bells.

Regina's gray eyes were wide.

"The full sensory experience," he clarified, unable to move his fingers away from her face now that he'd felt the smooth softness of her skin. "The kiss."

Her nod was almost imperceptible. But she let her eyes drift closed, the dark lashes fanning a sultry shadow on her cheek.

Hunger for her surged. He wrapped his arm around her shoulders to draw her close and tipped her chin up to taste her the way he'd wanted to since the first time he'd seen her.

Her lips parted. He breathed in the minty trace of toothpaste and a fruity hint of lip balm before he kissed her. Gently, at first. Her mouth molded to his, lips pillow soft as she sighed into him.

Her fingers traced over his jaw, back and forth, before her hand fell to the shoulder of his jacket where she gripped the fabric tight. She edged closer, the warm press of her curves against him a welcome weight that took the kiss from experimental to simmering.

Awareness flared hotter, and he angled her shoulders to deepen the kiss. The small, needy sound she made at the back of her throat was like a torch to dry timber, desire for her cranking into a slow burn. Devon knew that a sleigh in the middle of a snow-covered Montana river valley was no place to take things farther. Yet that didn't do a damned thing to impede the roll of red-hot thoughts through his mind, the need for her scorching away everything else.

Especially when she fitted so perfectly against him under the cocoon of the wool blanket. Hip to hip. Thigh to thigh. And before he allowed his thoughts to drift any more astray, he forced himself to break the kiss. Slowly he leaned back, inserting an inch or two of space between them where before there'd been none.

The cold December air rushed in, filling the gap. Reminding him how much he needed things to cool down.

"I see what you mean now about the dark heightening the senses," Regina told him as she opened her eyes, her gaze seeking his. "I'm in complete, one-hundred-percent agreement that it's a very real phenomenon."

Devon breathed in the snow-dusted air as the sleigh bounced over frozen ruts in the ranch trail, the big black draft horses never slowing. Long, spikey shadows of pine trees fell over them. He waited for his heart rate to even out after the head rush of kissing Regina.

"I honestly didn't expect to prove the point so thoroughly." He'd planned to woo her into letting her guard down. Letting him see a glimpse of what she was really about. He hadn't expected to be seduced by a kiss. "It was my intention to take you out and get to know you better."

Hell, it had been his plan to confront her about her real motives. Her real identity. Running a social media company had taught him that people in her age demographic rarely if ever left no trace online. Yet that was the case with Regina Flores. The text message from his private investigator had confirmed his hunch—Regina was a fake.

"You asked all the questions at our picnic," she hedged, her fingers threading through the fringed edge of the blanket. "It's me who doesn't know much about you."

"I'm an open book," he protested, not surprised that she wanted to sidestep talking about herself. Maybe he'd do better to share something superficial about his world, in the hope that it would prompt her to share something, too. Like why had she taken the job at Mesa Falls Ranch. And why she was interested in him. "What do you want to know? And would you like some hot cocoa?"

He reached under the seat and retrieved two thermal carafes, passing one to her. He used the time to think through topics he needed to avoid if it turned out Regina was a member of the media looking for a scoop about his father's book.

And, hell, if the conversation got too dicey, he could always kiss her again. The chemistry between them was hot enough to burn away everything else.

"Thank you." She twisted the lid of her thermos to

reveal the spout, and steam wafted out the top. "One thing I'm curious about is your job. Why did you start a media company?"

He seized on the topic to keep his thoughts from straying down the carnal path again. At least for the time being. Once they returned to civilization—maybe to the privacy of his cabin—he would be more than happy to revisit the temptation of Regina's lips.

"My brother, Marcus, has a gift for social media and a lot of ambition." Devon remembered seeing the kinds of things his brother posted in the early days of social media—innovative, creative content that people copied. "We've never had much in common, but I've always respected his intelligence. I had a strong feeling he would be successful, and I wanted to test my own ideas for growing a small business from the ground up."

Regina studied him for a long moment over the stainless steel rim of her drink. "Is it expensive to start a business like that? You must have been young."

"We both were. But there wasn't a lot of overhead at first—just the cost of manpower." He decided to mention his dad, if only to watch her reaction. "Our father invested in us, which helped."

Her head tilted a fraction at the mention of Alonzo. Was it polite curiosity? Or had she been waiting for a chance to discuss the author of the novel that had caused such scandal? He couldn't be sure.

"Nice to have a parent's support." She sipped her cocoa before continuing. "Is your dad an entrepreneur, too?"

"He was an English teacher, actually." He noticed how she peered down as he spoke, making it harder to gauge her reactions. "He died early this year."

"I'm so sorry." Regina's hand covered his, her tone undeniably sympathetic.

"Thank you." He missed his dad even though they'd never been close. If anything, that made it harder since he'd never have the chance to build a relationship with him now. "He taught at a boarding school on the West Coast. The same school the owners of Mesa Falls Ranch attended, in fact. My father remained in contact with them after graduation, visiting Montana whenever he had the chance."

He wondered about that. What had tied his father to the wealthy and powerful men who ran Mesa Falls Ranch? A small part of him resented the fact that his dad made time to see them, yet had rarely made the effort to spend time with Devon.

"No wonder the owners chose your firm to handle their social media as they open the ranch to private guests." She twisted the top closed on her drink and tucked the carafe into an open slot alongside the bench seat. "I'm sure it would make your father proud to know you and your brother are maintaining relationships that must have been important to him."

She sounded almost wistful as she said it, which made him wonder about her family.

"You said your mother lived in Tahoe," he said, recalling their conversation during the snowy picnic. "What about your dad?"

"We...aren't close," she admitted. "He was married to someone else when he had an affair with my mom, so I think I'm a reminder of his bad choices. Especially for my stepmother."

Before he could respond, she pointed into the field on their right. There, seemingly in the middle of nowhere, someone had decorated a pine tree with red and white lights. The blowing snow dulled some of them on the windward side, but the rest shone brightly.

"Are we close to one of the owners' homes?" he asked, trying to orient himself.

All six owners of the Mesa Falls Ranch had houses around the property. They'd seen a few of them on their horseback ride the day before.

She peered around the field, looking from the shadowed mountains to the river and back again. "Maybe Desmond Pierce's, although I don't think he's in Montana this week. And I don't see lights for a house anywhere nearby." She turned her gaze back toward him. "Although I've heard all the owners will be on hand for the launch event. How are the preparations going for that?"

Devon noted that she'd once again dodged the subject of her own life.

But now that she had nowhere to hide from his questions, he prepared to confront her with the bombshell that his investigator had shared with him.

"The preparations are running like clockwork. My biggest concern right now is you."

"Me?" She tilted her head, her expression questioning, but he didn't miss the hint of wariness in her eyes.

He met her gaze, the soft glow from the white lights on the sleigh helping him to see her even in the dark. "I can't figure out why you're hiding behind a fake identity."

Five

Panic bubbled up in her throat.

Not that she feared for her physical safety out here in the Montana wilderness, tucked into the back of the huge horse-drawn sleigh. Devon Salazar wasn't the kind of man to intimidate a woman; his demeanor was calm, his body language relaxed as he sat on the bench beside her. Plus, the sleigh driver from the ranch was right there, sitting high on his perch above the horses, a neutral party under his earmuffs and cowboy hat. He was far enough away from them not to hear their conversation, but close enough to remind Regina she wasn't alone with Devon.

So while she was safe, she was also well and truly cornered. There was zero doubt in Devon's eyes as he watched her every reaction to his accusation. And who knew how much she'd already given away in her shock? Her best option now was to tell him the truth.

Or at least enough truth to ease his suspicions.

"I have an excellent reason for hiding behind a fake identity." She retrieved the carafe of hot chocolate again, if only to soothe her dry throat—and to give her time to think her way through this. "I'm surprised you haven't guessed."

She twisted open the top and sipped the cocoa while the sleigh looped around an open field and turned back toward the ranch. A thin veil of snow kissed her cheeks as a cross breeze caught the flakes stirred by the runners. She welcomed the cooling touch against the knot of confusing emotions she had about this man. Resentment, anxiety and, yes, more than a little desire. She wished she didn't feel quite so much of the latter for a man whose father had been her worst enemy.

"I have ideas, certainly," he acknowledged as calmly as if they were discussing holiday decorations instead of her most closely guarded secrets. "And since you rifled through the papers in my jacket last night, you must know that I'm working with a private investigator, so I'll uncover the whole story for myself eventually." His level gaze revealed nothing. "But considering the draw between you and me, I'd prefer to hear the truth from you first."

Her stomach tightened. She could deny the sexual chemistry all she wanted, but at least he sensed it as much as she did. Why did she have to feel this way about the man she was spying on? Her relationships before now had been predicated on mutual interests. They'd been simple, sensible connections. They hadn't lasted long, but then again, they never stirred this level of heat and confusion.

Steeling herself for the conversation, she lowered her

drink and closed the top again. "I couldn't risk having you shut me out if you knew my real name," she admitted. "But I needed to meet you in person."

"Why?" he pressed. "What do you want from me?"

So many things now that she'd met him. She wanted his touch. His kiss. His eyes on her because he wanted her, not out of suspicion. But she was foolish to think about that when there was something so much more complex between them. Something painful.

"I want answers about your father, Devon. About the book he wrote that destroyed my life."

For a moment the only sound was the rhythmic clomp of the horses' hooves, the soft rattle of their dress tack against their bodies and the swish of the runners through powdery snow.

In the quiet, Devon looked at her with the same stunned expression that she suspected she'd worn just moments before.

"*Your* life?" He leaned forward, his knee brushing hers, the warmth of his body stirring her in spite of everything. "Who are you really?"

She wondered how he would react. Would he have her fired? Or would he leave Mesa Falls Ranch altogether and find someone else to oversee the launch event for his powerful client?

Those questions didn't begin to address the other fears and insecurities that came with revealing her identity. How many times had she been rejected because of her surname? Or turned into an object of scandal, ridicule or curiosity?

"I was born Georgiana. My original birth certificate had my name as Georgiana Cameron." She notched her chin higher, defensive of the girl she'd once been. "But in some ways, that name is far more deceptive than the one I'm using now."

Recognition flicked in his eyes. Something else flitted through his expression, too. Something dangerously close to pity.

"You're the daughter in that book?" He shook his head, eyes wide. "She was little more than a child—"

"I was sixteen when your father's book was released—almost seventeen by the time it was exposed that my parents were the key figures the novel was based on. And your father used a fake identity, too, I might add, for far more nefarious purposes than me. I need the anonymity to protect myself from the tabloids' relentless interest in me. But your dad? He used a pen name to hide behind. Plain and simple." She didn't have a prayer of disguising the bitterness in her voice. "I was twenty-one when I hired someone to investigate the pseudonym A. J. Sorensen, and it took two years to learn it was Alonzo Salazar."

"At which point, you learned he'd died." Devon put the pieces together quickly, but then, he was a sharp man to have taken his company from a start-up founded by two brothers to a globally recognized firm. "But why do you say your birth name is more deceptive than the one you're using now?"

The question tore at an old wound, one that had never healed. The anger it raised was never far from the surface, even in this beautiful, still Montana night.

"Because while I was born Georgiana Cameron, it was based on a lie." That was her mother's fault more than his father's. But there was plenty of blame to go around. "Have you read the book?"

A gust of wind whirled off the mountains and lifted

the edge of the blanket, causing the fringe to dance across her lap.

"No." Devon smoothed the wool back into place as he shook his head. "I read a few reviews of it to get up to speed once I discovered Dad's...connection. So I know the gist, but not all the particulars."

"Lucky you," she said tightly, her fingers fisting in her gloves. "In a nutshell, the book depicts a sordid love triangle between a powerful Hollywood producer, an LA singer and a Brazilian soccer star, where the singer passes off her lover's child as her husband's." How many breathless reviews had she read that said the world it painted was so vivid and real, capturing the seedy side of fame? Tension knotted her shoulders. "But a few details were so particular—like the singer being twice divorced and signing an ironclad prenup that gave her nothing if she cheated—that eventually a gossip columnist connected it to my parents. They were Hollywood actors and my mother's lover was an Argentinian polo player, but everything else lined up."

Her parents had met while her mother was in South America for her honeymoon, of all things, which was a tidbit of truth Regina wished she'd never learned. She'd loved the man she'd believed to be her father.

"It seems like a flimsy parallel—" Devon began, his expression thoughtful as the sleigh bumped from a field onto a path near the tree line.

His easy dismissal of that time in her life stirred a fresh wave of hurt.

"It became a national pastime to find other connections over the next six months. One of the tabloids offered a game with a huge cash prize for whoever found the most real-life similarities." It hadn't mattered for her by then, since her father believed the scandalmongers instantly. Her gut knotted. "But the most telling proof was the way my father—the man I'd believed to be my dad up until then—began divorce proceedings as soon as the story broke. I came home from dance practice one day to find a locksmith at work on the security system to ensure my mother and I weren't allowed back on his property."

She shouldn't feel tears burn at the back of her eyes about that anymore. But she rarely spoke about that day, and, yes, it still hurt.

Beside her, she heard Devon shift closer, his voice gentler. Kind.

"I'm sorry you had to endure that." He placed a steadying hand between her shoulders. "And sorry that you weren't ever able to confront my dad about his actions. Hell, I wish *I* could ask him why he wrote that damned book, and I've only known about it for a few days. I can't imagine how deeply it's hurt you to have no answers."

His empathy touched her, even though she told herself she shouldn't let it. Because she couldn't afford to lose focus on her mission in Montana—to find out where the proceeds from the book had gone. And taking comfort from Devon's kindness would only make her feel worse later if she discovered his business was built on the income from her heartache.

"Thank you for your sympathy." She gave a clipped nod to acknowledge words that didn't heal the hurt of having her past ripped away. "And to your original point about Georgiana Cameron, my mother's husband won a court order to change my birth certificate so that it no longer bore his name."

There'd been a time when she'd had grand visions for what she would say to the man who'd raised her when she saw him in court—for the impassioned plea she would make about how a family wasn't bound by blood ties but by love. In her girlish dreams, she'd thought that could change his mind and make him accept her again. But he'd sent his attorney to argue for him, robbing her of the chance to gain closure by speaking directly to him.

"So Flores is your birth father's last name?" Devon asked.

"No. It's Fuentes. When I came up with a name for myself, I used your father's trick of changing names just a little. In his book, my mother, Tabitha, was called Tempest. The man I believed to be my father, Davis, was called David." She shrugged, not owing him any more explanation than she'd already given. Yet now that she'd started talking about the past—about all the reasons she felt angry—she found it hard to stop. "Even as Georgiana Fuentes, the tabloids hounded me. It was so bad that I got into a car accident trying to elude a photographer. The surprise blessing of reconstructive surgery on my face was that at least I didn't bear as much resemblance to the woman I was before."

The surgeries had been painful. Recovery had been slow. But she'd used the time to formulate her plan for revenge. One that she couldn't abandon just because she was attracted to Alonzo Salazar's older son.

"Georgiana." He covered her hand with his where it rested on the blanket.

Even through her gloves she could feel the warmth of his palm. The sound of her name on his lips was oddly soothing. She hadn't heard it in so long. She'd isolated herself in so many ways, unhappy with the shreds of family she had left after the wreckage caused by that damned book.

"Please." Her throat burned with emotions as the sleigh hurtled faster toward the ranch. "Don't call me that."

She couldn't afford to let her feelings toward him soften. Part of her wanted to call an end to this conversation, but they were still too far from the ranch for her to get out and walk. She would have to sit tight, see how the conversation—and the attraction—played out.

"Regina, then," he corrected himself, the gentleness in his voice and his touch unnerving her. "I wish I could take back what he did. Or even help you to understand it, because I don't understand myself."

She willed herself to pull away from him but couldn't quite do it. Her emotions were ragged, and she feared one false move would dissolve all her boundaries and send her hurtling into his arms to seek what warmth she could in his embrace, to forget herself in the seductive power of his kiss.

She wanted the heat of their attraction to burn away everything else, if only for a few hours. And that was a dangerous desire when she should be focused on her end goal—finding out where the proceeds of that book had gone.

A goal she wasn't ready to admit to him. Because what if he thwarted her efforts to unravel the truth?

"So find the answers now," she challenged. "You said you hired a private investigator." She knew his budget would be far bigger than the measly amount she'd been able to pay someone to track the mystery author in the first place. "Why not ask the PI to find out your father's reasons for writing it?"

Devon studied the myriad emotions on Regina's face, visible even in the dim Christmas lights strewn around the outside of the sleigh. Her confession had rocked him, though he'd gone into the evening knowing that she wasn't who she claimed to be. Yet he hadn't expected anything like this—a revelation that she was a woman who'd been personally devastated by his father's book.

Even after all the ways she'd come clean tonight, Devon couldn't help the lingering sense that she'd held some piece back from him. Some part of the bigger picture he wasn't seeing yet.

Soon enough, he would. He just needed to bring himself up to speed on her and her family. Learn all he could about the Camerons, the Fuenteses, and about how his father's life had intersected with theirs. It seemed that the biggest mystery remained; Devon hadn't known his father at all.

For now, his need to stay close to Regina was stronger than ever. And not just because the air between them sizzled every time they looked at one another. But because he had to know what she was really up to in Montana this week. He didn't believe for a second that she'd come all this way, taking a job as a trail guide, just to learn more about his father's motives. Was she hoping to sue his family? Or look into his father's past for skeletons as some sort of payback scheme? She could certainly cause a scandal for him if she hoped to get even with the Salazars. There was more at play here, and Devon intended to uncover it.

More important, he planned to keep a lid on it until after his mother's wedding.

"Good idea about the investigator," he told her, still holding her hand. Still wanting her in spite of everything. "I'll ask her to explore my father's past and see what she can come up with. I wasn't aware he had ties to the show business community, so I'm not sure where he would have unearthed information about your parents' private lives."

For that matter if Regina was considering a lawsuit against his father's estate, it might be beneficial to have the investigator's findings ready to shore up a defense. But Devon hoped it wouldn't come to that.

Regina slid her hand out of his and hugged herself. He mourned the loss of her touch.

"When I came to work here, I thought you might have those answers for me." Her restless gaze roamed the lights of the guest ranch buildings in the distance, momentarily visible from a high hill. "Knowing the author's reasons for exploiting my family might help me finally gain some closure, so I can put the past to rest for good."

Her words sparked a feeling of defensiveness for his dad, but not strongly enough to outweigh the empathy he felt for what she'd been through. Besides, whatever wrongs had been committed didn't detract from the simple fact that Devon wanted her with a hunger unlike anything he'd ever experienced.

"I wish I had answers, but all I have right now are more questions." He shifted closer to her, resting his fingertips lightly on her cheek to encourage her to meet his gaze. A thrill shot through him to touch her this way; her skin was cool and soft. "And right now the most important of those questions is this. Will you have dinner with me?" he asked, looking deep into her gray eyes.

Her gaze lowered to his mouth and lingered.

"Dinner?" she asked after a long pause, pulling in a breath that huffed lightly along his palm.

Desire for her sharpened. Tightened. Crowded his chest.

"At my cabin," he clarified, wanting her to be very

aware they would be alone. "I ordered catering for our return, but I don't want to be presumptuous. We can go out if you prefer."

Her tongue darted along her bottom lip.

"You still want this to be a date?" she asked, her voice wary. "Even now that you know who I am?"

"Knowing your identity doesn't change the attraction." If anything, the outing had only reinforced it. The memory of that kiss had never been far from his mind.

He stroked a light touch along her jaw, feathered a caress over her lush mouth.

Her eyelids fluttered but didn't close. "But my name…complicates things."

The sleigh skidded to the left down a hill and her body collided against his. He caught her, held her steady just long enough to feel the rapid-fire beat of her heart, the soft swell of her breasts. He wanted to feel her naked against him just this way.

He burned for her, his skin on fire. He breathed in the slightest hint of her jasmine fragrance, different from the cedar and balsam all around them.

"I think the rewards will make the complications well worth it." It took a superhuman effort not to pull her closer. To slide his hands away. "But it's your call to make."

"You want me to decide." She worried her lower lip with her teeth in a movement as erotic as any touch.

He steeled himself, wondering how any woman could have this kind of power over him. Particularly a woman he shouldn't trust.

"I already know that I don't want tonight to end. But are you ready for more, Regina?" He kept his hands at his sides.

He knew his touch could sway her answer. That

wasn't egotistical. It was a simple fact that they com-busted when they touched each other.

And he refused to tip the scales unfairly. He needed her to be sure. To want this as much as he did.

The sleigh slowed down, and Devon knew they must be approaching the remote lodge where he was staying. The scent of wood smoke from a chimney fire teased his nose, reminding him he'd left a blaze burning in the river stone fireplace while the catering company set up service for the meal.

Fragrant cooking spices drifted on the breeze as the sleigh came to a stop. The driver remained in his seat, though he did turn around expectantly.

And still, Regina hadn't replied.

"Should we return to the ranch?" Devon didn't want to part company, but if that was her preference, he would wait.

Find a way to tempt her into another evening with him tomorrow.

"I don't run from complications, either," she finally said, certainty evident in every word as she peeled away the blanket and tossed it on the seat in front of them. Sitting forward, she gave him her hand. "And I signed up for a date tonight."

Six

Stepping over the threshold into the cabin perched above the Bitterroot River, Regina breathed in the savory scent of roasting spices along with the sweeter hints of nutmeg and clove. Devon took her coat from her before excusing himself to speak to the catering team.

In short order, the three staff members exited through a back entrance, leaving Devon and her very much alone. Warming trays filled the kitchen island, while the dining area table had been set with festive red candles and decorated with scattered pine cones on green boughs. The table was tucked into a nook of bay windows, but the sky remained too dark to see beyond the glass into the densely forested woods.

In the living area, a wood fire burned in the stone fireplace, casting an inviting glow over a deep leather sofa and a narrow holiday tree bare of all decoration except for white lights. The wide plank floors were covered with twill weavings in muted cream, gold and brown, in patterns she'd seen often in this part of Montana. Moose antlers hung over the fireplace.

Sliding off her boots, Regina left them by the front door and padded deeper into the lodge, pausing near the holiday tree. She tested the soft needles of the balsam pine, surprised to discover it was fresh.

A thrill shot through her as Devon's footsteps sounded behind her. She'd thought long and hard about his invitation here before setting foot inside. And now that she had made up her mind to be with him, she wasn't sure she could wait to kiss him again until after dinner.

"Regina." His voice was just over her shoulder.

His nearness made her heart gallop faster, the warmth of him close enough to make her nerve endings tingle with awareness. She was done questioning it. Done asking herself why she had to be so attracted to this man of all people.

The need for him was so strong she couldn't think past it.

She wasn't sure how to express any of that as she turned toward him. But when she met his gaze, she realized that she didn't need to try to articulate it. The sizzling connection sparked to life on its own, a magnetic draw so strong she couldn't say who moved first—him or her.

Their lips met. Fused. Arms wrapping around each other. Hers around his neck. His around her waist. The full-on impact of his body against hers was hot enough to take her breath away, stirring all her senses. She wanted time to appreciate every nuance of those sensations, and at the same time, she wanted more. Faster. Now.

His hands skimmed up her sweater, pressing her tighter. Her fingers raked through his wavy hair. The ripple of muscle under his shirt was enough to make her stomach tighten with breathless anticipation. Her pulse pounded harder in every tiny vein, making her whole body feel like a drumroll, a vibrating precursor to the big finish she craved.

When he broke the kiss, she made a sound of wordless protest, but then his lips fastened on her neck. She closed her eyes again to give herself to the feel of his tongue stroking along the exquisitely sensitive place behind her ear. Then the tender hollow at the base of her throat. Every sensual glide across her skin deepened the need to get closer. To be naked. To feel that good everywhere.

Tugging the hem of his shirt higher, she dragged it up and off. In the moment when his arms left her, she instinctively moved closer, craving his touch again. Her gaze fell to his broad chest, hands splaying over the bared skin. She would have kissed her way along one flat pectoral muscle, but with a low growl, he took her hand and drew her deeper into the cabin.

Following blindly—gladly—Regina passed the kitchen island into a darker hallway. Devon pushed open the door to the master suite. A desk lamp glowed on the far side of the king-size bed at the center of the room, the tan-and-gold-striped quilt half concealed by a rich red duvet folded at the foot of the mattress. She had a vague impression of high ceilings and dark wood beams, but then Devon's arms were around her again and she forget everything except for his touch.

His kiss.

Her lips found his with new urgency. The dance of

his tongue along hers ignited a sensual shiver. Her hips arched against his. Seeking. Wanting.

His arms banded harder around her in answer, every inch of him steely and unyielding, making her melt. He stripped off her sweater and she shimmied out of her jeans, a new tension building inside her. She hadn't dressed for seduction, and for a split second, she wished she'd draped herself in sexy black silk instead of staid pink cotton.

Her gaze flicked up to his. He was taking her in with a frank male appreciation that sent any doubts fleeing. His focus narrowed to her breasts at the same time he slid aside the straps of her bra. Her breath caught as his eyes darkened, his fingers freeing the clasp just before his head lowered to capture a nipple between his lips.

A paroxysm of sensations coursed through her. Her head tipped back, and she gave herself up to the wicked skill of the kiss. He lifted her, depositing her gently onto the bed before his mouth moved to the other breast. She felt the delectable muscles of his shoulders and back flexing as he moved.

The ache between her thighs intensified. She lifted her hips, wriggling against him where his knee pressed into the bed. With a hungry groan, he lifted his head and shed his pants and his boxers. He retreated to the en suite bath for a moment and returned with a condom in hand, the packet already falling away in his rush to roll it into place. Heat and longing flooded her, her breathing fast and hard even though she'd done nothing more than kiss him. She thought she'd come right out of her skin if he didn't touch her soon.

Sitting up, she reached for him before he returned to the bed, her fingers trailing along the shadowed, incredibly sexy striations of his rigid abs. She didn't have long to admire him, though, because he slid his hands under her thighs before walking his fingers up her hips to draw down her panties.

The last garment between them finally removed.

He lifted her off the bed and she didn't hesitate to wrap her legs around him, her eyes on his. When he sat on the bed, she was on his lap. Straddling him. Trembling like it was her first time because the sensations were so intense.

She wrapped her arms around his neck, kissed him while he edged his way inside her. Joining them.

Pleasure crowded out everything else. Every touch, every taste, every stroke tantalized her, the passion building fast. She locked her heels behind him, holding him close while they moved in sync. Over and over.

Heat seared her. She closed her eyes again, wanting to focus on the sweetness of what he was doing to her. On his hands cupping her breasts, thumbs teasing over the peaks, his thighs flexing beneath her in a way that drove her right over the edge.

Her orgasm blindsided her, her feminine muscles seizing again and again, wringing out every shred of possible pleasure. She felt Devon go still beneath her for a moment before the same wave caught him, too, his body going rigid as his release pumped through him. It was impossibly good.

Pure and utter bliss.

And all she could do in the aftermath was tip her head to Devon's shoulder and cling to him because there were no words for what had just happened. Other people had sex. This?

She was pretty sure the earth had moved.

After long moments wrapped in each other's arms, he found a way to disentangle from her, pulling her back to lie beside him on the bed. He drew the spare blanket over their bodies while she tried to catch her breath.

Reason returned slowly, bringing with it new worries about what had just happened. As Devon smoothed back her hair, she was grateful for the long silence while she collected her thoughts. Tried to figure out what happened now.

Because no matter how good it had felt, Devon Salazar remained a potential enemy, as well as someone who had the answers to the puzzle of her shattered past. And she couldn't forget that, even for the sake of the best sex of her life.

"I can hear you thinking," he said finally, his voice a sexy whisper against her ear.

For a moment, she wished that this could be just a normal relationship where she could lean into him and savor what had just happened instead of thinking through her every move. But she hadn't come to Montana for romance. She needed to be careful around him, no matter how amazing he'd just made her feel.

While she debated her approach, Devon spoke again. "Before we try to figure out where things stand, why don't we put some clothes on and go have dinner?"

As he took another bite of a spiced scone with cinnamon glaze an hour later, Devon studied the woman across the table from him. She'd surprised him in so many ways tonight. First, when she'd come clean about her identity, it had rocked him. He'd imagined plenty of reasons for why she was pretending to be someone else, but it had never crossed his mind that Regina Flores had been born Georgiana Cameron, a woman caught in the crosshairs of the scandal created by his father's book.

Then, before he could wrap his head around what

that meant, there'd been the unforgettable sex. Even now, after they'd enjoyed companionable conversation over roast duck, coconut-ginger yams and risotto with mushrooms, Devon's thoughts kept returning to what they'd shared. The connection had been unlike anything he'd ever known, scorching away the suspicions and deceits until there was nothing but burning need. And she had seemed as taken aback by their chemistry as he had been.

Now, after devouring the last of his dessert, he slid the dish aside and wondered how to proceed with the beautiful woman full of contradictions in front of him.

"More wine?" He lifted the bottle of port while Regina scooped up a forkful of gingerbread shortbread, one of three choices the caterers had left for them.

"No. Thank you." Her dark hair curled in waves around her face, the strands tousled from his fingers. "I have to be a trail guide early tomorrow morning."

She had put her jeans and sweater back on, and had the sleeves of the bulky knit pushed up to her elbows.

"You're going to continue your job here?" He wondered why, since her cover was blown. "I mean, now that your identity is out in the open?"

"I'm enjoying the horses." She swirled her fork through the whipped cream dusted with tinted sugar. "I didn't realize how much I missed the Arabian of my youth until I got into the barns here. And, as it turns out, I really believe in the ranch mission."

"The sustainable ranching?" Devon had spoken to a few of the Mesa Falls owners about that when he'd first arrived. Creating public awareness of the green initiatives on the land was the number one goal of the launch event that Salazar Media had been charged with executing.

He was drawn to the authenticity in her voice as she spoke, the passion for a cause he felt strongly about, as well.

"Yes." Regina moved one of the red taper candles out of the way so they could see each other better across the small table. "I know the practices aren't feasible for all ranches yet, but the more we learn about what works, the more we can incorporate holistic ranching ideas into livestock management everywhere. Someone has to go first."

"Agreed." He sipped the rich red port from a dessert wine glass. "You sound as prepared as anyone on my staff to write the talking points for the launch party speeches."

She laughed lightly, the candlelight catching deep shades of cherry in her dark hair. "I studied hard to convince the ranch manager that I was the one for the job. And as for my identity being in the open, are you sure you want it to be?"

"What do you mean?" Defensiveness had him sitting straighter in his seat.

"Georgiana Fuentes being out of the public eye has allowed interest in A. J. Sorensen's book to fade away." She set her fork crossways on her plate and leaned back from the table. "Are you prepared for the renewed media focus?"

Was she threatening to expose him?

"No one knows my father wrote it," he reminded her, treading carefully. "So public attention would likely be more problematic for you than for me, unless you plan to reveal Alonzo's identity as the author."

"Right now, I'm more concerned with finding my own answers before media interest clouds the path," she explained. "So I won't be sharing that information—

for now. But if you feel the need to out me, I wish you would give me fair warning. Tabloid media can descend with shocking speed."

He could see her point. But she'd also skillfully reminded him that she could send *his* life into a tailspin at any given moment if she blew the whistle on the author. All the more reason he planned to stick close to her throughout his stay at Mesa Falls Ranch.

"I understand why you'd prefer to remain anonymous. I won't share your real name with anyone." He wanted to touch her, to draw her against him, but the conversation called to mind all the thorny issues between them.

The mistrust.

"Thank you." She wrapped her arms around her midsection, the watchfulness in her gray eyes mirroring how he felt.

Dammit.

He reached for her in spite of the wariness, drawn by the connection that remained even now. He dragged his chair closer, his knee bumping hers under the table.

"It wasn't my intention to remind you of something painful." Covering her hand with his, he squeezed her fingers. "I plan to share with you what I learn from my private investigator about my father's reasons for writing the book."

He hadn't pressed her about her endgame in coming to Montana, about deceiving him to get close to him. Was her goal simply to gain information, like she'd implied? Or was it revenge?

With her body close to his, her dark hair spilling loose over one shoulder, and her cheeks lightly pink from the warmth or the wine, Devon found it tough to imagine her setting him up for some kind of payback plot. Especially after the feverish way they'd come to-gether earlier, like they were in the grip of something bigger than both of them.

"We could share our resources in that regard," she offered, taking a sip from her water glass while, just outside the windows beside them, the moon made an appearance above the trees. "The man I hired to find the author behind the pseudonym might have informa-tion that would help your investigator's efforts."

"I'm meeting her tomorrow. Should I ask her to con-tact you?" He hesitated. "For that matter, would you consider sharing your identity with her, if you trust her discretion?"

He could hardly renege on the agreement he'd just made, but no doubt Regina could help with April Ste-phens's efforts to follow the money trail from the book's profits.

She stared down at their joined hands for a moment before meeting his gaze. "As long as I can speak to her directly. Yes, that's fine."

He heard what she didn't say—that trust was going to come in degrees for both of them. It was the best he could expect, considering their tenuous relationship. He'd have to hope she didn't reveal his father as the au-thor of the book—at least not in the weeks leading up to his mother's wedding. And she would have to trust him to keep her secrets and maintain her privacy under the new identity she'd worked hard to build.

"Of course." He let go of her hand and slid his arm around her shoulders, feeling the silky warmth of her hair as it brushed his sleeve. "I'll let you make the call on how much you feel comfortable sharing with her. Just know that whatever you can tell her will probably help speed things along."

"Believe me, no one wants answers as much as I do." The fierceness of the words matched the spark in her eyes. Perhaps she heard it, too, because she smiled belatedly, as if to soften the tone. "And now, as much as I hate to end our date, I really should get back to the bunkhouse for the night."

"You're more than welcome to stay here, if you prefer." He stroked her hair behind her ear so he could see her face better. "For that matter, there's a spare bedroom if you'd rather have your privacy."

There was a pale red mark on her neck, an abrasion from his cheek, he guessed. He smoothed a finger over it, regretting that he'd marred her skin while he'd been kissing her.

"Thank you, but my gear is at the bunkhouse. And it's surprisingly fun rooming with a bunch of women. Sort of like the summer camp I never had." She shrugged, a small grin playing at the corners of her mouth. "Besides, I've got an ear to the ground on what's happening around the ranch that way. And from what you said about your father's relationship with the owners of Mesa Falls, it sounds like there might be more to learn about him right here in Montana."

Devon stilled, realizing that he'd allowed sex to scramble his thoughts. He mentally rewound to their conversation on their horseback ride the day before when he'd told her as much. What else had he revealed about his dad before he discovered her true identity? Of course, he'd known to be cautious around her, so he hadn't said anything sensitive. Still, it caught him off guard how quick she was to zero in on a detail like that.

He kissed her cheek to try to hide his momentary surprise, still struggling to negotiate the balance between wanting her and maintaining his focus.

"Good thinking." He felt the small shiver go through her and wanted to explore it. To undress her all over again. But he would wait until they had more time. "The sleigh driver has returned to the ranch for the night, but I can bring you back in the all-terrain vehicle."

All of the cabins on the property came with the added convenience. But Devon's thoughts were far from the corporate retreat's luxuries as he retrieved Regina's coat and hat, and they dressed to back out into the cold.

He couldn't help remembering her last observation of the night—that she planned to key in on his father's relationships with the ranch owners. There was no doubt that Regina was sharp and quick-witted. And very committed to unearthing the truth behind his father's book.

As was he.

Selfishly, he hoped that whatever they found wouldn't destroy the tentative truce they'd made tonight. But more important, he needed to make sure the truth didn't implode on him before his mother's Christmas wedding.

Seven

Seated in a private meeting room at the Mesa Falls Ranch guest lodge, April Stephens reviewed her notes as Devon Salazar continued talking.

She'd purposely taken a high-back leather chair facing away from the spectacular view of the Bitterroot Mountains. She might not have time to indulge in the outdoors again during this trip, and she didn't want to tempt herself with the sight of those peaks. Instead, she grounded herself in the space around her, the warmth of the crackling fire in the hearth and the calming decor. The meeting room was sleekly understated in pale grays and cream, the furnishings not detracting from the real visual interest of the snowcapped mountains outside the wall of windows.

Her client was paying her firm well, and she wouldn't disappoint him. She'd been fortunate to have this opportunity to work with a powerful and high-profile figure like Devon Salazar in the first place. Her agency's senior financial investigator had a death in the family and her boss hadn't wanted to turn down the business. He'd offered April a serious incentive on this case.

Crack the secrets of Alonzo Salazar and she'd get a promotion. That meant more money, more travel and more opportunities to escape the responsibilities of the smothering home life weighing her down more every day.

April would not fail. She'd maxed out her credit cards buying a few high-end outfits to get through this week, needing to look the part of a senior staffer.

Had that been pathetically self-indulgent? Or a wise act of self-care that would put her more at ease with the well-heeled crowd that could afford to stay in places like Mesa Falls Ranch? She didn't know. But the buttery soft wool of the jacket she was wearing made her feel like a million bucks. And it was a good thing, because she dreaded sharing some of her findings with Devon. What if he didn't like what he heard? Would he put a halt to the investigation?

Now, as he brought her up to date about "Regina Flores"—the woman April had warned him about—she took notes by hand on a legal pad. Apparently he'd uncovered the woman's real identity: she was none other than the elusive Georgiana Fuentes, living and working right here in Montana. Which was most certainly not a coincidence, given that Devon was researching his father's book.

The book that had ruined Georgiana's life.

April remembered the sudsy read well. *Hollywood Newlyweds* by A. J. Sorensen had been a huge bestseller at a time when April read anything and everything she could get her hands on. She'd gobbled that book up, and had followed the tabloid headlines afterward when the supposedly fictional story turned out to have a basis in real life.

But no one in the media had seen Georgiana in years. So for her to pop up here, using a fake identity and trying to get close to Devon, was about as ominous as April could imagine. Unfortunately, her client didn't seem to share her concern.

"Georgiana invited me to contact her directly?" April asked him now, glancing up at him from across the small conference table.

He was uncommonly handsome, tall and well built, with light brown hair and attractive green eyes. He had an easy manner that made him a natural leader—the kind of man people would want to follow. Not that she was in the market for romance—far from it. But if she had been?

Yum.

The fact that he'd taken a marketing start-up founded by two brothers and grown it to a globally recognized leader in the social media environment appealed to her on an intellectual level, as well. Studying business accounting and working in financial investigations had given her an appreciation for the savvy it took to do something like that.

"She prefers to be called 'Regina.' And, yes." He slid a paper across the table toward April, and she noticed how the sleeves of his black button-down were rolled up. "We would like to keep her real identity private. The longer Georgiana stays out of the spotlight, the more likely my father's connection to the book will, too."

The "we" was not lost on April. Something in his tone gave her the idea that he felt protective of the woman. Guilt, perhaps, since his father's book had sent

Georgiana's life into a tailspin? Or was there something else at work?

She planned to proceed carefully with the woman.

"Certainly." She tucked the contact information into a file folder. "I'll reach out to her as soon as we're done here."

"So my father was paying for a nominee service to collect his royalties on *Hollywood Newlyweds*?" Devon asked, returning to the information she'd given him earlier in the meeting. He flipped through web search results on a tablet before spinning his screen to show her a few prominent agencies.

"Yes." She'd invested far more hours than she would bill him to confirm it. "He set up his pen name like a corporation and gave it a director. The company collected monies from the publisher, and the nominee service oversaw the transactions and made sure taxes were paid."

A nominee service was extremely expensive, but it provided an unparalleled level of privacy.

"But the service must have expired with my father's death?" Frowning, Devon set the tablet on the sleek birchwood table. "There was nothing about that in the will."

"The service was paid for in advance. Given the precautions Alonzo took in order to keep his name away from the novel, I suspect he left explicit instructions for the royalty income after his death." April had chased the lead as far as she could for now, but she wouldn't give up. "Arrangements for future disbursements may already be in place and you weren't aware because you aren't a beneficiary. The other possibility is that the nominee hasn't learned of your father's death yet."

"Months after the fact?" Devon sounded skeptical. He glanced up from his tablet, one dark eyebrow raised.

"It's conceivable your dad only needed to touch base with the service once a year at tax time." She hesitated before sharing her biggest concern, not wanting to give him any reason to shut down this job. "And while I'm prepared to keep searching for information, you should know that in my experience, searches like this uncover illegal activity about fifty percent of the time."

Even though she hadn't taken the lead on an investigation before this one, she'd been in the weeds on similar cases at her firm for two years. And although there were highly reputable nominee services, the industry attracted its share of the criminal element.

"I appreciate the warning." Devon shut off his tablet and leaned back in the chair across from her, the afternoon sun gilding his features. He templed his fingers together, propping his chin on them. "My father obviously had a secret life we knew nothing about, but I still hold out hope that he had more altruistic reasons for hiding that income."

"So you're certain you want me to keep searching?" she clarified, needing his blessing before she unearthed news that could be upsetting on a personal level, or that had the potential to stir legal interest in the case.

"Absolutely. Whatever my father was up to, I need to know about it. And the sooner the better, April, so if you are in need of additional resources, don't hesitate to come to me."

She felt the thrill of victory at his words. She still had the job. The doorway for that promotion remained open.

"Understood." Hope filling her, she closed the leather cover over her legal pad and laid her pen on top of it. "I'll contact Regina Flores first, then begin contacting the owners of Mesa Falls Ranch to explore their connection to your father."

"And you'll continue looking into the nominee service?" he prompted, his words reminding her that she was getting into dicey terrain.

That information was well protected.

"I'll do everything in my power to find answers for you," she vowed, knowing she had to make it work.

"Very good." Standing, he ended the meeting with a handshake. "I look forward to hearing from you."

As he left the room, April's gut knotted tighter. How would she shake information out of a nominee service that sold complete anonymity to its clients? Her better hope was prying answers from Regina/Georgiana. Or the owners of Mesa Falls Ranch.

As she packed the file and her pen in her bag, April's gaze veered out the meeting room windows toward the mountains. One day, she'd have the kind of life that allowed her the freedom of wide open spaces and fewer responsibilities. A life where she didn't need to constantly walk the tightrope between taking care of her mom and hiding her mother's increasing trouble from the world.

Until then, she would just keep her focus on the task at hand. Starting with Regina Flores.

Three days after her night with Devon, Regina was keeping her eye out for him in the great room at the main lodge, knowing he'd arrive soon.

She'd just finished a snowshoe trek with a group of new ranch guests. Her duties as a trail guide had quickly expanded from leading horseback rides to hosting other winter activities on the trails. With the huge influx of guests arriving for the launch event this week, all of

the staff had been tapped to work extra hours. Now, as
she transitioned her group of guests from the snowshoe
activity to a whiskey tasting party in the great room,
she would finally have her first evening free since the
sleigh ride with Devon.

"The bourbons are on the bar and the scotches are on
the buffet," she explained to an older couple puzzling
over where to go next in the growing crowd.

Fires burned brightly in fireplaces at either end of
the post-and-beam-style room. A huge antler chandelier hung low over a game table already filling with
guests comparing tasting notes on preprinted cards.
A solo guitar player sat in a high-backed stool near a
stuffed grizzly bear. The scent of barbecue from the
hors d'oeuvres being offered by passing waiters mingled with fragrant woodsmoke.

Regina took a bottled water from a silver tub full of
ice near the whiskey display. Her cheeks were warm
from the change in temperature after being outdoors
for hours. She looked around the room, and somehow
felt Devon behind her even before she turned to see him
standing by the bar.

Her pulse quickened at the sight of him.

He wore dark jeans and leather loafers, but unlike
most of the other men wearing flannel shirts or sweaters, he'd paired his denim with a white button-down
and a gray tailored jacket. He didn't need a tie to appear like a man in charge.

Three days hadn't done anything to dampen Regina's hunger for him. But she'd spent every one of those
days reminding herself that she needed to be wary with
a Salazar. That she couldn't simply follow a compelling attraction to him; they had a far more complicated
relationship.

But right now, seeing him again, she could only think about what it had been like to be bracketed in his strong arms. To feel the intense passion. To melt under his kiss.

By the time he arrived at her side, her breathing was fast and shallow.

He leaned closer to speak words for her alone. "If I'd known it would be three days before I saw you again, I wouldn't have been so quick to let you leave my cabin."

A thrill shot through her—both at his nearness and at the idea that he'd missed her. Wanted her.

Her skin tingled with awareness and he hadn't even touched her.

"Buildup to your launch event is keeping all the staff busy." She opened her water and took a cooling sip. "I had no idea the ride two days ago would turn into an overnight event."

His gaze lingered on her lips. "I didn't know, either, or I would have signed up for it myself." The heat in his green eyes distracted her. It made her forget what they'd been discussing, even quieted her years-old need for revenge. The strong reaction he incited both tantalized and worried her. She couldn't afford to let her feelings distract her from her goal.

Around them, the strains of a cowboy folk melody, the clinking of glasses and rumbled laughter faded until she could only hear her own breath.

"Are you free now?" he asked, his hand landing lightly on the small of her back.

"I planned to meet with—" She lowered her voice. "That is, I have a call scheduled from our mutual contact twenty minutes from now."

She'd been trying to find a time to speak to the private investigator, eager to get back on track with what she'd come to Montana to accomplish.

"Of course." He nodded, his hand still on her back. "She told me she'd been trying to reach you. Until then, maybe we could step out into a quieter spot."

Capping her water, she let him guide her through the crowded room. A pair of younger women stopped her to thank her for helping them with the snowshoe trek—or possibly to ogle Devon—but eventually she and Devon emerged from the great room to head toward the saloon.

He bypassed the bar and continued down a hall that led to the bowling alley and screening room. The sound of an old Western film filled the corridor for a moment before he steered her into a den that functioned as a small library. The three natural log walls were covered with floor-to-ceiling bookshelves, while the fourth wall featured a stone fireplace flanked by tall, narrow windows. A painting of one of the original homes on the ranch dominated the space above the fireplace.

Regina set her water bottle on a side table and wandered toward the hearth, her eye grazing the collection of photographs on the mantel showcasing the development of the property from small working ranch to corporate guest facility. She noticed Devon had closed the door behind them. Not that it would necessarily deter guests who wanted to drop in, but most of the activity in the lodge was in the dining rooms and bars by this time of evening.

He joined her by the fireplace, his gaze following the direction of hers briefly before returning to her. The scent of old books and pine hung in the air, familiar and welcoming.

"Are you all right?" He tipped her chin up so she was looking into his concerned green eyes. "I didn't know how to read your retreat."

Her belly flipped at his careful scrutiny. At the feeling she thought she heard in his voice.

No doubt she was misreading him, seeing a level of emotion that wasn't there. She was only valuable to him because he wanted to keep his father's deeds on lockdown.

"I'm fine." Steeling herself, she ignored the fluttery sensations his touch inspired. "I told you, I got roped into leading a longer tour than I'd signed on for. I hadn't realized that accompanying the group to a local ski resort meant I'd be stuck there until the ranch bus picked everyone up the next day."

He regarded her thoughtfully.

"You're putting in a lot of hours," he said finally, his hand falling away. "Are you sure this pursuit of my father's motives is worth so much of your time?"

Even as she missed the feel of his fingers on her cheek, she felt indignation straighten her spine.

"I thought I made it clear to you the other night that finding out why Alonzo mined my family's secrets for his own gain is my number one priority?" The words came out with more bite than she'd intended, but it frustrated her to think Devon couldn't see how deeply the book had affected her.

How it had *hurt*.

"You have every right to know." His voice hummed along her nerve endings, seemingly calibrated to soothe her. "My point is that I can help you now. You don't need to do this alone anymore."

His calm, easy demeanor only reminded her that Devon had lived without any knowledge of his father's actions until recently, whereas she'd been keenly aware of them her whole life, even if she hadn't known whom to blame for them.

"Are you suggesting I give up my quest and go home?" With an effort, she held herself very still, ignoring the physical need to be close to him and restraining the impulse to run. "Trust that the son of someone who tore apart my family will turn out to be an ally?"

Frustration vibrated through her, making her limbs shaky while the sounds of the Western movie in the room next door briefly blared louder. A gunfight, maybe, with swelling, suspenseful music that hummed through the hardwood floor.

"Is that the real reason you've been avoiding me these last three days?" The muscle in Devon's jaw tensed. Flexed. "Because you're back to thinking of me as your enemy?"

"I never said that." Wrapping her arms around herself, she turned from the hearth to stare out the dark window at the stars dotting the horizon.

She recognized there could be a grain of truth in his accusation. She had gladly accepted the extra workload, telling herself she might have a chance to learn more about the elusive ranch owners who had a close relationship to Alonzo Salazar.

But was that the real reason she'd filled her calendar?

"You didn't need to." He remained by the crackling fire, his broad shoulders outlined by the orange glow. "And I understand if you want to pursue answers in your own way. But my offer still stands to share information and resources. April Stephens is going to get to the bottom of this faster than you or I could alone."

Regina bit her lip to keep herself from responding impulsively. Angrily. Yet the injustice of the situation wouldn't let her stay quiet.

"Her allegiance is to you, because you're paying her." She'd had a lot of time to think about it these past few days when she'd buried herself in the work of entertaining guests. "And you have to recognize the extreme financial disconnect between our stations in life right now. You're running a successful business, possibly funded by your father's ill-gotten gains. I'm seasonal ranch help after being disowned by my father thanks to your dad."

"That's not fair." Devon stalked closer, taking a breath as if he was about to expound on the point, but she held up a hand to forestall him.

"I realize that," she conceded, her pulse speeding up again when he closed the distance between them. "Your business has grown because of your talent and commitment. I've meandered around without a solid career direction. That's on me."

A log in the fire slipped, spewing embers and hissing softly.

"But you feel robbed of opportunities, while they've been handed to me?" He shook his head. "If my father had access to hidden wealth, he never spent it on his sons."

"Yet he was an investor in Salazar Media." She'd looked it up and the amount was staggering. "It's a matter of public record."

Devon's lips flattened into a line for a moment as he studied her. She wanted to reach out and touch his shadowed jaw, even when she felt an unreasonable resentment.

"True." He nodded in a distracted way, his gaze sliding from hers to peer into the distance. "Though the amount was funded from his retirement account. I worried about him giving us that money because it meant he'd have nothing to live on while waiting for the company to start turning a profit."

Turning on his heel, Devon paced away from her, clearly caught up in his own thoughts. It seemed that he was speaking to himself more than her.

"What is it? Did you remember something?"

She knew he didn't have to tell her. But maybe she'd catch him in an unguarded moment. Hadn't he just been asking her to trust him to share with her?

She followed him toward the sofa table that held a stone statue of a bucking bronc.

"Dad traveled a lot." Devon slid a sideways glance toward her. "Friends who knew about those trips used to joke that he must be a secret agent on the side."

"Trips where?" Anticipation curled through her that she might learn something.

And yet, would discovering the truth about the father alienate her from the son forever? It shouldn't matter to her. Except after what she'd shared with Devon at his cabin, she couldn't deny that it would.

"We didn't know." Devon faced her, the warmth of his body suddenly close to hers. "Since finding out about the novel, I thought maybe he was just seeking out quiet places to write."

"But now you're wondering if he was financing a more extravagant lifestyle you didn't know about?" A piece of her hoped that Devon truly wasn't aware of that hidden income.

"Not necessarily." He withdrew his phone from his jacket pocket and tapped in a note. "It's occurred to me that the investigator would surely be able to track some of those travel dates. Perhaps his destinations on those trips would provide more insights."

Regina chewed on that idea while he finished typing. No doubt he had a good point. She felt uneasy that she hadn't spoken to the investigator herself yet. What if she held the missing pieces of the Alonzo Salazar puzzle?

Nearby a wall clock chimed the hour.

"Speaking of which, I'm scheduled to talk to her now." She needed to get her own read on April Stephens and decide how much she could trust the investigator. "I don't want to miss her again."

Devon deposited his cell into his jacket pocket. "If you'd like this room, I can give you privacy. I need to go over some particulars on the launch event with the ranch manager."

"Thank you." She retrieved her water bottle from where she'd set it on a side table earlier. "That would work well. If anyone comes in, I can always take the call outside."

"Can I take you out tomorrow night?" he asked quietly, his green eyes darkening.

An answering shiver ran up her spine as her body reminded her how much she'd like that.

"Because you want to see me?" she asked, tempted, but needing to keep a level head around this man. "Or because you want to keep an eye on me?"

"I could ask you the same question about why you spend time with me," he reminded her, angling closer in a way that made her heart skip a beat.

Or two.

When his lips closed over hers, she didn't hesitate to kiss him back. The kiss was slow, thorough and sensual. A deliberate reminder of what it was like between them. Her arms wrapped around his waist, fingers curling into his shirt as hunger returned with an aching insistence.

As her breasts tightened, her nipples peaked against the fabric of her bra. She almost forgot everything else until he pulled away, his breathing ragged.

"You decide what you want next, Regina." His hands slid away from her, and it was all she could do to remain upright. "I want you, but only when you're sure about this. About me."

She blinked fast, trying to think of a response, but he was already walking away. He closed the door to the den behind him, leaving her beside the hearth while the fire blazed.

Regina bit her lip until it hurt and waited for her thoughts to reassemble themselves. For reason to return. She was turned on. Confused.

And very, very alone.

Eight

An hour later, Regina sat in a deep leather barrel chair kitty-corner to April Stephens in the Mesa Falls Ranch den.

The investigator had asked to meet in person once she'd discovered that Regina was at the main lodge, and within five minutes of the call, the two of them had taken seats next to one of the tall windows flanking the fireplace.

April defied every expectation Regina had of a female PI. The willowy blonde's long hair hung in full curls around the shoulders of a suit that looked right out of the pages of a fashion magazine. From her stilettos to her French manicure, April appeared more apt to step out of a limo on Park Avenue than sit in a stakeout. But maybe that was because her investigative specialty was financial forensics.

Now, taking notes in longhand on a legal pad, April paused to peer up at Regina.

"Did your mother ever speculate about who in her life might have betrayed her trust?" The woman had listened without interruption while Regina recounted growing up as Georgiana Cameron, daughter of the prominent film star, before getting iced out of her "father's" life once the scandal broke involving *Hollywood Newlyweds*. She should have been numbed to telling by now, but sharing about the betrayal still left her raw and vulnerable, perhaps because she was still unsettled by her last conversation with Devon.

A burst of applause erupted in a room nearby, then died down again. The entertainment areas of the lodge had remained busy throughout the evening, but no one else had entered the den except for a passing waiter who'd asked if they needed anything. Regina sipped her water and set it back on the small round table with a wagon wheel painted on it, which sat between their chairs. Her hand trembled enough to give away her fractured emotions, and she yanked it back fast.

"She said the only people who knew about her affair with my birth father were her two best friends and their yoga instructor." Regina hadn't thought back to that in a long time, and she appreciated April coming at the story with fresh eyes. But would it help Regina in the long run, or only serve Devon? "Eventually, Mom decided it must have been my father who'd let it slip to someone, because she trusted all of those women implicitly."

"Have your mom's friends ever been questioned?" April shifted in her chair, the red soles of her shoes flashing for a moment as she recrossed her slim legs. "By a professional investigator, that is?"

"No." Regina felt a surge of hope that maybe something could still be unearthed from one of them. "I'm the only member of my family who has ever paid anyone to look into the matter, and I didn't have the budget for it that Devon Salazar does."

"Will it create discomfort for your family if I question your mother's friends now?" April asked, pen hovering in midair over her paper while she waited for an answer.

"Not at all." She withdrew her phone and started typing in names. "I'll send you their contact information, but I should warn you that I've spoken to all of them before." Although, looking back on those conversations, she remembered how emotional she'd been at the time. It had been shortly after her high school graduation, when the realization had settled in that her life would never, ever, be the same again. "Come to think of it, they were probably all hesitant to share anything with me based on how personally involved I was. Am."

April remained quiet for a moment while Regina looked up phone numbers and emails, drawing comfort in the task, feeling proactive for once, rather than just reactive. Once Regina sent April the text with all the info, the investigator spoke again.

"I'm going to get to the bottom of it," she said, blue eyes unwavering, voice certain. "We'll have answers soon."

In that moment, Regina saw beyond the pretty, carefully cultivated exterior to the fierceness beneath.

And she believed her.

"I look forward to that."

They spoke for another quarter of an hour, going over details of Regina's past before wrapping up the interview. She assured April she'd never met Alonzo Salazar or even heard of him before her own PI finally turned up the name earlier in the year. When the woman seemed satisfied she had enough answers, the two of them parted ways. April strode out of the den on her elegant high heels while Regina stood on shaky legs to return to the bunkhouse for the night. She wanted to believe it was just weariness from snowshoeing, but it more likely had to do with dredging up the past. She didn't know if she could trust her feelings for Devon. Or his for her.

Strangely, April Stephens had seemed like an ally even though she worked for Devon. That was only an illusion, though, and Regina would be foolish to think otherwise. The investigator would have allegiance to the man who'd hired her—end of story. Which meant Regina needed to stay close to that man if she wanted to know what April turned up.

That had been her plan all along and, pride be damned, she was going to stick to it because she was finally getting close to having answers about Alonzo Salazar and his book.

Regina told herself that was why she was seeing Devon again tomorrow night. It didn't have anything to do with being wildly attracted to him.

If Devon had been an oddsmaker, he would have put the likelihood of seeing Regina tonight at 50 percent.

After the way she'd avoided him for days, then danced around the idea of meeting, he feared her conflicted feelings about their relationship had overshadowed the attraction.

Then, in the middle of a meeting with his planning committee for the Mesa Falls launch event, he'd spotted her text asking if they could get together.

"This was a fun surprise." Regina's face glowed in the firelight as she passed him an old-fashioned tin star for the top of the Christmas tree in his cabin. "I never guessed you would choose tree-decorating for a date night. Where did you get the ornaments?"

They were seated on the couch in the living area. Instrumental Christmas tunes played over the room's built-in speaker system, and the white tree lights glowed on the fresh balsam, which was tucked in the corner between the bookshelves and a wingback.

Regina's red sweater had a V-neck that framed a necklace of tiny silver jingle bells, and a slim black skirt hugged her curves in a way that drew his eye every time she moved. Her dark hair was pinned back in a green-and-red plaid bow. She seemed more relaxed tonight than when they'd spoken in the lodge the night before. The jasmine scent of her fragrance wafted under the stronger smell of pine in the room.

"I ordered the box last week from a charity I work with in New York. They provide everything you need for themed trees, and half the cost goes to holiday gifts for people in need." He set aside the star to save for the end. "To be honest, I was going to have my staff decorate for a photo op to post on social media. But when you messaged me, I thought it might be fun for us to tackle."

She grinned as she pulled a straw cowboy hat ornament from the box. "You must have chosen the Western theme."

"The official name is 'Cowboy Christmas.'" He peered into the box on the coffee table, full of rodeo-themed decorations along with a garland made of twine and tiny reproduction horseshoes. "I thought it would work well with the cabin's design."

"Are they a client of yours?" She sipped the champagne cocktail he'd made for her. Her silver bangle clinked against the base of the flute as she set it back on the table.

His gaze lingered on the long spill of her dark hair on her shoulder as she moved. He wanted to touch the strands, to breathe in the fragrance of the silky mass. To taste the delicate column of her neck.

But he was trying his damnedest to give her some space. To let her set the pace tonight after the way she'd seemed skittish about continuing their relationship.

"You could say that." He stood up to keep himself from following the impulse to touch her. Digging the garland out of the box, he started wrapping it around the tree limbs. "From the inception of the business, my brother and I wanted to allocate a percentage of company resources to community giving. The organization that sells the ornament boxes was just getting started in New York at the same time we were, so we approached them to see if they wanted some help."

The holiday music switched to a country tune, with steel guitars and more folksy vocals. Devon stood back to see how the garland looked while Regina joined him near the tree. Growing up, he had never decorated a tree with his family. In his grandfather's palatial mansion, trees simply appeared one day, professionally trimmed. Even as an adult, he'd found his decorating opportunities were limited to office parties, as a way to connect with his staff. But something had made him want to share this with Regina tonight. Maybe a sense that her family holidays had to have been painful after her parents' well-publicized split.

"That was good of you." There was a wistful note in her voice as she slid a velvety quarter horse decoration onto a branch. "You've accomplished so much between growing your business and giving back." She straightened the ornament, so the horse dangled the way she wanted it to. "And during that same amount of time, I feel like all I've accomplished is chasing my tail."

Regret for what she'd gone through rained over him. How could his father have published that damned book and destroyed her family?

"This week is going to mark a turning point for you, though." He couldn't help but touch her then, needing to reassure her. His hand went to the space between her narrow shoulder blades. "Once you have the answers you deserve, you'll be ready to move forward."

Her angora sweater was impossibly soft. Even so, he remembered that it didn't compare to the texture of the creamy skin beneath it. Thoughts of stripping her naked forced him to move his hand away again.

"I hope so." She found more ornaments to hang and they worked in tandem for a few minutes. "Have you heard from April?" Her gaze flicked over to his.

Wariness crept through him.

Was this why she'd wanted to see him tonight?

But then, he told himself it was only natural she'd want to know. He'd just told her she'd have answers soon, after all.

"She took a red-eye to the West Coast last night." He met Regina's surprised gaze. "To follow up on leads you gave her, apparently."

Devon hadn't asked the PI for details. His workdays had been crammed with the logistics of the ranch's launch event. He had a sizable staff on hand in Montana now, but the event included satellite parties taking place simultaneously on both coasts in real time. This would allow Mesa Falls Ranch to reach more potential clients, even if the expenses were high up front. Bottom line, he needed staffing in both cities, coordinating everything.

"Wow. That was fast." Regina held a pewter ornament shaped like a pair of cowboy boots in midair, as if she'd forgotten what she was doing. "I'm grateful for your support in helping her get to the bottom of this."

Something about the way she said it rankled. He took the boots from her and found a spot for them on the tree, then cupped her shoulders in his hands.

"I need answers as much as you do. It's not just kindness. It's good business to work together." He didn't want her gratitude. And damn it, he sure didn't want to think that she was only spending time with him for the sake of the investigation.

Her brows knitted together as she frowned. "In that case, thanks for doing business with me."

He shook his head, letting go of her. "Are you always so prickly, or is it just me who brings out the defensive side?"

Her sudden burst of laughter smoothed over his irritation, the sound far more melodious than anything playing on the Christmas music station.

"Maybe a little of both. I definitely have prickly down to an art." She bent closer to the coffee table and retrieved her champagne flute for another sip of her drink, the bubbles glowing golden in the firelight.

"And why is that?" he asked, genuinely curious about her.

"After the whole debacle of the book—and losing my old friends—it became a protective measure, maybe. It was just easier to keep people at arm's length rather than let anyone close enough to hurt me again." She set aside the flute and studied the tree. "And I've only started to recognize that tendency this week, as I grow closer to some of the women in my bunkhouse. It makes me realize I've gone a lot of years without friends."

The acknowledgement of her solitary existence saddened him as she took time rearranging a few of the tree lights so they illuminated some of the ornaments from behind.

"Will you go home for Christmas?" He hated to think about her remaining at the ranch during a time most people spent with their families.

She shrugged in a way that shifted the neckline of her sweater closer to the edge of one shoulder.

"It depends how much progress I make in finding answers about your dad and the book." Spinning to face him, she seemed to notice his careful regard, and her cheeks flushed a deeper pink. "If I think that staying here over the holidays will give me opportunities to speak to any of the owners privately, then I will stick around."

He wanted to reassure her. To give her some concrete findings from April's investigation that would ease Regina's fierce desire for the truth.

But what if giving her those answers meant she would turn on him? Would she sue his father's estate for defamation or drag the Salazar name through the tabloids?

When he didn't reply right away, she leaned past him to retrieve a package of ornament hooks. "What about you?" she asked. "What are you doing for the holidays?"

"My mother is getting married on Christmas Eve." Tension pulled his shoulders tight, the way it had all week when he thought about the wedding. Because his meeting with the PI—her warning that Alonzo hiding his money could indicate illegal activity—made Devon worry how soon something would leak about his father's hidden life. "I'm flying to Connecticut to be with her right after the launch party."

"That should be fun, right?" Regina's jingle bell necklace chimed softly as she moved to decorate the left side of the tree.

His gaze followed her movements as the tree's golden glow lit up her features. Thinking about the wedding forced him to consider what his life would be like once he left Mesa Falls and Regina behind. And the vision made him feel suddenly empty.

"It would be more fun with a date." He articulated the idea the moment it came into his head. Because why not? He'd started this relationship to keep an eye on her.

Just because it had grown into more than that didn't mean that the need to keep her closer had dissipated. Far from it. If she had any inclination to drag his father's book back into the public spotlight for some sort of payback scheme, he'd prefer to know about it sooner rather than later.

"Are you asking me to attend the wedding with you?" She frowned, clearly surprised.

Because she was ready for their time together to end? Or because she hadn't expected this relationship to continue after he left Montana?

"I am." He stepped closer, breathing her in. "I can already tell I'm not going to be able to walk away after the launch event."

She licked her lips. "Can I think it over?"

"Of course." He wasn't going to press her, especially since the wedding would mean spending Christmas together. "I need to fly out right after the launch party for some pre-wedding festivities. But my mother gets married on Christmas Eve, so you could wait and join me the next day."

She gave a thoughtful nod, lips pressed in a flat line. "Do you like the guy she's marrying?"

"I don't know him that well," he admitted. That was partly his fault for not making more of an effort, but also because his grandfather had claimed all the family's face time with the groom-to-be in order to strengthen Radcliffe ties with the international banker. "But I think having someone marry your mother is like someone marrying a daughter—no one will ever be good enough for her in my eyes."

Regina bent to decorate a lower branch. "That's a touching sentiment from a son." Her expression turned strained as she straightened. "Or a father, for that matter." She busied herself, adjusting things she'd already tidied. "Did you spend much time with your father as a kid?"

"No." His role model had been his cold and distant grandfather, who'd made sure Devon knew he would never be good enough because he wasn't a Radcliffe. "I visited the West Coast a couple times to see him, but mostly my mother insisted he come back East if he wanted a relationship with me."

As a teacher—even in an elite private boarding school—Alonzo had never had much money when Devon was younger. Later in life, when Devon was in his late teens, his father had had noticeably more disposable income. Now Devon knew that was thanks to *Hollywood Newlyweds*.

"What was he like?" She wandered over to the side table, where Devon had put out the offerings from the chef to accompany the champagne.

Plucking a dark salted caramel from a small silver tray, she nibbled on it as she watched him.

"An inspiring teacher." Devon had heard it over and over again throughout his life, and especially after the funeral, when former students began sending condolences. "He wasn't an involved father to my brother or me, and he didn't place any importance on marriage as an institution, which hurt more than one of the women he loved." He watched Regina's tongue sweep away a tiny spot of caramel on her upper lip, the movement igniting a fresh blaze of desire for her. "But he made a difference in the lives of his students and that meant something to him."

He forced himself to focus on decorating the tree to keep from touching her. Tasting her.

He'd been so damned determined to let this night move more slowly. To allow her to dictate how things went. But he'd forgotten the potent power of Regina's appeal.

"I read about that boarding school online." She retrieved a Santa dressed in chaps and spurs from the box and went back to the tree, her curves drawing Devon's eye as she moved past. "Dowdon isn't all that far from Hollywood in miles, but it might as well be on the other side of the globe for how much the community differs from the social scene portrayed in his book."

Devon had thought the same thing. "One of the school's biggest selling points is the remote location in a national forest, close to a protected wilderness area."

As a kid, he'd thought it sounded idyllic. His father lived on the campus, and was part of the horse program, which offered a mount to every student for the duration of their time at Dowdon. Learning to ride, caring for an animal and competing in horsemanship activities were all central to the experience.

"I wonder if he could have met my mother somehow." Regina's silver-gray gaze locked with Devon's. "He obviously knew a great deal about her private life."

Devon heard the resentment leak into her voice, and hoped to reroute the conversation before it turned more divisive.

"What's your mom like?" he asked to distract her. "I remember some of her films."

For a few years, Tabitha Barnes had been the queen of romantic comedies, but she'd stopped making movies after her affair began dominating headlines.

"Bubbly. Sweet." Regina seemed to take the question seriously, a slow smile spreading over her features. "Not all that different from the characters she played during her filmmaking heyday. Davis—the man I believed to be my dad for the first fifteen years—fell in love with her when he was making his directorial debut. He starred in the picture that was her breakout movie, and he directed it, too."

Devon thought he detected a begrudging pride in those words, and he recalled that talk about Davis Cameron hurt her most. No doubt because the man had cut ties so completely.

"It was unnecessarily cruel of him to push you out of his life." How could a grown man purposely distance himself from a daughter he'd raised as his own? From what Devon could gather, Regina had been close to Davis Cameron—perhaps even closer than she was to her mother. "In all the years since he ended things with your mom, has he ever contacted you?"

"Never." The answer sounded like it came from a ripped-raw place, but she cleared her throat and moved purposely back toward the box of ornaments. "At least he's been consistent about not talking to the media, either. There was a small amount of comfort in the fact that he never commented on the situation."

"I'm sorry I brought it up," Devon told her sincerely, intercepting her before she could pull more ornaments from the box. "I can't imagine how painful it was for you to have your world turned upside down by that damned book. But I'm confident we'll hear from April soon with some more definitive answers."

He took her hand in his, folding her fingers into his palm.

"The mystery behind *Hollywood Newlyweds* has dominated my life for years." She shook her head and huffed out a sigh, sounding upset. "And I'm not very good at putting the frustrations out of my mind once I start thinking about it. The resentment just festers."

He drew her closer, wishing he could absorb the hurt and take away that pain. His father had no business tearing apart her family or making them the center of public speculation for years. Devon wanted to make amends.

And right now, he had an idea how he could help, at least temporarily.

"Maybe you should let me distract you." He lowered his lips to her ear to speak softly against her skin. "Give you something else to think about."

Already, his heart hammered with wanting her. When she sucked in a sharp breath, the need for her multiplied exponentially.

"I thought you said I was too prickly and defensive," she reminded him, arching a dark eyebrow as she gazed up at him. "Are you sure you want to tangle with me?"

There was a light, teasing note in her voice, but Devon suspected she'd put it there to mask a moment of insecurity and doubt. Not that he'd let her see he recognized it for what it was.

A vulnerability.

So he skimmed his hands around her shoulders and sifted through the silky dark hair.

"It would be the greatest pleasure I can imagine."

Nine

Every day that Regina had been without Devon felt like years, making her question how she'd stayed away from him for this long.

Winding her arms around his neck, she sighed into him, letting go of all the excellent reasons she had for not trusting him. Tonight, he'd showed her a new level of caring, a kindness even more compelling than the red-hot attraction between them.

She lost herself in his kiss, his tongue sweeping over hers in a way that made her forget everything but him. How was that even possible?

But she didn't want to ruminate or overanalyze. Right now, when she had the chance to forget all the old wounds, to shut out everything else but this moment with Devon Salazar, she would embrace it.

His hands skimmed her curves, stirring pleasure. She arched closer, remembering how he could make her feel. How good they were together.

She broke the kiss, determined to make her desires clear. Breathing hard, she stared up into his green eyes that were so intent. So hungry.

"I'll take all the distraction you can give," she whispered, her voice a husky rasp of sound, before she turned and led him toward the bedroom she remembered well.

He caught up to her in a half step, plucking her off her feet and lifting her in his arms like a groom carrying a new bride over the threshold. Squealing in surprise, she shoved aside the romantic thought. His hold on her gave her the chance to appreciate his broad chest, though. She ran her hand over one muscular shoulder.

He entered the master suite, kicking the door shut with his foot, his focus on the bed in the center of the room. Her focus was all for him as she trailed kisses along the underside of his neck. She traced with her tongue, for only a moment, the place where his pulse leaped, before he set her on the bed with a bounce.

She toed off her shoes while he raked his shirt up and off, his movements visible in the light from sconces on either side of the mantel. He was built like a swimmer, tall with wide shoulders and a body that tapered to lean hips. Her gaze dipped lower as he flicked open the fastening on his jeans. She couldn't concentrate on her own undressing in her desire to watch him. The narrow line of dark hair disappearing under the cotton of his boxers tempted her to touch him there. But when she reached for him, he caught her wrist in a surprisingly strong hold.

"I really like what you're thinking." He loosened his grip as he pushed her back on the mattress, her head sinking into a down pillow. The jingle bells on her necklace slid along her neck to fall onto the bed behind her.

"But it's supposed to be me who distracts you. Not the other way around."

"How do you know what I was thinking?" She tugged the bow from her hair, then smoothed her hands over his chest, savoring the warmth of his skin.

"I didn't. I only knew I liked it." He lowered himself enough to kiss the patch of flesh bared by her sweater, taking his time to taste the lowest point of the V-neck. "There was something a little bit wicked in the way you were looking at me."

He nuzzled her sweater off one shoulder, then clamped his teeth on one black silk bra strap, dragging it down. An ache started between her thighs as he let go of the silk and reared back on his knees to look at her.

Their eyes met. Held.

Was there more between them than heat and hunger?

A moment later, he peeled off her sweater and bra, letting them fall to one side of the bed. He cupped her breasts, tasting each one in turn, teasing the taut peaks. When he drew one into his mouth, suckling, the hunger for him grew unbearably. She arched her hips into him, needing more. Now.

He slid her skirt over her curves, and the rush of lust made her dizzy. His hands skimmed her inner thighs before dragging her panties down and off. She twisted the fabric of the duvet between her fingers, muttering wordless pleas for more.

By the time his lips covered her sex, she was so close to release she had all she could do to hold on another moment, allowing the intense, heady pleasure to build more as his tongue traced her.

She let go of the duvet as his shoulder dipped beneath her thigh, positioning her where he wanted her. The stubble on his jaw rubbing lightly against her thigh proved the tipping point, the feeling so exquisitely sensual she went hurtling into a lush, endless orgasm.

Ripples of pleasure pulsed through her, over and over. She let the sensations have their way with her as her whole body seized with bliss. While she gathered her breath, Devon moved over her, standing to shed the rest of his clothes. She soaked in the sight of him, her heart pounding madly while he found a condom and rolled it into place.

He stretched out over her just long enough for her to feel the thrill of anticipation all over again. When he entered her, she wrapped her legs around his waist. Holding him there. Moving with him in a rhythm all their own.

She streaked her fingers through his hair, kissing everywhere she could reach. Nibbling. Biting gently. Then he took over the kiss, his hips and tongue moving in a tantalizing sync.

They rolled over once. Trading the top position, letting each other lead the way. It was all delicious. Exciting. So much more than she'd ever experienced before in a relationship.

Devon's breath went ragged and she closed her eyes, feeling how close he was in the tension along his shoulders. His hips rocked hard into her, the pressure stroking a place inside her that unleased a fresh wave of release. Pleasure uncoiled, and her body quivered from it. She knew the movement pushed him over the edge, too, his spine arching, his breathing turning harsh.

After long moments, they collapsed side by side, limbs tangled. She tipped her forehead into his chest, feeling the comforting thunder of his heartbeat before it slowed by degrees. Eventually, her skin cooled. Her inhalations slowed along with her pulse. But through it all, Devon's arms remained wrapped around her, holding her close.

A long, shuddering sigh left her, and she knew she could gladly remain tucked against him the whole night through.

As long as she didn't let herself think about what had brought them to this moment. His promise to distract her. Her willingness—gratitude, even—for his ability to give her that.

Devon stroked her hair from her face, his touch soothing her before her anxieties could ratchet up again. She told herself she could remain here another minute to soak up the sensation that felt close to... tenderness.

It was wholly unexpected.

And simultaneously undeniable.

She sat up, knowing she didn't dare indulge something that could come back to bite her in the long run. Devon straightened beside her, his expression puzzled. But before he could ask her anything, his cell phone vibrated on the nightstand table.

Once. Twice.

She felt relieved when he turned to glance at it. But some of the relief faded as he punched a button on the screen.

"It's April," he informed Regina a moment before speaking into the device. "Salazar here. April, I'm going to put you on speaker so Regina can hear whatever news you have to share."

Devon didn't normally make impulsive decisions. But he needed Regina to start trusting him if he wanted to get to the bottom of his father's secrets. Sharing the PI's findings with her seemed like a way to show her he was serious about uncovering the truth. And that he was as much in the dark about his dad's motives as she was.

The surprise in her silver-gray eyes as she sat up in bed told him that she hadn't expected this kind of primary access to the private investigator. He hoped it was a step in the right direction to winning Regina over. Because as his gaze fell to her bare shoulders visible above the duvet she held to her chest, he felt a surge of protectiveness toward her. A need to make sure nothing else hurt her.

Now April's voice sounded through the speaker on his cell phone as he held it between them.

"I'm still searching for answers about how Alonzo got access to Tabitha Barnes's story in the first place," April told them. "But I have one more interview with her yoga instructor tomorrow before I fly back to Montana."

Devon studied Regina's profile as she listened. Her shoulders were tense. She chewed her lip, still pink from his kiss.

"Maybe that will yield something," he remarked, if only to reassure Regina. "Any other news?"

"Yes, actually." April's cool, professional tone gave nothing away. "I discovered Alonzo's destination for many of his secret trips."

Regina's gaze flew to Devon's. She reached to grab his wrist. Was she hopeful? Nervous? Maybe a little of both.

"And?" he prodded, even as his stomach rebelled at the idea of his father being implicated in any wrongdoing. It was bad enough he'd written the book that hurt Regina in the first place.

"He frequently visited a cabin in Kalispell, Montana, that belonged to a woman I believe was a romantic interest." April paused, and in that moment of quiet, his phone chimed with a new notification. "I just sent you her contact information."

More women in his father's life. No real surprise there, since Alonzo had once told Devon's mother that he thought marriage "killed the creative spirit." Alonzo had long considered himself a lover and admirer of women in general, but never one in particular.

And damn, but Devon needed to keep Alonzo Salazar's name out of the public eye until after his mother's wedding. His mom didn't need any of the old frustrations resurfacing now. His father's choices might have soured Devon on relationships, but that didn't mean he couldn't applaud his mother's ability to find faith in love.

Beside him, Regina let go of his wrist, and the loss of her touch frustrated him. It reminded him she was going to slip away, too, if he couldn't figure out how and why his father had written the tell-all book about her family.

He glanced down at the incoming text on his cell.

"Fallon Reed." Devon read the name aloud where it flashed on his screen. "I don't remember him ever mentioning her."

He looked to Regina, but she shook her head.

"The email I sent to her came back with a notification that the account no longer exists, but I'll drive to Kalispell to speak to her if I have to." The investigator shuffled some papers on her end of the call. "But Ms. Reed is significant because she's related to one of the owners of Mesa Falls Ranch."

"Which one?" Regina asked before Devon could. Her fingers clenched the duvet cover again, dragging it higher against her bare body.

Devon could feel her anxiety in the way her muscles coiled as she went still.

"My mistake. Make that a relation to *two* of the owners," April corrected herself. "Fallon Reed is an aunt to Weston and Miles Rivera."

"Is there any reason to think this woman profited from Alonzo's novel?" Regina asked, her voice tinged with worry.

Or was it defensiveness? Restrained anger?

Whatever the emotion behind the question was, Devon could tell it was intense. She bit her lip, breathing hard.

"Not as of yet." April's tone was cautious, as if she didn't completely rule the idea out. "Tracing the payments from the book is proving difficult, as I explained to Devon."

He felt Regina's gaze land on him. Was the look in her eyes accusatory?

Something about her expression struck him as frustrated, almost as if he'd betrayed her.

April went on to outline her next steps—interview the yoga instructor, return to Montana, then speak to Weston Rivera and possibly visit Fallon Reed. Devon only half listened as she bade them good-night, however. He was more concerned with Regina's reaction that he couldn't quite read.

By the time he disconnected the call, Regina was sliding out of bed, wrapping a chenille throw around her shoulders.

"Where are you going?" He grabbed his pants and stepped into them, wondering what he'd missed.

"I thought you were sharing the information from this investigation?" She lost no time retrieving her skirt and sweater.

"I am." He followed her until she disappeared into the en suite bath, where he stopped outside the partially closed door. "That's why I took the call with you, so you could hear what's going on."

What was she upset about? He could hear her rustling around in there while he searched for his shirt.

"Yet you never mentioned one word to me about tracing payments from the book, let alone why it was proving difficult." She flung the investigator's words back at him before she emerged from the bathroom with her clothes back in place.

Her hair fell loose around her shoulders now. He also thought her sweater might be inside out, but he said nothing about that, seeing the emotions blaze in her eyes.

She really thought he was hiding things from her.

"There was nothing to tell," he reminded her, trying to put himself in her position. Trying to understand how she could be so defensive so fast. "You heard that for yourself from April."

"I disagree." Pivoting on her heel, she stalked out of the bedroom and back into the cabin's living area. "You could have explained to me why there is a holdup," she said even as she barreled around the room, finding her bag to toss her hair bow into it. "We could have had a conversation about why it's difficult, or you could have shared the obstacles with me. But I am in the dark, Devon. As I always have been where your father's motives are concerned."

"Whoa." He saw her silhouetted in front of the Christmas tree where they'd been having fun decorating just an hour ago. "Let me tell you now—I understand how important it is to you."

It hadn't been his intention to hide significant parts

of the investigation. And it saddened him to see how carefully she needed to weigh his words. To test them for truth.

No question about it, Regina had been hurt before.

He reached out to brush a touch along her shoulder. Gently. Carefully.

"Give me a chance," he said, not sure when it had become so important that she let him in. But somehow, it had. "If you don't like what I have to say, I'll make sure you get back to the bunkhouse safely. Okay?"

Another interminable moment passed. In the end, she nodded.

He reached for the remote on the side table to shut off the holiday tunes. With the room quiet and Regina listening, he shared what April had told him about his father hiring a nominee service to collect the payments from the publisher to A. J. Sorensen. Briefly, he explained how they worked, based on the research he'd done since then.

"Apparently, Dad contracted a nominee through a lawyer, which gave him attorney-client privilege, as well." He'd read over April's notes more carefully after their meeting to discover that, learning how it gave his father's pseudonym an added level of privacy.

Regina folded her arms around herself, her brows knitting in thought. She paced past him, setting her purse back on the couch now that she wasn't heading out the door.

He was relieved about that. Grateful to have her stay. And damn it, he wanted to get to the bottom of what his father had been doing—for her sake and, yes, for his own, as well. He just wished the timing had been better since he couldn't afford for the truth to come out now.

"So the nominee service is still active," she mused.

"And still covered by the attorney-client privilege." Pausing by a painting of one of the ranch's studs, she met Devon's gaze. "Which makes you wonder how she learned about it in the first place."

"I didn't question her methods." He scrubbed a hand through his hair, frustrated. "With everything it's taking to get the launch event off the ground, I really need April to do her job so I can take care of mine."

Moreover, as much as he wanted answers for Regina's sake, he wasn't in that much of a hurry for the truth to come tumbling out before his mother's wedding.

Not that Regina would necessarily run to the tabloids to share the news. But what if she decided to do just that?

"Maybe it's time we give April some backup." She picked up her purse again, a new spark of determination in her eyes as she hooked the strap over her shoulder. She looked like a woman ready to head out the door again.

"What do you mean?" Wariness crept through him even as he grabbed his keys from a hook near the kitchen counter.

"April Stephens has the best lead yet on your father's secrets." Regina was already moving toward the coat rack to retrieve her parka and gloves. "And while *her* hands might be tied with how hard she can push her sources as a professional investigator, mine are not."

"Just because you ask her to reveal her sources doesn't mean she will." He took the coat from her to help her into it, tugging her hair from the collar. "That could be proprietary information."

He didn't want their evening together to end, but he didn't plan on standing in her way when she was on fire to get answers to her questions. Even if that meant he had to face more hard truths about his father, the man he'd never known as well as he'd thought. The facts needed to come out before either of them could find peace. He'd bring her back to the bunkhouse and then figure out his next move.

As much as he didn't want to call his brother in Paris let alone admit Alonzo's murky past was proving tough to investigate, Devon wondered if he should give Marcus a heads-up about what April had discovered so far. Devon's longtime rivalry with his half brother needed to end if they were going to present a united front when the truth about Alonzo was revealed.

He hadn't wanted to believe his father was involved in anything illegal, but considering the lengths Alonzo had gone to in order to keep his secrets, it sure made Devon wonder.

"If April has run out of options for shaking more information free from her source, she might be glad for a new approach." Regina tugged on her gloves and studied him with a level gaze. "I got the impression that April has a lot riding on this case, too."

Devon thought back to his meeting with April Stephens. She'd been professional. Thorough. Committed. But he hardly got the impression she had anything personal at stake.

Not like they did.

Regina reached for the door, but he put his hand over hers, needing to slow things down. The feel of her sent a bolt of desire through him, but he restrained himself for now.

"I'm not so sure about that," he told her. "But I can promise you we're going to have answers sooner or later."

He didn't miss the shadows that passed through Regina's eyes as she stared back at him.

"It has to be sooner." She threaded her fingers through his, her touch as urgent as her tone. "I've been waiting far too long for answers already."

Worry gnawed at him as he opened the door and escorted her out into the snow. Regina was desperate for her quest to yield information. Now.

And more than anything, Devon needed time. To get past his mother's wedding, for damn sure. But maybe more important, he needed time to figure out why Regina had so thoroughly rocked his world and what the hell he was going to do about it.

Ten

Regina retreated to her trusty laptop, the same way she had for years every time she heard about a new piece of information that might finally solve the puzzle of why someone would write a book that ruined her life.

After she'd said good-night to Devon, she slipped into the bunkhouse bathroom and changed into flannel pajama pants and a long-sleeved thermal T-shirt. Combing through her hair—tangled from lovemaking—she couldn't help but feel a twinge of regret that the need to research the clues had sent her fleeing Devon's arms for the night.

She'd had a good evening with him. No, that didn't do their date justice. She'd had a special, amazing time decorating the tree with him and then retreating to his bed, where their sensual connection had blazed into a bond she would have never expected to feel for her enemy's son.

And that left her feeling more than a little unsettled. Confused. Full of what-ifs… Most of all, what if they'd met on even, uncomplicated ground.

Turning from the mirror, she emerged from the bathroom to retrieve her laptop, telling herself not to dwell on a relationship that could never go farther than this time together in Montana. Devon's launch event and his mother's wedding were both less than a week away, and as soon as everything was over, he'd be on a flight back East.

Without her.

She tucked her brush into her toiletries bag and hung her wrinkled clothes in the nook near her bed, trying not to think about how much that might hurt. They hadn't known each other long, after all. And yet he'd become more important to her faster than anyone she'd ever known. Who else had taken up her cause for answers the way Devon had this week? He hadn't protested when she'd left his cabin tonight. He'd understood her need to dig deeper for answers about his father.

Her gaze went to her laptop in its neoprene case at the bottom of her drawer, and she withdrew it slowly, thinking about all the times *Hollywood Newlyweds* had robbed her of real-life experiences. She still ached over how the book had fractured her family life, robbed her of friendships and nearly cost her her life in the car wreck. Therapy had helped, but she still hadn't found the peace she so desperately needed. And now she was spending her time picking apart the mystery of the author and his motives when she could be lounging in bed with a gorgeous, successful businessman who genuinely seemed to care about her.

How much more would she let the book steal from her?

Behind her, she heard the floorboards creak and

turned to see Millie wander in with a steaming mug in one hand and a paperback novel in the other.

"Hey, hon," the older woman greeted her, laying the book on an unused bed. A kitschy reindeer cocktail ring clanked against her stoneware mug as she wrapped both hands around the cup as if to keep her fingers warm. "How was your date?"

Regina smiled over how Millie had remembered she was seeing Devon tonight and cared enough to ask how it went. Touched, she set down the laptop and leaned her hip into the ladder on the sturdy built-in bunks.

"It's hard to say." She breathed in the scent of hot cocoa, soaking in the joy of a friendship from an unexpected source. "We had a great time decorating a tree and…" Her cheeks warmed. "Um. Getting close."

A wicked twinkle glowed in Millie's eyes. "Sounds fun. Which begs the question, what are you doing back home already?"

Was it a burning need to do April Stephens's investigative work for her? Or was there more to it than that?

"I thought I had a good reason." She'd attended enough counseling sessions to identify an attempt to rationalize her choices. "But I'm wondering now if it was old trust issues that sent me running."

Frowning, Millie took a sip of her cocoa before responding. "It's always a risk trusting people—friends, parents, coworkers…romantic interests."

"There's a high potential for hurt in those relationships." Regina should know. She'd been kicked in the teeth by life enough times to have all the survival badges. "Is it so wrong to want to spare myself that pain? To just have fun?"

Mille tilted her head to one side, her steel-gray ponytail swinging down. "But are you having fun?"

No.

She was mostly having stress.

"Sort of," she said finally, smoothing her hand over the peacock blue quilt on her bed. Her maternal grandmother had given it to her long ago, and the pattern was "double wedding ring." A romantic name for a pretty design. A dream that seemed far out of reach for her, considering her parents' spectacular failure and her experience with rejection. "I mean, I had fun tonight."

"And maybe that will be enough." Millie patted her shoulder, a brief, comforting touch. But as the silence between them stretched, she added, "Just keep in mind that if you always play it safe with people, you might miss out on the chance for deeper connections that can lead to something really wonderful."

Regina knew she could never put herself on the line that way with Devon. There was zero chance that their out-of-control attraction would lead to something "deeper." It was amazing they'd already found as much common ground as they had. Because even if she ignored the way the book put them at odds, they were still very different people. Devon was an entrepreneur with a company on the verge of international expansion and she was drifting through different jobs while she chased her dream of payback.

Regina hadn't even really figured out what to do with her life once she put the ghosts of the past to rest. Devon had a family to go home to back East. She was untethered, isolated from the only family she had left. Her real father didn't have room for her in his life, while she and her mother had never really put their relationship back together again.

"Perhaps you're right." Regina wondered how she

could move forward with her mom. Put the past behind them for good.

"Just remember to take some risks now and then," Millie encouraged her, warming to her topic and gesturing as she spoke, the crystals on her reindeer ring flashing in the glow from a pendant light. "None of us goes through life unscathed. We're all going to get banged up and bruised now and then, but that's part of the ride, honey. You take the risks to reap the sweet rewards."

They talked a little longer before Millie went back to the front room with her book. But the idea of taking chances stayed with Regina.

Once she was alone in the bunkhouse, she retrieved her phone and stuffed her arms into the sleeves of her parka before stepping out of the building into the starry night.

A light snow was falling as she dialed a number she hadn't used in a long time. She began to wonder if she'd get an answer when she heard a recorded voice and a beep.

Regina took a deep breath.

"Hello, Mom. It's me." She closed her eyes, wishing things were easier between them. "Call me back when you get a minute."

She didn't know if Tabitha would return the message, but Regina hoped so. She might not be able to smooth over things with Devon the way Millie suggested, but at least she could start rebuilding her relationship with her mother.

For now, it would have to be enough.

April Stephens had stalked men in her line of work before. A couple of cheating husbands in the early days before she'd specialized in financial forensics. Later,

she'd tailed some business types suspected of embez-
zlement. Sometimes she followed potential leads who
simply didn't want to talk to her.

None of those men had ever looked like Weston Rivera.

For that, she was grateful on her first full day back
in Montana after her trip to Hollywood. The Mesa Falls
Ranch owner was so absurdly good-looking, she was
distracted enough that she almost forgot why she was
following him. She'd been trying to find the right opportunity to approach him as he finished up his work
outside the stables, and somehow got caught up in
watching him. Her gaze drank in the ruggedly handsome profile, the hazel eyes and longish dark blond
hair, the powerful build and easy demeanor that let him
handle the agitated mount he was leading around the
snowy arena with a halter.

In the time he'd been working with the animal,
the huge black draft horse had gone from pawing the
ground and tossing its head to resting that same big
muzzle on Weston's shoulder. She didn't know how
he'd done it, but she felt as mesmerized by the man as
the gelding clearly did.

When Weston broke the spell with a soft whistle,
leading the equine into the state-of-the-art stables, April
forced her brain back into gear. She wasn't here to ogle
the man. Or to drink in the calming effect he had on her
nerves as he moved around the arena. She needed to
question him, since he'd refused to speak to her over the
phone. And her professional pride demanded she have
more information the next time she spoke to Devon.
Although she'd uncovered something significant in her
final interview on the West Coast, she knew it wasn't

enough. Her client wanted the full story, and to nab that promotion she needed, she would have to provide it.

Now she waited a few moments before following him inside the building that housed the ranch's business office. There were stables on the main floor, with cobblestone floors and polished wooden stall doors. The place looked more suited to hold champion Thoroughbreds than working animals like the draft horse.

Brass lanterns hung at regular intervals on the heavy beams that lined a walkway leading from the foyer. April waited until Weston climbed the steps to the second floor, where double steel doors bearing the ranch name stood half ajar. Once he disappeared through that entrance, she trailed him, peering inside to where a reception area appeared empty. The scent of coffee hung in the air even though it was late afternoon, and she saw a pot percolating in the corner on a gray granite wet bar.

Beyond the vacant reception desk and a wall emblazoned with another ranch logo, a second door remained partially open. Weston must be in there. She could only see a glimpse of a conference table with gray leather swivel chairs.

She was sure she had him cornered now. He couldn't make excuses about his horse needing attention, or edge past her into the barn where guests weren't supposed to follow.

Striding into the reception area, she stuffed her gloves into the pockets of her long down jacket as she closed the office doors behind her. She was unwinding her scarf from her neck when Weston emerged from the inner office, his focus on a sheaf of papers in his hand.

"Hello, Mr. Rivera." She left her scarf dangling free around her neck, her jacket open.

He stopped short when he spotted her, his hazel eyes

all the more compelling when they were turned on her. He'd removed his shearling jacket and Stetson. His well-worn denim and pale blue flannel didn't begin to hint at his wealth. With his dark blond hair brushing his shoulders, he looked like a misplaced surfer, right down to the bristle of a jaw he hadn't shaved for days.

"Can I help you?" His voice was deeper than she'd imagined. Low and melodic.

The timbre of it reverberated through her, resonating on a pleasing frequency.

"Yes." She wished they'd met under different circumstances, and she could have enjoyed the warm thrum of awareness. But since this job was far more important than the fleeting pleasure of a handsome man's voice, she came to the point. "I have a few questions to ask you about your aunt, Fallon Reed."

The look in his eyes went from warm and inviting to glacial in an instant. She could practically feel the chill of it.

"You're the PI who keeps calling me." He said "PI" like it left a bad taste in his mouth.

His tone was dismissive, as if he'd just seen her childhood home and the disaster area it had turned into these last few years.

She swallowed hard before she started again.

"It will only take a minute—"

"I have no legal obligation to speak to you." He brushed past her and approached the coffee maker. Turning his back on her.

She watched him take a cup from an overhead cupboard and fill it from the stainless steel carafe of the high-tech machine. When the ceramic mug was full, he sipped it before striding back toward the inner sanctum like she wasn't even in the room.

Aggravated, she hurried to step between him and his office door.

"Is that really how you want to address this?" She suddenly stood too close to him, but she didn't think backing up a step would be a good move when she was trying to press him for answers. "Because if you're trying to protect someone you care about, don't you think a PI has more leeway keeping an investigation quiet than a police department?"

She was taking shots in the dark since she had no evidence that Fallon Reed had taken part in any remotely shady activity. But Weston's scowl at least indicated she had his attention.

Better she ticked him off than he ignored her.

"You have no idea what you're doing, do you?" He glowered down at her while tapping into her every last insecurity about her ability to do this job. "Or what's at stake."

Unease curled in her belly. Given his harsh tone, she wouldn't have believed he was the kind of man who could soothe a thirteen-hundred-pound beast if she hadn't witnessed it with her own eyes.

"I know enough to recognize that you won't want your ranch associated with a man like Alonzo Salazar once his past comes to light." She hadn't learned everything about her client's father, but what she'd discovered so far didn't paint such a pretty picture.

No one kept that many secrets without very good reason.

"He has a lot of friends who think otherwise," Weston assured her as he straightened. "And now, if you'll excuse me, I have work to do."

"You consider yourself a friend?" She stepped sideways to remain between him and his office. "Then why not set the record straight to maintain his reputation?"

Weston Rivera's eyes narrowed.

Later, she realized that should have been a warning. But for now, she watched him set down his coffee mug and his papers on the empty reception desk.

"I'm calling security to see you out," he informed her as he picked up the handset on a desk phone. Then he slanted her a sideways glance. "Unless you care to leave under your own steam?"

His gaze lingered on her a long moment. Long enough to make her feel a surge of awareness for him despite her frustration. Huffing out a sigh to hide that unwelcome feeling, she realized she wasn't going to learn anything from Weston Rivera today.

"I'm going to find out what Alonzo Salazar was up to one way or another," she informed him, wrapping her scarf around her neck again, if only to hide the rush of heated color she feared was climbing up her skin.

If he said any more, she missed it in her rush to leave the office. She retreated down the stairs and out into the chilly wind blowing off the mountains.

Where she could breathe again.

Drawing in shallow breaths of crisp air, she tried to slow her racing heart. She feared she wasn't cut out for this kind of work. It was one thing to trace a paper trail from the safety of her Denver office. Being on the ground and mired in real detective work was far messier. Upsetting.

She'd had Regina Flores calling her repeatedly for the last twenty-four hours, wanting to quiz her about the investigation. And she'd fielded a half dozen messages from her mother's neighbors back home, threatening to take legal action if she didn't get her place cleaned up. April could manage it. She absolutely would get on top of it all.

Starting today, with a drive to Kalispell to confront Fallon Reed in person. She needed to make some headway on this case, not just because the job and the promotion were mission-critical to keeping her mother under her own roof. She also needed to see progress in order to experience the therapeutic effects of peeling away someone else's secrets.

That aspect of the job kept her working even on the days she didn't like it one bit. And if that put her at odds with the mesmerizing ranch owner?

She just needed to remember that she couldn't afford to get close to anyone anyhow. Her own secrets ensured that. No matter how much she might wish otherwise.

Heading for her car, she dialed Regina Flores to start ticking items off her to-do list. She would take back control of this case. April had already sent the information she had to Devon, but she understood why Regina wanted to hear all the nuances.

The woman answered even before April heard the phone ring.

"Hello?" Regina sounded as desperate as April felt.

Maybe that was why she found it difficult to talk to the woman sometimes. She empathized a little too well with Regina's difficult journey. April remembered what it was like to have control of her life wrenched out of her hands.

"Hi, Regina." She hit the fob on the keys to her rental car as she approached the parking area outside the main lodge. "I have an update for you."

Regina had thought Devon's PI was trying to dodge her. But after a thorough phone briefing with April Ste-

phens while the woman drove to Kalispell to interview
Fallon Reed, Regina recognized that April had simply
been too busy following leads to give updates.

Tucking her phone in her pocket, Regina went back
to prepping for a bonfire happy hour down by the skating pond. She owed a giant thank-you to Millie and a
few of her other bunkmates for pulling her share of the
work during her phone call, but she was learning that
was part of the employee code here. She'd covered for
one of the ski concierges the week before when she'd
ended up stuck overnight with a ski excursion. And in
return, her coworkers had finished Regina's chore of
lighting the antler Christmas tree they'd built out on
the skating pond.

Setup appeared complete now, and the bonfire was
lit even though the sun hadn't fully set. Regina could
see activity in one of the dining rooms overlooking
the skating pond. The waitstaff was preparing to bring
cold and hot carts down to the ice so skaters could help
themselves to cocoa, cocktails and appetizers. And, actually, as she peered up the hill toward the lodge lit from
within, she spotted a conference suite where Devon was
holding a meeting with the ranch higher-ups to finalize
plans for the launch event.

Even at this distance, Devon was easy to recognize,
from his broad shoulders encased in a custom-fitted suit
jacket, to the way he leaned back in the leather swivel
chair at the head of the table. His body was familiar to
her. The way he moved. His gestures.

He would meet her at the bonfire afterward, and she
was anxious to talk to him about the PI's revelations—
that Alonzo had had an affair with her mother's yoga
instructor, and the *yogini* had told him Tabitha's secret,
effectively giving him all his story fodder. April hadn't

yet figured out why Alonzo decided to write the story anonymously, but she'd asked Regina to weigh the possibility that he'd never meant for the story to be connected to the people it was based on in real life .

In other words, to consider the small chance that Alonzo had meant no harm with the book.

Boots crunching through the snow, Regina skirted the ice pond, remembering the unusual request, and how she'd rejected it out of hand. Why all the secrecy if he'd never meant for the truth to emerge? But the idea gnawed at her just the same, making her wonder what it meant if it turned out she'd chased down answers for years only to discover her life had been destroyed as collateral damage when Alonzo was only trying to tell a story.

But he'd done a poor job of disguising his sources of inspiration, and that felt damning to her. They'd know more about his motives, perhaps, once they could figure out where the profits of the book had gone, but April refused to share her information about the nominee service. Still, Regina knew they were getting close as her phone rang again. This time, her mother's number flashed across the screen, reminding Regina she'd been trying to reach her.

A mix of feelings washed over her. Nervousness. The old resentments. A tiny hope that one day they could have a relationship that wouldn't be overshadowed by the past.

Pressing the Connect button, she walked in the moonlight to the far side of the ice pond, where a gazebo provided shelter from the falling snow. She'd be able to see the skaters as they started to arrive. Devon had agreed to take a break from his work to meet her here later, too.

"Hi, Mom." Regina brushed some snowflakes off a picnic table under the gazebo before taking a seat on the wooden bench.

"Hello, Georgiana." Her mother's tone was cool. She sounded like she was in her car, or at the very least using her speakerphone. A rock tune played on a radio somewhere near her.

Regina bristled. "I'm not going by that name anymore, remember?"

"It doesn't change who you are, darling," her mom reminded her while a few car horns honked in the background. "And how's life in Montana? Are you honestly working at a horse ranch?"

Regina blew out a breath and tried to relax, remembering the whole reason she'd reached out to her mother in the first place. Hadn't Millie suggested she take more risks to build better relationships?

"I am." She'd imparted that much information in the message she'd left for her mother. Staring out across the ice pond lit with white lights strung from tree to tree around the perimeter, she couldn't imagine a more beautiful place to be right now. "It's peaceful here. I feel like I can think."

She hadn't realized how suffocating her life in Los Angeles had been back when she'd been trying to hold the threads of her unraveled life together. Back home, there had been reminders everywhere of all she had lost. The stores and restaurants she couldn't afford anymore. The parties that she didn't get invited to. And, of course, the tabloid interest in her story that made her feel like she was always running from questions.

"You needed *more* peace?" her mother asked drily. "I thought that's what counseling was for." There was a biting edge to her tone, reminding Regina how much her mom had resented the discussions of her daughter's therapy. Then her mother sighed, and some of the bitterness eased when she spoke again. "I was under the impression you'd forgiven me."

Regina closed her eyes, trying to remember the things therapy had taught her about her family relationships. She had traveled this road with her mom before, and was unwilling to fall into the same conversational traps.

Her mom's answer to the upheaval from *Hollywood Newlyweds* had been to retreat. Ignore. Move on. But that had never worked for Regina.

"I meant a different kind of peace, Mom," she clarified gently. "It's really beautiful here."

In the long, awkward pause that followed, she could almost hear her mother debating her response. Finally, she said, "What drew you there?"

Encouraged that maybe her mother was going to work on establishing a new peace between them, Regina decided to be forthright. She spotted a camera crew setting up to take footage of the bonfire party as it began. It was bound to be crowded, since the ranch's lodge was now full to capacity as guests and media convened for the coming launch event.

"I think I'm getting very close to finally putting the scandal and that damned book in the past, Mom." Her thoughts had been all but consumed by the new developments since April Stephens had taken the case. Or—perhaps more to the point—since Devon had decided to spare no expense in looking for the truth.

His contribution toward uncovering his father's motives only added to his undeniable appeal. If only she could trust what she felt for him. Or trust *him*. She'd been putting up barriers with people for so long she wasn't sure she knew how to relate to a man any other way.

"That would be good news. But why do you sound so sure?" Her mother switched off the radio, a drum solo ending abruptly. "What did I miss?"

The curiosity in her mom's voice reminded Regina that this wasn't just about *her own* past. The scandal and aftermath had affected her mother, too. Had devastated her, even. Tabitha Barnes had never returned to Hollywood. She'd never acted in another film.

Alonzo Salazar had stolen Tabitha's secrets and profited off them, wrecking her life in the process. Wasn't it only fair for Tabitha to know the truth? She might have put her anger behind her—and the hunger for answers that haunted Regina—but that didn't mean she didn't deserve to know the truth.

"If I tell you, will you keep it between us?" she asked, needing to keep the information out of the tabloids. Not just for Devon's sake, but for her own.

"Of course," her mother agreed. "I learned the hard way not to share my secrets," Tabitha continued, a hint of bitterness giving an edge to her voice.

Relaxing a bit, Regina told herself it hadn't been a mistake to reconnect with her mother. They could mend their relationship, couldn't they? Maybe Millie had a point about taking chances. Deciding to start with her mother, Regina brought Tabitha up to speed on what she'd learned so far, confident that her mom understood the hellish ramifications of having the tabloids involved in their lives.

"Who the hell is Alonzo Salazar?" Her mother interrupted midway through the story. "Hold on, Geor— Regina," she corrected herself. "I need to pull off the interstate so I can give you my full attention."

Waiting while her mother swore softly under her breath a few times, conceivably crossing multiple lanes to find an exit ramp, Regina's gaze traveled back to the window where Devon was still in his meeting in an upper-level conference suite. Seeing him there, remembering how supportive he'd been of her journey—with no thought to the consequences for his own family—made Regina realize that the progress she'd made in her quest for answers wasn't as exciting as she'd hoped it might be. Somehow, nailing Alonzo wasn't bringing her the peace she'd expected because he'd just exposed problems that were already there just under the surface of her family dynamics. She just hadn't known about them.

Like it or not, Alonzo Salazar had only spoken the truth.

"Okay." Her mother's voice sounded sharply in her ears. "I'm in a parking lot and I'm ready to hear it all. Spare no detail, Regina. I need to know all about the bastard who destroyed my family."

A twinge of worry passed through her that her mother sounded so serious about a topic Regina thought she'd put behind her long ago. Could her decision to share the news with her mom dredge up old unhappiness that Tabitha had put behind her? That hadn't been her intention. Maybe she'd just really needed to share the information with someone else—someone who'd been as affected by the scandal as her—because it was eating away at her inside to know the truth and not be able to talk about it.

"I'm telling you this in confidence, Mom," Regina reminded her. "I won't have the tabloids hounding us again."

"I know, sweetheart," her mother assured her. "I understand."

Satisfied, she took comfort in the words. "Thank you."

While she finished filling her mother in on the new developments in the investigation, Regina watched the camera crew film a few laughing ice skaters on the small pond, trying to reevaluate her feelings about the book and her family. It occurred to Regina that she was finally in the perfect position to unmask the author of the book that had ruined her life. She had a captive media audience. The storyline would be relevant since Alonzo Salazar had been a frequent guest at Mesa Falls Ranch, and his son was working with the ranch.

As tabloid news went, it seemed like a slam dunk.

It was an opportunity she'd been waiting for ever since she'd found the front door to her childhood home locked, her life as a pampered heiress—a beloved daughter—over forever.

Except, seeing the snow globe beauty of this place, seeing how her previously empty world had filled with friends and a warm, generous lover, Regina didn't feel the same thirst for revenge she once had. Because while she still wanted more answers about Alonzo Salazar's motives and where the profits from his book had gone, they no longer felt like the most important things in the world to her.

She'd placed all her anger on that one man—and things were more complex than that. *People* were more complex. Time to quit thinking of the past in terms of black and white and to see the nuances beneath. Her gaze flicked back up to the conference suite window, where Devon was passing his tablet to a colleague, pointing out something on the screen. He'd been so kind to her this week.

Even when she'd been spying on him and trying to wheedle information from him, he'd been supportive. So no matter how many issues from her past she dragged into this relationship, she knew he deserved better than what she'd given him in the past.

By the time she wound up her phone call with her mother, sharing more with her than she had in years, Regina felt ready to take a new kind of chance. A new risk.

And it had Devon Salazar written all over it.

Eleven

Devon's meeting ran long, making him late for his evening with Regina. He hadn't bothered to return to his cabin to ditch the business attire, or trade his overcoat for a parka, but at least he'd had a pair of boots in the utility vehicle he'd used earlier in the day. Now, as he trudged through the packed snow to where they'd agreed to meet, he could see the bonfire happy hour must have ended. The white lights over the skating pond were still lit, but the ice was empty except for a couple of antler trees twinkling in the dark.

He pulled out his phone to text Regina to apologize and see if he could still salvage some time with her. But before he could remove his leather glove to key in his password, a snowball pelted him between the shoulder blades.

Feminine laughter followed the ambush.

Tucking his phone back in his pocket, he turned to

see Regina peeking from behind a tall ponderosa pine. She stood mostly in shadow, but the glow from the skating pond let him see her smile. The red ski jacket she wore was different from the dark duster she favored for riding. A white knit hat covered her dark hair. Seeing her stirred him so much that the feeling stopped him in his tracks. It made him nervous that she had that kind of power over him. He pushed aside those sensations to greet her.

"Hello to you, too," he said, closing the distance between them. "I'm going to let you get away with that since I'm late."

He wrapped her in his arms, pulling her against him for a taste of her lips, grateful to lose himself in the feel of her. This, he understood. He just needed to keep things simple. Enjoy the physical connection.

Even with the wind blowing off the mountains and a light snowfall swirling around them, he was all in for this kiss. More than any wind or snow, he simply felt the arch of her spine toward him, the give of her soft mouth under his.

"Very late," she reminded him as she broke away to look up into his eyes. She didn't sound upset, though, for which he was grateful. "I might need to throw a few more rounds at you to even the score."

"I'm sorry." He brushed another kiss along her forehead, wondering how she could feel so right against him. "With the party day looming, we had a lot of details to finalize. I didn't feel like I could rush through the conference call with the staffers doing the heavy lifting."

"I understand." She slid one arm around his waist and ended up tucked under his arm, subtly steering him toward a couple of Adirondack chairs flanking a firepit.

"The one positive thing about being late for the party is that we've got a bonfire all to ourselves."

He'd rather have her in front of the fireplace at his cabin, where they could be alone, but he liked seeing her this way. She appeared happier than the last time they'd been together, when she'd rushed out of his cabin to dive deeper into April Stephens's latest findings.

"Sounds good." He followed the path around the perimeter of the ice. The catering staff was hauling the food carts back up to the dining area on the hill overlooking the pond. "Were you able to speak to April?"

He figured it would be better to dispense with the dicey subjects first so they could move past them. As they reached the stone firepit, he swiped off the snow from one of the seats for her.

"Yes." She dropped into the chair and leaned forward to warm her hands by the fire. "She was on her way to Kalispell to interview Fallon Reed and she got me up to speed while she was driving."

"I heard she didn't have any luck speaking to Weston Rivera." Devon had been receiving regular updates, too, and that one frustrated him. He took the seat beside her. "Which makes me wonder if the Mesa Falls Ranch owners are more tightly connected to my father than I first realized."

Peeling off her gloves, she laid them on the chair arms and held her bare fingers out to warm in the heat from the blaze. "I'm wondering if Weston said something to make April revisit her perspective on Alonzo. Because she asked me to weigh the possibility that your dad wrote the book without any intention of connecting to my family."

That was news to Devon. The idea sure as hell had

appeal. He grabbed a nearby stick and poked at the logs in the pit, stirring the flames higher.

"What do you think?" he asked, dropping the stick to study her expression in the brighter orange glow.

"At the time, I said 'no way.'" She gave him an apologetic smile. "But I've been thinking about it ever since. And I know that it's wrong of me to pin all the blame on your dad when it was my mother who betrayed my family."

The pain in her words was unmistakable. He reached to touch her, to soothe her somehow, his hand skimming her back through her parka.

"But it wasn't his story to tell," Devon assured her, empathizing with how much it hurt to realize the people you loved didn't share your moral compass. He'd struggled his whole life with forgiving his father for how much he'd hurt his mom. "I understand that. Though I guess the book wouldn't have experienced the level of fame or sales that it did without that gossip columnist getting involved and going public with her idea that the story was based on real people."

"No one made the connection to my family for eight months." Shifting in her chair, she turned toward him, shadows chasing through her eyes in the moonlight. "Maybe no one ever would have if not for that columnist."

He wanted to comfort her for all the ways her life had spiraled out of control. He stroked her back, wishing his father had left more clear answers in the paperwork he'd left behind at the ranch.

"No matter what his intentions," she continued, dragging in a deep breath, "I feel like the time has come for me to put it behind me."

As the light snowfall picked up speed, she lifted

her chin a fraction, and he saw the determined glint in her gaze.

"Really?" he said, feeling wary. He wondered what that involved.

"The biggest transgression was my mother's," she said firmly. "I've always known that, and that's why I started counseling, to try and work through my resentment at her. And my father was at fault, too, for just walking away. But even though I thought I'd gotten past it, I'm still here, spinning in circles looking for a way to blame my lack of family on someone else—anyone else—besides me."

"You've never been at fault—"

"Not moving on *is* my fault." From her pensive tone, she seemed to be at peace with the idea of taking full ownership. "I've seen that more clearly in my time here than I did in all the months I spent dragging myself through counseling sessions."

Weighing her words, he gazed at the skating pond, where the falling snowflakes sizzled softly when they met the bonfire's blaze. Then he turned back to her and searched her eyes, hating what she'd been through. His hopes for an uncomplicated evening together got more and more remote by the minute.

"That much I can understand. Being in Montana has given me a serious dose of perspective, too." He peeled off his gloves and threaded his bare fingers with hers. "As much as I want to support my mother at her wedding, I'm in no hurry to return to my grandfather's world, where everything is an excuse to network and get ahead in business."

Regina stared down at their joined hands for a long moment before raising her gaze to his. "Maybe it will be easier for you if I accept your invitation to be your date."

His heart slugged harder inside his chest.

"Are you sure?" He hadn't pressed her about continuing their relationship after this week, but he'd damn well been thinking about it.

A smile curved her lips. "Yes."

The light in her eyes called to him, making him realize how much he wanted to be alone with her. To spend more time with her. No matter what happened during the rest of their stay at Mesa Falls Ranch, at least he had that to look forward to afterward.

Edging forward in his seat, Devon captured her lips in a kiss. She sighed into him as her free hand wound around his neck, slipping under the collar of his overcoat to his bare neck just above his shirt.

She hummed a pleasurable sound against his lips, the vibration echoing through him and ratcheting up his need for her. It could be below freezing and he would still burn when she touched him.

"Come home with me," he urged her, scarcely breaking the kiss.

"Yes," she murmured back as the snowfall renewed its intensity.

Sensual hunger firing through him, he rose to his feet, lifting her with him, then peeled himself away. Blinking through the fog of red-hot attraction, he saw the same lust—or could it be more than that—mirrored in her eyes. Whatever was happening between them was moving fast.

As he led her to the utility vehicle on loan from the ranch, he told himself that as long as the fire remained purely sensual, there was no need to worry about it consuming them both.

But even as he opened the passenger door to help her inside, Devon wondered if he was only fooling himself.

* * *

Waking up beside Devon the next morning, Regina became aware of two things simultaneously.

First, she'd never felt this level of happiness in her adult life. Every cell in her body seemed to sing with contentment to be naked and lying next to this endlessly sexy man. He'd adored her from head to toe the night before, lingering in all the best places in between, until she'd drifted into deep, blissful sleep on a raft of happy endorphins.

Her second realization as the light of dawn streamed over the bed was that she'd never spent a full night with another man.

And as she examined that idea more closely, she acknowledged that was both strange and messed up. Somehow, she'd always found a way to distance herself from romantic interests, telling herself those guys in her past were never "the one," so it didn't matter. After the way her father turned on her, it wasn't easy to trust men. Yet her subconscious had quit blocking her from Devon, allowing her to enjoy the whole night in his arms.

Now, here she was. Naked. Happy.

And then realization number three hit: her heart was suddenly vulnerable.

Amazing how quickly realization number three could torpedo the first two.

Slipping from the covers, she retrieved her clothes to dress, worry spiraling out from that one thought like ripples in a pond. Millie had told her no one went through life unscathed. But was it so wrong for Regina to feel like she'd already had her cuts and bruises? She wasn't ready to take on more just when she was starting to let go of the need for revenge that had been driving her for too long.

She dug in her purse for enough toiletries to comb her hair and put herself back together, taking her time to try to steady her nerves, too. By the time she was ready to head out of the bedroom, she smelled the heady scent of coffee brewing and bacon cooking.

This man was too good to be true.

The feeling was confirmed when she first spotted him from the doorway of the kitchen. "How do you like your eggs?" he asked over the brim of a white coffee mug, the steam drifting up to caress his handsome features as he drank.

His flannel shirt was unbuttoned over his naked chest, his jeans low on his waist. Even after the supreme fulfillment of the night before, her gaze got stuck on the center ridge between his abs that ended in a sprinkle of dark hair above the top button on his jeans.

With an effort, she set aside some of the morning panic and uneasiness to enjoy his well-meaning offer.

"Over easy." Setting her purse on a chair in the living room near the cowboy-themed Christmas tree they'd decorated, she padded on stocking feet into the kitchen and helped herself to a cup of coffee from the pot on the breakfast bar. "You look decidedly comfortable in the kitchen for a man who grew up in a life of privilege." She realized how that sounded after the words left her lips. "No offense meant. I know I never learned to cook anything for myself until after my dad cut off my mom and me."

He grinned as he cracked the eggs into the skillet. "No offense taken. I had a brief notion that my father would let me visit more often if I was independent and didn't behave like a trust-fund kid." He shrugged as he tossed the eggshells in the trash. "So when I was about eight or nine, I asked our cook to teach me some stuff. And while my father never discovered my culinary skills, I've never regretted the lessons."

Eight or nine years old? She hadn't thought before about how his father's defection must have hurt at such a young age. Her heart ached for the boy he'd been… And the weight that he must still carry with him now.

"Consider me grateful to your cook." She helped herself to the cream and sugar he'd left on the counter. "And it must have been hard having so little of your dad's time growing up. As much as it hurt when my dad cut me off completely, at least I had him in my life until my midteens."

Devon shook his head while he dug in a drawer to retrieve a spatula. "I don't think anyone would say that the teens are an easy time to go through that kind of loss."

His words were yet more proof that Devon was a thoughtful man. Butterflies fluttered in her belly. She sipped her coffee to quiet the feeling while his phone rang. He silenced it with one hand and flipped eggs with the other.

"Do you have a lot of work obligations today?" She wondered about the schedule for the launch event. And their flight out afterward.

Last night she'd agreed to attend his mother's wedding with him, extending their relationship after the event ended. Her stomach knotted a bit at the memory. Not because she didn't want to be with him, but because of how very badly she *did*.

What if this risk exploded in her face?

Her belly tightened painfully.

"Yes. Although that message was from my mother, who's thrilled I'm bringing you to the wedding." His green eyes met hers for a moment before he plated the eggs and bacon he'd already cooked. "She's excited to meet you."

Her pulse raced at the realization that this was really happening. She was genuinely taking the next step with Devon, no matter that their relationship had started in such strained circumstances. Should she come clean about how she'd rifled through his jacket on purpose that first day?

She didn't want her first effort with a man who mattered to her to be marred by a lie going in. If she allowed that, she wasn't all that different from her mother.

The toaster popped near her elbow, startling her.

"You okay?" Devon asked as he set a plate in front of her and passed her a slice of toasted golden wheat bread.

"Sure." She nodded too fast. "Just realized I'm cutting it close to lead my first trail ride."

"I'll drive you back soon. I know we both have a lot of obligations today and tomorrow, but the day after that, you're all mine for the launch party gala." He took the seat beside her at the long breakfast bar, his green eyes turning a shade darker as his gaze smoldered over her.

She went from worried to keenly aware of him in the space of a heartbeat. How did he do that?

"I'd better start the search for a dress," she admitted, thinking how long it had been since she'd attended a black-tie event.

"I'm already on top of it," he assured her, straightening to dig into the meal.

"On top of dress shopping?" She gave a surprised laugh and nibbled at the bacon.

"You'll need a dress for the wedding, too, and I can't have you bearing the cost of that when I invited you so last minute." He tapped a screen on his phone to show her a web page for a well-known couture house. "So I messaged one of Lily's designer friends from New York to send you some samples."

Lily Carrington was his good friend and the COO of Salazar Media, who'd departed Mesa Falls Ranch after falling for Devon's brother, Marcus. Regina knew, because she'd spied on Lily and Marcus, too, in her quest to find answers about Alonzo. And despite the guilt that memory brought with it, she couldn't quite suppress a purely feminine rush of pleasure at the idea of wearing the gorgeous clothes he showed her on his phone. It had been so long since she'd had access to those kinds of garments.

"That's so kind of you, but—"

"I insist." He leaned over to kiss the back of her hand before returning to his breakfast. "I know the ranch has you booked for too many tours the next two days to give you enough time to shop. And for what it's worth, I appreciate your role in making this event a success."

She murmured her thanks before finishing her meal, trying to sort through all the feelings swelling like an incoming storm. Was she moving too fast in taking new risks? She'd been so sure she wanted to pursue this relationship with Devon, but the closer she got to him, the more she realized how devastated she was going to be if things fell apart.

And no matter how much she tried to focus on the positives of what was happening between them, she had the weight of a lot of frustrating years riding on her back, whispering that it would never work out. Even with the launch party to look forward to—surrounded by friends in a place she'd come to care about—Regina couldn't shake the fear that she was one step away from screwing it all up.

Twelve

After all the hours he'd put in the last two days, Devon was more than ready for his night with Regina. The day of the launch event, Mesa Falls Ranch looked like a scene straight out of a kids' picture book. The holiday decorations were heavy on the greenery and red bows. Even the four-rail fences were decked with pine boughs, and white lights were strewn along the private drive that led to the main lodge.

An event space simply called "The Barn" was a historic reproduction in turn-of-the-century style, with a giant wreath decorating the cupola. The whole building was lit with landscape lighting in addition to the Christmas lights, making it easy to photograph for the wealth of camera crews present.

Fat snowflakes fell from the sky, giving every photo a snow globe touch. Dark draft horses in full dress tack pulled the sleighs conveying the guests from the lodge to the party venue, dropping them off on a red carpet that led through the huge double doors.

Inside, Devon had checked and triple-checked the logistics of the social media tech. He'd done all he could to make this night a success, and he wanted the reward of time with the sexy woman who'd dominated his thoughts all week. He walked past the massive screen over the dance floor already broadcasting live video feeds from the simultaneous party events in New York and Los Angeles. Here, the focus was on traditional black tie, but in the other cities, there were ranching gurus on hand to narrate programs about sustainable ranching. They'd flown baby lambs and sheep across the country in both directions to make ranching issues more real, combining petting zoo opportunities with social media content moments.

The intent was to drive awareness about the benefits of making ranch lands greener and establishing greater harmony with the animals—both the livestock and the native species. Marcus had brainstormed it, but Devon had executed the bulk of the events. Now, with everything running smoothly, he could focus on finding his date.

Leaving the barn, he stalked out into the snowy night again, checking his phone for messages. There were none. He'd called Regina ten minutes ago, thinking she was just running late, but now he was concerned since they were supposed to have met half an hour ago. He hated not being able to pick her up personally, but he felt it was important to be on site before the event kicked off in case the ranch owners had any concerns. Three of them were here tonight: Weston Rivera, Gage Striker and Desmond Pierce. Two others were attending the party in Los Angeles, and one had flown to New York.

Frustration spiked that this event had required so much of his time during a week he would have enjoyed devoting to Regina. And while he understood his brother's wish to take time with Lily Carrington this week, Devon knew it was past time to confront Marcus about the simmering rivalry between them. He refused to let it destroy their company. He'd worked almost nonstop since starting Salazar Media, expanding the business during explosive growth in the field. What was the point of all that work—all those profits—if he couldn't take the time to enjoy what really mattered? Maybe Marcus had already figured that out for himself.

Even as the thought crossed Devon's mind, he tried to push it aside. Because if he admitted that Regina really mattered, he would have to confront the fact that his father's behavior had soured him on relationships. That he didn't trust himself, considering what kind of male role model he'd had. He'd always avoided serious relationships because he didn't want to put any woman through the hell that his father had wrought for his mother—and other women, too.

He looked up, straining to see who the passenger was in an approaching sleigh. It wasn't Regina. Then he scanned the crowd for her face. He didn't see her, but as the sleigh pulled up in front of him, he glimpsed April Stephens in a dark blue gown with a high neck and long sleeves.

"April." He went to the sleigh to personally help her down. "Have you seen Regina?"

April's blond curls fell in artful ringlets around her face. Other men turned to look at her. She was a lovely woman, and yet she left him cold because the only female who captured his attention was a dark-haired beauty with quicksilver eyes and fierce determination.

"I saw her at the spa earlier today." April smiled as she smoothed her long skirt and rushed to the temporary canopy to protect guests from the snow. "One of her bunkmates had a couple of openings in her schedule at the pedicure station, so Regina invited me to get my toes done with her."

"Did she mention her plans for the evening?" He couldn't imagine why she wasn't here. Had she backed out?

He'd sensed she'd been nervous about attending his mother's wedding even after she'd agreed to be his date. At the time, he'd told himself that was only natural, since going to weddings and meeting families were traditionally big steps in a relationship and he'd catapulted them straight into both arenas when he'd invited her to his mom's nuptials.

"Of course." April laughed, a dimple appearing in one cheek. "She seemed excited to go with you. She showed photos of her gown choices and let me help her choose."

Devon frowned.

So if something had gone wrong with Regina, it must have been after she'd seen April.

"Okay," he muttered distractedly, already straining to see if another sleigh was on the way. "Thank you, April."

Worried now, he was ready to ask one of the grooms about finding him a ranch utility vehicle when he saw one more sleigh headed toward the barn, horses trotting out in front.

She had to be in that one.

Waiting for the vehicle to arrive, he heard a commotion inside the barn—a subtle uptick in crowd noise as if they were reacting to a new band on stage. Or a speaker.

Which was curious, only because there was no change in entertainment scheduled for twenty more minutes.

He turned toward the barn, where one of the doors stood open despite the cold, thanks to the enormous heaters warming the space. A handful of people were moving purposefully toward the entrance as if something inside had captured their attention.

Curiosity turned to a bad feeling that something was going wrong inside. But he forced his feet to stay rooted outside for another minute so he could check if Regina was in the last sleigh. He waited until the horses pulled under the lights, where he could make out the faces of the occupants more clearly.

Regina wasn't there.

He began to feel downright dismal.

Had she blown off their evening together? Changed her mind about going to Connecticut with him for the wedding? Confused and still worried, he couldn't take time to hunt for her yet. Not when there was something clearly happening inside the barn.

As he jogged toward the entrance, he realized a hush had fallen over the crowd. In fact, as he stepped into the gala venue, he saw hundreds of guests in black tie all standing still, listening to a woman at the podium near the dance floor. Devon didn't have to crane his neck to see her; his company had installed a closed-circuit video system that was playing live footage from the three parties on a big screen.

Thirty feet tall, in full color, actress Tabitha Barnes—Regina's mother—had commandeered the microphone. She stared out at the crowd while she spoke, her gray eyes so like her daughter's.

"...and the author behind the book *Hollywood*

Newlyweds, which ruined my life, has been unmasked at last."

Devon's gut sank to his feet.

Not just because an audience in three cities was about to know the truth that would ruin his mother's wedding. But because he couldn't deny how the woman had learned this secret.

Regina had betrayed his trust in the cruelest way possible. No wonder she was nowhere to be found tonight. She'd been too busy orchestrating the revenge she'd craved for years.

The sweet smell of balsam and cedar turned sour as he took a ragged breath. He stalked toward the control board, edging through rapt listeners to turn off Tabitha's microphone and the overhead screen and switch the channel to any other feed.

It didn't take him long to attract the attention of the logistics coordinator. He gave her the "cut" sign that would kill the audio, but it didn't really matter. Because Tabitha Barnes was already dropping her bombshell.

"His name was Alonzo Salazar, father of the social media moguls who run Salazar Media—"

Tabitha's audio dropped. For a moment, there was silence, heavy and thick with the shock that could only precede an eruption. His gut twisted in anticipation a second before the burst of reaction came from the crowd. Just then, the image of the actress on the big screen switched to a feed from the Los Angeles party, where a rock star known for his philanthropy was arriving to support the party. But the damage had already been done.

A moment later, the chamber musicians scheduled to play during the welcome hour returned to their instruments. The violins blanketed the buzz of gossip, muffling the details somewhat but not nearly enough.

"Salazar" was the name on everyone's lips. He heard it over and over like an audio recording on repeat as he moved through the crowd to confront Tabitha.

And, more important, her daughter. Because he knew without a doubt where Tabitha had gotten her inside information about Alonzo, and it sickened him. He was mad as hell—and yes, hurt—to think how easily he'd been played and betrayed when he should have known better. He would find Regina and tell her exactly what he thought of this stunt and her.

After that, he would focus on tying up his business in Montana so he could put this piece of his life—and her—behind him for good.

"How could you do this to me?" Regina wheeled on her mother in the hallway outside the restrooms at the back of the event space. Framed photos of the ranch's public buildings covered the wall, and there was a black leather bench tucked into the far corner.

Her mother had never messaged her that she was on her way to Montana. She'd simply texted Regina five minutes before her date to say that she was going to use the launch event as a way to "set the record straight" about Alonzo Salazar.

Regina had been devastated. Hadn't she explicitly asked her mother to keep the information confidential? Her mother had agreed. And still, Tabitha had betrayed that trust. Even as Regina had scrambled to stop her mom, she'd assumed Tabitha would attend the party in Los Angeles since that was right in her backyard—the family's old stomping grounds.

In a panic, Regina had called and texted her mom

and her mom's friends. Then, when she'd gotten her
first inkling that Tabitha had actually flown to Montana, Regina had raced around Mesa Falls Ranch like
a madwoman in heels to try to stop the train wreck
before it happened. Her feet were still freezing from
tromping through snow in stiletto pumps, heedless of
the need to walk on the red carpets laid out for guests.
Her beautiful shoes and gown were ruined after she'd
spent all day primping for this night, eager to see the
look on Devon's face when he saw her. Instead of savoring that moment, however, she'd arrived with the hem
of the plum-colored velvet sheath rigid with ice from
her trek through the snow. But despite her best efforts
to stop her mom, she'd failed miserably, not locating
Tabitha until she was at the podium.

When it had been too late to protect Devon.

"How can I do this to *you*?" Her mother turned on
her, narrowing her gaze. "Do you think you're the only
one who has been affected by this nightmare? My life
was stolen from me, too."

Tabitha paced the narrow hall in a floor-length emer-
ald dress that was a size too small, a couture gown from
a long-ago film premiere that Regina had once paraded
around in as a child. Her mother's breasts swelled over
the bodice, her now softer physique straining the side
zipper. Poor dress choice aside, she was still incredibly
beautiful on the outside.

On the inside? Clearly, she still wrestled with dark
demons.

Regina could see that now with the perspective of
time and distance. Funny how much she'd gained of
both those things in her brief stay at Mesa Falls Ranch.
Especially since she'd met Devon. She understood now
that her mother's lies had hurt them both immeasurably.

Not just recently, in breaking the promise to keep the information about Alonzo confidential. The pattern of lies was more deeply rooted, dating all the way back to Tabitha's decision to pass off another man's child as her own. Alonzo Salazar had done a great wrong in revealing a story that wasn't his to tell. But he'd been able to tell the tale because of Tabitha's decision to live a lie in the first place.

"Mom, I thought we were going to try to rebuild a relationship." She thought back to that phone call when she'd shared the information about Alonzo with her mother. She'd really thought it was a turning point for them, an opportunity to share the hurt and move past it. "But that requires trust, and after what you just did, I don't—"

"You're a surprising person to tout the merits of trust." The masculine voice behind her was familiar, but the tone bore an iciness she'd never heard.

"Devon, I'm so sorry." She turned toward him, knowing this was her fault. Hating that she'd hurt him.

Desperate to fix it.

And yet the remote expression on his face gave her pause as he stared her down. Dressed in a custom-fitted tuxedo with a sprig of holly pinned to one lapel, he looked achingly handsome. But the coldness in his gaze sent a chill curling through her. Behind him, two burly ranch hands dressed in tuxes and cowboy boots stood at attention.

"Ms. Barnes." Devon's gaze flicked past Regina, landing on her mother. "There are still reporters out front. If you'd like more media attention tonight, I suggest you seek it outside the barn to avoid being escorted from this private event."

Her mother gave a harrumph of disapproval as she

brushed past them both. Regina noticed how the ranch hands followed in her wake, no doubt tasked with ensuring she didn't return to the building. Not that Regina could blame Devon for that. Her empathy with her mother ended tonight. She felt only guilt that she hadn't stopped her.

"I had no idea she would show up here—" she began before Devon cut her off.

"We can speak more privately back here." He pointed down the hall, toward a small cloakroom located near a back entrance.

She noticed he didn't touch her as they moved together toward the coat check, and that made her tense with worry. A quick glance into the main area of the barn showed the gala proceeding normally, although a few heads turned their way as they walked past. She overheard "Salazar" spoken behind someone's hand. She could see the way Devon's movements—already brittle—tensed even more.

Dread for what her mother had done multiplied.

Devon spoke in quiet tones to the young woman working the station, and she stepped aside to let him pass behind her into the coatroom. Regina followed him, stepping behind three rows of coatracks to see an assortment of folded tables, chairs and catering carts. The buffer of the coats filtered the noise from the party, making the space feel private. The scent of pine from the log construction permeated the room.

"You have every right to be furious," she said as soon as they were alone once more, her nerves wound past the point of tight.

And maybe it was easier to speak to his back since she was intimidated by the coldness in his eyes.

"Perhaps I do." He turned to face her, his face a neutral mask. "But since anger won't fix the situation, I have no intention of indulging useless emotions."

She drew in a breath, needing to explain what had happened. To apologize. But he continued before she could gather her thoughts.

"Since my mother is about to be besieged by tabloid reporters looking to feed off this story, I need to be at her side for damage control." His gaze narrowed, coldly assessing her. "And to personally apologize for my poor decision to trust you with sensitive information gleaned by my private investigator. How much does she know, by the way? Everything?"

Regina closed her eyes for a moment. She couldn't bear to see his disappointment in her. She knew he was hurt, and she hated that she'd been the cause. She ached to realize how badly she'd messed up. She'd been so resentful of his father for tearing apart her family. But now she was the one to cause pain.

"Yes." She wrenched her eyes back open. "I thought it would provide her the same closure as it has brought me." She had gained more than self-awareness these last weeks. She'd gained forgiveness. And that had been a beautiful gift she'd hoped to share with her mom. "I really believed we could put it behind us finally."

Devon's right eyebrow twitched, but his expression did not change. "Or else you believed you could finally have the revenge you've sought for years."

Crushed he would think that of her, she sensed there were far more emotions at work inside him, no matter what he said about not indulging them. She feared he was slipping away. That she wouldn't be able to fix this.

"I wouldn't do that to you." She'd grown deep feelings for him in a short span of time and she wouldn't just throw them away like that. She pressed her case, needing him to listen. "I didn't even know my mother had come to Montana until a few minutes before our date tonight. I panicked, but I thought I could stop her. With the benefit of hindsight, I can see I should have called you to help, but I didn't know she was *here*, in this state, let alone what she was planning. At the time, I was just so fixed on intercepting her."

When she paused in her diatribe, she peered up into his eyes and saw his expression hadn't changed.

A slow, dawning realization blindsided her.

"You really think I could stab you in the back that way, after everything we've shared?" Unshed tears pricked at her eyes as disbelief washed over her.

The anger at her mother stopped mattering. The frostbite in her toes from running around the ranch in the snow ceased to be a problem. Because the only thing she felt was a pain knifing directly into her heart.

Devon said nothing. If anything, his expression hardened a fraction, his lips compressing in a thin line.

"You're cutting me off." The realization struck her as she quietly said the words out loud, and she felt the ground wobble under her feet. She reached for the closest coat rack to steady herself, her hand falling on rough wool and cashmere. "Just like my father did."

"No." Devon's eyebrows scrunched together as he shook his head slightly.

But it was crystal clear to her. Her grip tightened on the wool coat and the wooden hanger underneath it, her reality rocking along with the seesawing garment.

"You might not lock a physical door to bar me from your life. But you're shutting me out just as effectively with the coldness and unwillingness to listen." The strategy hurt her so much more this time. Maybe because she'd believed Devon was a better man.

"That's not true," Devon responded finally. Starkly. But since he didn't have any follow-up to the statement, she took it for what it was.

A knee-jerk reaction.

"It is, though," she said softly, straightening herself despite the pain in her chest, desperate to hold onto her tattered pride. "And I'm more sorry than I can say. For both of us."

Awkwardly pivoting on her heel, she headed to the closest exit, knowing they were done. She'd taken the risk and put herself on the line like Millie had suggested, but it hadn't paid off, because Devon didn't love her the way she loved him.

And she didn't have any idea how she was going to recover from that.

Thirteen

How could it hurt so much watching Regina walk away when she'd betrayed his trust?

Devon stood immobile as she strode from the cloak-room, achingly beautiful in her deep purple gown, half of her dark hair piled on her head while the rest cascaded in curls around her neck.

Maybe it pained him so much because she might be telling the truth? Had her mother acted independently of her? Had Regina only been guilty of confiding in someone she should have been able to trust?

And the most painful truth of all? That Devon had been no better than her heartless father, blaming her for something she couldn't control.

Except she could have controlled this situation. She'd even admitted to telling her mom about the PI's report. Although if he could trust her reasons, Regina had said she did it in order to put the book in her past. For good.

Had she been ready to move forward with him?

Devon couldn't afford to dwell on the knot of questions or the cavernous ache in his chest. Not when he had an event to get through. And, far more important, he had to reach his mother's side to help her weather this latest Salazar scandal two days before her wedding, no less. Forcing one foot in front of the other, he began making his way back out to the party.

Swearing to himself, he paused near a stack of unused folding chairs to check his phone before he departed the privacy of the storage area. He'd already missed a video call from his mother.

His foreboding grew. Out on the dance floor he could see a few couples two-stepping, since the country band had taken the stage. He had to trust that his staff was keeping the event on track. Maybe his presence would only serve as a distraction since—inevitably—some of the media outlets would want a statement on the book.

He tapped the button to return his mom's video call, waiting in the shadows until the device connected. When the feed came through, he could see his mother on the other end. She appeared to be in the passenger seat of a vehicle wearing what looked like a cocktail dress with a heavy winter coat over it.

"Devon, I'm so glad you saw my message," she said in a rush, her phone unsteady in her hand and making the image shake. "I wanted you to be the first to know what's happening."

He ground his teeth together, hating that she had to deal with the stress of his father's mistakes. And Devon couldn't dodge that he'd been a part of the cause for her pain by sharing the PI's information with Regina.

"Mom, I'm so sorry about that—"

"Sweetheart, there's no need for you to apologize."

His mother cut him off. "You can't control the choices your father made. Besides, I think it's going to be for the best."

"For the best?" Devon asked, confused as hell. He tucked deeper into the storage area to focus on the call, gladly letting the gala event unfold without him.

A secretive smile curved her lips as she slid a glance to the driver's side of the car. In the background, Devon recognized her fiancé's voice.

"Damn right, it's for the best." At the man's gruff pronouncement, his mother laughed and glanced back down at her phone.

"Bradley and I have decided to elope. Tonight." She sounded genuinely excited. "We were getting ready for yet another one of Granddad's parties that turn into glorified networking opportunities when we heard about that actress's announcement."

From the other side of the car, Devon heard his mother's fiancé say, "And I said, to hell with it!"

Devon couldn't believe his ears. His mother was eloping? His grandfather would be furious. But if his mom was happy, that was all that mattered to him. Some of the knot in his chest eased a fraction.

His mother laughed again. She sounded sort of giddy. Full of joy. "I think Bradley was only too glad to have a reason to skip town. So we're going to Greece."

"I've said all along we should get married by a ship's captain," Bradley added, leaning into the frame quickly to kiss his future bride's hand. "We met on a yacht, right? This was meant to be."

Even when Bradley shifted out of the image, their clasped hands remained on screen, a silent testament to their solidarity. Trust. It made Devon glad because it showed how much this guy understood his mom.

Loved her.

Of course Devon was happy about that. But at the same time, seeing the way Bradley stood by his mother made him realize how much he'd just screwed up with Regina by not giving her that same kind of support when she needed it most. He'd shut her out. Refused to listen.

The pain in his chest worsened, a surefire sign that he had feelings far deeper for her than he'd been willing to admit.

"Mom, I'm thrilled for you," he said finally, grateful that she had someone looking out for her.

"I knew you would be." Her expression turned serious. "And I wanted you to know that there was no need to rush home to Connecticut for Christmas. Unless you really want to, of course."

She knew he'd never been close to his grandfather. And he appreciated the heads-up. If he didn't need to help his mother navigate the renewed tabloid interest in her ex, he could stay in Montana for Christmas.

He had to apologize to Regina. Make her see how sorry he was for being so rash in pushing her away. He would do whatever it took to show her how wrong he'd been. He could be a better man than her father.

Or his.

Especially when it came to the woman he loved. The realization pierced through the muddle of his thoughts, the one, clear, burning truth.

"I think I'm going to stay right here." Devon was already moving toward the exit. He didn't care about the gala party without Regina at his side. Right now, he needed to find her and do everything in his power to make this right. "I look forward to celebrating with you both when you get home."

"Thank you, Devon. I love you, son." His mom blew him a kiss. "Merry Christmas."

The video disconnected and he shoved the phone in his pocket. He had to find Regina so he could share everything in his heart with her. Tell her how wrong he'd been and how much he loved her, how much he wanted her in his life.

And pray she would hear him out even though he hadn't given her that same courtesy. Just thinking about it made him realize how much he'd need a Christmas miracle to pull this off.

After changing out of her party clothes, Regina found herself back in the stables at Mesa Falls Ranch. It was quiet there, with all the draft horses in their stalls for the night now that the sleigh ride portion of the launch event was done. The grooms had cleaned up well in the tack room, replacing the fancy dress tack on the hooks where it belonged. The scent of leather polish hung in the still air along with the sweet scent of hay. She'd been drawn here for the comfort of the horses after the heartache of the night.

After the betrayal of discovering that her mother was more interested in a media spotlight than in resurrecting a relationship with her. And the even more formidable pain of losing Devon.

She dragged in a sharp breath, stopping herself from dwelling on the memory of his cold rebuff. But the agony was still so fresh. The heartbreak so devastating. She caught sight of her reflection in a shiny halter plate bearing one of the horse's names. The woman's face staring back at her was growing more familiar as Regina Flores became more real to her.

For all the hurts she'd experienced tonight, Regina

was still standing. Not fragile Georgiana Cameron, the pampered Hollywood princess who'd lost the man she believed to be her dad. Not Georgiana Fuentes, whose birth father hadn't wanted anything to do with a daughter who reminded him of his mistakes.

But Regina. The woman who awoke from a car crash with a different face and a need for a name to go along with it. *That* woman was strong. And she was taking full credit for conceiving her, and for loving her. Because it would take all that strength to get over a heartbreak worse than she could have imagined. The heartbreak of losing a man who'd swept her off her feet in such a short time.

Leaving behind the tack room, she shuffled back into the stable to stroke the nose of Evangeline, the Appaloosa mare she'd saddled for Devon that day she'd taken him on a tour of the ranch. Memories swamped her, making her wonder how she'd ever sleep tonight without sobbing her eyes out.

She'd finally healed her past, only to be brought low by loving a man who didn't return her feelings.

"There you are." The voice startled her and Evangeline, too.

Hand falling away from the mare's soft muzzle, she turned to see Devon standing in the stable door. A tidal wave of complicated feelings threatened to knock her off her feet and drag her under. She tipped her forehead to the horse's cheek, taking strength from the animal's calming presence.

Devon cast a shadow over her since the only light she'd flicked on was a lantern near the entrance. He still wore his tuxedo from the party, though he now wore boots and a long duster over it. Snowflakes dusted the dark coat, and he stamped his boots to free them of icy bits.

"Here I am." She smiled sadly, unsure why Devon would seek her out but hoping she could hold back her emotions and save her pride if not her heart. "In the last place I thought I would see you." She hadn't wanted to run into him again before he left for his mother's wedding. Especially since she was supposed to have been accompanying him. She'd told all her bunkmates that she was leaving for the Christmas holiday. "You're going to miss your flight if you don't hurry."

"I'm not going to Connecticut." He hovered near the entrance, not getting closer, but not leaving, either. "My mother decided to elope instead."

Regina exhaled hard, twinges of guilt stinging her over the woman losing out on her special day. The news did little to alleviate her guilt. But then again, she hadn't been the one to hold an impromptu press conference during the launch event, so why should she bear that weight? She'd done her best to stop her mother.

"I've already apologized, but please know if this elopement has to do with my mother's announcement, I'm sorry for—"

"I know." He hung his head for a moment before taking a step closer to her. "And I'm sorry I was too much of a stubborn ass to listen to you then."

Now that caught her attention.

While it was hardly enough to soothe a broken heart, she liked to think maybe he knew how hurtful he'd been. She leaned on the wall between stalls, not trusting her shaking legs to hold her upright. "I'm listening."

"Regina, it was wrong of me to assume the worst of you." Peeling off his gloves, he took another step closer.

Close enough that she could see what looked like genuine anguish scrawled across his handsome features. "You gave me no reason to doubt you, and I got defensive right away."

She folded her arms across her chest to hold in the pain of the memory, needing to hear more from him before jumping in with both feet again.

"I'm done being judged based on the actions of my mother." She had thought she'd moved past the old tensions with her mom after the counseling sessions, but apparently, she'd needed this reminder to understand that sometimes you couldn't trust people who were supposed to love you. "I really thought she and I could resurrect a relationship, but tonight proved to me how wrong I was. And that hurts."

"I hate knowing that I only added to your grief after that painful realization." He stepped closer once more, bringing him within reach. He lifted a hand to touch her shoulder, his grip gentle and warm. "I don't expect you to forgive me for the way I behaved, but I had to find you to tell you how much I regret it. How sorry I am."

Hearing the heartfelt apology eased her misery a little. The physical contact helped, too, although she didn't dare let herself think there was anything more at work here than just that olive branch. She'd been through enough tonight.

"I appreciate you finding me and telling me that," she said, the words sounding stiff and formal since she couldn't let her guard down. Her gaze landed on his boots, which she now realized looked frozen. Her attention shifted back to his face. "How *did* you find me?"

"By looking everywhere. This was the last building on my list, but I saved it for the end so I could get a horse and start riding the trails if I didn't find you anywhere else. That was my next guess—that you took off on horseback."

"I thought about it," she admitted, feeling begrudgingly moved that he'd searched the grounds for her personally.

In a tuxedo. In December.

His hand on her shoulder was softening her defenses, his caress reminding her how much this man affected her.

"I should have come here sooner. I remember you saying how much you missed the Arabian of your youth, and that's why you wanted to keep this job." He shook his head. "But I ignored my instincts, thinking I should search the ranch more methodically."

It heartened her that he remembered her talking about the horse she'd had as a teen. She felt herself melting, hoping.

"You're a good listener," she acknowledged. "Most of the time. And, for what it's worth, I do understand what it's like to be so rattled you make poor decisions. I know it had to be awful to hear my mom at the podium tonight."

His green eyes tracked hers as he lifted his hand to her face.

"Nothing was as awful as losing you." The words stroked over her as tenderly as his touch. "Nothing else even came close."

Her heart pounded faster at the admission, a fragile hope taking root while Evangeline nuzzled the back of her shoulder.

"You seemed content enough with your decision when I left the gala." It had taken all her strength to walk away with her head held high. Where was he going with this?

"I never gave myself a chance to trust a relationship, in light of the twisted role model I had." His thumb brushed her cheek and she couldn't bring herself to pull away. "I told myself our connection was just physical, even when my heart knew there was far more to it than that."

She knew it, too. But hearing him say it, seeing the truth in his eyes, swept away the last of her pain and opened her heart to beautiful possibilities she hadn't dared to entertain before now. Before Devon.

"What made you change your mind?" she asked, still needing to hear the reasons.

He sounded more certain of himself this time. Outside the stables, a gust of wind battered the windowpanes, reminding her how cold the night had turned.

"My mother and I had a video chat." He reached to stroke the horse's muzzle as the Appaloosa nosed closer to them. "She told me she was eloping. She was already in the car with her fiancé, and they were going to catch a plane to Greece to get married by a ship's captain."

"That sounds wildly romantic." She was happy for his mother. Relieved that her mom hadn't totally wrecked the wedding plans with her ploy for media attention.

"It is. Even though the wedding plans were going up in smoke, she still seemed so happy they were together, because her fiancé turned a tough situation around for her." His brow furrowed as his focus turned on her, the truth of his emotions plain to see. "Seeing that bond, the unshakable connection, really slammed home how I'd failed you when you needed me."

Her throat burned with emotions as he shared the memory with her. She blinked through the feelings, not quite sure where it was all leading, but hoping desperately that his being here meant he wanted to fix things. Try again. She couldn't speak over the lump in her throat.

"More than that, Regina," he continued, his eyes locking on hers in the shadowy light cast by that single brass lantern, "it made me realize how much I wanted to bring you that kind of happiness. It made me understand that I love you."

The words reverberated as if he'd shouted them, even though he'd never raised his voice. The echoes of that simple, incredible statement burrowed deep into her heart. Her soul.

Unable to hold back another moment, she flung her arms around him and buried her face against his chest to feel the warmth of him against her. The scent of the holly berry sprig on his tuxedo lapel mingled with a hint of his aftershave, familiar to her after the nights spent in his arms. In his bed. She breathed him in along with his love as he kissed the top of her head.

When she had soaked up his strength, and reminded herself he was real—that all of this was real—she edged back to look up at him.

"Does that mean you forgive me?" he asked, his voice a raw whisper that revealed how much he meant what he'd said.

"Yes." Knowing how important this was to him soothed every hurt in her soul. "It also means that I love you, too, and it stole my breath that you feel the same way."

He bent to kiss her lips. The long and lingering kiss stirred her more than ever with the strength of this love firing through them.

"Everything else we can fix," he vowed as he pulled

back to look at her. "I promise I'll never hurt you like that again."

"I'm trusting you." She remembered how Millie told her that you take risks to reap the sweet rewards. She couldn't imagine a sweeter feeling in the world.

"I'm going to make sure you never regret it." He wrapped her in his arms, making her feel safe. Loved. Desired.

She arched up to kiss him again, her heart and thoughts full of joy over how she could look forward to repeating the pleasure.

"What are you doing for Christmas?" she asked, ready to have him all to herself for the night. "Because I have some free time I could spend with you before I have to be back at work."

"The cabin is mine for the rest of the week," he mused, a glint in his eyes. "And the tree is already decorated. I have an excellent idea for how we should spend the holidays, just you and me. Together."

"Perfect." Contentment curled around her. She would be able to see her friends, who'd become like family. But most important, she could be with Devon to plan for a future. "We can have a cowboy Christmas."

Epilogue

Two months later

"This view is so gorgeous."

Devon heard the awe in Regina's voice as she emerged from the bedroom to peer out the living area's bay window in the luxury cabin he'd rented them for the week. Glacier National Park sprawled before them, the cloudless blue sky making the mountains stand out in sharp relief above Saint Mary Lake.

"I'm looking at an even better one," he assured her, rising from the sofa where he'd been waiting for her to dress for an early dinner.

She took his breath away, the same way she had since they'd first met. For the last two months, she'd allowed her hair to return to its natural color, a pale blond that made her gray eyes all the more dramatic. She didn't seem concerned with hiding who she was anymore, even with the media's renewed interest in her family.

But she also seemed content to leave her identity as Georgiana behind. Tonight, with a diamond ring in the pocket of his jacket, he hoped she would consider taking a new last name, as well.

She'd chosen an amethyst-colored sweater dress that hugged her curves and sky-high gray heels that showed off beautiful legs. But the best part of this outfit was her contented smile, a radiant happiness he liked to think he'd helped to put there.

The investigation into his father's past continued—privately, thanks to April Stephens—but Regina seemed content to wait for answers about why he'd written his book and where the profits went.

"You are completely biased," she teased, turning toward him. A pair of heart-shaped diamonds that he'd given her for Valentine's Day dangled from her ears. "But thank you just the same."

"I'm a lucky, lucky man." He folded her in his arms, drawing her against him to savor the feel of her.

In the months since Christmas, they'd never gone more than three days apart, even though she'd wanted to stay on at Mesa Falls Ranch for a while to find her footing again. He'd respected that, knowing how much she enjoyed the horses and the sense of family she'd gained from the friends she'd made there—something she hadn't experienced since her youth.

But he'd brought her to New York on her days off, showing off the city to see what she thought, since his work was based there. His mom adored her, and had lobbied for her to move closer so they could see each other more, an invitation Regina seemed to be seriously considering. He'd move anywhere to make her happy, and find a way to do his job wherever he was now that he and Marcus had decided the only path forward for

Salazar Media was to keep the company together. To continue to run it as a team. The decision felt right now that they both understood brotherhood didn't have to be a competition. They could succeed together.

So Devon could work on the West Coast or in New York, and it didn't matter to him. Yet Regina genuinely enjoyed Manhattan, delighting in the luxuries that the city could provide. Tonight, he was going to see what she thought about a farm upstate where they could keep horses and he could commute in a few days a week.

If she didn't love that idea, he could see about setting up a presence in Montana, because this place would always hold a piece of his heart for bringing this woman into his life.

"I hope you still feel lucky now that your girlfriend is officially unemployed." She arched an eyebrow at him. "It seemed strange to pack up my things from Mesa Falls yesterday."

"I know it wasn't easy." He understood that she was more attached to the friendships than anything else. But he also wanted her to find whatever path in life brought her the most joy, and he had the feeling she was getting ready for her second act now that she'd put her past to rest. "But Millie said she'd come and see you no matter where you end up."

They'd talked about taking time off—together—to travel for the next two months. See new places. Explore the world. Find out what made them happiest. Marcus—already a married man since he'd tied the knot in Paris on New Year's Eve—had been supportive, assuring him the company would survive without him for eight weeks.

Devon hoped he would be as fortunate as his brother. He couldn't wait to ask Regina to be his wife.

"I know." Regina rested her head against his shoulder for a long moment, gazing out the window with him. "It's up to me to figure out what to do next."

"Are you okay with that?" He tipped her face up to his. "I know there's been a lot of change in the last few months. But I'll move mountains to make you happy."

He'd already helped her navigate a meeting with her father—the actor who'd raised her and then shut her out of his life. The guy had reached out twice after Tabitha's announcement at the launch event, expressing his regret that he'd handled his wife's betrayal so poorly. But Regina had been open to talking to him again, and Devon had hope that the two of them—not related by blood, but by a shared bond and obstacles—would heal.

"I know you would." Her gray eyes met his, her fingertip grazing his lower lip. "And I love you so much for that, Devon. Thank you for giving me a chance to find myself again."

"You're the woman I've been waiting for my whole life." He felt it deep in his heart. In his soul.

He never questioned the direction of their path. All that mattered was that they took it together.

* * * * *

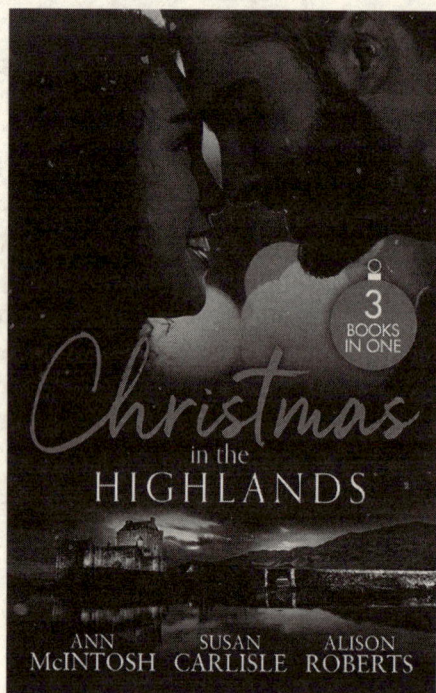

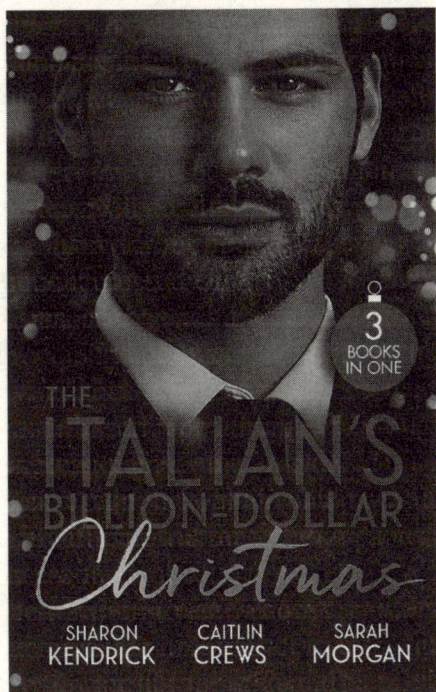

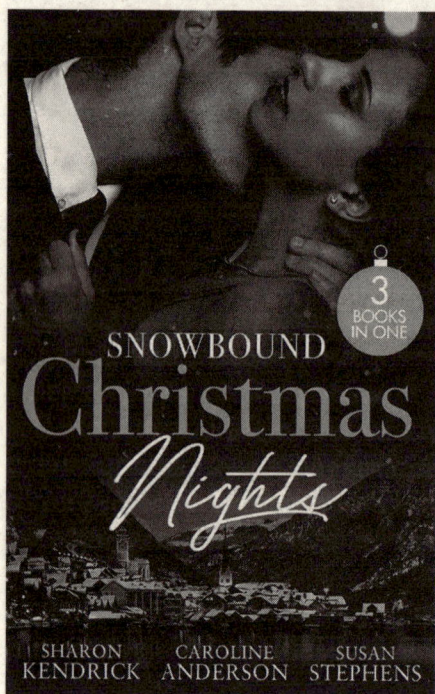

MILLS & BOON

THE HEART OF ROMANCE

A ROMANCE FOR EVERY READER

MODERN
Prepare to be swept off your feet by sophisticated, sexy and seductive heroes, in some of the world's most glamourous and romantic locations, where power and passion collide.

HISTORICAL
Escape with historical heroes from time gone by. Whether your passion is for wicked Regency Rakes, muscled Vikings or rugged Highlanders, awaken the romance of the past.

MEDICAL
Set your pulse racing with dedicated, delectable doctors in the high-pressure world of medicine, where emotions run high and passion, comfort and love are the best medicine.

Love Always
Celebrate true love with tender stories of heartfelt romance, from the rush of falling in love to the joy a new baby can bring, and a focus on the emotional heart of a relationship.

HEROES
The excitement of a gripping thriller, with intense romance at its heart. Resourceful, true-to-life women and strong, fearless men face danger and desire - a killer combination!

afterglow BOOKS
From showing up to glowing up, these characters are on the path to leading their best lives and finding romance along the way – with plenty of sizzling spice!

To see which titles are coming soon, please visit

millsandboon.co.uk/nextmonth

LET'S TALK
Romance

For exclusive extracts, competitions and special offers, find us online:

f MillsandBoon

X @MillsandBoon

◉ @MillsandBoonUK

♪ @MillsandBoonUK

Get in touch on 01413 063 232